BY ROSS RAISIN

A Natural

God's Own Country

Waterline

A NATURAL

A
NATURAL

a novel

ROSS
RAISIN

RANDOM HOUSE NEW YORK

A Natural is a work of fiction. Apart from the well-known actual people, events, and locales that figure in the narrative, all names, characters, places, and incidents are the products of the author's imagination or are used fictitiously. Any resemblance to current events or locales, or to living persons, is entirely coincidental.

Published in the United States by Random House, an imprint and division of Penguin Random House LLC, New York.

RANDOM HOUSE and the HOUSE colophon are registered trademarks of Penguin Random House LLC.

Originally published in the United Kingdom by Jonathan Cape, a division of Penguin Random House UK, London, in 2017.

LIBRARY OF CONGRESS CATALOGING-IN-PUBLICATION DATA

Names: Raisin, Ross, author.
Title: A natural: a novel / Ross Raisin.
Description: First edition. | New York: Random House, [2017]
Identifiers: LCCN 2017012177 | ISBN 9780525508779 | ISBN 9780525508786 (ebook)
Classification: LCC PR6118.A36 N38 2017 | DDC 823/.92—dc23
LC record available at https://lccn.loc.gov/2017012177

Printed in the United States of America on acid-free paper

randomhousebooks.com

2 4 6 8 9 7 5 3 1

First U.S. Edition

Book design by Jo Anne Metsch

For Toes, Maggie and Vic

A NATURAL

1

A few drivers had slowed to look up at the side of the coach as it circled the roundabout. Along one stretch of its window, near the back, three pairs of white buttocks were pressed to the glass like a row of supermarket chicken breasts. A car came past and the driver sounded his horn. The next driver repeated the action. When the coach lurched off the roundabout one of the pairs of buttocks momentarily disappeared, before returning emphatically to its place alongside the others.

Tom sat alone beside his kitbag, looking across the aisle at the hysterical gurning faces of the three mooners. The middle one had dropped his trousers to his ankles, his cock bobbing stupidly with the motion of the vehicle as it overtook a caravan onto the dual carriageway. Tom turned away, glad that the short journey was nearly over.

They were on their way to a hotel away from the town center—a preseason policy enforced by the chairman in the aftermath of one eventful weekend the previous summer. Tom had not been at the club then, although he had heard the story. He'd arrived less than two months ago, shortly after being let go by his boyhood club at a brief and tearful meeting with the new manager. The memory of that afternoon was still difficult for him to think about. All of the second-year scholars lining up in the corridor among the new man's cardboard boxes and whiteboards. The office and its

stale stink of the old gaffer's cigarettes. The sight of the new manager behind the desk, calling for him to take a seat.

"You're a good lad, from what I hear. Your parents should be
proud of you. You're going to be some player, when you grow into
yourself. I've got no doubt that you'll find another club."

Tom found out afterwards that he'd spoken exactly the same
words to all of them, except for the two he had awarded first-team
contracts to. Thirteen lads who had progressed through each of the
youth levels with Tom, all hoping now for another club to phone
them while they thumbed the jobs pages or took on work from re-
cruitment agencies, shopping centers, the multiplex, all waiting to
grow into themselves. Unlike most of them, though, Tom did get
approached. A small club down south. His agent called him one
morning to say that their chairman had organized a hotel for the
night so that he could come down and talk to them with a view to
a one-year contract.

"Who?" his sister asked when he told his family. "What are they,
non-league?"

"No, they just got promoted from the Conference. My agent
says they've got money behind them." He looked away, not wanting
to see her reaction, and clocked his dad already at the computer,
peering, slowly nodding at the screen.

The three backsides returned to their seats, laughing. The middle one, scanning around to see if anybody was still watching them,
caught Tom's eye, and Tom gave him a dumb grin before turning to
the window. Cars moved past them in the other lane. Out of some,
the blue and white scarf of that afternoon's opposition flapped and
spanked against rear windows. Inside a camper van, two young
children were sticking their tongues out at him.

The match had begun promisingly. It was Tom's first start of the
preseason friendlies, and the sick cramping tension of the dressing
room had left him the moment play started. During one early
scrappy passage the ball spilled out to him on the wing and he ran
automatically at the fullback who, stumbling, tripping, ballooned
the ball away over their falling bodies for a corner. Adrenaline car-

ried Tom towards the flag to demand the ball from the tiny ballboy. For the first time since he had left home he was liberated from thought, absorbed in the match. He struck the corner cleanly, and from the wrestling mass of the penalty area somebody headed the ball against the crossbar. In that instant Tom felt something inside him let go, an excitement, a lust, that left him almost dizzy as he turned and jogged back into position.

After that, though, most of the play switched to the other end of the pitch. A bungle between the central defenders, Boyn and Daish—who were sitting now on the seats in front of Tom watching a game show on a laptop—resulted in a goal for the home side. Confidence sank from the team. They lost 3–1. In the miserable sweaty fug of the dressing room afterwards Clarke, the manager, told them that they were a bunch of soft fucking fairies. When one of the younger players giggled, the manager stepped forward and kicked him in the leg.

The coach left the dual carriageway and joined the heavy traffic moving down a superstore-lined arterial road. By a set of traffic lights a group of home supporters stood on the pavement outside a pub, smoking. One of them noticed the coach and gawped at it for a moment until they all understood what was next to them and started into a frenzy of hand gestures. In front of Tom a few players turned to look at the group, but he pretended not to see them. At his old club even the reserve team coach had tinted windows. Now, outside the top flight, the supporters were an actual presence. They came up to him in the street and at the supermarket. Inside Town's small, tight, windswept ground, where they stood in little grimacing clusters along the terracing, he could already identify individual voices and faces amid them. The lights changed. He gave a final glance at the group, now rhythmically fist-pumping in an ecstasy of abuse as the coach pulled away in the direction of the hotel.

He was rooming with Chris Easter, the captain—a situation that Easter seemed none too happy about as he dumped his bag on the bed by the window, turned on the television, then pounded at the windowpane for a couple of minutes before eventually accepting that it was not designed to open. He remained beside it for some time, staring out at the flat-roofed view of a neighboring retail park, occasionally giving a small shake of his head.

Easter, Michael Yates and Frank Foley, the goalkeeper, were no longer allowed to room with one another, in any combination, and had all been paired with younger or newer members of the squad. Despite this, Clarke did not seem to have a problem with the three keeping company if there was a night out after one of the friendlies. They sat together that evening in the first of a convoy of people carriers, and they formed a small boisterous circle with a few of the other senior players by the bar of the first place the squad went into while everybody else piled into a large sticky red booth near the toilets.

There was nowhere left to sit when Tom got to the booth, so he stood behind the curved banquette alongside the other young players, most of whom had come through the youth team and stuck together, smiling and straining to hear above the music what was being said. Sitting immediately below him the right back, Marc Fleming, was telling a story. Tom could not hear a word of it. He kept his eyes on the top of Fleming's head, trying, in case anybody should look up at him, to appear coolly amused. The raw greased scalp shone through Fleming's hair. Whatever it was that he was saying, the seated players were gripped by it. At the end of the story Fleming bent forward and slapped both his palms onto the table. A wave of laughter coursed around the booth and Fleming pushed back, obviously unaware of Tom standing right behind him because his head bumped Tom's stomach and he twisted to look up.

"Christ, Tommy, that's the closest any of our balls has got to each other all day, that is."

In that moment Tom felt so grateful that he was almost moved to put his hand on Fleming's shoulder and attempt something funny in reply. Somebody else began speaking. Tom departed for the toilet. On his way back, in order to avoid being bought another drink, he went to the bar to buy one for himself. He did not notice until he got served that he was wedged up against the back of Frank Foley. Foley was talking to a tall young woman with bare pale

shoulders, and each time he leaned in to speak to her his large behind butted against Tom's hip.

The woman was frowning. "What?"

There was another press of the behind. The woman looked
briefly out at the room before turning back to Foley. "Sorry, mate,
I've never heard of you." She reached to collect three slim glasses of
dark liquid and squeezed out from the crush at the bar. Foley stayed
put, one arm on the counter, eyeballing his pint. When Tom moved
away he was still there, inert, a similar expression on his face to the
one that two and a half thousand other people had already witnessed, three times, earlier that day.

Back at the hotel, in the cafe-bar, Tom stayed on the periphery
of the crowd of players singing and tussling and drinking from the
bottle of rum that somebody had taken from behind the wrenched-
open shutters. He lingered for about half an hour before going up
to bed, where he fell into a deep sleep, held under by the fog of a
dream, a dim sense that something was not normal, that he had
done something wrong and he was going to be found out. His face,
his skin, beat against sheets that smelled unnatural, not his own—
and he had a shooting realization that he was in somebody else's
bed, they were coming into the room, about to find him there.

He woke, a seizing stiffness in both legs, his face damp. In the
beam from a security light in the retail park he could see the bag
still on top of the other, empty, bed. He stared at it for some time,
his eyelids heavy, gummy with perspiration.

Gradually, unmistakably, he became sure of a faint sobbing
noise out in the corridor. He closed his eyes and tried to shut it out.
It did not go away, though, and eventually he was forced from his
bed, pulling on tracksuit bottoms to go to the door.

He could see as soon as he came out of the room where the
noise was coming from. At the end of the corridor, in a leggy heap
against a wall and beside a fire extinguisher, a young girl was
slumped forward with her forehead resting against her knees. He
walked towards her. There was the smell of vomit. A dark tidemark
on her shin and calf where it had run down her leg. She continued
to cry quietly and did not look up at him as he knelt in front of her.

She did not respond even as he positioned one arm under her armpits, the other underneath the tacky back of first one knee, then the other, and lifted her up. In the brightness of the corridor lighting, with her eye makeup bleeding and a small pink rash on one of her temples, she looked to him even younger than his sister.

"It's OK," he whispered. "It's OK."

He carried her into the room and kicked Easter's bag off the bed, then laid her down and gently arranged the covers over her.

She was still asleep in the same position when, with sunlight filtering through the window, Easter came in. He leaned over Tom's bed and playfully clapped him on the cheeks until he was fully awake. When Easter then left the room, looking from Tom to the girl and smirking, an unstoppable sensation of pride flared inside Tom. The feeling, and the uneasy doubtful one that it turned into, stayed with him as he got up, showered and woke the girl—who moved silently into the bathroom to wash her face and leg before letting herself out into the corridor.

When he joined the squad downstairs she was nowhere to be seen. He did not ask after her, and he did not say anything about what had happened to any of the others. He kept slightly apart while they filed out of the hotel to the mellow tinkling of lobby music and the weary peeved faces of the reception staff. As he went through the revolving doors he noticed the sap leaking from a yucca plant, broken and lolling now beside the entrance, where Boyn and Daish had been play-fighting when Tom went up to bed.

After a long, drowsy coach journey, several of the new players were dropped off at a different branch of the same hotel chain. By now the staff of this hotel had become familiar with Tom's routine. They regarded him, because of his quiet, solitary way of going about the place, his separateness from the other players, with some intrigue. For almost two months they had observed his daily ritual: entering the breakfast room at five past nine for scrambled eggs, which he cut always into the same precise square inside the tray, toast, sometimes beans, orange juice, tea. He would sit down at the same table in the corner, partly secluded by a plastic tree and a life-sized cardboard chef holding up a plate of food unlike anything in the buffet trays, and finish his meal quickly before driving to training. He returned to the hotel in the early afternoon and generally kept to his room until the following morning; only when he came down to reception to receive his takeaway deliveries would there be any sign of him.

The hotel was a temporary arrangement while appropriate digs were organized for him, the chairman had told Tom, his agent and his parents when they came down to be shown around the club. They had sat in a wood-paneled room, at a large table with coffee and pastries, and the chairman had turned to his mum with a wet smile to say that when Town signed somebody as young as Tom, who had just turned nineteen, they made sure to do right by him. Unless it was agreed that he was mature enough to live in a place of his own, he had said, the club would find a good family for him to stay with in the meantime.

Tom had not spoken to the chairman, or any of the club staff, or his agent, about his accommodation since. But, as he explained to his dad every few days on the phone, now was not the right time, with the new season about to begin, to ask about digs. And living at the hotel had become normal now. He was vigilant of the other players and had learned how to pass through the public areas at different times to them. There were currently, including himself, four staying there. At various intervals there had been several others, all gone now to their own accommodation or to different clubs, or back onto the market. The remaining three carpooled to training and back, and Tom had seen them in the restaurant together, where he sometimes peeked in at them talking and laughing and wondered if they knew each other from previous clubs.

Near the beginning of his time at the hotel there had been an older trialist staying there with his wife and two little girls. The man and his family were friendly to Tom. On a couple of occasions they had asked him to join them when they had seen him sitting alone in the breakfast room. After some initial discomfort he had enjoyed being around them, their easy conversation, the noisy distraction of the children, and a few times he and the player had carpooled together. After a couple of weeks, however, the player was released, something that Tom did not find out until the following day when he was told by one of the receptionists.

For the final friendly fixture before the season opener Tom was a substitute. He sat on the bench, nervous energy tightening through his muscles, alert to every twitch of Clarke on the touchline in expectation that he might at any moment turn round and instruct Tom to strip off. He visualized himself coming onto the pitch, the tempo of the game changing as his teammates, the crowd, willed the ball towards him. The low urgent moan of anticipation from the terraces when it was at his feet—although in fact the ground was less than half full, and partly roofless—the scarce songs and shouts of the Riverside Stand floating up, disappearing into the hot bright sky.

They were up against a higher-division side, Coventry, and the mismatch was evident immediately. For the first twenty minutes Clarke did not turn round at all. When he did, with the team already two goals down, he looked dark and old with rage.

Tom was sent on for the second half. He did not receive the ball for some time and drifted infield from his position on the wing, eager to become involved. Coventry scored again before he had even touched the ball, and as his impatience grew he raced into an uncontrolled challenge on the opposition captain. He knew instantly, from the sharp pain in the arch of his foot, that he would have to come off. He lay there, an awareness of the manager, his teammates, his dad, knuckling his chest, pinning him to the grass.

In the treatment room after the match, Clarke's voice resonating violently down the corridor, the foot was already bruising. The physio sponged it clean, dressed it and told him to get home and put it straight onto ice.

The hotel receptionist misunderstood him. She went away for a few minutes and came back with a steel champagne bucket rustling with ice and a folded white cloth.

"It's for my foot."

"Oh, I see, sorry." She smiled. "Do you need some more?"

"No, thanks." And then, "I'll get champagne if we ever win a match."

She smiled again. "All right. I'll remind you about that."

He limped away with the bucket, grinning with unexpected elation.

"That is a superb cock, mate."

Foley stood, plainly assessing the scholar next to him in the showers. The boy, who had trained with the firsts that morning, angled his body marginally away and carried on washing himself, affecting not to have heard. Foley, though, stood motionless, water collecting on the large plateau of his head, looking down at him. "Hey, Yatesy," he shouted through to the dressing room. "You remember Davo's cock?"

Yates, from the bench, looked up briefly from lacing his trainers. "I do."

"That was some cock."

All around the dressing room the younger players waited cautiously for the right moment to laugh, but Foley and Yates continued to behave as though nothing out of the ordinary had just happened, showering, changing as normal, so the players turned automatically to the young boy hastening from the showers towards his space along the bench, wrapping a towel about his middle. Tom kept his eyes to the floor, anxious somebody might see him looking and bring the room's attention on him.

Prohibited from running or kicking a ball for at least a week, he was nevertheless required to come in daily for training. Like the other injured players, he had to get there an hour early and leave after the rest of the squad had departed. There were two others—Fleming and Boyn—both with minor knocks and bruises. All were kept, deliberately it seemed to them, out of the final preparations for the first match of the season. If they were not in the treatment room, being entertained by the physio's military fitness stories, they were traveling over to the stadium to use the gym for long sessions on the treadmills and weight machines to a constant backdrop of loud music and Sky Sports News. Or they were sitting on the bench against the wall of the clubhouse, looking across the field at the team going through their drills and shape preparations.

"It's a joke," Boyn said as the sound of Clarke shouting and clapping wafted across the pitches to them. "He thinks we're going to contaminate them or something."

"No, Boyney," Fleming said, without moving his eyes from the squad. "It's a warning. To the lot of us. Don't get injured."

Clarke came into the treatment room a couple of days before the game to tell all three that they would not be included in the party traveling to Cheltenham. They were to stay at home. Focus on their rehabilitation.

On the morning of the match Tom drove to the launderette. There was a laundry service at the hotel, he knew from his welcome folder, but he did not like the idea of somebody else handling his clothes, his underwear, so he returned each week to the same quiet place that he had found on the outskirts of town. He went inside and saw there were no other customers. Unhurriedly he bought some washing powder from the dispenser, loaded the machine, and went into the cafe next door to get some breakfast to eat in the car.

He put on the radio for the match buildups. He sipped his tea, unwrapped the warm sweating paper from his bacon and egg roll, Saturday excitement rising and tugging at his gut as the coverage skipped from voice to voice, ground to ground, deflating when he looked down at his injured foot. Forty minutes later he went back into the launderette, hauled his sodden mound of clothes into one of the dryers—noticing as he did so one of his sister's socks melded inside the sleeve of a sweater he rarely wore—and went out once more to his car.

When he reentered at the end of the drying cycle there was another customer, a man in gym gear sitting on one of the benches. The man looked up as he walked past, but Tom did not acknowledge him and headed towards his dryer. Some of the clothes did not feel fully dry. He pulled them out anyway, bundling everything into his Ikea sack, aware, through the glass of the dryer door, of the man watching him. He concentrated on his task, blocking the man out, his senses beginning to pulse with the echoed scrabble of his fingers against the drum, the thump of a washing machine behind him, until his clothes were all in the sack and he made his way down the thin aisle, certain that the man was about to speak or stand up and face him.

When Tom stepped outside into the cool street his chest and lungs loosened, expelling the stifling air of the launderette in long even breaths as he made for his car.

It was obvious, sitting next to the steaming sack on the passenger seat, that his clothes were still more than a little damp. On getting back to his room he decided that he would drape them over the radiators, but after a short search he realized there were no radiators in the room, only a climate control vent in one of the walls, quite high up. He thought about phoning his mum, but straightaway ruled it out. It would make her worry; make her believe that he was not coping. Besides which, he reasoned, she would be in a baby clinic, busy. He unthreaded the lace from a trainer and tied it to one handle of the Ikea sack. Then he pulled a chair over to the wall beneath the vent and stood on it to reach up and attach the lace to a bar of the grille so that the sack hung just below it. After tugging on it to see the lace held, he turned up the heating on the control panel and went to sit down on the bed with his back against the headboard.

He had fallen asleep in the warm smog of fuming clothes when his dad called at the regular time, ten minutes before *Football Focus*.

"Feeling good?"

"Fine, yeah, I suppose."

His dad laughed. "No point getting down about it. You're a footballer. Sometimes you're going to be injured. It's how you pick yourself back up that counts."

"I'm not in his plans."

"You're not in his plans today."

"Maybe." There was the buzzing of a vacuum out in the corridor. "Yeah, maybe."

"Talking of plans, I want to come down and see you."

"It's all right, Dad," Tom said as brightly as he could, annoyed with himself for sounding like a sulky child. "I'm doing fine. You're right. Another week of rehab and I'll be back training."

"I've spoken to the sorting office and they've said I can have the afternoon off to drive down on Friday."

"What, this Friday?"

"Busy, are you?" his dad said, tickled.

"No, no, that's fine, Dad," he said quickly. "That's fine."

He looked up at the bag of washing shackled to the vent and he had a powerful conviction that his dad knew what he had done. That he could see it all. The daft contraption of his moldering clothes on the wall. Tom dozing on the bed. The man in the launderette. A flickering perception came to Tom of the boy that his dad probably brought to mind when he thought about him, which he suppressed, pulling himself upright on the bed.

"I'll come straight down after work Friday, then. Might as well book a room in your hotel, keep things simple. Go to the first home match next day. We could watch it together, if the foot's still bad. Or would you need to be with the squad?"

"No. He doesn't like injured players in with the others."

"Right then. Sorted."

After they said goodbye, Tom thought that he probably should have offered to book the room for him, and he wondered if his dad had been expecting him to.

He put on the television for *Football Focus* and pictured his dad at home, watching it too. On the sofa, tray on his lap. Mug of tea. Fry-up. His sister upstairs, keeping out of the way until John from the sorting office arrived to pick up their dad. The drive to Uncle Kenny's, and the short chat in the kitchen with Jeanette before the three men went into the city to take up their positions at the bar in the pre-match pub. Everything normal, ongoing.

There was a knock on his door. The housekeeper, wanting to make up his room.

"No, thank you," he called out.

He moved to the wall and took down his clothes. They were no drier than before. Wetter, somehow. He tipped them all into the bottom of his wardrobe to sort out later and brought the sack over to the desk to collect up his takeaway boxes.

He went for a walk around the car park. He dumped his rubbish into the bulk bins at the back of the kitchens, something that he had taken to doing rather than leave his cartons and boxes around the tiny pedal bin in his room. He felt a bit weird at the thought of the housekeepers seeing them, dealing with them, just as he felt weird about putting up his posters or his speakers; leaving out his dumbbells, his cactus collection. He kept these things underneath the bed and when he returned each afternoon took them out, putting the cacti on the windowsill and a limited, alternating selection of his posters up on the walls until it was time to take them down again in the morning.

He followed the scores on his laptop while he watched the television. With a few minutes of their match remaining, Town were 2–1 down and Tom realized that he wanted them to lose. For his absence to be taken notice of, spoken about. When full time confirmed the defeat he refreshed the page, to be certain.

His dad arrived early in the evening. They went for a drink, then a meal in a pizza restaurant. He was doing well, his dad told him before the food arrived. Adapting, young as he was. He was proud of him. Tom did not know what to say. He looked across the table and saw his dad's determination to say these words to him, that he had planned them. Tom avoided his gaze and looked down at the tough broken knuckles of his dad's hands on the table, calculating how much this time off work would be costing him.

From the top of the main stand, with the high August sun on their faces, the formation and movement of the teams was starkly outlined. After half an hour Tom was too ashamed to watch. His view moved over the opposite stand towards the black flashing river and the plain of fields and houses and roads stretching away towards a range of hills—beyond which, although he had not seen it yet, was the sea. His dad, however, was watching the contest intently. He always watched football like this: hunched forward, elbows on his knees, studying the play. He spoke very little during the game, and Tom could not bring himself to look round and see his inevitable disappointment—at each broken-down move or misplaced pass, each booted clearance disappearing over the top of the Riverside Stand to the sarcastic cheers of the away supporters—that this, after all those years of outlay and sacrifice, was what Tom had amounted to.

After the defeat they went back to the hotel. Before his dad set off up north they sat in the cafe-bar and spoke about the match. His dad was not impressed with Clarke.

"It's big-man hoofball," he said. "It doesn't suit your game."

"It's League Two, Dad."

"Doesn't matter. Football's football. But a proper player will always shine through, even in a side like that."

"Not if he's in the stand."

"Come on, Tom. Don't be soft." He regarded Tom for a moment. "There's no use feeling sorry for yourself, son. You're at a bottom-division club. And you're injured. It's an education, is how to think about being here, on your way back up. There are plenty of others who've done it that route. You've just got to work that bit harder, is all." He looked past Tom towards the bar. "Tell you what, fancy a hot chocolate before I go?"

"All right," Tom said, smiling, secretly comforted by the childishness of the suggestion. "Thanks."

His dad got up to go to the bar, and Tom watched the Premier League results coming through on a television. His old club had lost, 2–0.

"You just need to be patient," his dad said when he returned with the hot chocolates. "You're only two matches in. Nine months of the season ahead of you. Plenty of time to crack on now the foot's on the mend. Just roll your sleeves up. Wait for your chance."

2

PLAYED 5   WON 0   DRAWN 1   LOST 4
DEFENSE = IMPROVE
ATTACK = IMPROVE
KEEPER = JOKE
RELEGATION. NON-LEAGUE. SCRAPHEAP.

was written on the whiteboard of the training ground dressing room, like an aide-mémoire. Clarke stood directly in front of the board, his number two off to one side. He was confused. He didn't know what the fuck their problem was. He was tearing his hair out. He was in at seven every morning, at his desk, wondering where their bollocks were. The number two remained silent throughout the whole of this speech. The players sat in a defeated semicircle, itching to get out onto the field. From them there was no noise either, except for the quiet grinding, like teeth, of their studs on the floor.

"You are a disgrace, every single one of you."

Those who had not played in the last game, or at any other point during the opening month, stared down at the floor with the rest.

"What's it going to take? Docking your wages? A bollocking?" Here he moved forward so that he stood in the center of them, and looked around from face to face.

As Clarke's small demented eyes flicked closer to him, a charge of anger moved inside Tom's chest. They had lied to him. To his dad. The manager, the chairman, they had both said that he was an important part of the club's plans, but he had been match fit for a fortnight and had not yet played other than a brief substitute appearance. The eyes took him in for an instant, then moved on. Earlier that same year he had been tipped off by his academy coordinator that he was under consideration to be a sub for a Premier League match. It never came about, but Tom knew, his coaches knew. If they were to look now—if they looked at all—they would see where he was and they would be in no doubt that they had made the correct final judgment on him: that he had not quite been good enough.

"You've got to talk to each other." He was back at the whiteboard. "Com-mu-ni-cate." With each syllable he beat the side of his fist against the board, smearing the writing.

"Easter, what the fuck is wrong with you?"

Easter looked up in surprise.

"You are the fucking captain of this shit heap. Why are you not shouting at them, organizing them? You're as quiet as a rapist out there."

Easter's heels lifted off the floor as his calf muscles clenched. He said nothing.

"Go on, then. Get up, all of you. Get out there. I'm going to make you work."

They emerged from the clubhouse into dazzling sunshine. On the warm grass they stretched in silence, guided by the number two, until Clarke came out, glaring at his watch.

"Twelve-minute run. Go."

The whole squad got to their feet and began sprinting around the nearest pitch. There was some bumping and hustling at the back, as no one wanted to be last. Tom, wary of getting trapped in the pack, kept to the outside. He ran hard, resolute that he would not be singled out. Already, these runs had become an accustomed part of Monday and Tuesday mornings. Any player who was seen to be running at less than full pace or who did not complete eight circuits of the pitch within the time would be made to go and train with the scholars. The side that ran alongside the clubhouse, where there was no relief from the sun and the touchline was baked hard, was the worst stretch, before the turn onto the goal line, past the taunting mist of the sprinkler watering the penalty area, and then the grateful turn onto the far touchline along the chain-link fence, shaded by the trees and scrubland that separated the four pitches from a thundering A road.

When they had finished they stood bent over with their hands on their knees, breathing, waiting to hear if he was satisfied.

"Good," he said. "Now go again."

By the end of the session, an hour and a half later, several of the players were nauseous with fatigue. As Clarke went ahead to the car park, still in his tracksuit, to go and attend to his van hire company, some put their arms around the strugglers' waists or shouldered their armpits, helping them inside.

In the dressing room, where they sat in silence along the benches or undressed stiffly for the showers, Tom went into his bag for his towel and saw that he had a text message. It was from the club secretary, letting him know that his digs had been confirmed.

The Daveys lived in a tall thin end terrace about twenty minutes' walk from the stadium. On match days Mr. Davey, the owner of a steel-wire manufacturing company and an associate director at the club, would drive to and from the ground, but if he was required for some vote or function during the week he made the journey on foot, enjoying, as he passed through the streets of hushed pubs and takeaways and ethnic shops on his way home from the stadium, the gradual easing of traffic and people, the transition into quiet, wide streets, trees growing up out of the pavements, postboxes, plant-tangled fences and the familiar old buildings lived in by families he had known for most of his life, until he reached his own house.

When the last of their three children moved out, the Daveys had spent a difficult six months contemplating whether the house had become too big for them. But then, with Town progressing up the non-league pyramid and recruiting more young players from out-side the area, the board had announced that they were looking for willing families to lodge these boys. Mr. Davey put himself and his wife forward without hesitation. It was a decision that they almost never regretted. The dozen boys they welcomed over the interven-ing three years had provided the house with a continual flow of laughter and activity, tantrums, anecdotes, broken curfews, not to mention the ninety pounds a week bed and board that the club paid out for each of them. Some stayed for a month or two, others for a whole season. There were sixteen- and seventeen-year-olds, joining the youth setup, and there were older boys who had failed to get senior contracts at other clubs, or were out on loan gaining experi-ence; boys from the north, from Scotland, Ireland, as well as one silent Hungarian who barely spoke a word of English and made cheese and cabbage scones in the middle of the night which he kept at the top of his wardrobe.

Tom's dad came down again. He drove them from the hotel and parked in the quiet turning by the side of the house, where they sat together in the car waiting for the club chairman to arrive and make the introductions. His dad kept looking up at the handsome old terrace or at the piece of paper that he had taken from his pocket and was squinting to read. The chairman's Jaguar pulled in behind them, fifteen minutes late. They watched his pained bulk appear slowly from the car, and got out to meet him.

"Ready?" the chairman said, already turning towards the house. They followed him through the gate and past the fat rhododendron which dominated a bushy green garden so unlike the neat lawn of Tom's parents' house, then up the few steps to the front door.

Both Mr. and Mrs. Davey were at home. They moved busily about the large kitchen, making coffee and plating biscuits while Tom sat at one side of a long table, between his dad and the chair-man.

"How's your foot doing?" Mr. Davey asked when the couple came over to sit down opposite them.

"It's fine now, thank you."

In his kitchen, jovial in jeans and a short-sleeved shirt, it was difficult to twin Mr. Davey with the featureless suited figure Tom had seen a couple of times in the players' lounge. He spoke to them at length as Mrs. Davey listened and smiled and got more biscuits. The chairman nodded occasionally, leaving the room at one point to take a phone call. Tom's dad had quite a number of questions, which Mr. and Mrs. Davey answered between them: he would have to do his own washing, of his clothes and his bedding; yes, there was a curfew, on the nights before training and matches, but he would have his own key, and on Saturday and Tuesday nights the Daveys allowed the boys more leeway. They trusted their lodgers to respect the house and behave maturely. He could cook for himself when he wanted to, and there was a shelf in the fridge for him, but there would be a meal provided every evening, which they all sat down to eat together. Tom grew increasingly self-conscious, watching his dad scrupulously write down all the information on his piece of paper. These were his mum's questions, he knew. He continued to sit there, like a child, saying nothing while everything was arranged for him.

When there was a pause, he spoke up: "Is anyone else lodging with you?"

"Yes," Mr. Davey said. "Two Scots lads. Both seventeen. A scout up there brought them to the club's attention earlier this summer and we had them down for a trial. Very impressive for their age group, played a few first-team games too for Partick, and now we've got them in with the second-year scholars. You wouldn't guess they were that young. Well, until you start speaking to them." He glanced at Mrs. Davey and they both smiled. "Shall we go up and show you your room?"

Tom followed the chairman's heavy buttocks up the narrow staircase. On the first floor he glimpsed through an open doorway of the first of two neighboring rooms—the walls gleaming darkly with posters of Celtic players, Parkhead, glamour models—before the party ascended the next flight of steps to the top floor.

The room was small but immaculate. They crowded in, and the sound of the chairman's breathing filled the space as they stood looking around: the bed, the small television on top of a chest of drawers, chair in one corner, full-length mirror in another; silently taking it all in as if they were imagining him inhabiting the room—sleeping, dressing, masturbating, combing his hair.

"Great view from up here," his dad said. They all turned to look out of the window set into the triangular far wall. The town spread out below the house. The cracked spines of terraced roofs fell away down a hillside. Satellite dishes blazed on the fronts of two towers bathed in sunshine half a mile away. Further on, the dirty boxed units of the central shopping area. Town's training ground, just visible beyond the edge of the town. And, looming at one side of the window, the football stadium. Out of nowhere an unexpected longing pulled Tom towards it—towards the floodlights, bulbs twinkling in the sun above the crumbling brick walls of the old part of the ground, floating him over the houses that obscured the main stand and the large new tiered structure of the Kop, until he could see all the glittering ranks of red and green seats.

"It's good, yeah," he said.

They left the room. Tom was the last through the door and he noticed, as the others made their way back downstairs, a couple of books propped against the skirting board, a Post-it note stuck to one of the covers: RETURN TO RICHIE B.

They sat again around the kitchen table. The chairman departed and Mrs. Davey offered another round of coffees. Tom expected his dad would want to be off, but he told her they would be happy to stop for another. Tom assumed he had more questions; however, instead, he started talking about Clarke's tactics with Mr. Davey, the team's chances of staying up. Mrs. Davey sat beside Tom and took the opportunity to ask him about his mum and his sister, what it had been like living in a hotel for all this time. "You must have felt like Alan Partridge," she said, and Tom admitted that he did not know who that was. "Nor do I, really," she said with a warm, complicit smile, "but Andrew, our eldest, used to be a big fan."

There was the sound of the front door opening and closing, then somebody moving about before a man appeared at the doorway.

"Dad. Oh, sorry, I'll get out of your way."

"No, don't worry. This is Tom Pearman and his dad, Ray. Tom's coming to lodge with us. Tom, Ray—this is our son, Liam."

Tom's dad got up to shake hands as the burly young man stepped forward, so Tom stood up too. He recognized him, he thought. The wide pale face and short sandy hair, gingerish, unlike his parents', both of whom obviously used to be dark. Tom wondered if he might be adopted. It seemed like that kind of family.

"How's the foot?" Liam asked. He smiled, noting Tom's surprise. "I'm a supporter."

"It's healed up."

"That's good." He turned to Mr. Davey as Tom sat back down. "Dad, I'm just after a plunger. Shower's blocked again."

"Under the sink."

Liam hunkered down to look in the cupboard. The sun streaming through the kitchen window was on his back. His shirt clung damply to him, glued to his vertebrae. After a moment he pulled out an old plunger, the wooden handle blackened with mold spores, and Tom realized that he had seen him before, at the training ground, tending to the pitch.

"I'll give it a go." Liam stood up. "Good to meet you, Tom, Mr. Pearman."

He left the room, inspecting the plunger, twisting it in his large hands as he walked through the doorway out of sight. When the front door closed Tom turned back to the conversation. His dad was observing him across the table. Tom looked sharply away and took a sip of his coffee. He kept his eyes on the other side of the room, on the sink, the window. There was what looked like a washing-up rota on the door of the fridge. A cluster of small framed photographs of players above the microwave, one of them Chris Gale, Town's left back.

"Well, Tom," his dad said. "Sounds good to me. You OK with everything?"

They were all looking at him now.

"Yes."

He drove his belongings over from the hotel the following morning, a day off, together with a few other bits and pieces that his dad had brought down in anticipation of the move. He kept to his new room for a long time, conscious of the other occupants of the house below him. He folded his clothes into the chest of drawers and put his dumbbells under the bed; then, listening to the voices of the other lodgers beneath the floorboards, he installed his cactus collection on the windowsill.

He was introduced to Steven Barr and Bobby Hart at dinner. Both of them were big and excitable, boyish, Bobby a world apart from the subdued youth that Foley had made a show of in the showers. They sat next to each other at the table, laughing and shoving and exclaiming in accents broad enough to make Tom feel slightly intimidated, although they were extremely polite to the Daveys, and to Tom they were immediately respectful because he was in the first-team squad. At the training ground they barely spoke. Now, bantering with Mrs. Davey, leaning over one another for more chili, salad, garlic bread, they could not seem to keep quiet, or still. The noise and laughter, drawing all the focus onto the two boys, gradually relaxed Tom. He joined in with a conversation about parachute payments to relegated Premier League teams. He gave a funny account of his time at the hotel. After the meal everybody moved through to the living room to watch television, and only when Bobby and Steven went upstairs to play a computer game did Tom start to feel awkward, sitting next to the Daveys on their large sofa. He waited a reasonable amount of time, then excused himself to go up to his room.

He began to settle at the house. The Daveys were kind, constantly good-natured. If he was quiet or over-polite, they never pointed it out. Mostly, they left him to himself. Since his recovery from the foot injury he had been working himself with relentless intensity, his dad's words in the back of his mind: *Roll your sleeves up; wait for your chance.* He drove back each afternoon, knowing that Mrs. Davey would be at the hospice kitchen where she volunteered and that the Scottish boys would still be training or studying, wanting nothing more than to sit in a cold bath and let his burning muscles give in to the water.

In the mornings he drove the boys in. They sat in the back of Tom's Fiesta showing each other videos on their phones, or leaned forward with their meaty white forearms up against the headrests to ask him what it had been like at a Premier League club. If he had met this or that famous player. He described for them just as he used to for his old school friends the experience of the few occasions he had trained with the first team: their technical ability, the skills and tricks that you would never see in matches, and the times that he had spoken to them. There had been a tiny boot room next to the home dressing room, where the scholars used to sit and chat and listen through the wall. Quite often a senior player would come in to talk or joke with them. Tom could see the keen, impressed pairs of eyes in the rearview mirror as he told the boys this, even though he could not escape a sense that he was telling somebody else's story. Some of the first-team players had spoken to Tom regularly. They knew he was a prospect, that he had played for England at his age-group level. He was one of the youths they had taken notice of in that leathery little room, a subtle respect which Tom thought he was never able properly to convey whenever he told people about his scholarship.

On Mondays and Tuesdays Bobby and Steven, sometimes with one or two of the other scholars, came across the pitches to train with the first team. On these mornings Tom could feel their restless enthusiasm in the back of the car. Once onto the field they concentrated, ran, played, with all-out commitment. Tom saw the attention they gave to the senior players, especially Easter, entranced by everything that was said, clamoring to be near when it seemed that some joke or prank was about to happen. They stayed close together, always a pair. One of the forwards, Charlie Lewis, declared in the dressing room that they should be called Neeps and Tatties. At this his striking partner Yates slapped his thighs and laughed loudly at what he was about to say: "Settled then. Nips and Titties."

In the revelry that followed the two boys stood still, unsure where to look. They both turned towards Tom, who smiled at them, instinctively protective, jealous.

Clarke rarely split them up. It was clear he approved of them. They were over six foot. Muscled. They told Tom one dinnertime that they both used to play as strikers. As a partnership they had broken school league scoring records. Now, though, Clarke had them playing as a central midfielder and a central defender, conversions to which they never offered a word of complaint, even to Tom in the safety of his car. They were grateful just to be there. Tom could understand that. He had been the best player at his own school, a striker too, like the majority of the exceptional school players he had come across. It was only when he progressed to county and club level that his various coaches decided he would be better placed on the wing, and he had stayed there ever since. Town had signed him as a winger. When he joined, Clarke spoke to him about the improvement he wanted his energy and crossing ability to bring to the team. The dovetailing relationship he could see developing between him and Fleming, the fullback behind him.

"I've been watching you," he had told Tom in the players' lounge that day. "Did you know that?"

Tom shook his head as the manager smiled at him disturbingly from the other end of the sofa. He was not exactly put at ease by this disclosure.

"Watched all the DVDs. Watched them a few times. And you know what I thought?"

Tom continued shaking his head.

"I thought, that boy's a player. A natural. And I'm going to turn him into a man."

There was nothing Tom could think to say to this.

"And fair play to you as well, because you could have sat on your backside and played for the development side there, the Under-21s, whatever fancy bollocks setup they've got, but you didn't, because you want to play."

"Yes," Tom said simply, and when they got up from the sofa he wondered if the manager was somehow under the impression that he had been offered a contract and turned it down.

Tom walked from the Daveys' to the stadium and made his way up to the players' lounge to join the other members of the squad not involved in the Oxford fixture. He was the only one to watch the game. He stepped out of the lounge into the small sealed-off area at the top of the main stand and followed the play absently while the muffled sound of everybody else watching a televised Premier League match came through the glass behind him.

The team achieved a 1–1 draw. Simon Finch-Evans, the right-winger Tom had been led to believe he'd been signed to take the place of, was one of Town's better performers, instrumental in the buildup to the goal and applauded off the pitch when he was substituted near the end. Tom had been in the shower that morning when Clarke had left a message to say that he was not going to be one of the substitutes. Oxford liked to play three in the middle, the short mumbled recording explained, so if he needed to make a change it would probably be to pack the midfield. But Tom would have to come to the stadium regardless, Clarke reminded him; he wanted non-involveds present for all home games if they were fit, he finished, for morale.

Tom came inside at the end of the match. He got himself a drink and looked for somewhere inconspicuous to sit. The players' lounge had been done up as part of the main stand rebuild, the chairman had told him and his family during their tour of the ground. It was flatly lit, fitted out with the same carpet tiles and plasterboard walls as all the other suites and function rooms, which gave the inside of the whole stand the appearance of cheap office space. Tom found himself a seat in the corner underneath the television. On the wall to one side of him were several canvas prints of players celebrating. All of them were recent. The biggest showed last season's promotion squad leaning deliriously from the upper deck of an open-top bus. Next to it was the FA Trophy triumph of the year before: Chris

Easter being carried aloft by his teammates, looking up at the sky in a moment of invulnerable joy. Tom tried to calculate how long it must have been after the picture was taken that Easter made his transfer to Middlesbrough. A couple of weeks, maybe. Easter did not yet know, in that golden still, the disaster that his time at Middlesbrough would be; that he would be let go within a year and eventually return to Town.

Suspense built in the lounge as they all waited for the first team to arrive from the dressing room. Tom was regretting the decision to seat himself under the television. In front of him a group of executive-box guests had gathered to stare above his head at the classified results, not speaking, swallowing their lager, encircling Tom with the bullfrog gulping of yellow flabby throats. His old team had won, he could hear, and for a moment Tom could see his dad leaving the ground with Uncle Kenny and John, the three of them talking happily among the swarm of the crowd as it poured down the narrow terraced streets and they made their way towards the pub, where, pint in hand, his dad would be waiting expectantly now for the League Two scores to be displayed on the television.

Some kind of altercation had started up over by the window onto the pitch. Outside, two teenagers in club replica shirts had climbed into the enclosed seating area. One of them was standing on a seat, pointing and chanting at Yates on the other side of the glass.

"You're shit, and you know you are" could just be heard above the sound of the television.

Everybody in the room was now watching the boy—and Yates, who began mouthing "Penis" at him. The boy continued undeterred as his mate climbed up beside him and joined in with the chant. Yates stepped so close to the window that his nose almost touched it, then moved his hand towards his trousers. The room went completely still as, from one pocket, he pulled out his wallet. With horrible exaggeration he licked the pad of his thumb and began to slide out twenty-pound notes, pressing them, one at a time, against the glass. He had got to eighty pounds by the time a detachment of stewards removed the incensed teenagers from the stand and a director walked over to Yates for a quiet word.

Tom went to the bar and bought another drink. He felt tired, a bit drunk. Lager went to his head; he was still not quite used to it. He remained by the bar, trying to decide how much longer he would need to stay before he could leave unnoticed. The double doors to the room opened. An unpleasant little official in a stained club tie entered, leading half a dozen women into the lounge. It took Tom a few seconds to register that these were the partners of some of the players. There were one or two small children with them, who ran ahead, and a baby in the arms of his mother. She was probably Price's partner, or Richards's, Tom presumed; her presence and that of the baby, the only black people in the room, heightening the oddness of the band of women. They followed the official to the far side of the bar—the powerful new smell of the group enveloping Tom as they passed him—where he left them and walked back out of the lounge with a wink for the men around the television.

Tom stared at the women. The sight of them jarred with the surroundings: the clash of shining tanned legs against the plum carpet tiles, the meticulousness of their made-up faces beside the bleary gaze of the men watching them. He had not seen any of the players' partners on match days before, and he wondered where they had been during the game. Two of the women came over to the bar. One stood quite close to Tom. When she was served she joked with the barman about there still being no proper beers on tap, and Tom was surprised to hear that she was foreign. European, he thought. The other woman was considerably younger. Tom knew her to be Easter's wife. She seemed less relaxed than the foreign woman. There was something pinched about her face as she ordered two bottles of wine. He checked out the floaty cream top, sequined leggings and heels, her uncomfortable veined feet glowing in the under-counter strip lighting. She looked round and Tom averted his eyes. Chemical curds of froth were floating on the surface of his pint. The thought of having to finish it made him even heavier with tiredness. When he looked up, Easter's wife was on her way back to the table with the other woman.

He had met her, once, at the beginning of the season, when he had been introduced to her by Easter as "the one I have to room with now." She had smiled at Tom and said, "I hope you make sure he behaves himself," to which Easter had jeered and told her that *he* was the one who had come back to their room to find a girl passed out in there.

There was an increase in the hum of noise and Tom saw that the double doors were opening again. Easter was at the head of the team. He led them straight across the lounge towards the women, some of whom sprang up to greet their partners with vigorous displays of affection. Tom watched Easter and his wife put their arms around each other's middles and fix each other showily with their eyes. They kissed, then Easter took her hand and walked with her to the bar to buy a round of drinks for the whole first team.

Tom joined the audience around the team and listened to the retelling of the match: their number ten was a handful, a nippy little sod; the officials had been half-decent for once; the home supporters were about as supportive as a pair of nipple tassels—a line that the whole group laughed at as if hearing for the first time.

Mr. Davey appeared at Tom's side. He greeted him with a look that Tom understood meant sympathy for not being selected again.

"Decent result," Mr. Davey said.

"They were all right, Oxford. I didn't know teams this level played that style."

"Well, there's not many of them. Will you want a taxi home?"

"I'm OK, thanks. I'll walk."

"See you back at the house then. I best go make sure that the money have drinks in their hands."

He moved away through the layers converging around the first team towards the small party that he was responsible for looking after, the match sponsors—today, two brothers in identical suits and muddied shoes who owned a light haulage firm, on their own over by the snack machine. Tom watched Mr. Davey gesturing to ask if they wanted another pint. They nodded, and he started back to the bar. Just beyond the sponsors, the afternoon's three mascots and their families were looking out at the pitch. Tom, vaguely aware that the number two had come into the room, looked out with them. He spotted Liam Davey among the scholars replacing divots in the grass. Liam said something to two of them, who then went in opposite directions for the corner flags while Liam started towards the goal in front of the Kop. He kept his head down, stopping sometimes to examine the grass. When he reached the goal he ran a hand up one of the posts, stretching the full length of his body to touch the upright with his fingertips, then, more slowly, he worked down it again, plucking, unfastening the net.

When Tom turned back, the mascots and their families had moved away. The number two was standing at one end of the bar, speaking to Easter. Whatever he was saying to him, Easter was clearly becoming aggravated. Tom was close enough, acquainted enough, to see the taut white maggots of flesh beading on his forehead. Before long, a few other people near to the bar were looking over. The number two continued to speak to Easter, who glared back with blatant disgust then abruptly walked away.

"Go crawl back under your rock, you useless little prick," Easter called loudly over his shoulder. A hushed excitement radiated through the lounge. The number two, flushing, cast a quick eye over at the team before going towards the door. Easter stepped with calm defiance back towards the players, and to his wife, who took hold of his arm and said something into his ear to which Easter did not respond. During the murmuring pause, while everybody watched for what else might happen, Tom glanced a final time out of the window then took his opportunity to leave.

3

Easter remained silently among the group as they continued drinking. His wife, Leah, sat beside him, her hand occasionally on his knee, turning towards him whenever he made some noise or response to the conversation. Nobody brought up the incident with the number two. At one point, however, Yates and Febian Price did perform their impression of the number two fawning to the manager—a routine in which Price stood up and faced away from the audience, hands on his hips, shouting, "Oi, Two," and Yates crawled around to kneel in front of him before thrusting his head forward so that his face appeared between Price's legs. Then, in a low, pleading voice, Yates whispered, "He doesn't mean it, really, he doesn't mean it," stopping, between repetitions, to arch his neck upwards and mouth kisses at Price's bottom.

"We don't have to stay, Chris."

He turned to Leah for the first time in the last half-hour. "You want to go?"

"No. I just think we don't need to stay if you're not in the mood for it."

"OK. Fine."

He kept his attention out of the taxi window while they moved past the dark shapes of the players' car park.

"What did he say to you?"

He did not answer. His eyes remained on the window. She could see the reflection of them in the glass, fixed, alert—and with a chill she sensed that he might be looking at her. She turned away and saw in the rearview mirror that the driver, somewhat less secretively, was looking directly at her. She rested her head against her window. Closed her eyes.

Once home, he went straight up to the bedroom. Leah poured herself a glass of water in the kitchen, loitering there a short while, and by the time she came upstairs he was already in bed. He was awake, though. She undressed and came over to his side. With one knee on the mattress she leaned over and gently ran her finger over a new cut on his temple. He reached out for the bedside lamp, presently on its dimmest setting, tapped it once, brighter, then brighter again—and for an instant she saw her exposed flesh flare luminously—until at the final tap the room fell to darkness, and she groped her way back around the bed to her own side.

When she woke in the morning she sat up and watched him for a while, still asleep, breathing lightly, peaceful. The cut on his temple had swollen overnight, and in the soft light from a gap in the curtains there was the petrol sheen of a perfect tiny bruise. She slid out of bed and got dressed quickly, quietly, leaving him there sleeping.

In the heat of her car she turned on the air-conditioning, then the radio for a little company, and set off for her mum's.

She knew he had not slept for some time after they went to bed. That was normal, though, after a match. His body would continue to buzz with nervous energy, twitching, turning, reliving the game. If he had picked up an injury, even a small one, it would be all the more difficult for him to get to sleep. This, he said, was why he needed to drink after playing. He would regularly sleep in the spare room, as he did before matches, or she would, but last night he had come to their bed and she had not wanted to leave him on his own. She had wanted him to know, whatever it was that was bothering him, that she was there.

Her mum still lived in the flat that Leah had grown up in. Her parents had moved into it shortly after the damp, thinly attended morning of their marriage ceremony, and Leah had been born there the following year. The block she was approaching now had changed very little since then: the echoing stairwell with its smooth discolored banisters, the smell of bleach, the heavy brown door to her mum's floor, the neighbors, whose hanging baskets creaked above a cheerful procession of welcome mats in the morning breeze of the balcony corridor.

The pram was outside her mum's. There was still no lift in the building, so when her mum had Tyler she usually enlisted the help of the Dynocks next door to get the thing up and down the stairs, and quite often the Dynocks ended up accompanying them on their outings to the shops or the play park. Sometimes, if her mum was working or being taken away for the weekend, the Dynocks looked after him themselves, and Leah wondered, noticing the two cans of Mr. Dynock's Shandy Bass in her mum's recycling box, whether in fact her mum might have been on a date with her new man last night.

She knocked and let herself in. She came through the tight corridor, past the dozens of photographs that covered both walls: herself as a baby, a child, a teenager swamped in Chris's debut first-team shirt, their wedding a couple of years later at the Cliff; Tyler on the facing wall in a Town romper suit, in the bath, at the Dynocks', cackling at their dog. She wondered sometimes what her mum's boyfriends made of this display—if they saw an over-the-top pride in it, loneliness, a warning.

Her mum was in the kitchen making tuna sandwiches. She finished spooning some filling onto a piece of bread and came over to kiss Leah.

"I'm making a packed lunch for me and Robert. We're going out later. I'm doing a packet for Tyler as well. You want one?"

"No, thanks, Mum." She looked over at the wall. "He asleep?"

"Went down about an hour ago."

Her mum went back to the sandwiches. Leah walked through the kitchen and put on the kettle. The window was open and a familiar draft touched her shoulder when she reached into the cupboard for the mugs. For a couple of minutes there was only the sound of the kettle gaining force. Her mum chopping a cucumber. Leah made the tea then stood against the counter and watched her. She might as well have been putting together her school lunchbox: the brisk, efficient movement of her hands, the weathered red plastic chopping board, the same ancient Tupperware. All that was missing was the ominous presence of Leah's dad.

"They drew yesterday." Her mum did not look up from her sandwich-making.

"They were unlucky. They should've won."

Her mum cut each of the sandwiches into four triangles, which she stacked and then cling-filmed. From the fridge, she took out a couple of yogurts, a pack of sausage rolls, a foil plate of quiche, a Kit Kat and, after a slight pause, another Kit Kat. He liked his food, Robert.

"How's he getting on, Chris?"

"He's OK." Leah placed the mugs of tea onto the small table in the middle of the room and the two women sat down.

"Robert says he's been playing well. Must be chalk and cheese after Middlesbrough."

"Yes. He's fine, Mum."

A babbling noise came from the baby monitor on top of the microwave. Her mum started to get up.

"I'll go," Leah said.

Inside the room she switched on the light and went over to the cot. Tyler broke into a simple, delighted smile. She picked him up and for a minute just held him, pressing the warm, hefty little body into her own, the sour stink of his nappy overpowering the room's faint cloying odor of her old perfumes.

When she had changed the nappy she carried him through to the kitchen, where her mum was still seated at the table in a rare moment of inactivity. Leah set Tyler on the floor and he started to crawl towards his grandmother.

"So what does your week look like?" her mum asked.

"Quite busy. College on Thursday, and there's a few people I've said I might meet up with."

"Oh, good." Her mum bent down to where Tyler had reached her toned legs and waggled a sandal strap at him. Leah wondered if she was going to press her further, but just then her mum's mobile vibrated on the table and she straightened up to read the message.

"Robert's about here. He'll be pleased he caught you," she said and went off to the bathroom.

A few minutes later the front door was opened. Leah waited, then Robert appeared at the kitchen entrance: tall, chortling, about to hug her. As he came forward she took in the fleshy eyebrows, the beer belly and, like last time, the disconcerting thin patent-leather maroon belt.

"Leah." He kissed her firmly on the cheek. Then he reached down to pick up Tyler from the floor and held him close to his face. "How's this guy doing?" Tyler pawed at his eyebrows.

"He's good, thank you."

Robert made a series of squeezed faces at Tyler. He touched their noses together. Leah watched, at first amused but increasingly uncomfortable, as her mum came to stand beside her, at the thought of how much time Robert had obviously spent with Tyler in the couple of months that he'd been going out with her mum. She should have been pleased, she knew. He was clearly good with babies, and her mum seemed happier now than she had been with any other of the string of losers since the bleak past of her dad. They went to dance classes. He had his own business, a commercial insurance firm. He had money, hobbies, no significant skeletons in his closet other than an ex-wife, but she was completely out of the picture, according to Robert, having left him two years ago for a strangely tanned Yorkshireman. "And what about Chris? How is he doing?"

"He's fine, thanks." She wondered what her mum might have said to him.

"Good. They played well yesterday, tell him."

Tyler was laughing uncontrollably now because Robert was balancing him on top of his belly. Her mum bent down to blow raspberries on Tyler's tummy. For a few awful seconds, as she looked up at Robert's contented face above her mum's hair, she pictured her head moving down over him. The eager unbuckling of the lady belt. The fat eyebrows creasing, bunching with pleasure.

"OK. Thanks, Mum. Call you in the week." She reached over for Tyler. "Have a good trip out, you two."

She drove home in the sunshine, thinking about the afternoon ahead. In a rare flash of inspiration a few days ago, she had come up with an idea of doing something in the countryside together, and on the Internet she had come across a petting farm only half an hour away from the house. She had not yet told Chris, but she imagined the three of them together, showing Tyler the ducks and chickens, watching his reaction to the donkey. The long expanse of the upcoming week, however, crowded her thoughts. She would do the supermarket shop tomorrow. On Tuesday morning baby music group, and in the afternoon, if she could put out of her mind the other mothers' furtive scrutiny of her figure, baby swimming. There was an away fixture that night, so Chris would be gone all day and not return until the early hours. Wednesday she would have to wait and see how he was—whether he wanted to be alone or to spend the day with them.

Thursday was the day that, privately, she looked forward to each week, guiltily anticipating the moment she would drop Tyler off at her mum's and be on her own, on her way to college, a whole day of workshops and people and thinking for herself before the tense ritual of Friday started to weigh upon her.

Arriving home, she could see when she came up the stairs that he was out of the bedroom and the door to the office was closed. She called hello and returned downstairs.

She began to make lunch. Cheese omelettes. Chris was extremely specific about his diet. In the early days of the week he kept his carbohydrate intake low, gradually increasing it in the buildup to a match, which was why, or at least she told herself was why, they often ate separately in the evening. At Middlesbrough, certainly at first, he had followed closely the advice of the performance nutritionist. Since promotion Town too employed a sports scientist, and preparing Chris's meals involved more planning than Tyler's did.

Tyler shuffled between his toys on the stone floor. She had attached padding to the sharp edges of the kitchen island, and in the spare, clean rooms, which had not yet built up the clutter of a home, there was not much opportunity for him to hurt himself, so she could quite securely leave him while she got on with other things. He would be happily occupied for long periods here with his squeaky animals, or scamper through to the large living space that adjoined the kitchen to sprawl over a carpet as creamy and luxurious as a polar bear, then sit in front of the digital fire and play with the pebbles or follow the flames on the screen with his fingers. In her mum's flat he was forever pulling at wires or fingering under the curled edges of the carpets. Here, though, everything was new, solid, bare.

They had moved in during the close season, soon after Town re-signed Chris. The club had approached him as early as May, the moment he was placed on Middlesbrough's released list. Town's interest had been at the chairman's instigation, she knew. Everybody knew. Clarke had not wanted him. Despite the drop in wages and despite Leah's reservations, Chris had refused to downsize and they had in haste bought this place, which was every bit as impressive as the house they had been renting near Middlesbrough. Why should he have to suffer, he had said, just because some monkey-faced nobhead wasn't going to give him a chance? Unlike the Middlesbrough move, when she had argued him out of buying a stupidly big property, this time she had not argued. She had been relieved simply to be moving back. To put behind her the whole experience of the Middlesbrough transfer. From the outset she had struggled to cope there: heavily pregnant, unable to get comfortable in the hotel room while she waited for him to come back from training, and when finally they did move into the rented house she gave birth the following week—exhausted, mostly alone, returning from the hospital to rooms full of boxes and shrink-wrapped furniture.

And she had thought too that coming back would make everything return to normal. That she would be able to step straight into her old life. But they had been home for almost four months now and so far nothing was like it used to be. This house in the middle of nowhere. Her days spent drifting between it and her mum's and the baby groups in town, where she sat at a remove from the impenetrable chatting clutches of mothers, readying herself for the next moment her isolation would be shown up by Tyler barging over one of their children.

She could hear Chris moving about upstairs. A door closing. The flush of the toilet. She turned on the hob and began whisking the eggs.

When he came down he was dressed and seemed to be in a good mood. He walked over and kissed her on the forehead before going to pick up Tyler, who was crying for her attention at her feet.

"Cheese, is it?"

"That all right?"

"Yeah, cheese is good."

He stayed by the island, letting Tyler chew at the cords of his hoodie while she cooked and served the omelettes.

"How's Donna?" he asked.

"Fine. Good, actually. She looks happy."

Chris put Tyler into his high chair and they sat down at the kitchen table. "What's his name again, the new bloke?"

"Robert. She's into him. More than the last one, anyway."

He snorted. "No shit."

She looked at him across the table. "I found this place on the Internet I thought we could take Tyler this afternoon. This farm for kids, it's not that far a drive."

"A farm?"

"A petting farm. It's not actually that far away."

Tyler took apart his tuna sandwich and threw one of the pieces of bread to the floor. She bent to pick it up and put it on the table.

"No, let's go into town," Chris said. "There's some things I need to get."

Tyler was peering quizzically at his remaining triangle of bread. He revolved it a couple of times in his palm, then pushed the whole thing into his mouth.

Chris laughed. "Just some stuff that I need to finish off here before we go. He can sleep in the car, right?"

She knew, as she cleared away the plates and heard him going back up the stairs, the office door closing, that he would be some time. He was relaxed, though, she placated herself. That was enough.

Tyler fell asleep straightaway in the car. They decided to drive around for a while to let him nap, rather than head straight into town. They took the road towards the coast, and she began to hope that they might end up spending the afternoon there, in the sunshine, but Tyler woke up and started crying before they got that far, so they turned back for town.

She had an intuition, even before he spoke to the supporter in Foot Locker, the old man on the escalator, the group coming out of Burger King, that he would not avoid the fans today. During these conversations she stayed by the pram and waited, glad at least that she was invisible in public when he was with her. They always said the same things: how pleased they'd been when they heard he was coming back, that they weren't convinced Clarke was up to it at this level, and could he maybe sign something for their dad, their brother, their little boy?

She watched from a short distance as he chatted to three teenagers, a boy and two girls, outside Burger King. The girls' smiling faces never leaving his, Chris clearly ignoring the boy. After a few minutes she began to get embarrassed and moved further away, crouching to talk to Tyler inside the hood of his pram.

In the days that they used to go to clubs together, she had become used to this. There had been many times that she had stood beside him as brigades of girls came and talked to him, bought him drinks, touched his stomach, his bum, and she would grow unsure whether they were even aware of her there, holding his hand. Once, when she had left him to go to the toilet and come back to discover that he had moved from their table, she had searched the bar and the dance floor of the club until she found him in a passageway near the exit doors with a girl that she did not recognize. Their faces had been close together. She could not be certain if they were moving towards or away from each other, or if their hands had been touching. She had watched them for a few seconds, then left, afraid of being spotted, to go and join the other players in the chill-out room.

When he returned from Burger King he said that he wanted to buy her something. What would she like? Shoes? Something for her course? For Tyler?

He bought her a top, himself a phone upgrade. When they got home she tried on the new top and showed it to him. It looked good, he told her. They ate with Tyler and sat watching cartoons with him before she bathed and changed him and got him to bed.

In the living room, the television on in the background, they sat together on the sofa and she rested her head on his shoulder. He put his hand to her hair and began to stroke the side of her face with his thumb. She let her eyes close. Briefly, she thought she might go to sleep. He moved position, though, gently shifting her head from his shoulder and lowering himself until he was laid out on his front over the sofa. She got up and knelt down on the carpet. Starting at one end of his body she gave him a leg, back and shoulder massage, for a long time, until eventually he turned over and, to her tired relief, took hold of her hands, sliding them slowly across his stomach.

4

In the gastroenterology unit of the district general hospital a consultant with a lazy eye was explaining to her small following party the nature of the work that her team performed. She had only been briefed by the ward manager at the start of her shift that three footballers would be visiting that afternoon, so had been required to cut short the daily review with her house officers and forgo lunch. Nonetheless, she managed without rush or irritation to show them around the department before passing them on to the sister who would lead them through some of the patients.

This was Tom's first community visit for the club. He, Yates and Ashlee Richards, the friendly young left-winger, had driven separately from training and met in the hospital car park.

"Come on then," Yates had said on the walk towards the entrance. "Let's go see them before they die." He was not enthusiastic about community visits. The previous season he had cost the club a considerable amount of unfavorable coverage, and complimentary tickets, when he told a pupil at a local secondary school that he kicked like he had a golf club up his arse.

He was staring now with sullen boredom at the consultant and her peculiar eye, while Tom and Richards listened respectfully then followed her down the busy, bright corridors. When the consultant left them, the sister, a giggling middle-aged woman with long withered fingers, called Sabihah, led them into a large room. Exhausted-looking old men were sitting up in their beds. On the screen of a television on top of a wheeled cabinet by the wall, a teenage boy and girl were kissing in an empty classroom. Sabihah gave each player a different starting point and arranged a circuit for them around the room, as if they were at a sponsors' function.

Tom sat down at one after another of the low chairs by the beds, unsure what to say. With the first two it was not a problem, as they were happy simply to talk: they had supported Town all their lives, they missed going to the games, they wanted the toilet but they didn't want to say so to the Asian nurse. But his next two just lay there, their eyes goggling at him or across the room. Yellow flagging chests gaped from the slits in their gowns. Spiny hands trembled on the sheets. One had no chair by his bed so Tom stood awkwardly beside him for the three minutes, filling with a grave urge to find something to speak about.

The stubbly old boy on the next bed, though, chuckled when Tom handed him one of the signed match programs that he had been instructed to give to each patient.

"I know. Sorry."

"No, no, not to worry. Not to worry. This will help pass the hours. Let's see."

He opened the program with exaggerated fascination. Through his thin hair there was a dark cut, newly clotted. "'View from the dugout,'" he read aloud. "'I'd like to take the opportunity to extend a warm welcome to today's opponents, Exeter City, their manager and visiting supporters.'" Tom wondered if he was going to read out the whole piece. He stopped there, however, and read silently for a short time before speaking again: "'I honestly believe we have the players in the building to get out of this difficult spell. Tonight's cup tie gives us a great opportunity to pick ourselves back up and it's all the more significant because this will be the first time of course this club has ever competed in the League Cup. But we all have to pull together. So let's get behind the team tonight and hope that first win is just around the corner. Spectacular achievement is born of unity alone.'" The man looked up at Tom. "What happened in this game then? Spectacular achievement?"

"We lost 4–1."

The man went back to the program. He flicked through until he got to the center pages.

"Is that you?"

It was a double-page picture of Easter, his head down, about to strike the ball.

"No, the captain."

"Oh." He appraised the picture. "What's he like, then?"

Tom looked over at Richards, sitting in animated conversation with one patient, and Yates, who had his chin in his hand, staring with his own man at the television.

"Actually, he's a dick."

The old man, and Tom, began to laugh—loudly enough for some of the patients to look over and Sabihah to smile from the doorway.

"I don't know anything about football," the man said. "I never liked it." He considered Tom calmly for a moment. "Don't mean to be rude, but I'm not sure you look like a footballer to me."

Tom smiled. "What does a footballer look like?"

The man turned his head to Yates, who was getting up from his chair and looking through the doorway at two nurses walking past. "That one. He looks like a footballer."

"Well," Tom said, "I'm more of a substitute."

The man patted the bed in appreciation. Tom stood up. It was time to move on to the next patient but he felt reluctant to leave.

"Do you enjoy it?" the man asked.

Tom looked down at him. Through his nightshirt he could see his breasts rotting like old fruit.

"It's what I always wanted to be."

The man clucked admiringly. The sheeted mound of his body stirred at the shaking of his left leg. Tom suddenly imagined his dad lying there, old, dying. "There's not many of us can say we've achieved that." He patted the program. "Thank you for this. I'll stash it away with my pornography."

———

The official photograph of the visit was published in the local paper the following day: the three players standing together next to the bed of a baffled old man.

"We'll put it up, then?" Mrs. Davey said at breakfast.

Tom shook his head but Mrs. Davey and the two boys protested, so the photograph was torn out and pinned to the large corkboard on the back of the kitchen door, alongside the youth and first-team fixture lists, the washing machine schedule and the tear-outs of bits and pieces that had taken anybody's fancy. Mrs. Davey liked to put up recipes, hospice newsletters, articles that she had read in the *Express* or in the local paper, and Bobby and Steven liked to push their luck with her by displaying page three models, their nipples obscured by drawing pins.

There was an atmosphere of unceasing noise and motion about the house. Tom enjoyed the mealtimes: weekday roasts, pies, fish and chips that Mrs. Davey made herself. When they finished eating, the household moved through to the living room to watch the television, and after a little while, depending what was on, the Scottish pair would go upstairs to play on Bobby's Xbox. They usually asked Tom if he would like to join them, but mostly he declined, even though he always left the living room shortly after they did to go up to his own room.

He went regularly to the cinema—most Wednesday afternoons and, a couple of times since his arrival at the Daveys', after dinner with Bobby and Steven. One night he walked with them to a pub on a nearby street to play pool. He had been given firm instructions by the Daveys not to buy them drinks. Against the pair's pleadings, he did not, and they drank several Cokes while he slowly finished a single pint of lager, conscious the whole time that one or two of the people in the pub had identified him. While they were at the pool table a man came up to speak to him. He was amiable and introduced Tom to his wife, but all the same it made Tom uneasy to think that people might know who he was, be looking at him as he went about in public. On one of his first trips to the cinema a group of boys not much younger than himself had spotted him in the foyer. He had tried to ignore them repeatedly looking over from the popcorn counter, and in his haste to get away he had slipped into an auditorium and sat down in front of a film that, despite the title, turned out to be foreign.

Andrew, the Daveys' other son, came to visit for an afternoon. He was very chatty with all of the lodgers, and made a joke of the fact that he knew nothing about football. Both he and the middle child, Sarah, had left town some years ago. Sarah was married, lived in London and had not visited since Christmas, something that was mentioned three times during Tom's first couple of weeks in the house. Liam, though, lived somewhere nearby. He came over occasionally, never for long, usually to eat.

He was at the house the Sunday after Tom's hospital outing, when the whole household sat down to three roast chickens.

"How was it?" he asked Tom during the meal, pointing at the newspaper cutting on the corkboard.

"All right," Tom said. "Bit stupid, giving them signed programs."

Liam kept looking at the newspaper. "How were Yates and Richards?"

"Richards is all right."

"Yes," Liam said. "I've seen what Yates is like."

Mr. Davey, at the head of the table, cleared his throat at this point. "Michael Yates is a class-A bighead."

The Scottish pair looked at each other and sniggered. Mrs. Davey caught her husband's eye very briefly and raised her eyebrows.

"He is," Mr. Davey carried on. "He's your typical loudmouth. Always giving it this and that and winding people up because he knows he's not very good and he's scared out of his tiny brain by it."

Tom noticed that Liam was watching his father with amusement during this speech. There was a twitch of his lips, pursing into a smile, which lingered even as he placed a forkful of chicken into his mouth and started, slowly, rhythmically, to chew it.

"He couldn't work the vending machine at the hospital," Tom said to Liam. "I went to the toilet and he was trying to get something out of it, and when I came back he was just pressing all the buttons. I don't think he knew you've got to put money in it." He had made the last part up, but Liam laughed, the whole table laughed, and Tom looked down at his plate to hide the obvious pride on his face.

The easiness of the house was in contrast to the fraught daily battle of training and match days. He pushed himself to impress. He competed with breathless application in practice games and aimed always to be one of the first or the fastest during fitness work. As a result he was left alone—his effort quietly respected by some, distrusted by others, and it seemed in the case of the manager both.

For endeavor only Bobby and Steven could equal him. Like the other couple of scholars who sometimes joined first-team training, they were fitter than most of the seniors because the youth team's sessions were longer, harder, geared towards endurance. It made them a target. A number of the older players routinely made sure to assert their physical and vocal superiority. Sometimes, after a heavy challenge or sudden abuse, Tom imagined speaking out to defend them, but did not. They were shouted at, elbowed, kneed in the back, all under the eyes of Clarke, who wanted them prepared for the same in real matches, and all just as Tom too had undergone as a scholar.

One afternoon, behind the clubhouse, Bobby was given the boot polish treatment. Easter appeared with the brush and tin and held the boy down on the grass himself while several others stripped him and pinned his frantic spatchcocked legs for Price to apply the polish to his genitals. Tom moved inside, into the corridor, from where he listened to the sound of shouting and hilarity coming through the fire exit. Moments later the group barreled inside, Bobby at the front of them, naked, grinning and pale. In the middle of his white body was the shocking sight of his black, oiled penis, his thighs blotchy with scarlet finger marks.

After the squad had changed and gone to the canteen, Tom turned back to look into the dressing room. Steven was sitting on a bench, staring at his phone. Beyond him, Bobby was still in the showers, desperately sponging himself. There was nothing, Tom thought, that he could say. Their status would improve at a stroke, he could tell them that. But it was better to say nothing, he decided, and of course the incident could never be brought up at the Daveys', so he left them to themselves.

On the days that Bobby and Steven trained with the seniors they usually sat next to Tom in the canteen at the far end of a long bench by the milk fridge and the recovery shakes table, after queuing up patiently for their food and giving up their position every time a first-teamer joined the line. Today, though, they did not come in. Tom ate slowly, glad that this was not one of the afternoons that he drove them home, until eventually most of the squad had left and the backroom staff began arriving for their lunch. One of the last to come in was Liam. Tom wondered whether he had seen anything of the boot polish scene. He chose his food, chatting a while to Lesley the cook over the top of the glass counter before turning round and, on seeing Tom, hesitating momentarily before walking towards him.

"You're in late. Mind if I join you?"

"Go ahead." Tom scanned behind Liam to see if any of the few remaining players had noticed, knowing that it would look unusual.

Liam began eating hungrily. "Mum's wrong. I think Les's food is really good."

"I had chicken," Tom said. Then, worried that he had just made himself sound like a thickhead, "It was good."

Liam kept his eyes on his plate, continuing to eat. "She gets a bit competitive. You've seen the effort she makes with the coach food. She doesn't have to do that, you know. She loves helping out. You know she used to wash the kit?"

"Mrs. Davey?"

"Before we had a kit man. She used to hang it all out in the garden."

Tom looked about the room. The rest of the players had left.

"I was in the youth team then," Liam said. "Keeper. Bet you didn't know that, either."

Tom regarded with intrigue the broad, flat face. Liam was finishing his food already. His hands, wrists, were smudged with soil.

"Same time as Boyn and Easter. Chris was a cock back then too." For a couple of seconds he observed Tom's reaction. "He was good, though. To be fair. Made the rest of us look like park players. He got offered schoolboy terms at Tottenham, but he didn't take them. Right move, probably. They just get lost, those kids."

Tom turned his face away, embarrassed.

Liam started into his bowl of stewed fruit and custard. "You played for England Under-18s, didn't you?"

Tom gave a sniff of surprise.

Liam smiled. "Google."

Tom wanted at that moment to tell him about Bobby. But he could not. A confusing barrier of shame held him back—an instinct as well that it was not for Liam to know, that what went on among the squad was not for people on the outside. Liam was getting up now anyway, wiping his mouth and picking up his tray.

"Back to it then. See you around."

Tom watched him stack the tray on the tower by the door, saying a few words to the goalkeeping coach. Before Tom could look away, Liam glanced back in his direction, then left.

The canteen was deserted. Through in the kitchen, Lesley was wiping the surfaces, humming to a song on the radio. For a few minutes Tom stayed where he was, one hand still around his glass on the table, then flinched as Lesley suddenly appeared smiling in front of him.

"Come on then. You ready to let me go home?"

The players' car park was nearly empty. Only the injured players' vehicles remained. A small paper notice rested on the window of Boyn's silver Mercedes: £40 FINE—PLEASE PARK IN SQUAD NUMBERED BAY. Tom walked on until he reached his own car. Getting into it, he felt jittery, inexplicably in need of something to do with his hands. He took a CD from the glovebox and popped the disc out of its case, then back in again, out, in, out, the rhythm of the action focusing, soothing him, until the plastic inner of the CD snapped and flew off.

Further down the lane he could see the minibus in the staff car park that would soon take the scholars into college for their BTEC, and he considered waiting for them to come out of the clubhouse, to see Bobby and Steven with the others, talking, being normal.

He started the car and drove away. Before he had even reached the turning onto the main road, though, restive at the thought of going back to the house, to his room, he made a spur-of-the-moment decision to drive to the coast.

He followed the signs until, through a windswept avenue of faded houses and hotel fronts, the sea became visible. He parked at a pay and display. When he got out, the air was fresh, inviting, and he made towards the seafront. Not many people were about: a woman on a bench beside a boy in a pram, both eating chips, an old couple sitting in their car, two young women in aprons and hairnets standing talking outside a fish and chip shop. He went towards an ice cream van near the seafront. When he got to the window it appeared at first that there was nobody in it, but then a girl his own age came out from behind a screened compartment.

"Sorry," she said. "Fag break. You caught me out. What would you like?"

He studied the board behind her, aware of her eyes on him.

"You got a choc ice?"

"Sure."

She turned away towards a large chest freezer. As she reached into it her earrings, like tiny wind chimes, dangled against her cheeks.

"Thanks," Tom said when she handed the choc ice to him. There was a moment of stillness in which they looked at each other. He felt his veins thicken and knew that he was blushing. "Must get boring, days like this," he said.

"Hell, yes. I'll be out my mind by four thirty."

"Yeah, I bet."

He gave her his money. She took his change from the till and smiled at him as she put it into his hand. For an instant he thought to say something about the earrings. He smiled back at her. "Thanks," he said and walked away onto the promenade.

A little way along, three teenage lads were sitting atop the backrest of a bench. At his approach they stopped their conversation to look up at him. He lowered his choc ice away from his mouth and continued past them. When he was a little way on he stopped, inciting himself to return to the ice cream van. Seagulls screamed above him. His heart began to race, and he turned—only to see that one of the boys was coming towards him. He changed direction again and hurried away.

"Mate." The boy was close behind. "Hey, mate."

There was no choice but to turn and face him. The boy advanced and stopped a couple of steps away. He looked around to his friends and when he turned back to Tom the remains of a smile were on his lips.

"I know who you are."

Behind him, his mates were angled towards the scene, nudging at each other and laughing.

"You're Tom Pearman, aren't you? Bet you're pissed off, going from Premier League to here. Can't even get in the team either, can you?"

"I've been injured."

His choc ice was dripping onto the ground.

"Things not going so well, are they?"

"It's going all right."

"Oh yeah, it's going fucking great."

"I need to get on, sorry."

"Fine. See you then, mate."

When the boy spun round, his friends burst out laughing. Tom began the long loop back round to the car park. Behind him, a few seconds later, he heard one of them shout something, the words lost to the wind and the movement of the sea.

He was picked to start in the first round of a Johnstone's Paint Trophy tie, at home against Stevenage. Clarke had taken Tom and a few of the other squad players aside a week earlier to tell them that he was planning to bring them in—he would have rested the whole first team but the rules did not allow him to, he said. It was their chance to impress, he drummed into them, especially as the game was to be shown live on Sky.

As soon as Tom entered the dressing room and saw the rows of carefully arranged place settings, each shirt on its hanger above a neat pile of shorts and socks and folded underpants, two nestled bottles of water and a banana, he could not get out of his head the thought of his mum. He went into one of the toilet cubicles and locked the door. He sat down and gripped the sides of his head, concentrating on regulating his breathing. Nerves—burning, liquid—plummeted through him. He could see her, with the rest of his family, all gathered in Kenny and Jeanette's living room, probably with a few neighbors, waiting for the match. He tried to remember when he had last spoken to her. Two weeks ago, on the phone. She had been in the middle of cooking tea and they had spoken for only a minute or two. He thought back for the time before that, but he could not bring it to mind.

When he came out of the cubicle the dressing room was jumping with the sound of voices. Laughter. Spanked flesh. Loud chart music from one corner, some of the players singing along. Boyn dancing. The smell of Deep Heat. Tom walked to his kit and sat down on the bench. Directly in front of him, Daish was laid out on a massage table, getting a rub from the physio. Some of the players were sitting at their places, quiet and alone, headphones on or reading the program. The kit man was on a chair near the door, polishing footballs with a shammy. Tom watched him, the man's face engrossed in the task, his eyebrows twitching with each turning of the ball. A couple of minutes later the kit man got up and went towards two large metal chests against a wall. He opened the lid of one and Tom was able to glimpse inside—a treasure trove of chocolate bars and cereals, chewing gum, Jelly Babies. He did not at first realize that Price, sitting on his left, was talking to him.

"You all right, bud?"

He was close enough for his knee to be touching Tom's. On his top lip there was a slender mustache that Tom had not noticed before. "Fine, yeah."

"First start, isn't it?"

Tom nodded.

"I still get nervous before matches, you know," Price said. "Every time. Even Paint matches no one cares about. Always been the same. Gets five minutes to kickoff and I'm bricking it." He gave Tom a light slap on the leg and stood up. "You'll be fine, bud. You've got talent, you know. More than I have." He walked off whistling, and disappeared into a toilet cubicle.

When, after Clarke's blunt unspecific team talk, the buzzer sounded on the wall above Tom's head, he at once needed to go to the toilet again, but the other players were already getting to their feet so he filed out close behind Price, replicating his actions: shaking the hand of Clarke, the number two, the goalkeeping coach, then high-fiving along the line that had formed at the opened door, where the noise of the crowd was coming down the tunnel to mix with studs and shouts and the murmuring incantation of sixteen players telling each other, "All the best, all the best, all the best."

He knew straightaway that the small hesitant youth he was up against would not be able to cope with him. His teammates knew it too, and played him in at every opportunity. The boy panicked each time, clinging to Tom's shirt, stabbing his child's feet at the ball, missing. Tom controlled a long pass from Fleming, heard a quiet mewl of "Oh shit" behind him and turned to set upon the boy again.

He began to play with a confidence that he had forgotten. He shouted for the ball. He took a shot from distance that was deflected marginally past the post and sprinted to take the corner himself—his senses alive to the urging of the crowd, to the blood throbbing through his limbs, to the rousing warm drift of onions and pies from the tea bar at the bottom corner of the stand.

Town won 3–1. Tom almost scored a fourth in injury time, with a shot from just inside the penalty area that scudded off the top of the crossbar and into the closed-off stand behind the goal. For the thirty seconds that it took the clambering ballboy—tasked with standing alone on the terracing to wait for off-target shots—to retrieve the ball, Tom's body felt so light with adrenaline and awareness of the crowd, the cameras, his family in Kenny's living room, that he had to force the smile from his face.

The euphoria of the win survived for several days. A new noise and energy surfaced. Tom was in the clubhouse lounge with Bobby and Steven one morning when some kind of festivity became audible outside, and they went with everybody else to find Boyn at the entrance to the clubhouse, wielding a five-foot-high rectangle of card that he was trying to get through the doorway. "What the hell's he doing?" someone whispered. "What's that?"

"Not a clue."

"It's a check."

"It's what?"

"It's a check. Bank check. Look."

And as more of them herded into the reception area while Price took one end of the thing, helping Boyn maneuver it like a piece of furniture through the doorway, Tom could see that it was true.

"Fuck's that, Boyney? Community this afternoon?"

Boyn smiled. "Nope."

Slowly he lifted it up for them to read. The check was for forty pounds, made payable to the club. At each corner was an image of Boyn, sitting on a chair in swimming shorts, spooning out a coconut.

"It's my fine. I got it done on the Internet. I'm going to give it him now."

There was a rash of gaiety; guarded silence from those who still did not understand.

"He'll go ape shit."

"Well," Boyn said, starting through the crowd, "let's see, shall we?"

They streamed from reception, following the wibble-wobble noise of the great check quivering along the corridor. When they approached Clarke's office everybody else held back, watching Boyn knock on the door, then, upon a dim shout, disappear.

He came back out a few minutes later. Clarke's arm was around his shoulders. Both men were grinning.

"Brilliant banter," Clarke said to the group. "Bloody brilliant banter."

They looked at Boyn, trying to discern whether this was some kind of trap, but Boyn looked almost beside himself with exultation. Clarke gave in to a new impulse of laughter, pulling Boyn into a constrictive embrace, mock-punching him in the stomach. "Fucking check cost him more than the fine," he said, punching him again.

Clarke was, however, careful to balance the mood of victory with a warning that nobody should get ahead of themselves: "It was only the Johnstone's fucking Paint, remember. You're still shit. You'll be back in the reserves next week," he told the cup team playfully, and although Tom was sure that he had played well enough to be excluded from this rebuke, he found out soon enough that he had only made the bench for Saturday.

He sat slumped in the dugout, willing the team to fail—and he experienced a sly satisfaction when they did. The match appeared to be heading for a draw, but a late miscommunication between Boyn and Foley allowed a Shrewsbury forward to nip in and head the ball into an unguarded net. The Town supporters turned on Foley, then Clarke—"You don't know what you're doing!"—and then the Shrewsbury manager when some fans in the main stand detected from a joke with his substitutes what they took to be mirth at Town's situation. As he sent on the two very young subs for the remainder of injury time, he was subjected to a chant of "Sit down, you pedophile" until the referee blew the whistle and the stadium imploded with booing.

Town went bottom of the division.

Afterwards, as Tom left the ground to begin the walk back to the Daveys', he saw a knot of half a dozen players in the car park. He pretended not to see them and walked on, but Richards caught sight of him and called him over.

"We're off to the Beach Hut, Tommy." Richards looked to the stadium behind Tom. "Clarke's not to know, right? Up for it?"

It took him a couple of seconds to respond. "OK."

He got into one of the two cars and texted Mrs. Davey to let her know that he would be late back, angling his screen away from Boyn and Richards next to him on the backseat.

The Beach Hut was the larger of the two clubs in town. The players went there infrequently. When they did socialize together, which was not often, they mostly traveled to one of the big city nightclubs an hour or so away. They were known at the Hut, which—although that presented its own attractions—meant that whatever they got up to there would be known too.

The minute they entered the club, Tom already reeling from the lager and shots they had drunk quickly in the bar on the other side of the road, it was obvious they were being looked at. Tom stayed close to Richards, who bought him a drink. It was dark and loud. He felt bewildered, a little intoxicated, by it all. He had heard some of the players talk about Hut girls before, and had assumed that they were exaggerating. But he watched now as one girl, talking to Charlie Lewis, indicated with her finger for him to turn round, then squeezed his bum, an action that Lewis then repeated on her. There were several young women, and a few young men, around their group. One of the women looked at Tom and smiled. Richards, watching, gave him a thumbs-up. The woman came forward and said hello to Tom, but then Boyn stepped in to talk to her. Boyn led her towards the dance floor and the woman turned, gesturing with her head for Tom to come too. He smiled at her but hung back. The group of players had fragmented by now, and Tom found himself apart from the others. He moved back to the refuge of the bar. He could not make sense of things, his head spinning. For a while he stared out at the heaving mob of bodies and remembered vividly the night that he had got together with Jenni Spoffarth. The huddle of his mates egging him on. His best friend Craig, before Craig puked up in the toilets, shoving him towards her and the strange, proud feeling as her tiny figure had pressed against him.

He picked up his vodka and Red Bull from the bar counter, downed it and made for the dance floor.

By one o'clock the club was a sticky mess of legs and faces and spilt drinks. The area around the food kiosk was trodden with chips and burger droppings, mayonnaise skids. Two men had been thrown out after a fight started in the toilets when one of them made a joking threat to the young African student dispensing hand towels and aftershaves by the sinks and the other demanded that he apologize.

Some of the Town players were standing in a circle just outside the railing around the dance floor, clapping and stamping at a young woman wearing a belt of brightly colored liquids in thin test tubes. A small posse of other women was gathered nearby, watching and cheering as the men drank down a round of tubes, then moving forward gamely when the players bought a second round for them.

One teenage girl, during the distraction of the footballers laughing at each other, tried to pass her tube back to the shot sales rep, but Yates, who was making a joke of unbuttoning his shirt and encouraging the women to lick off the clammy substance he poured onto his stomach, spotted immediately what she was trying to do and started up a clap-chant with the other players: "Drink. Drink. Drink." The girl held the tube aloft and to a loud cheer took it in a single gulp.

In the hugging and jostling of everybody moving towards the dance floor, nobody noticed the momentary buckling of her legs. She gave a small retch, but nothing came up, and with one hand she held onto the lacquered railing while one of her friends supported her other arm. For a few seconds she dropped to her knees, the friend saying something into her ear and somebody else holding a plastic cup of water in front of her. On coming to, she drank the water, scrambled to her feet and pulled away from the hand on her arm to move out onto the dance floor.

A few of the players were doubled over with laughter, pointing through the mass to where Tom was dancing, energetically and alone in the middle of the floor. He was lost in the music, clapping, jumping, then repeatedly punching the air to the song's chorus.

The girl had begun dancing now too, in a fashion, unable to hold her head up, her eyes cast down towards the whirl of ankles and dirty shoes. Boyn pushed through the dancers towards her and took hold of her upper arm. He tilted her face up and pointed at Tom, shouting something into her ear as he steered her towards him.

When Boyn released her, the girl grabbed Tom around the waist. He placed a hand on her back and continued to dance, holding her to him. She looked up at his face and leaned her head into his neck but stumbled. He caught her, pulled her towards him and they kissed messily, his bottom lip sliding against her nose before he lifted her head back up. They kissed again, for longer, the girl's eyes closing as he pressed his hand against the small of her back.

Tom let her forehead rest against his shoulder and gripped her tightly as they swayed to the music, the girl completely oblivious, unlike him, to the leering faces on the other side of the dance floor.

5

The starting eleven and substitutes were made to undergo a video analysis of the Shrewsbury match. Each section of the team came in separately to examine its own particular failings: the front two, then the midfield, the defense—working backwards through the lineup to conclude with Frank Foley grimly following a looped sequence of his own large form watching the flight of the ball from a corner, leaping, punching, missing, flattening Boyn, then watching again from the ground as the ball was nodded into the goal.

The midfielders came in for the heaviest criticism. They entered the small darkened room inside the bowels of the stadium to sit on a bench surrounded by the shadowy ghosts of whiteboards and motivational posters. Unconsciously, they took up their on-field formation—Richards on the left, Easter and Price in the center, Finch-Evans on the right, and the midfield substitutes on chairs either side—while Clarke moved to stand behind them, ready with the remote control. Loud bursts of windblown footage came onto the screen, punctuated, as Clarke rewound, by heavy silences inside the room and the faint drone outside of the rotary mower going up and down the pitch.

"What are you not doing?"

The midfielders stared at the frozen image, searching for the answer somewhere amid the disjointed figures.

"What, that I tell you every week—every fucking day—are you not doing in this picture?"

"Moving?"

Clarke glowered at the back of Easter's head, unsure if this was a joke. "Squeezing," he said. "You're not squeezing the pitch. They've got the ball, and you four aren't fucking doing anything." He replayed the passage. Then he walked round to the front of the bench. Only Easter looked up to face him. Clarke showed them more examples, which took some time to achieve because he twice pressed the frame skip button by mistake—advancing to the defense section, then to Foley's misadventure—his irritation mounting as he struggled to find the correct clips. "You don't want to play league football, is that it? You want to go back where we were? Do you? Dog shit on the pitches? Changing in car parks? Crowds you could fit in the back of a van? Do you, Pricey? Finch?" He stared at the impassive faces of the pair, ignoring Easter, who had been at the club before either of them. "Because if this doesn't improve then that's where you're headed, even if by some bloody miracle I manage to keep us up."

He pressed for the next clip. "Given away." Then the next—this one accompanied by the background groan of the cameraman, the youth welfare officer, part of whose job it was to compile these recordings. "And again—given away."

"I thought we're supposed to get the ball forward early."

Clarke looked down at Easter. "You are. To one of *our* players."

"Yes, but thing is, gaffer, if we're just hitting it long as soon as we get it then the ball's just bouncing off heads."

Clarke said nothing but stepped forward slightly.

"What I'm saying," Easter continued, "is how can we pass if it's in the air?"

Clarke placed his foot on the edge of the bench in between Easter and Price.

"Are you taking the piss out of me?"

"What?"

"Are you taking the piss out of me?" There was an arch, oddly flirtatious, note to the repeated question. "The rest of you can go. Tell the defense to wait outside."

Once they had gone out Clarke closed the door and switched on the lights. The small dark eyes shrank further into their crumpled pockets, fixing on Easter from above two little beards of ruined skin.

"Do you want to play in the reserves, you stupid boy?"

The sound of the mower, advancing towards them, grew louder.

"Or somewhere else, maybe? Pack your bags again?"

"You're the gaffer. You do what you want."

After a pause Clarke smiled and stepped aside. He pointed at the door. When Easter reached it there was a hurried shuffling on the other side before he let himself out.

He was too worked up to go straight home. He drove away from the stadium, the town, seeking open roads, fields, the coast. He had wanted to be hit. Just for a moment, there in that room, he had wanted Clarke to punch him. To feel the sharp red pain of a blow to the nose and not budge. To take it calmly and walk away. But it had not happened, and now he needed to feel the power of the car, to run into something even—a rabbit, a fox—and hear the impact of it on his bonnet.

It was half past three, however, and the car idled in school traffic. He closed up to the vehicle in front, revving, goading his anger, trying to sustain it, already fearful of what he knew would follow.

Finally out onto country roads, he felt the surge of the engine responding to his foot. When another car or a tractor slowed his progress he pestered at their rear bumpers, relishing the fury that rose in him when they did not speed up. He moved alongside an estate car on a long, unsighted hedge bend, his hands getting hot and rigid on the wheel, until the straight road ahead suddenly appeared, clear.

He climbed into the hills near the coast and parked at a deserted viewing point. From inside his car he looked out at tiny ships, a ferry, which barely seemed to be moving.

A single faraway patch of light shone on the water for a couple of minutes, before the ceiling of clouds closed around the sun. He texted Leah to tell her that he had stayed on at the ground and wouldn't be home for a while. For a long time he stared at the sea. A light rain started to fall. The horizon was blurring. He could feel a heaviness pulling him down and he tried to bring to mind some thought or image that might rile him back up: he pictured Foley's error, Price not tracking back, all those other useless fuckers' mistakes that were not flagged up like his own. Clarke smiling at him. Today had been the first time that Clarke had threatened to get shut of him himself, rather than getting his little prick of an assistant to pass on the message for him: that he had been at fault for a goal; that his form wasn't good enough; that if it didn't improve they might have to think about their options.

He put on the windscreen wipers and he directed his sight on the ferry, trying to recall the times that he had played well, to visualize what he had done. He went backwards through the season, recollecting each match and his part in it, but he could not bring to mind his last good performance; he could only see the mistakes he had made.

He thought back further, to the previous season at Middlesbrough, and was instantly put into the same state of fretful unhappiness that had followed him—them—for the whole of that period—from car journey to car journey, to the training base, to the oppressive bowl of the stadium, to the hotel room and the queasy company of Leah lying enormously on the bed next to her phone and a bucket. That season, he was certain, he had not played well once. For the most part he had not played. After the first dozen games, in and out of the team, the manager made a comment on the club website about his needing time to adjust to the slower, more controlled pace of Championship football; that he would have an important role to play as the season progressed and injuries and fixture backlog took their toll. Such a role never materialized. He spent the season on the bench or, more often, not on the bench or even at the grounds—instead at the hotel, then the expensive rented house surrounded by boxes and baby clothes, looking on at the helpless veined creature in the bed with his wife that responded more to the various nannies and cleaners who came and went than to himself.

The thought of telling Leah about the confrontation with Clarke passed through his mind. He knew, though, that he could not. The idea of admitting that he had failed, again, that she might have to move, again, was simply not an option. He kept his eyes on the ferry, advancing unstoppably towards him through the relentless brutal sea—and panic entered him, his every sinew hardening against the sensation of being out of control. If he let his hold slacken, even for a moment, he was sure that he would never regain it and his weakness would be exposed—to Leah, his teammates, the fans. Not good enough. Not man enough. His world collapsing from all sides in on him.

He fired the engine and turned the car round.

Below him, the open country of his drive home was fleetingly lit up in a snatch of sunlight: a flat panorama of patchwork farmland and the dotted islands of woods, hamlets, one of them his own, merging further on into a belt of suburbia—the faceless mass of mediocre idiots who drove in once a fortnight with their scarves and their sons and their pretend shirts towards the dark blot of the town in the distance, which was falling now again back into shadow, the matchsticks of the stadium floodlights disappearing from view as he pulled out onto the road and descended towards home.

He came into the living room, where Tyler was sitting on the rug, repeatedly face-planting into a cushion.

"Mate, what are you doing?" He walked towards him, smiling, and bent to pick him up. When he put his hands around the small body, though, Tyler went rigid and began to cry. "It's all right, mate, it's all right." He lifted him, patting his back, but Tyler bucked, kicking his feet, so he dumped him back down on the rug and went into the kitchen.

Leah was sterilizing feeding bottles in the microwave.

"Want a coffee?" he asked.

"I will, thanks."

He filled the kettle, watching her take the steaming plastic bottles out of the microwave, screwing on teats, caps, moving about the kitchen, and he wanted right then to take hold of her, to detain her against him and not let her go. Then Tyler blared into the room, the kettle clicked, at which he made their coffees and headed for the door, avoiding Tyler, to make his way upstairs to the sanctuary of the office.

Who do you think should be captain?		
Started by Bald and Proud	Replies:	55
17 Sep 2011 ≤ 1 2 3 ≥	Views:	612

He clicked on the thread.

Bald and Proud   **posted Sat at 11:46pm**

After today I'm convinced that Easter isn't the right player to lead this side, it needs someone with more league experience who hasn't got issues with their own performances.

Riversider   **posted Sat at 11:53pm**

Totally agree, Bald and Proud. Easter's head isn't right, hasn't been since he came back. Get shut if you ask me and bring in an older head who can help the younger players along better.

Voice of Reason   **posted Sun at 12:10am**

Easter's head isn't right!!! Nice one, don't make me laugh. His head was never right, the guy's a ****ing nutcase! It's not his head it's his legs that've gone. Got more than he was worth for him last summer . . . never should have signed him back. Overrated.

Dr. Feelgood   **posted Sun at 12:52am**

Bald and Proud wrote:
After today I'm convinced that Easter isn't the right player to lead
this side, it needs someone with more league experience who
hasn't got issues with their own performances.

The trouble is, Bald and Proud, to get someone experienced and quality in like you say, we'd need to free up Easter's wage, and who realistically is going to sign him from us? Besides which he's the chairman's monkey and no way is the Fat Controller going to let him go now when he made so much noise about getting him back in the first place.

Town Legend   posted Sun at 1:03am
Don't hear the chairman making much noise about him now though do you?

Road to Wembley 2010   posted Sun at 9:02am
John Daish should be captain.

Lardass   posted Sun at 10:35am
What short memories people have. It wasn't that long ago that everyone was singing Easter's name from the rooftops. It was always going to take him time to adjust, coming back, especially with so little first-team football under his belt last year. It's only September, folks. We're not even two months into the season. Keep the faith!

Jamesy1987   posted Sun at 11:38am
Chairman's monkey! 😂 😂 😂

Each new post sent a sharp thrill through him. He read the thread to the end then began it again. Leah called from downstairs but he ignored her, moving on to new threads, firstly on the official message board, then on the other Town forum, and finally to the comments following that day's article in the local paper. When he had read each entry he went back onto the official message board and stared at it, refreshing the page every couple of minutes, waiting.

It had rained through the night and was still coming down in patchy showers while they ate breakfast. When they set off, though, the sky began to clear, and a weak sun followed them on the drive to the coast. It had been Leah's idea to go there today, Chris's day off.

She had prepared the suggestion in advance, waiting for an opportune moment to ask, and when in the end it came, massaging him on the sofa while they watched a film, he had agreed readily, had even seemed pleased at the idea of a day out.

Tyler was happy in the wet sand. They carried him across the beach and set him down in his waterproof all-in-one to sit at the edges of pools. He reached in and clawed fistfuls of thick paste, holding his hands high above his head to watch the sand dollop and splatter into the water. Chris's attention was on him. A smile broke over his face and Leah moved closer to put her head against his chest. When she looked back at Tyler his mouth was covered in dark sludge. "He's eating sand, isn't he?" she said.

"Yep."

"We should probably stop him, shouldn't we?"

"Probably." He walked over to Tyler slowly, crouching—then scooped him up and sprinted with him in his arms towards the sea. Once he was at the edge of the water he turned Tyler upside down and held him by the ankles, lowering, lifting, and she could hear through the lapping waves the gleeful screams of Tyler each time Chris pretended to drop him in.

They walked to a beach cafe, where they sat waiting for some time before a waitress appeared, apologizing, from the kitchen. They ate prawn rolls, feeding mouthfuls of prawns to Tyler, who closed his eyes in anticipation when each fork came towards him. Leah noticed the waitress smiling over from the counter. A little flush of pleasure came, then went, as she turned her attention back to the table and saw in Chris's eyes, his lips, that it was him she had been smiling at.

It was past Tyler's nap time when they finished eating, but Chris suggested they go for a walk along the front to buy sweets. After they had got them, Chris let Tyler suck on a fizzy dummy. At his perplexed reaction they both smiled and Chris put his arm around her. The moment they got back into the car, Tyler fell asleep. Drizzle built up on the windscreen as they drove away. She was about to drift off herself when Chris mentioned that Town were at home against Aldershot on Saturday, and Jamie Atwell, an old teammate from his first spell at Town, was going to be playing. Jamie and his wife were staying down for the rest of the weekend in a hotel, he said, and Boyn had been talking about having them, with the Easters, over for a meal after the match.

Before they had even reached home she was taut with anxiety. They were rare, these occasions, but she dreaded them. She never had anything to say, especially once the meal was over and the partners moved into the kitchen to talk about their jobs and their friends in common while the men disappeared for endless computer games or darts or drinking games with their shirts off.

When Chris went upstairs she called her mum, hoping that she would be unable to babysit. She was free, though; she was only too happy to take Tyler so that Leah could see her friends.

She tried not to think about the meal even as she prepared herself for it. She got her nails done at college and on the Friday afternoon went to her hairdresser for a fringe cut while Tyler crawled about the salon reception charming the stylists, playing peekaboo behind the products stand. On the day of the match she did not get to the stadium until a few minutes before the final whistle. She had told Chris that her mum was not available until later, so that she would not have to spend the game in the family room with Alison Atwell and Boyn's girlfriend Clare.

When she did arrive, the two women were in the players' lounge, bunkered in one corner on a sofa, chatting, a bottle of wine on the low table before them, paying little attention to the small monitor by the bar that was showing the match. They did not see Leah until she was right in front of them. Clare got up to lean over the table and kiss her on the cheek. Alison repeated the gesture. Leah noticed that each woman, beaming, toned, childless, gave her a quick look up and down as the other greeted her. She declined the offer of a wineglass to share their bottle and went to the bar for a tonic water, explaining to the others that she was driving. She knew— sitting down in the uncomfortable slouching armchair opposite them, nodding and smiling when they took up again their conver-

sation about the difficulties of arranging Wednesdays off work—
that she should have bought another bottle of wine for the table,
and that Clare and Alison were probably driving too.

When the players arrived the mood in the lounge became lively,
bullish. The match had ended in a 3–3 draw, Jamie Atwell scoring
two of Aldershot's goals. He came into the room and shook the
hands of the directors and backroom staff who had been at the club
during his time there, and then turned to look with them at the
monitor by the bar as it showed a replay of his first goal—which, in
a self-conscious demonstration of respect towards the Town fans,
he had responded to by picking the ball out of the back of the net
and lowering his head to walk soberly back to the center circle,
staggering under the weight of his teammates as they bounded on
top of him.

Only later, in the privacy of the house, did he celebrate openly:
loudly reenacting both of his goals amid the chrome and glass and
brown leather furniture of Alek and Clare's living room. Chris had
not played. In the players' lounge, when Leah had gone to the bar,
she had seen him on the monitor, emerging from one end of the
dugout to warm up with the game about to finish. From outside the
window she had heard the muted strain of some supporters chanting his name; the scattered shouts too of those closer to the window, making him the object of their stock accusations: lazy, greedy,
not fit to wear the shirt.

As they sat down to their starters he was alert to the others'
banter. He appeared relaxed, but Leah could see how aware he was
of them. They ribbed him at length for being dropped. "I wouldn't
mind two and a half grand a week to sit on the bench," Jamie pro-
claimed.

"It's because he can't afford my appearance bonus if he starts
me."

Leah felt a dart of pride at the comeback and the raucous reaction to it around the table. The conversation turned to the manager. Alek was of the opinion that he was an evil idiot. Clare, to
cries of laughter, did an extremely accurate, confident impression
of him. Leah could not think of anything to add that wouldn't

make her sound like a fool. She remained silent, smiled, drank. When eventually she had prepared something to say, about him being more interested in his van business, the conversation moved on. Alison Atwell began talking about her own boss. She had been a police constable when she met Jamie but had recently been promoted to sergeant; she could always be relied upon for a good story and, after she had got up to help Clare bring out the main course, she was persuaded by Jamie into a long comical tale about a Polish man who had attempted to hold up a pharmacy with a water pistol.

Leah was mindful of not speaking since the nibbles in the living room. The longer she did not contribute, the more she retreated into herself and took care not to do anything that might draw the group's attention. She was missing a coaster. All the others had the same patterned fabric coasters that matched the tablemats, but hers had either been forgotten or had got lost beneath the assortment of breads and stuffed olives. As a result it was difficult to put down her icicle-stemmed wineglass without a loud clang on the glass table. She did not pick it up for long intervals and, when she did, took quick deep slugs, fully aware that she was getting too drunk to drive and that Clare and Alison must surely be making some judgment about her given that she had refused to drink with them in the players' lounge.

They were back on Clarke. "He'll be gone by Christmas if we're still in the relegation zone," Clare said, to which everybody agreed. "All those years, all that money it's taken to get into the league, just to go down at the first time of asking—it'd be a fucking catastrophe. There's no way the chairman would continue that level of investment. It'd be the end. Clarke's got to go."

"I almost had a fight with him on Monday," Chris cut in. "Real one. He near as anything punched me."

There were aghast expressions from the other women. Leah tried to act as though she already knew.

"If he had, I would have taken him out. Serious. I'd have knocked him cold."

"I knew this lad," Jamie said, "played for him a few years ago.

Told me Clarke had a massive falling-out with the club's owner and pinned the guy down on a weight bench right in front of the whole team."

"I'm not joking, I'd smack his lights out if he tried anything on me."

"Clarke's just a cunt," Alison said.

Leah felt a shock of heat at the word. She watched the others smiling and got up as soon as Clare did to help clear the plates. In the kitchen she told her that the food had been lovely.

"Thank you. Alek made most of it. He loves cooking, believe it or not." She took a stack of bowls out of a cupboard. "How's your course going? Remind me what it is again—fashion design?"

"Textile design, yes."

"Are you enjoying it?"

"Yes. It's nice to be creative for a change," she said and straight-away hoped that this would not sound like an insult to Clare, who was a restaurant reservations manager.

"You must be very good at drawing."

"Not really. We do most of that part on computer."

Clare handed her a large bowl of pavlova. "Mind taking that through?"

Leah liked Clare. There were, in the past, several friendly talks that she could recall having with her, and she always asked about Tyler. In the players' lounge earlier, when Alison went to the toilet, she had told Leah that she and Alek had been trying for a baby themselves but had decided now to put it off until next summer so that they could time the birth for the end of the following season.

When they brought the pudding to the table there were two different discussions in progress. Leah sat down, hoping that she and Clare might continue their own conversation, but Clare immediately joined in with Alek and Alison's dialogue about how far the chairman's money could take a club like Town. Leah listened, noticing too the intense private discourse on the other side of her, before she excused herself to go to the loo.

On the walls of the toilet corridor were numerous silver-framed photographs of Alek in action, each with a small engraved inscription: DEBUT FOR TOWN; FA CUP AGAINST READING; WINNER AGAINST LUTON. She felt a sudden sad tenderness at the proud little exhibition, the effort that must have gone into obtaining the photographs. She was pissed. She went in and sat on the toilet. She suspected that Chris felt ashamed of her. He had barely looked at her all through the meal, while the other women had joined in with the banter and impressions. She wanted to go home. She wanted to go to her mum's and be with Tyler, to put him into her old bed with her and go to sleep. When she had peed she went to the sink and fumbled for the soap dispenser along a shelf of purple glass vials and jars, realizing at length that they were all decorative, and eventually washed her hands with what turned out to be a scented candle.

Outside the bathroom door she paused. She could hear the ebb and flow of conversation from the other end of the corridor. There was no knowing how long the night would last, and clearly she could not be the one to bring up the suggestion of going home—practically her first words of the evening: "Can we leave now?"

When she retook her seat, Alison was lifting up her top to show a tattoo above her hip.

"I know. What the fuck was I thinking?"

"What is it?" Leah asked.

"A phoenix. Rising from the flames. Aldershot. Not like he's going to be there forever or anything, but it seemed like a good idea at the time. I tell him it's because I wanted to impress him," she said, simpering at Jamie, and as they all looked over at him, Leah felt Chris's hand press softly onto her own on top of her knee.

She tried not to dwell on her performance at the dinner party. She focused hard on her college assignment—finding natural images to mirror the appliqué designs she had been given—and Tyler. She spent concerted time with him, playing, reading, making him healthy, inventive meals, and she put considerable effort into regulating his sleeping patterns, determined that these at least were tasks at which she could prove herself capable. Tyler was usually a reliable sleeper, but for the last couple of weeks he had been struggling to drop off at his normal nap times and was waking up four or five times during the night. Teeth, her mum thought. During one particularly wearing campaign to get Tyler down, she received a text from her friend Shona, saying that she and the others were going out on Friday; did she fancy coming?

Since the return from Middlesbrough she had not seen her old school friends as regularly as once she used to. Chris had been unwilling for her to, especially at first. "You can't leave Tyler," he had said, "waking up in a new house, finding out his mum's gone missing." She had been out with them a couple of times more recently, but it was still so uncommon to leave the house without Tyler or Chris that there was something slightly unreal about the thought of traveling into town on her own now, in a taxi, stepping into her old self. When she had mentioned Shona's invitation to Chris she had said she could get her mum to take Tyler, but he had been surprisingly against that idea, affronted, even: he would be in anyway, having a quiet one, preparing for Saturday, so why should it be a problem?

Nonetheless a niggling worry beset her when she left the house—that Tyler would wake up and Chris would not know how to soothe him; that his pre-match routine would be disrupted and he would get frustrated, angry—and the thought was still with her when she got out of the taxi and walked up the steps into the bar.

They saw her come in and waved her over. All four were there already, smiling up at her as she approached their table in the middle of the noisy room.

"Lucky you." Mark, wearing a designer T-shirt and a careful new beard, stood up. "You're just in time for my round."

When he had gone off to the bar, Leah sat down in the place they had saved for her beside Liam. "So," she said. "How is everybody?"

There was some trace of the way she used to hold attention in the looks from around the table.

"Gem's going to be fired and Mark is shagging a teenager," said Shona, and the others fell into easy, familiar laughter. Shona went on to explain both pieces of news, with occasional objections from

Gemma and loud, delighted laughter from Mark when he returned from the bar. They wanted to know how she was doing. What she was up to. Almost immediately she began an account of the dinner party. She told them about the phoenix tattoo. Washing her hands with a candle. They could not get enough of it, begging her for more. Ever since the summer she left school, when Liam had brought some of the Town youth teamers along to Katie Wheelwright's end-of-GCSEs party and Chris Easter had kissed her in the downstairs toilet, they had reveled in her footballer stories. She knew they did not like Chris. It had been a surprise, even then, when she started going out with him, and even more of a surprise that they had stayed together, married, had a baby—all before the rest of them had even begun to consider settling down. They thought he was arrogant. In the early days, whenever she persuaded him to come to one of their houses or the shopping center, and he kept silently and impatiently to himself, she used to explain to them afterwards that he was shy, that he got nervous around new people.

They thought he cheated on her. The allegation had last come up a couple of years ago at a New Year's Eve party. She had lost it then, telling them they could all go and fuck themselves, and leaving the party before midnight, getting home and in a fit of door-slamming waking Chris up, ruining his sleep the night before a big match. "Just because he's a footballer doesn't mean he's a dickhead," she had shouted at them. "There's a lot you don't know about him."

Here, now, among her friends, she felt herself begin to relax. They got back on to the story of Mark and the teenager: how he had met her in the club one night and not twigged how old she was until after she had given him her number and met up with him the next day. How he had checked her Facebook profile to make sure that she was not even younger than she said she was. Leah told him he was a pervert—a pervert with a beard, she said, which made it worse. She was pulled, as they moved on to Shona's new job, deeper into the conversation of the group, distracted, for a spell, from having to perform a mother, a footballer's wife; from the constant fear of failing, in public, in private, to be that person.

When their drinks ran low she took the initiative to get a round in. Liam came to give her a hand.

"What's it like then," she said as they waited to be served, "turning out a league pitch?"

"Be better if it wasn't on a non-league budget. Don't suppose you're down there much?"

"I don't think he'd want me to be. Not at the moment."

"No, bet not. What's going on there? He fall out with Clarke or something?"

A reflex of loyalty made her hesitate. "Not that I know. Have you heard anything at the training ground?"

"Right. Yes. Me and Chris were chatting about it the other day when he came into the ground-staff shed for a cup of tea." He looked pleased at his joke. "What do I know? I cut the grass, mate. I don't talk to them. I've been at the stadium the last couple of weeks anyway. But no, I've not noticed anything. Apart from Clarke being a tosser, but that's not exactly news."

The barman came over. Liam reminded her what the others were drinking. When the barman went to pour the drinks Liam looked at her directly, his big open face taking her in. "Things been difficult?"

"No. Not really. Good as can be expected. This season isn't exactly going like he wanted."

"It's not exactly going like anybody wanted."

The barman was speaking to two customers further down the counter. Both men glanced round at her before the barman came back with the last couple of drinks and took her money.

"He'll be fine soon enough," she said. "You know what he gets like."

They both smiled, recognizing together that Liam did not in fact know what he got like—not since they were teenagers, friends in the youth team together before a falling-out that had endured ever since—other than what he gleaned through club gossip, the Internet and the cautiously divulged information that Leah had shared over the years.

"There has been a bit of talk that Clarke's looking to send him out on loan in January," Liam said. She did not respond. Liam moved forward to cradle three of the drinks in his hands. "I heard that from Pete, though—you know, my assistant groundsman Pete—and this is the man that thought Noel Edmunds was buying into the club, so it's obviously bullshit, unless you know better. Come on, let's take these over."

They stayed until closing. She promised that she would come out again soon and said goodbye, Liam's words staying with her as she walked the short distance to the taxi office. She knew it was unlikely to be true. Town had only recently signed him back. The chairman would surely not agree to it. And yet the prospect of it—the upheaval, the confusion for Tyler, the incessant phone conversations with his brainless cocksure agent—was difficult to ignore.

The house, to her relief, was quiet when she let herself in. He had left the hall light on for her. She went upstairs and pushed open the door to Tyler's room. For a minute or two she listened to the steady heave of his breathing until she had satisfied herself that everything was normal, then she went to peek into the spare room at the dark humped shape in the bed, before going through to the bedroom and falling promptly asleep.

Loud wailing woke her. She sat up and let her senses gather themselves. There was a run of wretched little sobs, then it stopped. She lay back down, listening. It was difficult to keep her eyes open, and soon she let them stay closed, sleep taking her, until the sobs came again. She dragged herself into an upright position, facing the wall that backed onto Tyler's room, the muddled shape of the wardrobe becoming more defined in the gloom as his crying continued. She looked at the alarm clock. 02:26. She waited for one minute to pass. It was getting louder. She fixed her eyes on the clock and timed another minute. There was a desperate, hoarse note to the cry now, interspersed by short silences that she knew were jerking breaths of air, and then a dull rhythmic clatter as Tyler pulled himself up and shook the bars of the cot. She knew that she had to resist. She lay there convincing herself of it as a new wave of crying filled the room. It seemed louder, somehow, than if he was in there with her. 02:30. She was doing the right thing. She repeated the thought over and over. There had to be one thing, she kept telling herself, one single thing that she was any fucking good at.

She got out of bed and crept out until she was by the door of Tyler's room. This close, the screaming was impossibly loud, monstrous. She could imagine his face, confused and contorted, his neck and the hem of his sleep suit becoming sodden. For a long period—she tried to time it, five minutes, ten, but lost track—she stayed where she was, her forehead thrust against the door, willing herself to remain firm, until finally the jolting of the cot ceased. He was still crying, but more quietly—a small drained whine, gradually diminishing.

Chris must surely be awake, it struck her as she was about to return to bed. A quick spiteful thrill that his sleep had been broken passed through her, but when she looked towards the spare room she noticed, with sudden cold trepidation, that there was a crack of light under the door of the office.

6

As the season entered October the bright, immaculate pitches of summer were already beginning to thicken and spoil. Goalmouths knotted with mud, and the lower-lying areas of many of the division's slanted, undulating grounds were turning yellow with drowned grass. The non-league pitch on which Town played their reserve fixtures was even worse. During these matches Tom found it impossible to develop a settled rhythm. He would try to deceive himself into the actions that he had once done by instinct, conjuring the vision of belting down the smooth swathe of his academy-pitch wing, but whenever he tried to run with the ball now it would be up against his shins and knees, bobbling out of control.

The reserve starting eleven was as unpredictable as the pitch: a mixture of eager scholars like Steven and Bobby—who sometimes, to the annoyance of the older pros, captained the side—trialists and fringe players desperate to impress but at the same time reluctant to commit themselves for fear of getting injured. Tom, who was playing in most reserve games and also as a substitute for the first team, was sometimes involved in two encounters a week now, yet did not feel like he belonged to either side. He was determined not to be associated with the seconds but performed erratically. In four reserve matches he had drifted in and out but had still contributed the assists for two goals and scored once, a strike that he celebrated with the same muted animation as did the few dozen obsessives, scouts and parents in the crowd, who greeted each goal with cheerful seated applause, as if at a sports day.

Apart from the scholars, with whom he tried to appear confident and senior, Tom seldom mixed with the other reserves. Instead he increased his efforts to be around the first team. Ever since that fuzzily remembered night at the club he found that he could hold the attention of most for brief conversations while stretching or taking fluids or changing. He joined the back of huddles to look at images on phones, laughed, hand-clasped, always feeling like a fool and a fraud but reasonably certain that nobody noticed.

He ensured that he was one of the last to board the first team coach to Southend and sat himself with a rehearsed nod next to Richards, who nodded back but did not take his headphones off. When, nearly an hour into the journey, he did finally lift them from his ears, Tom was careful not to speak to him immediately, instead continuing to look at his laptop for a short time before turning towards his neighbor. "You seen this? It's fucking class."

Richards leaned in to look at the YouTube video that Tom had picked out the previous evening: a rival squad cheering and dancing in their training-ground lounge after hearing their manager had been sacked.

Richards laughed. "Yeah, I can guess how that feels."

They watched a couple more videos together, then Richards got up to join the group of players standing about the back stairwell, idly watching the Sky match on the monitor while they queued for the microwave to heat their Tupperwares of Mrs. Davey's chicken pasta.

They lost. Afterwards Clarke refused to speak to them—in the tunnel, the dressing room or on the coach, where Tom, like many of the others, sat alone, staring out of the window at the burnished golden estuary mudflats.

Because of the length of the next away journey, to Morecambe, Tom did not this time intrude on Richards. He sat instead across the aisle from the table of card players, occasionally joining in a

game of brag and, in the quiet spells between their playing and betting, offering them funny videos that he had spent several evenings
finding on the Internet.

"What's that faggot's problem?" Easter pointed at Lewis, a few
rows down by himself. "You and him have a tiff or something,
Yatesy?"

"Maybe his shrink's told him to steer clear of us."

A few days earlier Lewis had let slip that he had started visiting
a sports psychologist. To help him prepare mentally for games, he
had explained while they fell about laughing.

"Hey, CL," Price shouted. "Your shrink told you yet why you
never score any goals? It because your daddy never loved you?"

Lewis's head appeared above a headrest. "He does have a theory
about it, as it happens."

"Go on. Enlighten us."

"He says it's because our midfield is shit."

Lewis, to a hail of peanuts and an energy bar, ducked out of
sight.

The goalkeeping coach had arranged, by calling in a favor, for
them to use Blackpool's academy base that afternoon, then there
was an hour for a nap at the hotel, followed by dinner. On these
Fridays they were the perfect guests: quiet, preoccupied, sober.
They ate all together around three large tables in the restaurant
before going up to their rooms just after nine o'clock, leaving the
traveling directors to eat and drink themselves into a state of pink
untucked recline in the hotel lounge.

Tom still roomed with Easter. He knew that this continued arrangement was to do with the manager, and he wondered sometimes if it was the main purpose of his place in the traveling party.
They had established a routine: on going up to the room after dinner, Easter would immediately leave again, sometimes for a short
while, sometimes for longer. Tom would switch Easter's bedside
light on for when he came in—quietly if Tom was asleep—to undress in the bathroom. In the morning they used Easter's phone to
wake them, then Tom went first for a shower while Easter sat on his
bed and drank coffee, watching the television. They did not speak

much, but Easter did not seem to resent Tom's presence. He was quiet, considerate even. Tom suspected the reason he had grown not to mind the arrangement was because Tom left him alone. He had come to understand, with a certain amount of hidden pride, that there was a side to Easter, reclusive, reflective, that only he among the squad knew about.

So it came as a bit of a surprise that night when Easter got into bed and leaned over to hold out his phone.

"That's my son."

Tom looked at the bug-eyed thing on the screen. He did not know what to say.

"He's big."

Easter appeared not displeased with this response. He looked at the phone himself, smiling. "Fat little bastard, isn't he?"

Tom was in two minds about whether or not to laugh at this so he took the opportunity to go and get them each a glass of water, staying in the bathroom until he was sure that the color on his cheeks had died down.

They were both on the substitutes' bench. Tom was not used, but Easter came on to score the equalizer, a frantic scrambled effort inside the six-yard box, in reaction to which he sprinted the full length of the pitch towards the eighty away supporters and, in the fervor of the moment, turned round once he was before them to stretch down his shirt and thumb blindly at what he intended to be his number, but was in fact the lettering above it: YDV FINANCIAL SERVICES.

With no league wins, five draws and seven defeats, firmly planted at the bottom of the table, out of the League Cup, attendances dwindling and the board increasingly agitated, Clarke pulled off, as he himself described it to Peter Pascoe in the local paper, something of a coup. He signed a very reputable higher-division midfielder, Andy Jones, on a three-month loan. He did not state openly that he was signing the player to replace Easter, but the interview with Pascoe left nobody in any real doubt: "Andy is somebody who will run through walls for you. I've had him at previous clubs and I've always made him run through walls. That's exactly what we're needing now. I'd love to sign him permanent come January but the budget's not there for it yet. If we can clear some of the wage bill by then, hopefully we'll see what we can do with Andy."

These words caused apprehension to ripple through the squad. Even the established first-teamers who played in different positions to Jones became unsure of their places. The January transfer window, still over two months away, loomed ahead of them, and they viewed Jones with caginess because, in their eyes, he had arrived as the embodiment of it.

Jones needed no time to settle in. He took charge straightaway, demanding the ball constantly during practice matches. He let them know if they were not working hard enough. He injured a scholar. He stayed behind after the rest of the squad had left the field to talk privately with the manager, and returned to the dressing room to plunge into the vacated ice bath, wincing and groaning in there for longer than anybody else ever did before rising enormous, glistening, his skin blue and purple with bruises that gave him the appearance, under the stark dressing-room lighting, of butchered meat.

He marked his debut by galvanizing the team to its first victory of the season. Tom, next to Easter in the away dugout, applauded Jones's first goal but did not stand as the others did, yelling, slapping the roof. When they settled back down Tom looked round at Easter. His elbows were raised, head clamped between his fists, obscuring his face. For a second Tom thought about catching his eye, but the idea immediately dissipated and whatever sympathy he might have tried to communicate remained unexpressed save for the hot squash of their thighs, minutely increasing.

Upon Jones's second, decisive goal the tight pocket of Town fans came alight—dancing, jumping on seats, rushing down the aisles towards the pitch, and a steward sprinted all the way from his position by the dugout to accost a young boy on the grass in front of the advertising hoardings. He caught the boy unawares, lifted him in a bear hug and began dragging him across the side of the pitch towards a solitary policeman, all the while pursued by a group of fellow stewards who had realized, along with most of the crowd and the overjoyed away dugout, that the detained youngster flailing in the big man's arms was not in actuality an away fan, but a ball-boy.

Hope grew that the team's fortunes might be on the turn. Training sessions took on a new competitive edge. Every player apart from Jones lived under the permanent threat of being bombed out if Clarke thought they were not keeping up to the new standard. Even Boyn was punished, judged not to be running fast enough between cones during a doggies drill. The squad all stood and watched him walk over to the scholars, who paused their session under the huge balding sycamore tree to let him join their number. When the squad turned back to resume the drill Clarke glared, with a slight smile, at Easter. Easter did not meet the challenge but continued to stretch, waiting for his turn to sprint. The others had begun keeping their distance from him in the dressing room and around the ground. If Clarke was present they avoided speaking to him, or even, except in the moments that he and Jones fought for the same ball, looking at him at all.

The improvement in the team did not bode well for Tom's standing either. Finch-Evans had played well in the win, replaced by Tom for only the last three minutes. Not enough for Tom to get into the game, barely enough to touch the ball. He had come in at the final whistle with his kit unmarked, ashamed to shower. A few days later he was not even picked to start in the next round of the Johnstone's Paint despite his convincing performance in the first, which seemed to him now like a dream, and he walked off the pitch at the end without joining the celebrations of the others following another victory. In the showers afterwards, rinsing off a cursory lathering of soap, he realized that Easter, under the neighboring shower head, was laughing quietly.

"What's the fucking point?" He did not move his gaze from the wall. There was nobody else left near them, and Tom could not tell whether Easter was speaking to him. "Seriously, what's the fucking point?"

"Showering?" Tom said.

Easter turned to look at him. "Yeah, if you like, showering."

"Don't know."

"No, me neither." He moved away and reached for a towel to wrap about his waist. Tom did the same. "Seriously. Tell me. What kind of operation is it he thinks he's running here?"

"Van hire?" Tom said on a whim, a remark that Easter found improbably hilarious, stepping forward to give him a short aggressive hug.

"You're all right, you are, mate." He laughed again. "Van hire."

Tom paused for Easter to go ahead of him into the dressing room, grateful that they had been alone in the shower room, that they had been wearing towels.

To Clarke's fury, the team's momentum was curtailed by a period of heavy, near-continuous rain. Within three days the lower half of the stadium pitch was submerged. A home fixture had to be called off. A section of the car park wall collapsed. Brown puddles formed on top of the Portakabin club shop, leaking into the stock room; water ran down the steps of the two uncovered terraces to collect in secret pools in the foundations; cascades from the corrugated roofs of the Kop and the main stand poured down in windblown torrents that left a flotsam of litter and bird shit over the pitch.

The training ground, however, held out for longer. The squad continued to slog and slide, Clarke refusing to give in to the rain. He walked the touchline in his wellies under a giant golfing umbrella, bawling commands into the drenched air. Daring them to complain. One morning the players stood by the side of a pitch, water up to their bootlaces, waiting for Liam to finish clearing the area near a corner flag with a brush mounted on the front of the compact tractor. He drove off around the edge of the pitch when it was done, but instead of continuing on across the floodplain towards the ground-staff shed, he turned the tractor again, and came straight at them, speeding up. The others scattered, but Tom could only stand exactly where he was, anchored, Liam coming directly for him, his eyes fastened on Tom, until at the last moment he swerved away, creating an arc of spray that showered several of the players and caused the flock of seagulls around the goalposts to launch themselves into the air.

Some of the squad chased halfheartedly after the tractor as it roared away, Liam standing like a jockey, one arm raised in the air. The players soon gave up and trudged back. Liam slowed the tractor down and, on reaching the ground-staff shed, cut the engine, turning round as he did so to look back briefly to where Tom stood now in the midst of the group.

For the final two mornings of the week training moved to a local secondary school. In public view the sessions were less intense, less combative, than usual. The size of the sports-hall pitch allowed only for small-sided games, and each time there was a break in lessons an ebullient pack of children crowded onto the two balconies, where, to the disbelief of the squad as the hall echoed with shrill cries, Clarke let them remain and sometimes even looked up to joke with them or offer a criticism of a player. Two Year Seven boys, arriving early for lunchtime basketball practice, ran into the changing rooms while the players were still there. For a few seconds they stood dripping in their coats by the door, completely stationary. Men walked about the room in complete nakedness. One was sitting on a toilet, the cubicle door open. The smaller of the boys nudged his mate to leave, but the other stood hypnotized.

"Hey, Yatesy, I think he's got a thing for you."

Yates, drying himself, stepped towards the boys. He moved his towel aside. "What, you never seen one this big before?"

There was some giggling.

"I thought Asian lads were supposed to be huge. Bet your daddy's got one like a baby's arm."

The two boys turned and fled. There was an eruption of laughter, joined in with by Price and Lewis stepping through from the showers, although they had witnessed nothing of the scene, and by Tom, staring through the doorway after the boys, away from Yates.

———

After a series of sucking footsteps and easily inserted fingers, Saturday's referee declared the Swindon pitch unplayable. Tom, the whole weekend free in front of him, rang his dad and within minutes of the call ending was in his car on the way home.

On the motorway his mind turned to the past couple of days at the school. Being in that hall had felt achingly familiar. The squeak and scuff of the AstroTurf. The rubbery smell of the storage rooms. The constellation of shuttlecocks and soft tennis balls caught in the ceiling nets. He slowed to watch a column of Aston Villa coaches come past in the other direction and wondered how so much could have changed. It was not so long ago—school. Everything had been so clear to him then. All he had wanted—to play football—and never a doubt in his mind that he would make it. Another sound he remembered from those days, so well that he could hear it now: *Give it Tom*. Every lunchtime, every PE game, bouncing off the walls for years. *Give it Tom. Give it Tom.*

He arrived home to the sight through the kitchen window of his mum chopping vegetables. She waved when she saw him getting out of the car and moved to the sink to wash her hands as he came through the gate. The small lawn was waterlogged. Damp little flowers stood in solemn lines along both sides, like Town supporters. The image of his dad hunched with his trowel came to Tom, the door opening now, his mum waiting there, and it was an effort to hold himself together as he stepped into the house, her arms closing around him.

They pulled apart and she looked at him. "Are you allowed a beer?"

"There's no match, Mum. And it's not like I'd be playing anyway."

She smiled, shaking her head. "No point feeling sorry for yourself. Go say hello to your dad. He's in there, wrecking his head at the football. Rachel's upstairs." She turned round. "Rach! Tom's here." But his sister was already coming down the staircase, bounding towards him, hugging him. For an instant, her skin against his face, he remembered the girl in the nightclub.

"So, the fourth-division footballer returns."

"League Two."

"Fourth division. Dad's been explaining it to me."

Their father was coming out of the living room. He shook Tom's hand at the same time as pulling him in close. Squeezing knuckles pressed against Tom's stomach.

"Heard the Chelsea score?"

"I was listening in the car," Tom said. "Crazy game."

His dad was studying him. "Very crazy game. Beer?"

They ate a late lunch, sitting on the two sofas of the living room, talking, the television on in the background. It made a nice change, he told them, not having to eat around a table. When nobody responded he feared he might have offended them, so he went on to say how good the shepherd's pie was, how much he'd missed his mum's cooking. He told them about life at the Daveys', concentrating on the lack of privacy, the Scottish pair playing Xbox into the night, the waiting for the bathroom. He felt somewhat sheepish pointing out these things, especially as it quickly had the effect of worrying his parents that he might not be happy in this place they had sent him to. They wanted to know if he was getting on with the other lodgers, if he was sleeping enough. He looked tired to them.

"He's fine, Dad," his sister stepped in. "He's only tired because he's out on the pull every night."

Tom was at once hot with embarrassment. He was aware of his dad watching him, waiting for what he would say.

"I'm fine. Seriously. I'm not tired. It's a good place to stay. It's the club. The manager. That's the problem."

His dad seized on the change in direction: "Clarke's teams have always played the same way. Fine if you're winning, but if the results aren't coming he's got no plan B."

"He's brought in Andy Jones, to be fair," Tom said.

"Yes. I remember Jones from when he was at Blackburn. Dirty player. Just the type Clarke likes."

His mother and sister, with nothing to add to this conversation, began talking about the upcoming wedding of one of his mum's colleagues, another health visitor alongside whom she had run a baby drop-in clinic for years. When there was a lull and he was sure his dad had finished his point, Tom turned towards them on the other sofa. "How's A levels, Rach?"

"Hard. Coursework never stops. I shouldn't even be down here now. You should feel honored."

"You still planning on John Moores?"

There was a moment of silence. "I'm not sure yet."

"Thought you were dead set?"

"Well, I was. Bloody Tories, though."

They all looked at the television. Tom did not understand, but he said nothing more. He had always been proud of his sister's cleverness, never threatened by it, because he had football. For as long as he could remember there had been an unspoken assumption in the house that they would both be successful. She wanted to do an events management degree, as far as he could recall, and he wondered now if he had got that wrong. But as he observed the look that passed between his parents, he thought that maybe he did understand; that it was about money.

He perused the small immaculate room while they listened to the half-time reports coming in. It was a world away from the busy clutter of the Daveys'. The pert, vacuumed sofas. The remote controls lined up on the television stand. His dad's neatly organized plastic desk tucked into one corner of the room; wage slip, bank and utilities files boxed underneath it next to a pile of printed-out Town match reports that Tom had noticed the second he came in, which he knew his mum or sister must have shown him how to do. His dad was listening to the Bolton–Everton report. His plate and tray were on the floor by his feet. It struck Tom for the first time that he probably earned more than his dad. Barely playing, in League Two. He thought about the box upstairs, with all of his photographs and press cuttings and England age group caps. For years his dad had driven him to school matches, county matches, Centre of Excellence and academy matches, England matches, reserve matches. Taking time off work. Paying for kit. Overnight stops. Relocating the whole family. All while Rachel had never asked for anything, never been given anything.

His mum collected the trays from the floor. "You got plans for later, love?"

"Here, I'll do that, Mum. No, I've not told anyone I'm up. Thought I'd stop in, watch *Match of the Day*. I'll stick around tomorrow too, if that's all right."

He followed her into the kitchen to help her with the dishes. He had thought about texting some of his old friends but decided against it. The last time he came up he had gone out and it had been awkward. Not at first, when they came to the door to say hello to his parents, lingering for an appearance from his sister, and his dad had made them stop for a beer, but later, when they had exhausted all talk about football and what the other former scholars were up to. The conversation of the other three then was about the gym that they worked out in—they had all put on muscle—and girls. Tom wanted to entertain them by taking the piss out of Town, but they didn't ask about his life playing football, and Tom did not feel that it was his place to bring the subject up.

He dried up the plates that his mum washed. He heard his sister going upstairs. In the other room his dad was on the phone.

"You can go out, you know, if you want," his mum said.

"No, it's fine. Don't worry."

"OK. But we won't be put out if you change your mind."

His dad came into the kitchen. "Just been speaking to John. There's a guy off sick at the sorting office and he's picking up the shift tomorrow. Says you're welcome to his ticket if you want it."

After *Football Focus* his dad drove them over to Uncle Kenny's. Jeanette made coffee and they stood around in the kitchen, Jeanette and Kenny wanting to know all about his life down south, how he was getting on at his digs, what it was like playing senior football. Jeanette gave him a third cuddle as they were about to leave. "Oh, Tommy. My Tommy. You're a man, look at you," she said, and Tom looked down at the polished floor, feeling every inch a child.

Most of the familiar old faces were in the pub, his dad and Kenny's crowd, though Tom was glad that none of their sons was there.

"You drinking, son?" Kenny asked him, turning from the bar. Tom looked instinctively at his dad.

"Yes, he's drinking. Not playing this weekend, is he?"

Kenny waited to be served and Tom stood back from the group at the bar alongside his dad, hoping that they would move over to a quieter area of the pub where he would not have to speak to his dad's friends and hear, in their questions and their joking, the unspoken pity behind their words at his failure to gain a contract.

"First match in a while, isn't it?" his dad said.

"Since last season."

His dad nodded. "Must feel a bit strange for you." He nodded again. Tom did not say anything and they both turned to look at the television above the pool table. Outside, a small group of Arsenal fans was coming towards the pub, the bouncer smiling, shaking his head at them. Kenny was approaching from the bar. He had three pints of lager in a careful stranglehold.

"It's all right, lads, don't give me a hand or anything." He smiled, offering Tom the first pint, and they moved away from the bar.

As soon as they left the pub, Tom felt the old excitement start to build. The routine of the walk to the ground automatically made his senses tingle with anticipation, heightening at each of the normally empty pubs now overflowing onto the pavements, the stalls crammed together on derelict scraps of land selling programs and badges and sweets, the tide of people thickening down the road, horse shit, police wagons, car horns, the tops of the floodlights appearing and the noise of the growing crowd riding on the air, soaring over the city. Throughout all the years no aspect of it had ever changed. The pre-match sausage roll from the tea bar. The queue to buy a program, which he would take home afterwards to pore over in his room. He followed Kenny and his dad into the toilets for the customary piss at the packed urinal, before hurrying out, up the steps and through the gangway for the sublime moment of seeing the pitch, the crowd.

They made their way to their row. The team was being announced on the Tannoy. There was the smell of pie fillings, Bovril, farts. Old men and women, families, were in the same positions they had sat in since Tom was little. All of this was deep inside him, ingrained yet altered now by the knowledge—shared by his dad, Kenny, all of the season-ticket holders they nodded past on the way to their seats—that Tom was not part of the club anymore. He was not going to play for it. He sat down in John's seat. Kenny, beside him, held out a Yorkie bar for Tom to break off a block.

"We're very proud of you, Tom, you know, me and Jeanette," he said. "Very proud." And he turned to the pitch, where the players were coming out of the tunnel to an escalation of noise. The Town players did not know what this was like. None of them would be able to handle it, Tom thought as he gave himself up to the mass of the crowd, becoming a part of it, the collective voice entering him, joining with the increased pumping of his heart and his lungs.

One of the scholars that Tom had played with was on the bench. Jamar Daley. At each break in play Tom looked over at him among the substitutes. He had been given a one-year deal. Inevitably, he would play only a handful of games, mainly in the cups, probably go out on loan and be released at the end of his year, but still the unfairness of it kept pulling Tom's attention away from the game. Jamar had been good, a tidy midfielder, strong, competitive, but through all their academy years together he had never been as good as Tom. He was on five thousand a week now, according to one of the old scholars Tom had seen the last time he came up. If not for the couple of goals Jamar had scored in the FA Youth Cup semi-final he would probably not have got the attention, or the agent, that had followed, although it was Tom who had been given the man-of-the-match award for that game. Everything he had done that afternoon had come off. Every dribble, every through ball, every decision the right one because he had not hesitated or over-thought any action, he had played purely on instinct—and it had been obvious, to the large crowd, to the agents waiting in the car park, his family, his teammates bouncing and shrieking in the dressing room, that he was the one, out of all of them, who was going to make it.

A quick throw-in caught the Arsenal left back by surprise, and Kenny, Tom's dad, everyone around them, were all onto their feet as he slipped and handled the ball just inside the edge of the area. The referee straightaway indicated a penalty and a bellow went around the stadium. Tom remained standing, his stomach knotting. Kenny was making a low guttural sound as the crowd became quiet, waiting.

The ball went underneath the goalkeeper's dive. All around Tom people were jumping about, doolally, released from themselves. Kenny was shaking his fist in the air. He turned to Tom and they put their arms around each other, bobbing up and down, fastened together, Kenny's nose pressing into his cheek—"Yes, Tommy! Yes! Yes! Yes!"

The rain eventually gave way to a cold dry spell. Tom stood by his bedroom window and viewed through the night sky the glowing cigarette tips of the weekend's rearranged bonfires on the hills. He drove Bobby and Steven to the stadium the following afternoon to look with the other players over the wasteland of the pitch. They walked up and down, shaking their heads, imagining injury. There was an atmosphere of abandonment everywhere. Small heaps of rubbish had accumulated on the grass and the terracing. Mildew flowered across the plastic roof of the dugout. Inside the bowels of the main stand the air in the dressing rooms and tunnels hung with damp. When they came past the referee's room, a rat skittered across the floor just in front of Steven, who yelped and jumped back.

"You little fairy," Boyn, following behind, shouted. "Look at the little bloody fairy, pissing herself." And he got down on his hands and knees to give chase to Steven, pretending, it only dawned on Tom when Boyn was some way down the tunnel and he started sniffing at the concrete, to be a rat.

Tom sat in thermals then played for the last ten minutes of a heavy Tuesday-night defeat in Dagenham. The small flame of hope, ignited before the rain came, was put out by this loss to another relegation-threatened side—extinguished, if not by the first four goals, then by the fifth and the ensuing squabble between Daish and Gale as the teams left the pitch to the backdrop of "Girl fight, girl fight, girl fight" from the rapturous home support.

They stopped for takeaways on the way back, and the air of the coach became thick with the rich cheesy stink of two-for-one pizzas. Tom ate his slices slowly, looking out of the window at the hurtling dark while Clarke proceeded up the aisle, stopping at each seat to say, softly, "Cunt" to every player along the way.

The squad was ordered in on its day off. They gathered together outside the clubhouse and one or two players took shots at the crowd of seagulls that still loitered after the flood while they waited for Clarke to arrive. As soon as he appeared, gray and faintly unsteady, he made them start running.

The ground broke up like cake under their feet and a track began to blacken around the perimeter of the pitches. Two players collapsed and were removed to the clubhouse. Tom, however, had no difficulty coping and found himself wanting more, and it to be harder. He stayed at the front of the group, forcing the pace—past the clubhouse, the fencing, the hulking sycamore, the grass-wet mower outside the open doorway of the ground-staff shed—as if by running hard he might distance himself from the anxious mood that had settled on him since the visit home. He shut it out, focusing solely on the satisfying action of his heart, his blood, his limbs.

When the squad limped in to shower and change, Tom jogged over to the reserve goalkeeper, Hoyle, and asked if he would be up for staying behind to practice a few crosses and catches. Hoyle wavered a moment but agreed. A few of the others, near the back of the group, turned to look and exchanged words. They probably thought he was trying to impress the manager, Tom realized, regardless of the fact that Clarke had already left to drive to his van-company premises.

They practiced together for about twenty minutes, at which point Hoyle said that he was done.

"OK," Tom said. "I might stay out a bit longer, though. Do a few drills."

Hoyle laughed. "You're not in the Premier League now, mate."

When Hoyle had left, Tom spaced out half a dozen cones along the right-hand side of a pitch where the grass was still fairly smooth and emptied a bag of balls by the cone furthest from the goal. He repeated a shuttle: dribbling around each cone until he reached the dead-ball line, looked up and swung a cross in, aiming every time for the same spot at the near post. He did this until all of the balls were gone, scattered over the neighboring pitch, which he now saw that Liam was approaching. Liam stepped towards one of the balls and, when he reached it, booted it. Tom ran to apologize and collect them all up, but Liam jogged to kick another ball, then another, and as Tom got closer he could see that he was enjoying himself, firing each ball with deliberate aim towards the goal.

When all of the balls were returned, many of them into the net, Liam came over to where Tom stood watching at the side of the pitch. "Don't want to try a few penalties against me, do you?" He was striding towards the goal before Tom even replied.

Tom struck his first attempt low towards one corner, but Liam was quickly down to stop it. The second he aimed for the same corner and this one went in, just, despite Liam sprawling to get a touch on it. Tom smiled to himself as he turned to get another ball. Liam was surprisingly agile, even in his heavy boots and canvas trousers. For five penalties Liam threw himself about, attempting to get one of the leathery palms of his groundskeeping gloves to the ball. He stopped three.

"You're good, you know," Tom said when they had finished.

Liam was sweating. He wiped a long muddy smear over his forehead with the back of a glove. "Too good for you lot." He grinned and walked away. Tom watched him go, then collected the balls and the cones and returned to the clubhouse.

The other players, including Hoyle, had all left, so he took his time getting changed, enjoying the quiet echo of his studs on the floor and the still-steamy warmth of the shower room.

Afterwards, collecting his things, he began to feel a sluggishness descend through him, as if the strength was being sapped from his arms and legs. He sat down, staring ahead at the pool of shower water struggling around the drain. When he tried to get up, his kitbag was a lead weight. For some time he stayed there, watching the last of the water eddy and choke down the hole, before he forced himself to stand.

He went out onto the field. All he could hear was the noise of cars in the distance beyond the fencing and undergrowth. He started towards the breeze-block outbuilding at the far side of the pitches, trying to ignore the exposed, self-conscious sensation of walking across the expanse of reeking cut grass.

As he got closer he could see Liam through the doorway. He was pouring the last of one pot of white paint into another on top of a trestle table. He looked up in puzzlement and, Tom thought, amusement.

"What, more penalties?"

He looked down again to shake the last of the paint into the pot. Tom stood in the doorway. The roller shutters of the tractor entrance rattled momentarily beside him. He knew he should say something but he did not know what. Liam, however, did not seem perturbed by the interruption and carried on with his work. On the walls, among hanging rakes and shelves of canisters, paint, pallets, balls of string, there were old team posters and a dirty red and green scarf nailed to a ceiling joist. Somehow the sight of these things filled Tom with a distinct but unplaceable sadness. He watched as Liam pressed the lids onto the paint pots then took the empty one towards a dustbin by the door.

Liam was about to open the dustbin when Tom reached forward to clasp his arm. Liam shifted his eyes to him. Tom let his hand fall to his side and gazed down at the paint pot still in Liam's hand, his boots, at his own trainers, stained green. He was conscious of how fresh and clean he was, this close to Liam's work clothes. A dim thrum came from the road. He could not bring himself to look up. Liam moved away and Tom watched him step back to the table, hearing then the unbearable clunk of the paint pot being put down.

Tom turned to stare, for a long time, out of the doorway at the wide abandoned field. He heard Liam's boots on the concrete floor. Then he felt the warmth of his body behind him. A hand touched

Tom's side, pressing, gradually, against it. Tom pulled himself away. He twisted to look directly at the large face and he was charged with a sudden glorious sense of risk as the man stood there, inspecting him.

"I have to go," Tom said.

He made for the clubhouse, not deviating to avoid the patches of mud. Above the road noise, the baying of seagulls, was the sound of blood in his ears. His vision was constricting, the sky, the world around him, closing in until all he could see was the door of the clubhouse ahead.

7

Bobby and Steven did not seem to notice how withdrawn Tom was the following morning. They largely ignored him, arguing excitedly in the back of his car about each other's chances of being picked for the upcoming area quarter-final of the Johnstone's Paint. The discussion had started over breakfast and was still going when Tom pulled off the road onto the training ground lane, which he drove down slowly, trying to not make obvious his glance over at the staff car park.

Inside the clubhouse, while Bobby and Steven helped the other scholars lay out the boxes of cereal and porridge beside the tea urn, Tom went to sit at the far end of the lounge, where Richards was on his own. Richards handed him the paper and he stared at the football stories without taking them in, fighting against the urge to look out of the French windows onto the field.

"You all good, Tommy?" Richards asked.

"Fine, mate."

"I know you're quiet, man, but you look a bit zombied out, you know?"

Finch-Evans, on the tea run, approached with two mugs. He stood above them. "Carry on, ladies. Don't stop your chinwag on my account." He gave them each a mug, tousled their hair and walked off.

"You get to see your family much?" Richards said. Tom's body immediately tensed at the mention of them.

"Saw them a couple of weekends ago."

"Swindon postponement? Me too. Miss them like hell, to be fair. My brothers, they think I've got this footballer life and all that, and I'm telling them, nah, come on, most of the time I'm just playing *Call of Duty* with Hoyley."

"Could be worse."

"Right, like if he tried to engage me in conversation or something."

Tom sipped his tea. A memory of the visit home stirred: Rachel joking about him being out on the pull every night, and the way his dad had looked at him. A paranoid idea went through his mind that the thing in the ground-staff shed had already happened then, and that his dad had been looking at him so closely because he had understood; he knew what Tom had done.

The room was filling with noise. There was a movement outside the French windows and Tom's eyes darted towards them, only to see a scholar dragging a bag of balls across the concrete.

They assembled for the ten thirty meeting to talk about why they weren't able to replicate their Paint form in the league, before going outside. Tom kept his eyes on the ground. They warmed up alongside a gang of rusting wire mannequins, which the number two started to position inside a penalty area after the players were sent off around the pitches. Tom stayed in the middle of the line. He focused on the rhythm of Boyn's flashing heels. His breathing, coming thickly, was drowned out by the noise of their footfalls as they skirted the long side of the pitches until, up ahead, he heard the distant sound of the tractor starting up.

Only when they had completed the full circuit did he let himself look through the mass of panting bodies at the tiny figure on top of the tractor, moving slowly over the furthest pitch. Even from this distance, he could see that it was the other groundsman.

———

Tom arrived each day and scanned the pitches. Once he had identified the squat shape of the assistant groundsman he would go in to
change and stretch and then surrender himself to the training, driving his body to its limit until every part of him ached and cramped.

On finishing, he took off in his car. He filled the enclosed space
with music or talkSPORT and drove, it did not matter where; he
just needed to be alone. He often took the same road, turning over
and over in his head whether it was just because of a normal schedule rotation that Liam and his assistant had swapped over. On these
drives he timed the exact moment that he would need to turn round
and go back to the Daveys' in time for dinner.

One day, after again shunning the canteen, he got onto the motorway. A couple of junctions down it, ravenous, he pulled off into
a service station.

He sat down in the central seating area shared by the outlets and
ate a clumsy damp burger. The place was busy. Lone men in suits.
A group of teenagers in rugby tracksuits. An old couple grappling
with a jumbo road atlas. On the other side of the seating area a
man in a gray shirt and gray tie met his eye for a second and Tom
had the flinching realization that he had been staring in the man's
direction. Tom lowered his sight, holding it on the family of legs
arranging themselves under the table opposite him. His face was
hot. His fingers, on the dirty tabletop, trembling. He let the bland
muddle of noise wash over him, trying to block out the fear of what
his eyes would do if he allowed himself to look up at the man—
resisting the horrible compulsion to do so, to see if the man was
still looking.

His mobile was ringing. He took it out of his pocket and
breathed deeply before putting it to his ear.

"Mum."

"Well, here's a turnup. He answers. We've been thinking there's
something up with your phone. Your dad's left quite a few messages."

"Is everything all right?"

"Everything's fine, love. Did you not get them?"

The smell of the opposite table's paninis reached him. Across the seating area, the man was gone. Tom looked around—at the entrance, the toilets—but could not see him.

"Sorry, Mum. It's been really busy with games and training and that. Can you tell Dad sorry?"

His mum was quiet for a moment, and Tom wondered if she could tell that he was lying. "Yes, I'll tell him. But you're OK?"

"I'm fine, Mum. Everything's fine. You don't need to worry about me."

After the third Wimbledon goal a few drunk youths moved to the bottom of the away terrace, directly behind the dugout, and started to chant, "Clarke out." When the team left the pitch at halftime the boys shouted and gesticulated at the substitutes surfacing from the bunker. Yates looked round, mouthing at them to fuck off, and the teenagers were seized with such disbelieving rage that more supporters were attracted down the steps and a nervous delegation of stewards came to stand nearby.

By the time the players reappeared, a small mob had formed, which, ignoring the stewards, sang lustily for the manager's sacking. Clarke did not acknowledge the insults; he maintained his normal routine, stalking the technical area, abusing the officials. After one penalty claim was dismissed he charged at the fourth official and, as the referee later described it in his match report, "acted in a manner that was above and beyond the understandable tensions of competitive football," calling the man "a disgrace," "a bender" and "a ginger nonce" in one particular outburst. He was banned from the touchline for two matches. For the first round of the FA Cup he sat high in the main stand, sheltered by empty seats and a docile buffer of season-ticket holders. For ninety minutes, Town's third defeat in succession, he wrote furiously in a notebook, giving no attention to the chants of "Remind me: how do I spell shit?" and "You'll be sacked in the morning" from the away, then the home, supporters.

Clarke was called to a meeting with the chairman. He sat in silence, picking at the frayed vinyl of an armchair. The chairman recommended that he play Easter. Clarke continued to pick at the vinyl as the chairman stood at the side of his desk, looking down at his manager. "We're paying that much for him, Paul. It's making us look stupid, keeping him on the bench."

"Making who look stupid?"

"All of us."

The fingers went still on the armrest. "What does it make me look like if I put him back in the team now?"

The chairman moved round to perch on the front of the desk. His trousers pulled against the soft straining beef of his thighs. "You could play Jones and Easter together."

"You are fucking joking."

The chairman appeared taken aback. Then he laughed. He shifted his legs and slid down from the desk. "Well, you're the manager."

Clarke said nothing. He watched the two moist receding marks on the desktop and stood up, leaving the room without looking at the chairman.

The number two rounded up the squad in the clubhouse lounge.

"Paint next week—the gaffer wants to put as many fringers in as he can again. I've got the team for you here already." He took out a notepad. "Hoyle, Jamie F, Bobby Hart, Chris Easter, Boyney, Tommy Pearman . . ."

Nausea climbed the insides of Tom's stomach. He shut his eyes, and on opening them again looked at Bobby, who, to a murmur of surprise, had been named captain. Despite the instant sick antici-pation that had taken hold in Tom's gut at having to appear before hundreds, maybe thousands of people, he felt a needle of jealousy at the wide childish smile that Bobby was not attempting to con-ceal.

The Paint team lined up against the rest of the squad. Bobby was everywhere, directing play, shouting, relishing the contest alongside Easter with Jones in the center of midfield. He got onto the ball at one point and looked up towards Tom on the wing.

"Go," he mouthed, signaling the area ahead of Tom. He played it into the space, but Tom held his position and the ball went out of play, rolling off into the bushes at the foot of the fencing.

"Eyes open, Tommy. See the pass." Bobby stood with his hands on his hips, his face all comic bright cheeks, ridiculously serious.

"Too heavy," Tom muttered.

Everybody else was watching. Nobody had gone to retrieve the ball. Bobby gave a loud clap and addressed his team: "Right, boys. Got to communicate. Move for each other, OK." His breath came in a jet of condensation. It clung about his head in a dumb fog. He turned to look at the bushes, then at Tom. Tom stayed where he was. There was a slight but unmistakable shake of Bobby's head before he sprinted to the fence, scooped the ball up and ran back with it. "Let's go. Come on."

Gale, Tom's opposing left back, was standing near him. "That's you told, mate," he said and jogged back into position, laughing. From the throw-in, play drifted towards the other wing.

The match was likely to be on television. His family would watch it. His dad—and sudden dread came over Tom at the thought that his dad might come down for it. Gale was powering towards him with the ball. He kept coming, confident of running right by him. Tom, in a flare of decision, dived in. He felt first the ball against his left foot then the tender tearing flesh of some part of Gale with his right. There was a hot sharp pain in Tom's ankle as he fell, Gale tangled and falling with him.

His first thought, as a hand clutched his forearm and held it to the grass, was that he would not have to play in the Paint match.

Players were leaning over them.

"You fucking clown, what was that?" came through the mist of collected breath.

Tom's ankle had gone numb. He could hear Gale whimpering beside him, and he turned over—their faces, before Tom drew back, almost touching—to see him looking up at the sky, his eyes bright, confused, like a stunned animal. Tom propped himself onto his elbows. Through the scrum of faces he could see Bobby, and a contraction of pleasure passed through him when he understood from the look on Bobby's face that he had no idea how to deal with this situation.

By the next morning the ankle was too swollen for Tom to drive or wear trainers. However, a scan that afternoon revealed that the injury was not serious: a sprain, with only minor damage to the ligament fibers. His foot and ankle were wrapped and strapped, and he was instructed to report for training half an hour early until he had recovered.

For the next few days, Mr. Davey drove him in with Bobby and Steven. There was something different about the way the Scottish pair were behaving around him. They were even tighter than usual—closed off. Tom did not care. He ignored them, trying to occupy his thoughts with the radio until they had passed the staff car park and Mr. Davey let them out in front of the clubhouse.

He watched the squad train from the bench, next to Price, who had a thumb fracture and fingered miserably at his phone with his good hand. By the end of the week they'd been joined by Gale, now with a deep gouge in his thigh muscle. On his return he promptly sought Tom out and held out his hand. "No grudges, yeah?"

"No grudges."

The three of them sat and watched the others going through their routines.

"I'm bloody freezing here," Price said, scratching at the dead crust of his cast. "How's this going to help me recover?"

Tom and Gale said nothing.

"They link up all right, you know, Easter and Jonah," Price said, and all three stared at the shape drill going on across the field. Away towards the other side of the pitches, the tractor engine started up, and Tom turned towards it. Liam was there. "I thought they'd be too the same, but it sort of works, never mind they want to kill each other."

"Maybe why it works," said Gale.

Price made a noise of agreement. "Think he'll start them together Saturday?"

"Got to," said Gale. "Pretty obvious the chairman's leaning on him to, if you read what he said in the paper yesterday. And then it'll be Easter and Hart for the Paint on Tuesday."

"Well," said Price, "that's me bombed out then, isn't it?"

The session was ending. The three waited for the squad to leave the field before going in themselves. They sat in the unlit passage outside the dressing room until the squad came out for their lunch. When Price and Gale got up to go with them, Tom slipped into the empty dressing room. He took off his tracksuit and went to shower, turning the dial colder and colder until he was nearly unable to breathe.

Zoning out of Price and Gale's conversations, Tom watched with silent creeping animosity the lumbering figure going about his work every day just as normal. He never appeared to look up from the tractor, the mower, the line marker, working slowly, methodically. Even when he came closer to the clubhouse he always remained totally focused on the ground, though when he got to within a pitch's distance Tom would go inside to sit in the treatment room and let the physio talk at him while he gaped at medication and military fitness certificates and anatomy posters, taking in the bright musculature, the exposed systems of blood and tubes and bones.

In the lounge one morning Tom picked up an old newspaper from underneath a chair by the breakfast trolley and it occurred to him that he had paid no attention to the Paint result a couple of nights ago. They had won, he read. Easter had scored the only goal, which probably explained why he was still in such a good mood as he moved about the room doing the tea run, humming a song of his own name that Tom presumed to be from his first spell at the club.

Tom went for a review of his ankle. The swelling had reduced and he felt no discomfort when the physio began changing the strapping, peeling off the layers of bandages until his foot appeared, gray and stinking as a fish. He was not yet able to kick, so he was employed later that morning fetching any balls that strayed beyond the touchline as the players attempted cross-field passes to a partner. Within seconds, three or four balls had sailed past him and he shuffled onto the neighboring pitch to collect them. Approaching the furthest ball, he raised his head. Liam was standing by the ground-staff shed, looking in his direction. Tom picked up the ball and walked back to the others.

He entered the canteen that lunchtime to a chaotic scene. The youth team coach had cut short the scholars' session so they were in early, massed near the doorway waiting for the seniors to get their food, filling the room with banter, deodorant. Price and Gale were among them, waiting too. The two stood close together, stiffly protective of their damaged body parts. Tom walked past and nodded; they nodded back.

He placed himself at the end of the furthest table and began cutting into his pile of rice with the edge of a fork. From his isolated position he observed all the comings and goings, quietly eating, aware of Liam the moment he came into the room. He joined the back of the line, patient, undistracted, and once he got to the front stayed a while by the glass counter, staring down at the bowl of rice, then at the remaining jacket potatoes sitting in the cracked dishes as soft and rumpled as toads.

He took a seat near the counter, facing away from Tom, and began to eat slowly, his head moving rhythmically towards his plate each time he took a mouthful. Tom continued to fork rice into his mouth, dry, chewy, taking draughts of water to swill it down. By the time he moved on to his fruit salad the canteen was less full. Scholars were bunched around one table but most of the firsts had gone. Only one group of five was left, on the table in front of Tom, crowding around a newspaper that Fleming was reading aloud from. Tom was still eating when Liam got up to leave: he finished his drink standing at the table then moved away to the door without looking round once.

A thin cold rain had set in by the time Tom left the building. He hobbled hurriedly towards his car, not wanting water to soak through the holes in his plastic cast.

"Tom."

He kept walking.

"How's the ankle? I heard you tore Gale open."

Liam caught up and walked at his side. Tom did not look at him; he kept going, listening, watching for anybody else who might be about, until he got to his car. His ankle was twinging. He needed urgently to be inside the car, driving off.

"Tom?"

"This isn't your car park."

Liam gave a short laugh. Teeth. The ugly insides of his mouth. "Clear off then, shall I?" he said but stayed exactly where he was, standing next to the bonnet, fidgeting inside his pockets, the scrunching noise of his hand clenching and unclenching a set of keys. The last group of players was coming out of the building. Tom reached for his door handle and as he did so Liam touched him for an instant on the arm. Ignoring him, Tom opened the door, lowered himself inside and shut the door.

He drove away down the lane, putting the radio on. There was a discussion about music played over the PA after goals. Listeners were tweeting in with suggestions of the perfect song. He stopped at the road junction, waiting for a gap in the traffic, letting the sound of the radio drain through his brain, not permitting the violent desire that was ripping at the inside of him to take hold, trying to block out the sensation in his forearm that felt as though it had been trapped in the car door.

8

Jones or Easter—if we could only keep one?		
Started by Town Legend	Replies:	11
5 Dec 2011	Views:	94

Town Legend   **posted Mon at 7:22pm**

Open and shut case for some of you on here a few weeks ago but since Easter's come back in the team who would people choose if the budget's not there to retain both of them come January?

Road to Wembley 2010   **posted Mon at 7:30pm**

Easter is contracted until the end of next season so this topic is redundant.

Mary B   **posted Mon at 7:55pm**

Andy Jones every day of the week. Best player to sign for Town since Our Glorious Leader and his chequebook arrived at the club.

Riversider   **posted Mon at 8:41pm**

Dead right, Mary B. Jones covers every blade on the pitch and it's obvious that the other players look up to him. Him and Easter playing together just shows the gulf between them. Just because Easter's had one mediocre game doesn't mean he's back to the player he used to be.

Jamesy1987   **posted Mon at 9:12pm**

Road to Wembley 2010 wrote:
Easter is contracted until the end of next season so this topic is
redundant.

Doesn't mean that nobody will buy him Road to Wembley (unlikely), or
take him on loan (more likely).

Onetoomany   **posted Mon at 9:18pm**
Jones. We all know Easter is only here for the pay packet.

Town Legend   **posted Mon at 9:40pm**
. . . and what do you think Jones is here for then?

Dr Feelgood   **posted Mon at 10:08pm**
In my eyes, this is what the team should be—
                        ~~Yates Lewis~~
                Richards Jones Hart Pearman
                    ~~Easter Price Finch Evans~~
                ~~Gale~~ Daish Boyn Fleming
                          Hoyle
                          ~~Foley~~

Jamesy1987   **posted Mon at 10:11pm**
Er . . . your team's only got eight players in it.

Tommo   **posted Mon at 10:40pm**
I was on Maygate the other day and I saw Easter out with his kid and
his wife (who's seen better days . . . remember what she used to look
like when CE first broke into the team?! 😉) I was a few tables away
from them in Costa . . . and is it me or is he heavier now than when he
left?? Definitely looked to be carrying a few pounds.

Voice of Reason   **posted Mon at 10:51pm**
Get shut. Never should have signed him back.

Towncrier Ian   **posted Mon at 10:58pm**

Chant for Plymouth match tomorrow: "He's fat, he's round, he's on two and a half thousand pounds!"

He could not get a foothold in the game. The ball seemed always to go to Jones, who, even when Easter was standing free, in space, turned away from him every time as if he were an obstacle in the way of the right pass.

"Free. I'm fucking free," he shouted as Jones zigzagged, chased by two opponents, towards a dead end. Jones ignored him and dispatched the ball high into the air, to no one.

Preoccupied with forcing himself into the game, Easter abandoned all tactical discipline. He failed to track his opposite number's runs into the box and eventually watched from the eighteen-yard line as the talentless little meathead scored, unmarked, with a header into the corner.

He was on the other side of the pitch when the board was held up with his number on it. Before he even reached the center circle his legs felt as though they might cave under him. He walked the final stretch, picking out the odd abusive shout from the main stand until a wave of booing and sparse clapping and the new chant—"He's fat, he's round . . ."—increasing in vehemence, engulfed him.

Any shred of form he had started lately to hope that he could piece together, since his surprising reinstatement in the team, now vanished. He was substituted at halftime two games in a row, and as Christmas approached he was again out of the starting eleven, his place taken by Bobby Hart. Even in training the others sensed his indecision. Targeted him. Scholars who would not long ago have stood off now wrestled him for the ball, unafraid to go in with their slight shoulders and hips or pull at his shirt, his shorts.

He was summoned by text to the stadium, to Clarke's office.

"You've not been in the team much the last few games."

"I noticed."

There was a pause during which he wondered if he had made a wrong move.

"You want to play football, yes?"

He did not know how to respond. He cast his eyes over the mass of papers on the desk and the floor, the unshaven Adam's apple scraping at the collar of Clarke's faded polo shirt, and wondered if the question was tactical.

"Of course you do. You want to play football. Well, I'll tell you one thing: you're not fucking going to do it here."

Easter relaxed a little in his chair.

"I'll tell you how it's going to go. Put in a transfer request, and I'll give you some games, get you in the shop window, then we'll—"

"No."

They looked at each other.

"You'd rather sit on your arse not playing?"

"There's a year and a half left on my contract. If I put in a transfer request, you don't have to pay it up." He dared a smile.

"So you'd rather sit on your arse for a year and a half. Then what? Who's going to want you then? That'll be three seasons and counting since you were any good."

Easter thought for a moment. "My agent needs to be here for this. I don't know why you got me in here without my agent."

"Because your agent is a penis."

Both men went quiet. Easter scanned the few photographs on the walls. The new stands under construction. Wembley—the FA Trophy final, one neat segment of the stadium awash with red and green. The arrival of the subsequent victory parade at the town hall, before the meeting with the mayor and the incident with a waiter on the fire escape. He had got drunk in this office that night. The same man who was now eyeballing him across the desk had cradled his head in both hands and brought their faces together to tell him that the two of them were the beating heart of this club, that together they would take it into the league and they weren't fucking going to stop there.

"How much do you want?"

Easter stared, at a loss.

"Severance. How much? Fifty grand? I'll write you a check for fifty right now."

"I need to talk to my agent."

"What about Leah? She wouldn't be happy with fifty grand?" Clarke opened a drawer in the desk. Easter's heart accelerated. Clarke took out a tube of Polos. He wiggled one loose to put into his mouth. A passing thought came to Easter of telling Leah that he had stood up to Clarke, put him in his place. Demanded fifty thousand from him.

"I'll talk to my agent," he said.

"Fine."

Clarke sucked on the mint. He rolled it around the insides of his cheeks. His lips briefly parted and the tip of his tongue appeared, protruding through the hole like the moist inquisitive nose of a rodent.

"Paint area semi in a couple of days. Leyton Orient. I'm putting you back in. Way I see it, if somebody doesn't take you this transfer window then that's you finished."

He knew, as soon as he sprinted for the first loose pass, that he was nowhere near match fit. After only five minutes, when the ball cleared the wooden-gabled roof of one stand, he knelt to retie the lace of his boot and lowered his face to hide his labored breathing. But when a new ball was obtained and the throw-in taken, the Orient player who ended up with it blundered into his rising figure, the ball rolling free in front of him. Easter advanced and clipped a pass into the path of Bobby Hart, who ran unchallenged all the way to the edge of the box and scored with a long wrinkling shot that bounced over the goalkeeper's outstretched arm. Bobby, as surprised as anyone, froze—then bounded towards the stand behind the goal and spreadeagled himself on the grass. It took him several seconds, lying prone while his teammates rushed towards him, to become aware that the Town fans were in fact in a different part of the stadium, and the provocation of the Orient supporters ensured that the rest of the half was played out in a new atmosphere of noise and tension.

The team entered the dressing room revitalized. Clarke, moving around as he read out his key performance notes, stopped in front of Easter. "Keep it up, son," he said and winked.

The second half, however, did not continue like the first. A few minutes in, Easter attempted a long diagonal pass back to Hoyle that was not hard enough and was intercepted by an Orient striker, who flashed a shot into the roof of the net. That was all it took. His confidence was sucked from him. For the remaining forty minutes and then the never-ending half-hour of extra time, he ached for each respite of the ball going out of play. He no longer seemed to be in control of his body. Every time he received the ball, what should have been automatic—trapping, looking up, passing—was now complicated by thought: which part of the foot to use, which part of the ball to touch. By the time he had command of it he would look upfield and see only a blur of bodies and an opponent would be harrying him for the ball.

When the final whistle sounded, the teams lined up along the halfway line, arms linked around each other's waists, for penalties. They watched the first Orient taker walk up to the spot. A cheer echoed around the stadium when he scored, then low taunting suspense as the crowd waited for a Town player to move. Fingers dug into his flank. There was no planned sequence. Whoever is man enough to step up, Clarke had said during the exhausted coming-together after the final whistle. Boyn came forward. His strike went in off the crossbar. Easter knew that if he had not been supported by the hot, damp sides of Bobby and Lewis he would not have been able to stand. He remained rooted to his position as Richards, then, following seconds of stillness in the line, Yates and Daish went up and scored.

With the score level, the final Orient taker drove his penalty down the middle, high into the nearly empty family stand behind the goal to cannon against the corrugated back wall.

Easter sensed his body refusing, shriveling into the earth. Bobby, though, was pulling free of his arm, stepping out from the line. Relief, shame, flooded him. He felt weak with a need to be away from there, to be at home, in his office. Bobby bent to place the ball. Retreating in preparation for his run-up, he glanced at his teammates, his face white, hard to read. He spun and trotted up to the ball then sent a low curling shot beyond the reach of the goalkeeper. It was all Easter could do, while the team sprinted to Bobby and clambered on top of him, to stay on his feet and not vomit onto the pitch.

Leah was still up when he got home at just gone half past one.

"I've made you a sandwich," she said when he came into the living room.

"A sandwich?" He looked through into the kitchen to where it was cling-filmed on a plate on the island. "Mind if I don't have it now? Stomach's in bits."

"Course. You OK? You won."

He poured himself some wine into her glass and sat down next to her. "Yes, we won. Penalties."

"He didn't pull you off, then?"

"Nope. Played the full hundred and twenty and I had a fucking shocker."

"It can't have been that bad or he'd have taken you off."

He put his head back against the sofa and closed his eyes.

"Want a massage?"

"Yes," he said, his eyes still closed. "Thank you."

She waited for him to pull off his top and tracksuit bottoms. She could tell from the way he removed the clothes and lowered himself onto his front that he was in some discomfort. She knelt down beside the sofa. He had put on a bit of weight, she noticed. She wondered when that had started.

She began at his feet, pulling at his toes so that they clicked, then worked her way up, kneading and sliding, over his calves, hamstrings, buttocks; his back, which, the moment she pressed on it, caused him to let out a small desperate sigh. It had always been a miracle to her, this body. When they had first got together she used to find herself staring at it while he got changed or walked naked across her bedroom, every supple part stirring with design

and purpose, like the body of an animal. Sometimes he would notice her looking and grin, and she would smile back or look away
in embarrassment. It was the same body, even now. Only a little
thicker. A few increasing signs of wear: the broken capillaries that
threaded the backs of his legs, the twists and lumps of calloused
skin and scar tissue, unexpected knots in his back that gristled beneath her hands. They comforted her, these parts of him. There
was a solace in her intimate knowledge of them, an assurance that
they were aging together.

She came to the top of his body, circling her thumbs into the
nape of his neck and behind his ears. "Are you going to sleep in the
spare room?" she asked.

"No. I'll stay with you."

When she had put the sandwich in the fridge, brushed her teeth
and joined him in bed, he tapped the light out and moved on top of
her.

She watched the dark outline of his face going up and down.
She exhaled audibly in answer to his own short, rhythmic moans,
until she realized that he was making the sounds because some re-
gion of his body was in pain. Gently, she took hold of his sides and
whispered for him to stop. He let her turn him, carefully, so that he
was lying on the bed. She kissed his forehead, stroking his hair off
it, and repositioned herself over him.

In the morning he was dead to the world. He lay flat on his
back, legs apart, arms by his sides under the covers. She ran her
hand down his torso and touched the waistband of something that
felt unnervingly like a pair of her tights, but then it occurred to her
that he must have put on his recovery skins at some point during
the night. An unexpected spur of playfulness made her sit upright.
She took her glass from the bedside table and dipped her fingers in
the water. She held them above his face, letting a couple of drops
fall onto his nose. When he did not rouse she dipped again and let
more drops fall, then again, until his cheeks were wet and his nose
crinkled at a droplet of water that hung, quivering, inside a nos-
tril. She examined the motionless face. His mouth. The thin purple skin of his eyelids. She put her lips to his forehead, then

resettled the covers over him and left the room, quietly closing the door.

Four hours later, once it was clear that her plan to go to a soft play center would have to be aborted, she decided against going alone with Tyler and instead got him ready for a trip to the super-market.

Leah manhandled Tyler into the foldout seat of a trolley and went inside to find the place was heaving. She considered turning straight back round—they barely needed anything anyway; she had come two days previously—but she was nonetheless sucked in, past the plastic Christmas tree and the fat festive newspaper bundles into the maw of the entrance hall and its Tannoy dream of Christmas music. Tyler was twisting to get down from his wire throne. She seized hold of him, straightening him up. There were tears in his eyes and a scowl on his face. He was looking up at her with such accusatory hostility that it must have appeared, as she moved into the fruit and vegetables, that she had been harming him.

"Sorry, Ty." She pinched a glob of snot from his nose with a wet wipe. "You're just going to have to deal with it. We won't be long."

She waited behind the dithering horde selecting from a landslide of easy peelers, and grabbed two bags as soon as a space appeared. She ripped open the netting, peeled and offered one to Tyler, but he batted it away, so she pressed on into the cold meats aisle. At a car-ton of Peperamis she stopped, took one, opened it there and then in the aisle and handed it to Tyler. He shut up at once, and she car-ried on, trying to think of things that Chris might need while Tyler sucked away at his meat stick. In the frozen section she heard an older woman openly tut to her husband at the sight of Tyler with his Peperami. *Fuck you,* she thought, but even in her head she could not compose a better comeback. Tyler's mouth and chin were dis-colored. She pulled out another wet wipe and rubbed him hard. He squealed in discomfort.

"Do you want me to take it away?" She brought her face level with his. "Do you? Mummy take it away from you?"

A teenage boy and girl were up ahead of her, in front of a DVD stand. The girl was sliding her hand inside the boy's front jeans pocket. She pulled out a chocolate bar, all the while looking into his eyes, smiling. She opened it and took a bite, then held the bar up to the boy's mouth, touching his lips with it. Leah stood by a line of chest freezers, halted by the scene. Shoppers shunted past her on either side, but she continued staring over the head of her son at the young couple. She was not more than four or five years older than them. The thought of behaving like that with Chris in public was unimaginable, and yet they must have done—they did, once. Kissing on the dance floor of the Hut. Whole days at the coast messing about in amusement arcades. In her bedroom while her mum was at work; in his bedroom before his mum moved abroad and the club put him in digs. But even as she reached for these memories she could not avoid others, things that had so often followed the good times. The fights he had got into, in those same arcades, in the Hut. The argument with the youth coach in a car park that got him suspended for a month and resulted in the same period of silent grievance which she had not known how to coax him out of. The falling-out with Liam during their final year in the youths, which to this day had not healed over.

But she could also remember the fight with her dad, on the weekend that her mum finally left him. How Chris had pushed him to the floor in reaction to some snide comment he had made about Leah, then stamped on his hand—*Who's the big man, now, yeah? Who's the big man now?*—and told him that if he ever spoke like that to Leah again he'd break all his fingers. The weeks afterwards were the happiest she could remember of their time together. He had not wanted to be apart from her. He had told her, drunk, at the Hut, that he loved her, he didn't give a shit about anyone else, he loved her and the rest of the world could go fuck themselves.

But again she could not hold on to the memory. She started to push the trolley again, coming closer to the teenagers. The girl was chewing, looking up with a playful smile at the boy's face, and as Leah went past them it was not the memory of herself behaving like that with Chris that she could recall, but the thought of other girls doing it.

Two men were looking at her, smirking across the freezers. She moved away, ignoring Tyler's anguish that his Peperami was gone, dropped somewhere. She got to the end of the freezers and turned the corner, coming back the other way along the next aisle, pulling random items from shelves—olives, brandy butter, a Christmas cheese board with a miniature bottle of port squeezed into its heart—but Tyler was thrashing now, screaming, and she had to stop and get him out of his seat. She held his head against her chest, shushing him. The men were there again, at the far end of the aisle, watching her. One of them said something to the other, which made them both laugh. With one arm around Tyler, the other on the bar of her trolley, she turned and walked away. Half a minute later, when she looked round again, she saw they were following her. She sped up, her heart beating harder, but it was difficult to manage the trolley and Tyler together, so she abandoned the trolley, people looking at her, judging her. She hastened on past them, past the shelves full of relaxed competent mothers on the sides of nappy packs, and as her anger mounted she wanted to stop and scream—at the shoppers, at the men, at Tyler—but she knew what would happen if she did. It would be Chris who would be punished for it. An Internet telltale. A chant on the Kop.

The men were blatantly pursuing her now, marching down the central aisle a little way behind her. She hurried towards the exit. The tutting woman had recognized her as well, it crossed her mind, another of the army of anonymous eyes that followed her about in public, willing her to fail. She stopped. For a few seconds she did not move. Voices, laughter, blurred past her.

When she turned round, the two men, taken by surprise, both looked down at the floor. As she stepped towards them they hesitated, then veered towards the closest rank of shelves. They were pretending to look through a box of wrapping paper rolls when she got to them.

"Enjoying yourselves, boys?" she asked, taken aback that it was her voice saying this.

They blanked her, and she realized that they were younger than she had at first thought.

"Get off on this, do you?" She was speaking loudly. Other people had noticed.

One of them made to walk away, but they were surrounded, blockaded by trolleys, a small intrigued crowd already gathering. Tyler made a sudden lunge downwards, so powerfully that she almost dropped him. There, poking out of his left welly, was the Peperami. She took it out and handed it back to him. Instead of putting it in his mouth, he held it out, offering it to one of the boys. The fleshy little nub of meat protruded obscenely from its slimy plastic sheath. She laughed, and some of the other shoppers joined in, while the two boys, clearly terrified, gave each other a look but remained frozen where they were.

"It's all right, Ty," she said. "I don't think they'd know what to do with one that big. They're only used to each other's."

In the ballyhoo that followed she walked away, the crowd parting to let her through, her legs transporting her weightlessly towards the exit, electrified, abruptly alive.

9

		P	W	D	L	F	A	GD	Points	Form
1	Crawley Town	21	14	4	3	44	26	18	46	DWWWD
2	Southend United	21	13	3	5	37	22	15	42	WWDLL
3	Cheltenham Town	21	13	3	5	34	20	14	42	WWWWD
4	Shrewsbury Town	21	12	4	5	33	20	13	40	WWWLW
5	Swindon Town	21	11	4	6	34	17	17	37	WDWDW
6	Burton Albion	21	10	6	5	33	30	3	36	WWWLD
7	Gillingham	21	10	5	6	37	26	11	35	WWDDW
8	Oxford United	21	9	6	6	30	23	7	33	LLLDW
9	Rotherham Utd	21	9	6	6	38	35	3	33	WWLWW
10	Port Vale	21	9	5	7	38	29	9	32	LLDWW
11	Morecambe	21	8	7	6	35	24	11	31	DLLDL
12	Torquay United	21	8	7	6	33	29	4	31	WWDWL
13	Accrington Stan.	21	7	8	6	25	24	1	29	WDWWW
14	Crewe Alexandra	21	8	3	10	24	29	-5	27	LWWDD
15	Macclesfield Town	21	7	5	9	21	21	0	26	LDLDL
16	Aldershot Town	21	8	2	11	24	28	-4	26	LLLWL
17	AFC Wimbledon	21	7	5	9	29	38	-9	26	DDLLL
18	Bristol Rovers	21	6	5	10	26	37	-11	23	LLDDL
19	Barnet	21	5	5	11	26	41	-15	20	DWWLD
20	Bradford City	21	4	7	10	22	29	-7	19	LLDDW
21	Hereford United	21	4	6	11	19	36	-17	18	DLLLD
22	Northampton Twn	21	4	5	12	24	42	-18	17	LLLDL
23	Plymouth Argyle	21	3	5	13	20	40	-20	14	DLWDD
24	Dagenham & Red.	21	4	2	15	19	39	-20	14	WLLLD
25	Town	21	1	7	13	17	42	-25	10	LLLDL

"Christmas. Listen up." Clarke looked away from the sheet of paper stuck to the whiteboard and folded his arms across his bosom. "We've got four matches coming up in the next ten days. Pitches are going to be frozen. Some of you are going to get injured. Some of you are going to have to play through injuries, and some of you who've been out of the team are going to get some minutes. All of you will train Christmas morning. And you better believe that if anyone so much as looks at a drink, I'll know it. I don't need telling what a hangover looks like."

And as he moved away to the tea urn, his eyes yellow, his nose spidered with veins, it was a brave or unwise player who could doubt that this was true.

"Christmas party, gaffer," Yates called out as the number two was about to take them through the upcoming schedule. "We've been holding off. When can we have it?"

Clarke stepped back in front of the number two.

"January. And that's if you've improved what this bastard table looks like by then. And"—his lips stretched into a deformed jovial smile—"if you invite me."

Later, in the dressing room, Yates slapped his legs and got up from the bench. "Right then. Party. Who's sorting it?"

For a few seconds nobody said anything. Apart from Bobby and Steven and one or two other young players looking eagerly about the room, they all avoided beholding Easter, whose head was lowered, his hands compressed between his knees.

"Come on, boys," Yates continued. "I know there's sod-all time but it's not that hard. Venue, girls, Jägers."

Jones stood up. "I'm on it."

There was some clapping, a few shouts.

"First thing's money," Jones said. "Fines need calling in, pronto. Who's up for it?"

A few hands went up.

"Stevie Barr. Good boy. You need to write out the fines board and go round collecting. Any of these faggots give you any trouble, you come to me. All right? Done."

Talk about the party soon dominated most conversations. The

most sensible plan, it was decided, by Jones, was to have it well away from town. No chance of supporters, press, partners. They were playing Oxford on New Year's Day. The party could be held there after the game. Jones, who had played for Oxford at one point, put in a call to a contact in the city and made a deal to hire a club for the night. Extras he negotiated separately, through other contacts.

Tom attempted to join in with the banter. He laughed at each new jibe at the manager. He made a cumbersome joke of his own one lunchtime about drinking games, which nobody seemed to hear. All the while, though, thoughts about the party hung over him. His fear—having been to the last Christmas party at his old club, when one of the other scholars was forced onto the stage and had ended the night sobbing and retching on a pavement—was that he would be singled out, brought into the spotlight. Living with the Scottish boys did not help. They spoke about little else. Steven had thrown himself into the role of kitty man. The money was stuffed into an old ale jug of Mr. Davey's on the kitchen worktop. Mrs. Davey tried to ban the subject from the dinner table but the two boys were so unable to stop themselves that she relented.

Tom found out, with a stealthy peep at the noticeboard in the club office when he came in under the pretense of wanting some match-day programs for his family, that the staff would be holding their own party separately, at a pub in town.

In the fortnight or so since his attempt at contact in the car park, Liam had not tried again to speak to him alone. Tom had made sure to avoid any situations which might have given him the opportunity, keeping away from the car park and the canteen except at busy times, never training alone, staying out of the Daveys' kitchen as much as he could. He was up in his room late one afternoon, though, when he was alerted to the sound of Liam's voice downstairs. He went to his doorway to listen. Liam was talking to Mrs. Davey, although it was difficult to make out what they were saying. He came quietly down the staircase, checking that Bobby and Steven were not in their rooms, and stood against the wall of the bathroom, close to the first-floor landing.

". . . just into town. Not a late one."

"How's he getting on, Mark?"

"Mark's just Mark. Never changes, to be fair."

"And what about Leah? You're seeing more of her these days?"

"A bit. When she's allowed. She's out tonight, she says."

There was a break in the conversation and Tom thought they were going into a different room. He moved back from the landing.

"Tom?" Mr. Davey was coming up the stairs. "Everything all right?"

Tom jumped. He looked towards Bobby's and Steven's rooms, then at his watch. "Just seeing if the boys were back. There's a magazine I was coming to see if they've got."

"Right-o." Mr. Davey gave him what Tom was sure was a doubtful look on his way past him to the bathroom. Tom went to knock on both bedroom doors then back up to his room, where he lay on the floor, his eyes shut, trying to regain himself.

He was often irritable with the Daveys. It would not take much—the sight of them chuckling on the sofa, a jokey conversation with the Scottish pair over dinner—and he would become silent and go up to his room at the first opportunity. They had noticed the amount of time he was spending in his room. The silences. Mrs. Davey cornered him in the kitchen one icy morning, freezing fog pressing at the windows, while he was waiting for the toaster to pop. She sat down at the table and started leafing through the post.

"Will you come and sit with me while you eat your breakfast?" she said when he turned round with his plate.

He ate his first slice quickly, aware that she was looking at him.

"How are you getting on at the minute, Tom?"

He waited to finish his mouthful. "Not bad."

"I've had enough boys through here to know how difficult it can be. Tom. Look up, please. Look at me a moment."

He did as he was told. Her face, soft and lined under the kitchen light, made him suddenly furious.

"You know you can talk to us? We've seen it all before, believe me. It makes no difference if you're nineteen or you're twenty-nine, if you're out of the team or you're injured, that's not easy for anybody. It doesn't mean you've failed."

"I don't think I've failed."

"No. You shouldn't. Nobody else does. You're a very talented boy. You can go as far as you want in the game, Tony thinks. So go easy on yourself, Tom. You've got your whole life ahead of you." She reached across and held his hand. "Talk to your folks, sweetheart. Don't bottle it all up."

With that, she let go of his hand and left the table, smiling. One job down, he thought cruelly, now to the ironing.

As well as the party, for which the idea of going in costumes—as each other—had to Tom's great relief been jettisoned, the other topic of discussion was the January transfer window. Every day there would be a new rumor on the Internet message boards or Twitter or in Pascoe's column, which one or other of the players, usually Yates, would make sure to bring up. Easter, although nobody spoke about him if he was present, featured prominently in these rumors. So too did Clarke. To a lesser extent, Tom's future was also under debate: he was going to be sent out on loan for first-team experience; Finch-Evans was going to Aldershot and Tom would be given a run in the team; a club in the Conference South had made an inquiry.

Tom read all of these rumors, worrying in his room, desperate to stop himself, to turn off the laptop. He occupied himself almost constantly in an effort to distract his thoughts, as he always had, with football. But it felt hollow. He was back in training, though he had long forgotten what it was like to play. To be worked up at the prospect of a match. For nothing else to matter except stepping onto a pitch with his instructions about the fullback's weaknesses, expecting to beat him, knowing that his teammates expected him to. The muscular effort of riding a challenge. The release of sprinting, of striking the ball. He wanted to be able to close his eyes and remember all of that, to lose himself in it, but whenever he closed his eyes he felt lost, afraid, as though something was waiting for him in the dark.

He was already awake on Christmas morning when his parents called. The Daveys had set the heating to come on in the early hours and his room was uncomfortably warm. He stood by the window in his underpants with his forehead against the glass, looking out at the frosted town dotted here and there with busy windows smoldering through the mist, damaged frigid Santas, reindeer, hanging from the frames.

"You're having lunch at the Daveys', then?"

"After training. Then we're off down to Torquay early tomorrow."

"So no celebrating then?"

"No."

"But you'll have a drink tomorrow night, after the game?"

"Depends, Dad. I doubt we'll be celebrating. We'll probably have lost."

"Hey, none of that. It's Christmas." There were voices in the background, laughter. "Your mum's tipsy already."

Tom listened to the muffled fuss of his mum protesting. She came to the phone and wished him happy Christmas, giggling at something his dad was doing next to her. She told him to have a good day and handed the phone back.

"Well, look at this," his dad said. "It's up. Your sister wants to speak to you, Tom. I think she's still drunk from last night, looking at her. Here she is. Happy Christmas, mate. Chin up, eh?"

There was the crackling sound of the phone being passed.

"Hi, Tom. Make them stop, please."

Tom smiled. He shifted his forehead on the glass. "Happy Christmas, Rach. You had a late one, then?"

"It was ugly. City center was a wreck. How are you? Happy Christmas. You got to stay off it today?"

"We've got training in an hour. Torquay tomorrow."

"No Christmas pudding for you." She paused. "Christ's sake, it's carnage here. Mum is actually pissed." She was laughing, her mouth turned away from the phone. "Are you OK?" Down on the pavement, Tom could see two old men with dogs, shaking hands. "Tom? You still there?"

"Sorry, I thought you were talking to Mum. I'm fine, yes. You know. Christmas is crap being a footballer."

She was quiet a moment, probably considering a remark. "It

must be. Hang in there, though. OK, Tom, I should go. Happy Christmas. I hope you play tomorrow. I'm sorry you're not here."

He stayed by the window for a while. On noticing that some of his cacti were looking out of condition he moved the whole collection an inch further from the glass and, after putting on some tracksuit bottoms, waited at the top of his staircase with the elegant little copper watering can that his sister had given him a year ago until he was sure that there was nobody in the bathroom below.

Mrs. Davey made them pig-in-blanket baguettes. There was a single glass of Buck's Fizz each. All along the kitchen worktop lay ordered piles and bowls of chopped vegetables. A turkey sat in a gigantic tray on top of the oven. Tom stared at the meal preparations while he drank the last of his Buck's Fizz and the Scottish pair badgered Mrs. Davey for a second glass, going over in his mind once more his strategy for the day ahead.

Training was an hour early to give the players more time with their families in the afternoon. The number two brought in a box of Santa hats. They were worn by one of the teams during a seven-a-side but came off too easily and were soon discarded. Only the seniors were there. No scholars, no staff. Lesley had left plastic trays of Christmas dinners, like airplane meals, for those players who were not hurrying home after the session. This group, most of whose wives and girlfriends lived in other parts of the country, numbered only half a dozen, so the canteen was unusually quiet. There was some difficulty operating the microwave: Richards and Hoyle had gone ahead to warm up the meals, but when the other four arrived at the table they found in front of them a line of shrunken trays, the meat stained brown with evaporated gravy, sprouts withered and steaming, and cranberry sauce melded to the buckled plastic. Tom joined in the banter of the others, but he did not care and barely took notice of the food. Afterwards, the group was going to the house that three of them shared, for darts and computer games, and for a second Tom considered joining them, but then he thanked them for the offer and said he was going to go back for Christmas lunch at his landlords'.

"Don't blame you," Richards said, "after that circus."

Tom drove the empty road to the coast. All of the shops and cafes were closed, something which he had not considered, so there was nowhere to buy a drink or a snack, but it suited him fine—the peaceful streets, the boatless sea. A week ago he had told the Daveys that Richards had invited him to Christmas lunch. They were disappointed, he knew, but at the same time it was obvious how pleased they were too, as if they were his own parents, at this sign that he was mixing with the other young players. He felt some guilt, deceiving them. This was overridden, though, walking onto the beach, by the knowledge of how out of the question was the alternative. He kept going down the coastline, over rocks and gullies, across wilds of sand whipped into a haze by the swerving wind, until he had to turn back before it got too dark to walk safely.

He sat in his car in the empty car park. Unbidden, crawling possibilities passed through his imagination. Liam's big lumpish body pressing up against one of the Scottish pair. Some sordid little note waiting for him in his bedroom when he got back. But when he did return, after nine o'clock, the kitchen spotless, Bobby and Steven in their rooms, the Daveys asleep on the sofa with the television on and the remains of a board game on the carpet, there was no note or any other sign of Liam in Tom's room or any other place that he searched.

The day after Town's Boxing Day defeat in Torquay, Tom was sitting on the floor of his room wrapping up presents to give to his family that afternoon, when it began to snow. Lightly at first. He looked up at the tiny floating flakes, which turned to water the moment they touched the window. He imagined the warm car journey ahead of him. The unwrapping of presents on the living-room floor while his dad went around topping up drinks to the smell of the roasting turkey crown his mum had insisted they were having, despite his dad's and his sister's complaints that it would only be two days since their last one. But the snow started to come more thickly, falling over the town in soft heavy waves. Just before ten there was a knock on his door, and Mrs. Davey came in to tell him that there were severe weather warnings already, advising against motorway travel.

The snow continued to fall, on and off, into the next day. The sky had cleared by the morning of the home match on the 29th, but the subzero temperature prevented a thaw. At the ground, ice nested in lines along the stand roofs, and dense snow had settled on top of the pitchside rows of seating. A smooth compacted layer of it shone across the pitch. A message was put out that morning calling for volunteers to clear the playing surface. There would be a free ticket in it for anybody that came down. By nine o'clock some thirty or forty people, many with their own shovels, were dispersed over the pitch: fathers and sons, club staff, scholars, groups of teenagers, stiff laughing old men, couples—all working under the cheerful direction of the two groundsmen. They dug in teams, wheelbarrowing the snow to dump against the advertising hoardings. The referee, who had set off from his home at 4:30 that morning to brave the roads, watched and waited in his overcoat, preparing for his eleven o'clock pitch inspection. Cheers broke out each time a patch of grass was revealed. After an hour of clearing, the chairman and the club secretary appeared, to more cheers, with flasks of tea and large foil platters of bacon sandwiches.

Steven, on finishing his second breakfast, followed Bobby onto the pitch and threw a snowball that hit him on the back of the head. Bobby turned to return fire, at which all of the other scholars ran to join in. As the rest of the volunteers watched the escalating snowball fight, Liam walked over towards the boys. Once he got close to them they stopped, eyes to the ground, shamefaced.

"What do you think this is doing for the pitch, lads?"

"Sorry," Steven said.

Liam pointed at Bobby. "You. Come and look at this."

Bobby walked slowly to where Liam had knelt on the ground to scrape aside a little pile of snow, understanding only when Liam cupped the pile between his gloves and rose smiling that he had been hoodwinked. He sprang up and sprinted away. Liam gave chase, throwing his snowball, clipping Bobby's arm.

"Hey," Bobby called over his shoulder, laughing. He stumbled, almost falling, and Liam gained on him. "I'm going to do my ankle here," Bobby shouted as Liam caught up and rugby-tackled him into the bank of snow at the side of the pitch.

By five to eleven, large areas—the center circle, the corners, both penalty boxes—had been cleared. Viewed from above, the field, with its shoveling figures moving at the edges of these dark patches, looked like an archaeological site. The referee stepped onto the pitch. He had changed into his match boots and, to the amusement of the hopeful huddled audience, his shorts. He walked slowly over the grass clearings, stooping here and there to prod at the ground or perform a sudden battery of stamps with the serious head-cocked scrutiny of a burrowing animal.

His decision was announced at midday: match postponed. Even though the snow, at the current rate, would be cleared in time for kickoff, the surface was dangerously hard. The volunteers departed, disheartened, but, after a minor quarrel with the chairman over the free ticket offer, reasonably content, moving carefully away from the stadium with their shovels over their shoulders and warm clouds of conversation about their heads.

The Daveys held a small party on New Year's Eve for their friends the Whittells and the Beeneys, and their lodgers, who had to stay sober because of the match the next day. Tom spent most of the night near Bobby and Steven, and joined them in Bobby's room at one stage to play on the Xbox. When they came back down Ray Beeney trapped him on the far side of the kitchen table. He thought Tom had ability, he said. Real ability. He hadn't got to many games this season but he believed Tom had not been given a fair crack of the whip. "It'll come, son. It'll come." He repeated this a number of times. "It'll come." Then he wandered off, knocking a bowl of bread-crumbed prawns onto the floor on his way out of the kitchen.

Tom rode out the long stretch to midnight, feeling as out of place as a child. Shortly after the clinks and hip-hoorays and a short boisterous "Auld Lang Syne" led by Bobby and Steven, he saw Mrs. Davey hold up her phone to show Mr. Davey before turning to Ray Beeney: "He's in town with Mark and Shona and the rest of his crowd. He says happy new year to you all."

"Good boy, good boy," Ray Beeney said. "Happy new year, tell him."

A few minutes later Tom left, unnoticed, to go up to his room.

He thrust his face into his pillow. When he brought it back up he was gasping for breath. He waited a moment before standing and reaching for the magazine at the bottom of his wardrobe. When he sat down on the bed his breathing was still irregular. Mark. Shona. The names held him captive, as alien and shocking as the staring faces and wet cramping tongues of the women in the magazine before him.

Clarke forbade any mention of the party until the final whistle at Oxford, but its unspoken proximity charged the atmosphere inside the dressing room, rippling through the squad's preparations— from the increase in the number of non-starters requesting a rub from the physio to the quicker than usual emptying of the caffeine-tablet boxes going around the room.

The surface was difficult, the referee inconsistent. Oxford scored three late goals to win 4–1 and keep Town, at the halfway point in the season, bottom of the table. The defeat, however, did not dampen the excitement. After an initial period of silence during which the sound of the Oxford players celebrating bled through the wall, the mood soon swelled with energy and banter. Players queued at the mirrors and watched each other's deft practiced movement of combs and fingers and hair dryers. When Clarke left, not to be seen for the rest of the night, Jones brought out a bottle of champagne and Yates performed a long thrusting dance on top of one of the benches. Tom watched and laughed with the others, swallowing deeply from the bottle when it came to him.

Back at their hotel, Easter spent a considerable amount of time in the bathroom while Tom sat on his bed and drank from the bottle of vodka that he had stuffed into a compartment of his bag, until the bathroom door started to open and he slipped the bottle back.

When Tom had finished in the bathroom himself, Easter was sitting on his own bed, looking at his phone, scrolling, Tom saw as he came past, through photos of his wife and son. Tom sat down opposite him. He put on his shoes and set to lacing them.

"Looking forward to this?" Easter asked without looking up from his phone.

"Yes."

Easter began to rock very slowly on the edge of the bed. "Easy enough for you, I guess, isn't it?"

Tom did not understand, or ask what he meant.

"Fair play, though. Fair play. I remember that." He took up the sports jacket from beside him on the bed and slid it on. The top of his chest, above the collar of his T-shirt, was shining. He looked up at Tom. "You know I could have gone to Spurs? Got offered a place in the academy there."

"I heard that somewhere. Why didn't you?"

Easter shrugged and started rocking again. "Don't know. Seemed clear enough at the time. All of it."

It hit Tom, watching Easter's eyes as he went back to the phone, that he was drunk. Music started up in the room next door: Richards and Hoyle.

"Here," Easter said, letting the phone drop and crawling to the far side of his bed to reach for something on the floor. He lifted up an almost empty bottle of champagne. "Want some?"

"No, thanks," Tom said and bent down for his vodka bottle. He held it up to knock against Easter's.

"Cheers."

Jones stood by the door of the first, then the second, of the minibuses conveying them to an Italian restaurant, ready with an encouraging word or a squeeze on the bum for each embarking passenger. When they arrived Tom hung about at the rear of the throng in the restaurant lobby, backed up against empty dust-covered wine bottles, so that he would not end up in the middle of the table or next to anybody who might resent sitting next to him. The high spirits increased during the meal. Champagne buckets were strung down the length of the table and the waiting staff given instructions to maintain a flow of bottles throughout the meal. Before the starters arrived, Tom, at one end with Bobby and Steven and the first-year pros, felt something hit his left cheek. He saw with panic that a gang at the other end was laughing in his direction. He had been struck by an olive. Automatically, he grinned back. Another olive flew towards him, but missed to the side of his face. Then another, which missed to the same side, and he realized with a rush of joy when Bobby was hit on the forehead that he was not the intended target.

"Come on, boys," Price implored from behind them, ruffling the heads of all of the young players as he walked round the table, "get your banter up."

A doorman welcomed them at the entrance to the club. They followed him in single file down some steps and along a passageway with the careful tread and close-guarded mental preparation of the walk down the pitch tunnel. The passage ended at a large dark room, empty apart from three staff behind the bar busily stocking fridges and, at one side of a bare stage, a DJ at a mixing console nodding to the music on his headphones. An arrangement of champagne buckets was balanced on the bar counter. There was a smell of bleach. The throb of music above their heads from the main part of the club. One of the barmen came over to speak to Jones. The players were still standing about in the middle of the space when the DJ set to work at his mixer and loud music issued from the speakers around the walls.

With nobody there but themselves, the players quickly grouped into familiar cliques. Tom stayed around the young players, his mouth pinching with champagne, taking in the faded black curtain behind the stage, a formation of small round tables in front of it, the chairs lined up on one side of them to face the stage.

There was a sharp change in Steven's expression. The circle turned to see what he was looking at. Other people, young women, were entering the room. Jones, then Yates, moved across the floor to greet them. The pressing inescapability of the night closed around Tom. He went to the toilets and as he entered them imagined locking himself inside a cubicle, unnoticed, until it was over. When he came back into the room he saw that his group had gravitated towards the busy area around the bar. A woman with short side-parted dark hair was among them. She was talking to Steven as Tom rejoined the circle.

"Who's your captain?"

Steven paused for a moment. "Depends."

The woman smiled quizzically, thinking that he was being playful. "Depends on what?"

"Depends what you mean. Supposed to be him." He pointed over to where Easter had isolated one of the women on the other side of the bar. Then he turned to point behind Tom. "See, these days really it's that guy." They all turned to look at Jones. "He's the captain."

"Sounds like a strange setup."

"Oh, it's a shambles, aye."

They all laughed, including the woman. Several others nearby looked over and identified, by the expression of proud surprise on his face, that it was Steven who had made a joke. Another woman came to join them. She held up a bottle of champagne by the neck and topped up their glasses. She moved in beside the first woman and the Scottish boys, falling in with their conversation. Tom was drunk. His forehead ached with the heavy tender weight of his eyeballs. He could not understand who they were, these women—if they had been persuaded down from the club upstairs or if they had been invited, paid, to come here.

A low expectant clamor was growing around him. A thin, very white girl stood in the center of the stage. She was in a close-fitting green dress, her hands clasped together behind her back. Beyond her, a whorl of dust from the still-moving curtain was caught in the shaft of a spotlight. Tom tried to remember whether she had been one of those around the bar, who were now walking with the rest of the crowd to take seats at the tables in front of the stage, but she seemed new, younger.

Tom sat down near one end of the row. He looked down it briefly for Easter but could not find him. He turned his face to the stage. From his position, he could see the girl's fingers struggling momentarily with the zip at the back of her dress before she guided it up over the protruding contours of her spine. She walked slowly to one edge of the stage, then the other, and back to the middle. Her face was flushed but expressionless. She let the dress collapse to the floor. A few shouts went up. Fists banged on the sturdy little tables. The girl removed her bra and dropped herself to the boards, where she lay front down with her hands positioned as though about to go into press-ups. Her neck tautened as she lifted her face, then her chest—her palms, stomach, thighs still flattened to the dirty black-painted wood of the stage.

A tray was being passed along the row. Tom watched it glinting in the stage lights with every exchange. He thought at first that there must be shots on the way, but as the tray got closer he saw that there was money on it, a pile of notes.

"Silver platter," he heard from a few seats down. "Get in."

By the time the tray reached him and he lifted the black and gold leatherette cocktail menu that weighted the notes down, there looked to be a few hundred pounds on it. He took out his wallet, confused because he thought that everything had been paid for already, and added a twenty. Another girl, shorter, slightly older, with a dyed red bob, came onto the stage. She danced, worming out of her clothes alongside the thin white girl. Fervid excitement was building along the row. The two girls switched positions. Tom noticed the blackened soles of the younger one's feet as she moved away. His own body was shutting down, weak with pathetic complicity. Hoyle tapped his arm, urging him to look down the line to where first Bobby, then Steven, were being pushed, dragged, onto

the stage. Somebody touched Tom's shoulder. His hands tightened
to the seat of his chair. "Amazing." Price was behind him, moving
down the line. "Fucking amazing."

Yates leaped onto the stage to pair each boy with one of the
girls. Following their new partners' leads they began to dance—feet
planted to the floor, both punching the air with uncontrolled nervous vigor. The audience, delighted by the two stern faces, started
to clap in unison. Tom, delirious with relief, joined in. He laughed
spontaneously with those around him at Steven, nearest to his own
side with the younger girl. Steven did not know what to do with his
arms: they fell prone by his sides one moment then all at once were
fisting the air again whenever he looked across and copied Bobby at
the other side of the stage.

The girls, moving to the front of them, set to unbuttoning their
shirts. The two boys exchanged an unsmiling look over the girls'
heads: determined, together. There was a loud cheer when the
shirts came off, revealing their glaring white bodies, hard new muscle packed over childlike frames. They stopped dancing. Their trousers were being unbelted, pulled down. In tandem they lifted one
leg, then the other, so that their feet could be pulled free, like two
brothers being undressed for bath time.

Their underpants—from the same shop, or pack—were lowered. Tom looked away. The line of faces, interspersed with those
of the women from the bar and the obvious terror of the odd player,
was transfixed, straining with a force of unbending will for this to
happen, for it not to stop.

Penises. One erect, the other not. Steven, grinning manically,
possibly crying, pumped his arms above his head in response to the
shouts of insult and encouragement from the audience. Tom
pressed a hand against his mouth as his stomach retched. He made
himself look away again. Crumpled heaps of clothing lay scattered
across the stage. A chant of "Bob-ee, Bob-ee, Bob-ee" was rising,
the rhythmic thump of the word hammering inside Tom's chest.

The younger girl got to her feet, embarrassed, and danced a little way apart from Steven. The other girl, though, was kneeling on
the stage, hunched towards Bobby. The tag of her underwear was

untucked, irritating a small red patch at the base of her spine, which was rolling fleshily up and down now in time with the slow sad rhythm of the back of her head. The only other movement of the two bodies, barely visible past her ear, was the faint tremor of Bobby's left leg.

Nobody appeared to notice Tom get up from his seat. The doormen said nothing when he reached the top of the stairs and moved past them onto the street. He kept on walking, then ran, not stopping for some time, his nose streaming, until he had composed himself enough to squat against the wall on a pavement a short distance from the bustling crowd outside a fried chicken shop. He knew he could not return to the hotel. He wiped his face, realizing that he had left his jacket behind, and stood up to hail a passing taxi.

Numbness filled him the moment he sat down and closed the door. Only later, during the long disorienting journey, distantly aware of the sound of the radio and the suspicious glances of the driver, the steadily climbing unset fare—£200, £300, £400—did it start to turn to shame.

The driver parked to accompany him to the cashpoint. He stood close by, watching Tom withdraw a stack of notes with his bank card, then another with his credit card.

"You sure you know where you are?" the driver asked when the money was in his hand, but Tom ignored him and walked away. He proceeded down empty streets, past darkened shopfronts. Through the wasting light of an upstairs window he could make out the lagging end of a party. His head smarted. The desire to cause himself damage kept seething up from somewhere inside him. He imagined stepping into the path of a car, his ankle crushed by a tire, his pelvis shattering. But there were no cars, no people, nothing.

He let himself into the Daveys' house very quietly. Inside, it was completely still. He sat down at the kitchen table, listening for any sound upstairs. After a few minutes he stood abruptly and began searching through the post on the kitchen table, then, his chest heaving with terrible excitement, a drawer under the kitchen counter.

He left the house as silently as he had entered it. Holding a piece of notepaper in one hand, he took out his keys and his phone and got into his car.

The cul-de-sac when he turned into it was lit but unstirring. He moved automatically, without pausing: out of his car, down the pavement, through the gate into a dark garden. He located a doorbell and rang it. There was a long wait, then the door opened.

"Tom? You OK?"

Tom remained on the doorstep. He was bewildered, unable to comprehend what was happening.

"Is it Mum and Dad?" Liam was wearing a blue dressing gown. His concerned face stared at Tom. "Jesus, you're hammered, aren't you?"

For an instant Tom thought he was about to take his hand, but instead Liam reached behind him for the door handle and motioned him inside. Tom followed him into a living area. "All right, what's going on?" He looked round at the staircase then back at Tom. "You know what time it is?"

Tom lurched towards him. "Come on then, queer. Come on." He latched a hand onto the back of Liam's neck and tried to pull his face forward but Liam held him off easily. Tom's strength gave. He stumbled and was caught. Lifted up.

"Jesus, Tom, don't be a twat," Liam said in a low voice, shooting another look at the staircase. "You're embarrassing yourself."

Liam's chin was on the top of Tom's head. His Adam's apple bore down on Tom's temple. "You're pissed, mate." He clinched Tom's arms tightly to his trunk, restricting any movement. The smell of him was overpowering. "You're pissed, mate. You're just pissed, that's all."

When Tom woke, aching and shivering on a sofa with a blanket over his legs, the curtainless room was filled with dim light. There was a tang of vomit. He turned over slowly and examined the cushion behind his head, his clothes, the small, peeling plastic sofa, but he could find nothing. He tried to sit up but was prevented by a wave of nausea.

It took some time, his eyes not leaving the staircase, before he was able to get up from the sofa. He moved himself to the kitchenette at one side of the room and got himself a glass of water. Three dirty plates were stacked in the sink. The counter was cluttered with pans and a sieve and several full shopping bags. In a large clip frame above the fridge there was a wide-angle photograph of a football pitch, taken from low down, which Tom recognized from the advertising hoardings as Town's. He drank the water steadily, listening for any sound above his head. He checked his pocket for his car keys and stepped towards the door, then, after a short panicked fumbling with the lock, he let himself out.

10

Gale, on the expiration of his deal, was released. A couple of first-year pros who had never played were transported to the Scottish third division on three-month loans. Charlie Lewis, moments before a short assault on the filing cabinet in Clarke's office, had his contract terminated "by mutual consent" and three days later signed part-time terms with Hendon.

There was no buildup to these departures. The four players were present for training one day and gone the next. The first that anybody knew about Gale leaving was in the lounge during breakfast when Richards spotted it on the rolling news at the bottom of the Sky Sports screen that played continuously in a corner. A nervy atmosphere crept into breakfast times over the coming days. The squad watched for every entrance into the room and followed the tiny gliding text above their heads, forever adding and looping, adding and looping.

They waited for new signings. The chairman declared in the paper that there would be three or four additions to the squad before the close of the January window. The existing players remained on guard for their arrival, increasingly anxious with each day that nothing happened. The mood lifted only occasionally. A surprise draw against Swindon. Reminiscences about the party, often in the form of already well-worn impersonations of Steven and Bobby dancing.

The two boys smiled at these moments but said nothing. An awkwardness had inserted itself between them. They could no longer always be found together, even in the house, which, as the Daveys pointed out to them with good-humored concern, had become blessedly quiet. Bobby was often among a small crew of young players, playing cards, in the gym, and had become more noticeable around the club, in part because of the new game that accompanied every training session and shower and coach journey—for which somebody would call out, "Sex face," and everyone else would assume the same contorted expression—and in part because Steven kept more and more to himself. He moved from his usual position in the clubhouse dressing room. Quietly, without reaction, he removed the Viagra and the dead earthworms from his pigeonhole. When he got to Tom's car one afternoon and saw the opened magazine pinned under the windscreen wipers he looked on impassively, barely registering the image of the wet, veined penis poised beside a man's face, before Tom pulled the magazine out and flung it to the ground.

A full week went by with no more departures and still no new signings. The players were restless, distrustful. They eyed Clarke closely. During a practice match Yates pretended not to hear him call for a substitution, and when he shouted the instruction again Yates walked off the pitch so slowly that everyone turned to look at Clarke, who stared into the trees and appeared not even to notice.

That evening every player received a text message from the club secretary informing them that the board had, after careful deliberation, decided to relieve the manager of his duties.

The number two took training as normal the following morning. They watched him, and each other, with cagey excitement, not daring to utter a word about Clarke's departure, as if for fear that he might at any moment appear from behind a tree or stride out of the French windows onto the playing fields. It only took a day or two, though, for him to be forgotten. In the cold, still air of their final preparations for Crewe away, the sound of seagulls overhead, the incessant murmur and little rainbows from the tractor sweeping dew off the pitches, whenever they paused for a break there were bursts of speculation about who the new man might be. It was as if the old manager had never existed. The memory of him lurked only in small hidden places, for those who knew where to look: the chipped crater in the wall of the dressing room, the unmoved magnetic counters on the tactics whiteboard. The folded pile, when they arrived one morning, of "PC" monogrammed tracksuits and waterproofs that the kit man had placed on a chair in the reception of the clubhouse.

The number two was placed in temporary charge. He contrived, either through design or loyalty to the departed manager's methods, to alter nothing. He picked the same eleven for his first match as had played the last and achieved the same result: a 1–1 draw. They started calling him "gaffer." It began as a joke but very quickly, with nothing else to call him, it felt perfectly normal. Day-to-day life carried on, but within the squad there was a deepening sense of uncertainty—over who the new man would be, whether he would take charge before the transfer window closed, how big a budget he would be given if he was. All of these questions were put to the temporary manager.

"Just keep on as you are," he answered them. "That's all you can do—keep doing what you're doing." Words that were reassuringly conventional enough to feel correct, in spite of the fact that they were still bottom of the table. "Messing everything about right before the new manager gets here isn't going to do him or anyone else any favors."

Boyn seized on these words: "So you know who it is, then?"

He shook his head. His eyes closed weakly. "No. Believe me, I'm the last one they'll tell."

He was wrong, as it turned out. Ten minutes before the kickoff against Bristol Rovers the chairman slipped unannounced into the dressing room. He stood beside the door while the room fell silent, the squad becoming aware of the fat suited man attempting to appear at ease among the half-dressed and naked bodies. His lips, purple from a pre-match meal at which he had just shared his news with a banqueting suite of sponsors and box holders, squeezed against each other with pleasure. "Boys," he said, "I've come down here for two reasons. First is I wanted to wish you good luck tonight." He looked about the room, at the battered hi-fi that Richards had just turned down, the signs on the walls: DESIRE . . . FOCUS . . . BE ALL THAT YOU CAN BE. "The second is I wanted you to hear from me that we've made an appointment I think everybody is going to get behind." He smiled again. "Aidy Wilkinson is in the stands tonight. From tomorrow morning, he will be your new manager."

He stayed where he was, clearly expecting some reaction to his words, but when none came he gave a nod to the temporary manager and left.

Throughout the first half the team scanned the main stand for the face that would be looking down, judging them. Most, however, had never heard of him so could not locate it.

"Row in front of the chairman," Fleming informed them at the interval. "Ginger. Young. Looks like a player. I played with him a few years ago. He's different, you'll see. He'll want his own around him, that's for sure."

Wilkinson introduced himself the following day at breakfast. He walked into the lounge and stood in front of the tea urn while the temporary number two dithered, unsure whether to stand alongside him or with the squad, and Lesley peered in from the doorway to the canteen, clearly impressed by his confidence, his youthfulness.

"I'll keep it simple. Steve is going to take training today as normal, and I'm just going to observe. No pressure. Just get on as usual. Right?"

They marked the bright mouth and alert watery gaze, the pullover and tie, the shiny black shoes, the thick plastic folder tucked under his armpit. Those who had googled him the night before tried to match him with the former defender who had played most of his career non-league, who had desired a "simple, on the ground style" from the team he had guided into the Conference Premier last season, and whose son, Ryan, had Down syndrome.

Out on the field he was always on the move—up and down the touchline as they went through their drills, walking over to the scholars' pitch, inspecting a sprinkler—and talking, to everybody: the first-team coaches, the youth team coach, the groundsman, the physio. At the end of the session he spoke briefly to the temporary number two then departed for the clubhouse, his shoes caked with mud, specks of it up the back of his trousers.

He went to the stadium in the afternoon to conduct a series of one-to-ones with the players. Tom was among the first to see him. When he arrived at his office the new manager was ready at the door to greet him with a handshake. "Sit down, Tom."

There was a sheet of paper on the desk that had a small photograph of Tom paper-clipped to the top. It was an old one: the website shot for his former club, as a second-year scholar. Wilkinson assessed it for a moment before looking up, perhaps trying to recognize something of the goofy, smiling boy in the photograph in the pallid watchful figure on the other side of his desk.

"How would you describe your first—what is it, eight months or so—at the club, Tom?"

"I don't know. I've not played much."

"Did you expect to? Is that what they told you when you signed? You must have. Look at your pedigree: FA Youth Cup final, England Under-16s, -17s, -18s. What happened?"

"Don't know. Big-man hoofball."

Wilkinson laughed. "Well, I'll tell you one thing: big-man hoofball's out the window. We start afresh. Everybody will get the chance to prove themselves. And from now on we're going to be using the grass."

Tom turned his eyes away. Under the desk a pair of muddy shoes was set to one side on top of a newspaper. On the other side, a cardboard box loaded with new laminated motivational posters.

"OK, then. Done."

They both stood up. At the door he shook Tom's hand again. "By the way, I don't want you calling me gaffer. I don't believe in all that bollocks."

By Saturday's trip to fellow strugglers Northampton the players had passed through an initial period of waiting to hear what any-body else would call him to calling him boss, and finally, at the manager's own suggestion, Wilko. He sat at the front of the coach, working on an iPad. The number two sat across the aisle from him, staring out of the window at the countryside. Behind them card games were being played quietly. Some slept. Others listened to music. The physio moved down the aisle, gently rousing players to offer pink pills or blue pills in little plastic sacks, like party bags.

Tom leaned his head against the window. In the glass he could see the reflection of Richards's headphones. He listened to the soft insistent pulse of music. Even in his increasing separation from the others there was never a moment that he could be alone, not on display; but at the same time there was always the disquieting in-evitability of the return to his bedroom, of being unable to sleep, vulnerable to the dark. The image of himself at Liam's door, ring-ing the bell, being let in. Drunk as he had been, he could remember exactly the words that he had spoken to Liam. Every time he went over them they shocked him. And he could remember too his un-natural excitement at the Adam's apple against his temple, which he had to force himself, with other thoughts—racing to the byline to whip a cross in; his dad filing match reports at his plastic desk—to repel.

The team went in at halftime leading 1–0, and the new manag-er's name rang out from the small freezing band of away support-ers. The goal had come from a practiced delivery by Easter. He had started the game and was playing well—with energy and aggres-sion, winning the ball and moving it on quickly.

"Our possession is good," Wilko said in the dressing room, "but I want us to move it twenty yards up the pitch, where we can hurt them more. We can win this. Come tomorrow morning these will be looking over their shoulders at us." His lips were plump, brown-ish, like minuscule kidneys. "And Chris Easter, that is exactly what I was asking for. More of the same from you, please."

He instructed the substitutes to go out onto the pitch and warm up. Tom followed the other four out of the room and into the tun-nel. From one habitual point to the next: pitch, dugout, dressing room, coach. It drugged them, this routine, was meant to drug them, Tom was sure, so that they did not have to think—the next instruction always ready to be called out, texted, written on a whiteboard. But as the noise of the crowd echoed down the tunnel he could feel his heart rate quickening and his legs turning to heavy jelly. Every face, every pair of eyes, he became more convinced with each step, would be able to see it in him. They would know what he had done.

Into the light, the sudden exposure to the crowd, he focused on one specific area of the pitch and made his body move towards it. The goalkeeping coach was untying a bag of balls. They spilled like guts over the grass. Bobby fetched one of the balls and pointed for Tom and Yates to form a wide triangle with him. Bobby tapped the ball four or five times into the air without letting it drop then lobbed it to Yates, who controlled it on his chest, let it fall to his right foot and kept it up for a long time, alternating his feet, before kicking it to Tom. The ball skewed off Tom's foot onto the grass. The next time it came round to him he managed to control it and kept it up twice, but his cushioned volley to Bobby landed short. Yates made a noise of displeasure, audible to Tom despite the crowd. The game, one that he had played almost every day since he was a small boy in the garden, was now a trial. He could sense the eyes of the crowd on him. A couple of times Yates and Bobby reversed direction, passing between themselves, cutting him out.

"Going to do some shuttles," Tom said and jogged towards the halfway line.

A raffle was being drawn. A Northampton player, injured and in a suit, drew numbered balls from a cloth bag and handed them to an enormous stoop-shouldered man with a microphone to read out over the Tannoy. Tom sprinted back and forth between two points. Even this, though, made him feel that everybody was looking at him. He glanced at the scoreboard. There were still six minutes until the second half. He lay down and stretched his back, his glutes, keeping his eyes away from the crowd and the other players. A schoolboy penalty competition was taking place in the other half. A dozen eight- and nine-year-olds in immaculate baggy shorts were shivering inside the center circle, waiting their turn to take the very long run towards the penalty spot. Each one set off determinedly, arms and twiggy legs flailing, looking as though they might at any moment fall over. Most of their shots went wide of the goal. A couple went in, slowly looping beyond the goalkeeper's scurrying efforts. One shot failed to reach. Then a tall black boy who had his socks pulled above his knees ran in a wide arc towards the ball and struck it with surprising power into the very top corner of the goal. Tom's final thought, before the blissful yell of the goalkeeping coach calling them in, was one of wonder at the boy's pureness of concentration, and that he could not imagine striking the ball like that himself, so cleanly, so decisively.

Town continued to press. Richards scored a second goal. Tom, enclosed by the dugout, tried to follow the game, but his mind kept returning, inexorably, to the night at Liam's house. Near the center of the pitch half a dozen players were gathering around somebody on the ground. More distant players from both teams began to run towards the scene. One of the Northampton defenders looked in and at once turned away, his hands going to his face. Jones shouted for the physio to get there quicker; he broke into a squat pumping sprint, and as the players parted to give him access Tom saw Easter on the ground. Two stretcher bearers ran onto the pitch. On the other side of the pack, Boyn was walking away. Jones came across to put an arm around his shoulders, talking closely into his ear.

After a long wait the stretcher was raised and began to move slowly towards one corner of the pitch. The procession moved past the dugout. The physio looked up at Wilko and gave a short distinct shake of his head. Then he turned his attention back to Easter, who was gaping up at the sky with one arm dangling down from the stretcher like a sunbather, seeming not to take in the constant soft stream of words from the physio walking alongside him, stroking his hair.

11

A team meeting was held on Monday. The room was hushed, every-body staring up at the television until the manager came in. He stood by the breakfast table and poured himself an orange juice. He had been to the hospital on Saturday night, he told them. He hadn't stopped long because Easter's wife was there but he had passed on the best wishes of the squad. The tibia and fibula of his left leg were fractured. He was sedated, although understandably emotional, and Wilko had reassured him that he would receive the full support of the club for however long his recovery took.

"How long do they think that's going to be?"

Wilko shook his head. "Too early to say."

There was silence as the same dark thoughts passed unspoken like a current through the room.

"Do we send him something?"

"Like what?"

There was another pause as they considered this.

"Or send his wife something?"

"One-way ticket somewhere?"

Nobody laughed. They decided, after a short discussion, to send her some flowers. As for Easter, Boyn had the idea, generally supported, that he would probably most appreciate messages of encouragement.

"Who's got his number?"

Most did not, so Boyn read it out for them to put into their phones. For a few minutes they consulted over what to write. Lesley came through to see if the fruit juices needed refilling. She observed the pensive faces with puzzlement and looked for some explanation to Wilko, who ignored her.

Once the texts had been sent, the players relaxed somewhat. There was a little conversation as they piled out of the room. If any of them was still dwelling on the thought of Easter in his hospital bed, his phone now convulsing to the arrival of twenty-two identical messages, they did not let it show. They had done the right thing. They moved eagerly into the dressing room. There was a buzz of anticipation about the first full week of the new era. The club secretary could deal with the flowers.

It was soon evident, though, that this morning was going to be unlike the few others that had followed a victory. A cloud of fear weighed over the session. They held back, reluctant to throw themselves into it—attentive to the intricate mechanics of their bodies as they ran, jumped, collided. The straining hollows of each other's knees. Flexing, jackknifing ankles. These bodies were managed and monitored more than anything else at the club, the physio always at hand for a massage or a tablet or an injection, their fitness levels charted, urine samples given up. All they ever needed to concentrate on was applying themselves on the pitch. But the careful order of things had been unbalanced, despite the encouragement of the new manager and his sprightly drills. Now they could not stop thinking.

Another victory followed nonetheless. The largest crowd of the season turned up for an unexpected 1–0 win over Charlton in the first leg of the Paint area final. Tom played for the last four minutes. When he returned home, Mr. Davey and Steven were watching the highlights on the television.

"I knew it was a penalty," Mr. Davey said as Tom sat down next to him. "They just showed it. Blatant handball, clear as day."

The remaining highlights were all of Charlton's late pressure. At the final whistle the Town players and coaching staff ran towards the home fans behind the goal. Tom could see himself hesitating by the center circle, being passed by the departing Charlton players.

"Next stop Wembley, maybe," Mr. Davey said, getting up to go to bed. "You never know." When he had gone upstairs Tom went through to the kitchen to look for the date of the second leg on the calendar and his eye was immediately drawn by the coming Sunday: LIAM FOR BREAKFAST.

From the moment he entered the house to a flurry of plates and kettle and toaster, Tom was determined not to look at him. He made sure to say hello at the same time as Bobby and Steven, but with his back turned, getting cutlery. He kept his eyes down or on the others throughout the whole ordeal. He heard Liam give his opinion on the Charlton game, Wembley, the new manager, as if everything was normal. He listened to the enthralled responses of the blind adoring Daveys. Liam did not once attempt to get his attention, to speak to him.

Only towards the end, when they had finished eating, did Tom momentarily falter, peeking over as he collected the plates. Liam was looking at him. Not smiling or communicating, but watching him directly with an unreadable expression until Tom turned away to the sink, needing, in the action of twisting on the tap then scouring at the egg-congealed plates, to work off the muscular agitation of his hands and forearms.

A low bright sun flared between the office buildings and industrial units on the far side of town. His dad had called just before they left. He had a plan to visit him with his mum and sister. Rachel had agreed to the weekend of the Crawley home match in a couple of weeks. "It doesn't matter if you don't play," his dad had said. "It's you we're coming to see." Tom pulled down the windscreen visor, anxious to put the prospect of the visit out of his mind. In the rear-view mirror he watched the Scottish pair, busy at their phones, and it occurred to him, from their fixed expressions, that they might be watching one of the videos of themselves. There were three, of varying duration and focus, but all with the same soundtrack of pounding music and manic laughter, which was instantly recognizable whenever it erupted from some part of the canteen or the coach. Both boys had their headphones on, though, so Tom could not tell.

He turned onto the lane. The pitches were flooded with sunshine. It burned on the windscreens in the staff car park. He slowed into his bay, and they got out without talking, at once buffeted by a strong wind that had picked up in the short time since they had left the house. Liam was by the near wall of the clubhouse. He was talking to a couple of scholars, telling them something. When he had finished they both laughed then moved off, and for a moment Liam watched them as they jogged away.

All morning Liam was occupied with aerating the pitches, drawing slow columns up and down, his big head barely moving, contemplating the grass, and Tom began to bridle at his total ease—chasing a pigeon, in the canteen tucking into a fish pie, casually chatting to Lesley when she came over to speak to him. As if it was all so simple. Typing on his phone, tucking into the large helping of dessert that Lesley gave him with a wink, drinking the last of his tea to go back out onto the field and get on with his jobs, whistling, his sure routine continuing freely under the cold winter sun.

The roller shutters had been left up to accommodate the tractor's roll bar and a bitter wind poured into the ground-staff shed. There was nowhere to sit, even if he had wanted to, so Tom stood against the far wall, facing the entrance. The sound of the tractor faded, or got suddenly louder, carried by the wind. A gust bristled through a rack of birch brooms. Above his head, the club scarf trembled between its two nails along the ceiling joist.

On the wall near where he stood, between two posters of former players, was a photograph. He stepped over to look at it: a youth team, the page neatly torn out of a black-and-white match-day program. The picture was grainy, but he recognized Liam immediately, at the center of the squad, the taller of two goalkeepers. His face, his haircut, exactly as now. He looked older than the other boys, most of whom—cheeky, skinny, acned—seemed like young children. It took Tom a moment to spot Boyn, then Easter. Easter's head was shaved and he was smiling. The front row had been instructed to place their hands on their knees and Easter's extended arms looked frail and boyish next to the coach's. There was a noise behind him and Tom swiveled round. An empty canister scraped at the floor, shunted by a new spurt of wind. He moved back to his position against the wall, working to recover his composure.

Even though Tom was standing in clear sight of the entrance, it took Liam a few seconds to notice him. He locked his eyes on Tom for a moment, then concentrated on parking the tractor. The sound of the engine thundered inside the shed. When he turned it off, there was ringing silence.

"Tom." He climbed from his seat. "Cup of tea?" He gestured towards a small filthy kettle on a shelf beside a sink. Two tin mugs hung from nails in the wall.

"No, thanks."

"Sure? I'm having one." He walked to the sink, passing Tom closely.

Liam bent towards a trestle table on which were collected washers and bolts in different-sized jars and a sprinkler head. Under the table he opened the door of a rusted mini fridge. He was like a tramp in his domain, Tom thought, surrounded by his hoarded junk. He took out a pint of milk and Tom noticed a couple of cans of lager inside the door before it closed.

Neither of them spoke while the kettle boiled. Liam perched on a pair of upturned wooden pallets wrapped in sacking and bound with twine. He did not point for Tom to sit anywhere so Tom stayed where he was. The tractor engine ticked and gurgled in the middle of the shed floor, spent.

Liam was winding a piece of string around his finger. "Those two." He poured the milk into his tea. "Bobby and Steven. What's the story there? They're like two puppies every time I've met them before, but there wasn't much banter between them on Sunday. It because of Bobby being in the team now Easter's out?"

"I don't know. I think they're fine." He would not tell Liam anything about the party. To expose the pair further. To let him imagine them up there on the stage, Tom watching.

"I saw the picture there," Tom said. "You in the youth team."

"Glory days," Liam said, moving over to a shelf, from which he picked up a wooden box. Inside it, heaps of assorted tines glinted in the dark of the divided sections. The cords of his neck showed as he lifted the box and carried it over to the aerator mounted on the front of the tractor. "Never stood a chance, did I? Keepers never get taken on." He released the tines from the aerator and knelt to the floor to collect them. There was a heavy metallic clatter with each handful that he dropped into the box. One of the tines had rolled underneath a stand of rubber rakes. Tom moved to pick it up. It had the weight and shape of a bullet. He walked over to Liam, still on the floor, and stood over him. A fine trail of gingery hairs ran along the back of his neck. Tom handed him the tine.

"Cheers."

The wind had lessened and the only sound in the shed, in the silence between the tines dropping, was the ticking of the tractor engine. Something livid surged through Tom, watching Liam carry on with his machines and his boxes in this private shithole, forcing him to stand there like the queer. He wanted to hurt him, to push him to the ground and press his head against the concrete. Liam stopped boxing the tines as Tom's fingers moved slowly around his neck, finding the soft hollow of his throat, the delicate spokes beneath the skin. Liam stood up. Tom could see the movement of his breath through the wide pink nostrils. A spasm of disgust leaped inside his stomach at the touch of Liam's fingers on him, moving aside his shirt and resting on his stomach. Liam was pushing against him now. Tom closed his eyes against the heat and the smell of his face, the deviant excitement of their stubble coming together. Their lips touched, then came apart, and as they touched again Tom was certain that he was about to be sick into the man's warm stinking mouth.

They were both in some pain at first. Tom stopped, not knowing what to do. This had happened the other time, two years ago in
the bedroom of an empty house, neither boy sure how to go on, so
they had not and had tried other things instead, frustrated. But
now, after a moment of calmly guiding Tom's fingers, Liam moved
once more up against the tractor's side, drawing Tom's hands behind him, one at a time onto his waist—and Tom let himself suc-
cumb to whatever ugly thing was within him, released, until it was
over, from caring.

He sat in his car for some time with his hands closed around the
steering wheel. He could still see the grass cuttings in Liam's hair,
working themselves loose. The thick stench of diesel when his nose
had pressed into the back of Liam's head had been so strong that
he could smell it even now, filling his car, coating and seeping into
every part of him.

12

"I only sign players who fit the right mold," Wilko told the assembled media in the directors' lounge. The BBC correspondent put down his doughnut and asked what the fans could expect from the two new signings, recruited hours before the close of the transfer window.

"Honesty, integrity, excitement. Jay Beverley is an attacking left back I've worked with before so I know exactly what I'm getting from him. As for Jacob Gundi—goals. He's a big fast boy and he'll always get you goals at this level. It's a real testament to what the chairman wants to achieve here that we've got him, believe me."

"Michael Yates—a word about him?"

"Michael Yates has gone out on loan to Luton for the remainder of the season with a view to a permanent move."

An hour later, Jacob Gundi, a once-prolific forward who had been third on Wilko's target list due to a recurring back problem, sat in the main stand posing for photographs at the side of his new manager. Peter Pascoe loitered by the edge of the pitch in a shirt so threadbare that his cold pink skin shone through it, waiting to secure a quote for the next day's paper. When the photo shoot was over and he did manage to catch Gundi in a stairwell it was apparent that nobody had informed Gundi who he was. It was later adjudged by the paper's sports editor that the quote—"It's good to be here. Peterborough can get stuffed"—was not quite suitable for use.

On the coach to Port Vale, Wilko assigned Beverley to Tom as his new roommate. Beverley ate the evening meal on a different table to the one at which Tom sat, silent and detached, so the two spoke for the first time only when they were in their room together. They quickly agreed on which bed they would each take. Tom said that Beverley could go into the bathroom first. When he came out sometime later in his boxer shorts there was a pack of wet wipes on the mirror shelf.

When Tom had brushed his teeth, Beverley was sitting up in bed.

"How are you finding him, the manager?" Beverley asked.

"All right. Anything's an improvement on Clarke."

Beverley smiled. "Yeah, I've heard some stories about him."

Tom moved over to his bag and turned away from Beverley to pull on tracksuit bottoms before getting into bed.

"Tell you what, though," Beverley continued. "Wilko's got some fire in him too when he wants. Just wait. You don't see it much but when you do . . ." He pursed his lips, shutting his eyes and blowing out. Tom noticed a collection of items lined up on the floor at the base of his bed: a banana, headphones, protein bar, white socks tucked into a pair of slippers.

"Night, mate." Beverley's bedside light went off.

"Night."

Town were leading when Tom came on. He stationed himself near the touchline in a daze of uncertainty, letting the pulse and heave of the match pass him by until a headed clearance from Bobby spun in his direction, dropping at his feet. There was space in front of him, so he ran into it. Nobody closed him down so he continued, the suddenness of the action preventing him from thinking about it. He cut inside—there was noise from the Town fans at the other end of the ground—and was into the penalty area. He swung his left leg to shoot and, as he did so, felt the bite of studs on his standing foot.

Gundi took the penalty and scored. He ran across the pitch to the away fans and planted himself before them with his arms out-

stretched while his teammates jumped onto his back and supporters streamed down the terracing towards him.

Some of the others came up to Tom in the dressing room and
the showers to praise him. He smiled and turned to the wall. When
an unseen hand patted him on the bottom he let out a small terrified sound, which was lost in the happy steaming commotion.

Tom walked with Beverley and the last remaining group out of the
clubhouse. When they were as far as the car park, Tom stopped.

"Damn. Forgot my skins."

He moved quickly through the empty corridors, not looking up
as he passed Lesley mopping the floor inside the doorway to the
canteen. He let himself out of the back of the building. The pitches
were deserted. He continued at the same pace, checking often over
his shoulder, the sour fragrance of cut grass all around threatening
to overwhelm him.

Liam looked up from where he was kneeling in the shed, pulling
tangled stalks from the wheels of the rotary mower. He returned to
his task, and Tom felt his entire body shudder. He stepped forward,
pushing out of the way some piece of equipment that blocked his
path. Liam's eyes shot up, and for a split second Tom savored the
alarm in them.

He did not let Liam lead this time. He was unhesitant, aggressive, forcing Liam's cheek flat against the top of the trestle table
and watching with hot revulsion his pale lips stretching, catching
against his teeth. Liam's shirt had ridden up and Tom fastened
his grip on the flesh of his side until the skin darkened. He moved
his hands to Liam's neck and felt the breath constricting inside his
throat, the need rising again to make him hurt, to make himself
hurt, to know without any doubt that he was abnormal, worthless.

Liam straightened his clothes without looking at Tom. He reor-
dered the top of the trestle table. There was the gentle rattling of
the shutters on the other side of the shed. Tom, not wanting to hear
Liam's voice, to talk to him, left.

As soon as he was outside, self-loathing enveloped him. There was no relief in the walk to the car or the drive back, entering the house and locking himself in the bathroom to scrub at himself in the Daveys' shower, scouring his penis and the insides of his thighs until the skin gave and bled.

He found antiseptic cream and bandaging in the medicine cabinet. He attended to his legs, then spent a long time kneeling on the carpet removing any traces from the shower tray.

A replacement coaching team was present at the training ground one morning: a new number two, fitness coach, and a goalkeeping coach who had retired as a player only a couple of seasons ago after a long and successful career in the Premier League but whose face and body were already so swollen that none of the squad recognized him until he was introduced.

The new number two spoke to them before the session. He was considerably older than Wilko. Standing together—both tall, arms folded, thick uniform haircuts—they looked like father and son.

"I've got no time for reputations, good or bad," he said, pacing the breakfast table with the bunched, sprung knees of a long-retired player. His face was weathered, the back of his neck rucked with folds of skin. "I'll be taking training from today, and I'll be assisting the manager by having a good look at what we've got in the building." He looked about the squad. The pouched apparatus of his neck drooped vulnerably beneath his chin, like a testicle. "There's talent here. We shouldn't be where we are in the table, I'll tell you that right now."

The number two supervised the session with little pause or interruption. He took them through the existing drills and set plays for the weekend. His instructions were short, clear, authoritative. When finally there was a break he walked over to Wilko on the touchline and the two men exchanged a few words, looking over towards one group of players. The duo and the goalkeeping coach—on the next pitch now firing low shots at Foley and Hoyle—had worked together with great success the previous season. There had been some difficulty negotiating their release because their pre-

vious club had wanted a considerable sum in compensation, but
Town had wanted to pay none so had ensured that the matter was
handed to the FA. Now that they were here the players were keen to
find out from Beverley what life would be like under the new re-
gime.

"Organized," Beverley told them, brushing his teeth at one of
the dressing-room sinks. "That thing about not having time for
reputations is right enough. Drury will take you as he finds you.
Which means if he decides you're a prick, then you're a prick."

Tom waited for everybody to leave. He was supposed to go and
see the physio, he said to Beverley and Richards.

He crossed the field, spotting Liam at the entrance to the
ground-staff shed, disappearing inside. When Tom got there Liam
was on the other side of a workbench, looking inside a toolbox.
Tom went towards him. He moved around the bench, carried now
by a momentum that seemed to be coming from outside him. He
put his hand on Liam's shoulder and drew it towards him, but Liam
resisted. He took hold of the upper part of his arm instead and
Liam put his hand over Tom's to remove it. Their hands fleetingly
locked and pulled against each other, and dark excitement moved
inside Tom at the awareness of Liam's strength.

"I don't want this, Tom."

In the trough of a wheel-transfer marker machine a thick rubbery skin had formed over the pool of paint. There was a writhing
wood louse in the middle of it, stuck.

"You can't just come in here like this," Liam said. "And what if
somebody saw you?"

But Tom was backing away, pushing between pieces of machinery, mumbling that he had to go. All the force of earlier had left
him.

"Fucking kidding? You're running off?"

There was a whiny note to his voice, Tom judged, his heart
jumping at the fierce metallic screech of a mower on the concrete
when he pushed past it, that he could not put from his mind even
after he had retreated across the field and got away in his car.

Two days later, when Tom returned home and went straight through to the kitchen to get himself a drink, he was there, sitting at the table.

"Thought this would be the least weird place in the house for you to find me," Liam said.

Tom walked around the table to the sink and made himself a glass of squash. He stayed there, drinking. "Why are you here?"

"To talk to you. I knew they'd all be out." His eyes were away from Tom, on the corkboard on the back of the door. He was shaking his head slightly, half smiling to himself. "I get it, you know," he said. The washing machine, which had been quietly sucking and rumbling, jolted to life. The unexpectedness of it made them both start. For a while the spinning was too loud to speak over. When eventually it quietened Tom could feel the throb of it still, as if the reverberations had passed into his body.

"Why are you here?" he asked again.

Liam looked down at the table. Directly in front of him was one of Mrs. Davey's farmyard table mats, a picture of a sheep with the word SHEEP underneath it. Tom registered the mat next to him—COCK—and wanted suddenly and bitterly to laugh.

"You want to keep it separate," Liam said. Tom wished there was some way to stop him talking. "This is all sort of new to me, you know," he continued. Then, after a pause, "We could meet somewhere else."

Now Tom did laugh—quickly, sarcastically. "Where?"

"I don't know. Just for a drink."

"That's worse."

"We don't have to hold hands, mate. We can just talk about football."

Tom looked at him, horrified. The washing machine exploded into action again and Liam jumped noticeably. Again they waited, both watching the drum going round. Mrs. Davey would be back from the hospice soon, Tom kept thinking.

Liam stood up. "I'll give you my mobile number." He tore a strip from the newspaper on the table and instinctively Tom was afraid that Mrs. Davey would understand why it was missing. Liam placed the strip on the table and wrote his number on it. "You can text me or something."

When he had gone Tom sat down at the table. He stared at the line of numbers. After doing nothing for some time he folded the paper over and over, until it was very small. He got up and put it in the pedal bin. He stood there, hovering by the bin, his foot still on the pedal, before reaching inside to retrieve the bit of paper from where it had stuck to the greasy wrapping of a slab of butter. He went to the shelves, picked up a lighter from one of them and set fire to it over the sink.

The gray flakes swirled in the water from the tap, disappearing down the plughole until nothing remained but the creamy smoking smell of burned butter.

He met his family at their hotel before the Crawley match. They had set off from home very early to avoid the traffic, and he could tell immediately on entering the foyer just what his sister thought about the dawn start. She came over to greet him. As he hugged her, turning their bodies so that he was not facing his parents, a wave of desperation spread through him.

"Decent place, this," his dad said, shaking his hand. "Comfortable enough."

"Yes," said his sister with a small motion of her head at reception. "They've got a dispensing machine that does toasted sandwiches."

His dad gave her a lighthearted flick on the arm. Tom looked about him. The hotel was a grade down from anywhere that he had stayed in for some time. There was no restaurant or bar, plants, windows. He followed them through a number of corridors to their rooms to fetch coats and bags. His sister split off for her own room and he walked with his parents to theirs, where he sat on the bed while his dad took his wallet from the safe and his mum occupied herself in the bathroom rinsing cups. There was something uncomfortably intimate about sitting in somebody else's hotel room, even his parents', whose bedside arrangements—the neat stack of pillboxes on one side, the heavy paperback and reading glasses and immortal travel alarm clock on the other—had not changed from the earliest memories of his childhood, and he was glad when his dad said that it was time to get going.

Tom drove them all to the ground, conscious the whole journey of his dad inspecting his driving and, when they arrived, fearful of somehow bumping into Liam, even though he had already worked out that there was no way they could. They stopped for an age to admire the cars in the players' car park. Price, getting out of his four-by-four, smiled over. Mr. Davey had offered an executive box but his dad had declined—"No special treatment"—even though Tom knew that he would have relished it. Tom then went to the main reception to collect their tickets and was thankful to take his leave for the dressing room.

The game ended in a draw. Tom did not play. He met his family afterwards in the players' lounge, where he found them chatting with Mr. Davey.

"First out?" Mr. Davey stepped forward. Tom saw his dad watching as Mr. Davey put a hand on his shoulder.

"Not like he needed a shower," his sister said.

"Drink, everybody?" his dad asked, intent on being the first at the bar.

They all sat together and discussed the match. The result had put Town within two points of getting out of the relegation zone. His dad was impressed with the new manager's playing style, and with Gundi, who had scored again. The other players started to come in. Tom noted his sister watching them. Automatically he was about to tease her, but he stopped himself, wary of what she might say in reply. The players dispersed around the room. Gradually they began to take notice of Rachel. Boyn caught Tom's eye and winked at him, and Tom flushed with ludicrous delight.

He only drank one pint, then drove his family to the restaurant that his dad had booked in the town center. Tom knew, from his dad's comments when they were seated, that he had specifically requested a good table. They ate and talked and began to get quite pissed and at moments he relaxed—until the main courses were cleared and his mum started to cry, saying how proud she was of him, how much they missed him. He at once felt the acute need to comfort her but found himself unable to. He could not even look at her. He stared at the waitress's hands removing the plates. "I know, Mum, I know." His dad and his sister, however, to his profound relief, began ribbing her, and by the time the waitress returned with the pudding menus she was laughing again.

When his dad, adamantly, had paid, they walked the short distance to the hotel. Tom said goodbye to his parents in the foyer and left with his sister for a drink.

"Go on then." She leaned across the soft black sofa towards him. "You can tell me now. Mr. Davey's a dirty old pedo, isn't he?"

"He's really nice. They both are," Tom said, almost shouting. The bar was very busy, the music thumping. His sister's choice. "They seem good, Mum and Dad," he said.

"They've been excited to see you. You know Dad will be going on about being in the players' lounge for weeks. Kenny and John are never going to hear the end of it." She smiled. "They're going to help pay for me to go to uni, you know. We went out to the pub, and Dad got all serious and I thought he was about to tell me he was dying or something, but then he said that him and Mum had been talking about it and they'd decided it wouldn't be fair if they didn't give me the opportunities they've given you, so they're going to help with my funding."

"Great," Tom said, but not loudly enough that he could even hear it himself.

"I'll still be in a load of debt when I finish," she said. "But fuck it."

A couple of young women came past. One of them glanced down at Tom; he looked away.

"They think *you're* a pedophile."

"Yeah, right. You look older than me," he said, not joking. It had not been nine months since he left home, but she had changed.

She was more at ease, more confident. He looked at her quick, attractive face and again felt gratified that people might see them together.

"Are you seeing anyone, then?" she asked.

"No."

She laughed. "It's all right, I won't tell Mum and Dad. I bet you've got girls coming on to you all the time."

"Not really. Sometimes."

"Don't worry. You don't have to tell me."

At her faithful smile shame penetrated him, alongside a deep but impossible need to confide in her. Once, two years ago, drunk in his bedroom, he almost had, but then immediately had clammed up in confused panic.

"What about you?" he said. "Boyfriend?"

"Sometimes."

"Not at the moment?"

"Not at the moment, no." She said something else that he could not quite hear above the music. "Anyway, go get me another drink. And try not to get mauled by those two at the bar."

By the time they left they were both drunk and tired. He helped Rachel out onto the pavement, letting her lean into him. She almost fell over at a crossing, tripping on his foot, and he had to catch her to prevent her from falling into the road. She wanted to go to a club. "There must be somewhere," she kept saying, "even here there must be somewhere." He walked her back to the hotel.

In the foyer, when they said goodbye, she would not let go of him. For a moment he thought that she had gone to sleep. He held her, progressively tighter, burying his face in her neck until she started to tip over.

"See you, then," he said.

"Come home and see us more."

He watched her stumble away to her room. Only when she was long gone did he become aware of the receptionist watching him through the doorway of the back office.

Leaving, he started back in the direction of where they had come from, carried onwards by a resolve that he was going to return to the bar and find the two women, but when he reached the entrance and saw the short numb queue outside, the bouncer, he could not make himself go through with it. He stood there on the pavement. Through the window he could make out one of the women at the bar. He eyed up her face, her legs, willing himself to feel something, to want to go inside and talk to her. But he was already turning away, walking off, hating himself, hating the bouncers and the bar and the town and its stupid horny coatless people.

He found his car, got in and closed the door. He turned the engine on, the heating, and the warmth and stillness made him want to sleep. The smell of his parents, his sister, was still in the air. He should get out, he knew, find a taxi. Or sleep. There was nobody about, though. He put the car in gear, pressed the accelerator and took his foot off the clutch. The engine stalled, and he eventually worked out that he had left the handbrake on. He looked at himself in the rearview mirror. He looked normal, he was certain. He moved his eyes away to the dashboard, then back up again, trying to view his face as somebody else might, the women in the bar might.

He started again. Once onto the road he felt sober, in control. There was not much traffic about—taxis mainly, which he steered around safely whenever they pulled up outside the bars in the town center and expelled their passengers. He braked alertly when a people carrier halted without warning in front of him. Swerving past it he fumbled for his indicator, but flicked on the windscreen wipers by mistake. For some reason, as he passed from the center into darker, tree-lined residential streets, they would not turn off. Eventually he gave up and let them be. Their rhythmic dry shrieking filled the car. He made himself focus on the road, the quiet black expanse of night above it, broken every few seconds by a streetlamp through the trees.

His sister would be long asleep by now. Left to herself she would stay in bed until the afternoon if not for the inevitable knock at the door hours before that. There was something different about her and their dad, he had noticed. The way they were with each other now, the teasing, the teaming together, their difficulties of the past year seemingly forgotten.

There was a loud noise outside. The car juddered, a hubcap, a tire, scraping against the curb. He felt the side of the car—with the weightlessness of a fairground ride—lift, and he gripped the steering wheel, powerless to stop the back of the vehicle swinging round, veering into the road.

He thought he saw a house window brighten, but when he looked again the street appeared dark and dead. He did not recognize where he was. He tried to move the steering wheel but it was jammed, so he sat still, trying to work out whether or not he was injured, loud blood churning thickly through his head and the windscreen wipers continuing unabated, the ugly wrenching of them across the windscreen, back and forth, back and forth.

13

Leah arrived home with the shopping. The house was noiseless, but the kitchen light was on. She put Tyler down on the floor with the carrier bags. He pulled himself up on a cupboard handle and took a few heavy steps before dropping onto his bum. She began to put things into the fridge and the cupboards, and onto the growing pile on the island of miscellaneous requested items—sports magazines, DVDs, Rice Krispies Squares, ibuprofen—that would vanish almost as soon as she left them on the carpet outside one of Chris's two rooms.

He had spent every night of the past four weeks in the spare room. He needed the extra space to stretch out his leg, he said, with no risk that she might turn over onto it. He stayed upstairs for most of the day, as far as she knew, only coming out of the office to go to the toilet or come down for his enormous silent lunchtime sandwich.

Briefly, as she continued putting things away, she paused to read a text from her mum: "Robert free any of those Sundays for lunch. Suggested meal out but told him you wanted us round to yours." She did not reply and finished with the shopping. It had been her mum's idea to have Sunday lunch, her mum's idea too that it might be nice to have it at hers, to which Leah had made a small noise of agreement. The relationship with Robert was showing no sign of slowing and her mum wanted him involved in things, in her family.

It would also be an opportunity, Leah was well aware, for her mum to get a sense of whether everything was OK with them. The thought of Robert there, in the kitchen, his big hands buttressed on the kitchen island, looking about the place, eager to talk to Chris, rattled her. She could not imagine Chris at the table eating with them, but equally she did not want to think about him upstairs, alone in the office while they sat downstairs, Robert and her mum making small talk and ignoring the fact that he was not coming down to join them.

They had not once spoken about all the time he was spending holed away in there. Sometimes she listened to him watching television programs, or football matches, often back to back, and she felt a stupid gratitude whenever she heard these sounds, safe in the temporary knowledge that he was not on the Internet. When all that had started, at Middlesbrough, she had asked him what it was he was doing for so long on the computer, teased him about it even, and at his increasingly evasive responses she had grown anxious about what, who, he might be looking at, communicating with. But by the end of that season it had become such an everyday thing that she was usually able to bury the thought, leaving him to himself, and since the injury she was mainly just glad that he was not in the living room.

Early one morning, though, when he was still asleep, she had gone into the office to collect any plates and mugs that had accumulated and she had noticed that he hadn't shut down the laptop. She had swiftly rebooted it. As it began to stir into life, instantaneous suspicion, fear, had moved through her as she braced herself for the image of a girl, a message, but when she had looked round to check the landing and returned her eyes to the screen she saw that it was some kind of fans' forum. Without pausing to read it she had stepped away, her body relaxing, and carried away the dirty crockery.

On only one occasion since the injury had she come home to find him downstairs. He had been on the sofa, watching a German second-division match, so lost in it that he did not at first notice her come into the room, and she had wondered later if he had been betting on the result. In the weeks since that afternoon, however, he had barely left the office. One Thursday, on leaving the house for college without for once making him his lunch, she had put a small stuffed rhinoceros against the bars of the gate at the top of the stairs. On her return, seven hours later, it had still been there in the same position.

She put Tyler down for his nap, and over her lunch she tried to think of how she would fill the five hours before she had to take Chris to the stadium for a sponsors' function. There were no baby groups on, and Tyler was not at nursery until tomorrow. He had started going two mornings and one full day a week. These sessions broke up her own days. She woke on each nursery morning already disoriented at the prospect of being without him but at the same time guilty about making the choice to be so, the pressure of how she should better be using her time pursuing her during the drive to drop him off, in the shops, the gym.

She would have liked to go to the gym this afternoon, but her mum was away for the day with Robert and she could not leave Tyler with Chris, especially when he was preoccupied by the sponsors' function. Twice over the past fortnight they had gone to the gym together. Both times she had found it difficult to exercise, so conscious had she been of him in the weights room beyond the opaque glass wall, overworking the upper parts of his body, his cast jutting into the gangway for afternoon bodybuilders and pensioners to step respectfully around.

She knew that he did not like being reliant on her for lifts. On both gym visits, and the appointments at the hospital and the club, he had sat staring out of the car window, his seat pushed right back to accommodate the stretched-out leg, any possibility of talking to him made all the harder by the fact that she could not see his face. He rarely left the house. He dressed every day in the same pair of shorts, or in the giant tracksuit bottoms she had bought for him in the hope that he could get the cast inside, but which he had ended

up having to cut off at one knee anyway, the final result so ridicu-
lous that in the past they would probably have laughed at it.

There was nowhere, he had told her in a single moment of openness soon after he was discharged from the hospital, that he didn't
feel useless. And the club, she sensed, was where he wanted to be
the least. She would have liked, as she once had been able, to tell
him to stop feeling sorry for himself and get his act together. It felt
like so long since she had been able to talk to him like that—as she
had the summer his mum moved abroad and he went into digs, or
the difficult final year in the youths—that it was hard even to remember the person she had been then. Now, she was constantly
mindful of keeping her own act together. Only sometimes, as she
drove to college, leaving behind her the weight of her duties, did
she let herself pretend that there was no one else to think about;
that this was her life, the one that faintly she could remember wanting.

Amid the busy colorful world of the studio she was transported—
dyeing, bonding, felting, alert to the gunning of the sewing machines, the heat and stink of irons and glue and solder, the strange
thrill of using her hands for something other than cooking and
nappies and massaging her husband's backside.

Because Chris had been loath for her to take up the full-time
course option that she had once intended, before Middlesbrough
and Tyler, it had not been easy at first. Only coming in on Thurs-
days, she had felt nervous around the other students. Most of them
were younger than her. They knew each other; they lived and went
out together. It had taken her a few months to become comfortable
enough among them to join in the conversations around the large
worktables, or to talk in more than snippets to Maria, with whom
she had been paired to work on a computer-aided design project.
Instead of eating her packed lunch on a bench in the entrance hall
she now regularly went to the canteen with four or five of the others, who talked enthusiastically about designers and career plans,
and about the trip, scheduled for the beginning of the second year,
to a trade fair in Milan.

When they asked her one lunchtime if she was going to come on it she told them yes, probably, if she could arrange childcare, though the possibility of her actually going was so remote that she had not in fact given it any thought. She nearly told them then, as talk moved on to their ambitions for the second year, about a daydream she sometimes indulged in—of developing her own designs, of starting up a small business from home—but she did not in the end mention it, feeling, in the hub of their eagerness and confidence, a fraud. Back inside the studio, Maria had opened a packet of biscuits in the workspace the two of them shared and pushed it towards her. "You've got to come, you know. Milan. It's going to be amazing."

"No, I want to. Just it won't be easy with my little boy and everything."

"There's no one can look after him for a few days?" Maria was looking at her, munching a biscuit.

"Not really. I've not left him that long before."

"I don't want to be rude, but what about your husband? Couldn't he look after him?"

"Oh, he could, of course he could. It's just that he's a footballer and there'll probably be a match while I'm gone."

"He's a footballer?" Even though she had avoided saying much about Chris before, she could not arrest the jab of pride at how obviously impressed Maria was by this information. "He professional?"

And as she went on to tell Maria about him being captain, about him having played in the Championship, she realized that she was not going to tell her that he was injured, that he would not have to go to any match while she was away—and the unspokenness of it only made the reality of the situation more stark: the many months that he would remain at home, torturing himself, shut away in his rooms, the only solace for her the pathetic consolation that she at least knew where he was.

He came downstairs ready for the sponsors' function at half past five, while she was still giving Tyler his dinner. She laughed without thinking when she saw him. He was wearing the giant tracksuit bottoms with a smart black shirt, ironed, and a sports jacket. On his right foot was a brown leather shoe.

"You look like a manager."

He smiled. "Sharp, eh?"

She wiped Tyler's mouth and set him down on the floor. He tottered immediately towards the cast and flung his arms around it. "Lif, lif, Dadda." He gripped delightedly to the monstrous ski boot as Chris raised his leg up and down a couple of times.

"You about ready to take me?"

"Yes. I'll just get him in his pajamas. He'll probably fall asleep on the way back."

In the car Chris was withdrawn again, breaking from his trance only to shush Tyler, who was fussing in his car seat.

"You don't need any food doing?"

"No. It's a sit-down. Thanks."

"Who's it for?"

"Fuck knows."

Tyler started crying. He was getting tired. By the time she got back it would be past his bedtime.

"Shall I text you when it looks like I'll be able to leave?"

She turned instinctively to where his face would normally be. "I can't pick you up, Chris."

"Oh, right. Why not?"

"Tyler."

After a moment he said, "Can't you get your mum round?"

Tyler was still crying. The cast in the footwell twitched as he stretched to find where the dummy had fallen.

"You'll have to get a taxi, sorry."

They stopped outside the reception entrance of the main stand. Leah got out to fetch his crutches from the boot and waited for him to get unsteadily out of the car.

"See you later, then," he said.

She watched him swing-plonk away, and some old part of her went with him—reaching to be at his side, helping, joking, united, as he negotiated the heavy glass doors of the entrance.

There was a squeal behind her. She turned to get back into the car, saw briefly to Tyler and set off on the journey home.

A boy he vaguely recognized hurried towards him from behind the reception desk.

"It's all right," Easter told him. Then, looking up the flight of stairs, he said, "You can carry this," and gave him one of the crutches.

The boy followed patiently a few steps behind. The muffled din of the function swarmed towards them from beyond the stairhead. At the top he took the crutch back and, when the boy had gone, paused outside the swing doors to the Williams Suite.

He entered to a rush of noise. Suited men filled the room. They stood in the gaps between the large round tables, lined the walls, curdled thickly around the bar. The retractable divider between the two banqueting suites had been pushed back to make one open space, the semicircles of the drinks service areas now joined into a round at its center, like a beach bar. There was the smell of meat. Gravy. It was too crowded for him to pass through—there must have been a hundred and fifty, two hundred people there—so he stayed by the door, unsure what to do, claustrophobia rising as he failed to make a decision. A sea of men. One woman, deep within the crowd in a vivid red dress, showing through the dark mass like a wound.

The operations manager was coming towards him.

"Chris." He inspected the tracksuit bottoms. "Come with me."

Big men squashed against chairs and tables to let him through. Some of them clapped him on the shoulder. He heard his name a few times.

"Here we are. Enjoy your night."

Ten or so men were standing around the table, all with pints of beer or lager in their hands, evaluating him. PEEL DAVIS LOCK AND KEY SOLUTIONS was typed on a square of card clipped to a stand at the center of the table. The tall, ill-looking man beside him offered his hand. When he smiled his mouth opened to angry, withered gums. "Terry. MD. Meet the lads, Chris."

The men moved around the table, shaking his hand in turn, until they were all back in their original positions.

"So, how's the leg?" Terry lowered his eyes, and the rest of them looked down together at the injured limb.

"Improving. They gave me a plastic cast walker, so I'll be able to take it on and off to start my physio soon."

The men nodded approvingly. On another table he could see Jones. Further out, Fleming. Pearman. Terry started saying something to him but was cut short by the loud crackling voice of the chairman on a microphone.

"Ladies and gentlemen, your seats please."

The room sat down to the sound of cutlery shuddering on black cloth over folded-out plywood tables. The chairman, on a small stage that had been erected at the far side of the room, outlined the order of the evening. Easter zoned out until, in the details of the prize raffle, it was announced that he would be drawing the ticket numbers. His table were all looking at him. He avoided their gaze, keeping his eyes on the stage, trying to conceal his quickened breathing, his fists clenching beneath the table. The chairman finished speaking and moved tentatively off the platform. There was no step up to it, as far as Easter could make out. He imagined himself up there, revealed, the absurd leg on display like a beacon.

But when he turned back to face Peel Davis Lock and Key Solutions a bolt of pleasure passed through him, viewing the other players, none of whom had been chosen.

Creamed salmon tartlets came out. Terry asked him various questions about the injury, the team, the new manager. At each of his responses the circle of grinding pink mouths confronted him. He tried to be interesting, to make it sound as though he was passing them privileged information, but he heard himself telling them much the same as he had told Peter Pascoe in a short strained phone interview the previous week. They made noises of appreciation and fingered stray flakes of pastry back into their mouths. He was conscious of the fact that, technically at least, he was hosting their table. They had paid for him. There would have been a choice, maybe even a price list, as if he was an escort or a dinner magician.

By the time the roast beef was served they were having conversations among themselves. Terry, though, had no end of small talk for him. He asked if he had seen the win on Saturday. No, Easter told him, he had been at home, and when Terry found out that he had a son, he thought of a new wave of questions to ask about Tyler, many of which, to Easter's disguised humiliation, he did not know the answer to.

After the beef the booming mustached football-in-the-community officer gave a lengthy account of two Christmas holiday soccer camps, and the catering staff came round with raffle tickets. Easter visualized the long walk across the room. The hundreds of eyes upon him when he hesitated in front of the stage. His stomach dropped. For a second he imagined that Leah was there with him, the room empty, nobody but them. Sudden hooting laughter made him turn to look over at another table, where sponsors were rocking and clutching at themselves because of something that Jones, erect and leering, had said, and when he turned back round Terry had begun talking to the man on his other side.

He tilted his head back and let out a long breath. There had been a time, before the injury, before Middlesbrough, when he used to look forward at these bullshit events to telling Leah about them afterwards. But when he considered what he might say about tonight all he could think was how pathetic it would sound. That he had not been man enough to go up unafraid onto the stage. That he did not know where his son went to nursery.

Directly above him one of the ceiling panels was missing. Empty black space gaped beyond it, rising past foil-wrapped pipes and dustballs and the cold rusting girders of the main stand. A fantasy that he used to have came into his head again: Tyler coming onto the pitch, the last game of the season, toddling towards him across the grass for him to pick up and kiss and put onto his shoulders to parade in front of the crowd.

Dessert was quieter than the other courses. Terry found less to speak about, and he was able to sit unnoticed for long spells, drinking, laboring at his treacle tart, before the chairman came onto the stage again.

"Gentlemen. I'm delighted, absolutely delighted, to introduce for you now our guest of honor for this evening. What can I say about him? Twenty years of management experience across the top four divisions. Respected pundit. Unafraid of controversy. Successful businessman. Ladies and gentlemen, Doug King."

There was applause as Doug King toiled onto the stage.

"Fuck me," he said when he had got there and taken the microphone. "That's not done my hernia any favors."

The room was at once alive with laughter. The tea and coffee carts clattered between tables, and the sponsors adjusted their trousers, eased back into their seats.

"Do you know what wins you trophies?" He paused, resting the microphone on his gut to survey his audience.

"Money," somebody shouted to a burst of cheering from his table.

"Money? Fuck money. Spirit. That's what wins you trophies. Spirit."

There was general concurrence. They commended this, even if many were surprised by the implication that Doug King had won trophies.

"Every club I've been at, we've had this tradition. Laziest trainer. You know that one? Laziest trainer? What we do, end of a session, we take a vote on who's trained worst—not got stuck in and all that—and the lad that gets voted has to wear the laziest trainer top for the whole of the next session. That top was pink, and the boys could write any abuse they liked on it, and it never, ever got washed. By the end of a season it could pretty much stand up by itself, and I'm not bloody joking."

The room was captivated. He went on to speak frankly about the winning mentality, relegation, the death of his father, the damaging effect of foreign players. When he finished he received such a long and clamorous ovation that a waiter had to be called to one sodden table which had been slapped overenthusistically by a sponsor, and he was still on the stage when the operations manager came up to announce the drawing of the raffle.

Easter bent for his crutches under the table. He stood up and set out towards the other side of the room. There was a hubbub around him, outbreaks of laughter. Legs reluctantly drawn back. He came past a couple of the other player tables and inadvertently caught the eye of Tom, who nodded slightly then looked away.

By the time he had picked his way around the tables, careful to avoid the trailing wires gaffer-taped to the floor in front of the stage, the noise was dying and all he could hear while everybody watched and waited for him to get there was the thudding of his cast on the thin burgundy carpet.

When he reached the stage, Doug King, still on it, was quick to figure out that he would not be able to get up. He took the microphone from the operations manager and passed it down, pausing briefly as he did so to speak into it himself: "You're better doing it from there, son. You look like you've been gang-raped by a herd of elephants."

The ensuing laughter was still going when he read out the first of the numbers, and resurfaced, every now and again, throughout the draw and the handing out of the costly unremarkable prizes.

He headed away the second he was done. In an alcove outside the kitchen, beside towers of dirty plates, he called for a taxi. He was told that he would have to wait forty minutes. A waiter, clearly not recognizing him, came out of the kitchen and told him that he could not stand where he was, so he moved out from the safety of the stacked plates to the edge of the mingling crowd, imagining Leah seeing him there, irrelevant.

He turned to see Tom hovering close by. "All right, mate?" He gave Tom a wink. "Fucking hate these things."

Tom looked at a line of nearby men with their backs to them, then stepped towards him. He had a half-empty pint glass in his hand. He seemed drunk. "You got a drink?" Tom asked.

"Left it on the table."

"Here." Tom proffered the remains of his lager.

Easter laughed, pulling a face at the glass, but took it. "Fuck it," he said and downed what was left. "Cheers. What was your table, then?"

"I can't remember. Something to do with windmills."

"Windmills?"

"Yeah, windmills. Something Windmills. Or Windmill some-thing, maybe." He pointed at the cast. "How's it doing?"

"Uncomfortable as hell."

"It was horrible," Tom said. "Seeing it happen."

"You were on the bench, weren't you?" The line of men had spotted them. "What did he do—Wilko? When it happened."

Tom angled his body away from the men. "I don't know. I was looking at what was going on. He was the other side of the dugout from me."

He wanted to press for more—to ask what they had said in the dressing room, how often they had mentioned him since, but he held back, and now the men were beginning to sidle towards them. He moved in beside Tom as they closed around them, offering drinks, gesticulating at the leg. More men drew near, and though he tried to stay close to Tom and sensed Tom wanting to do the same, they quickly became separated. Sponsors converged on him. A drink was put into his hand. He was able to escape only when the operations manager came for him and directed him back towards the stage for a round of photographs with the shirt sponsor, the program sponsor, the stadium sponsor, the Riverside Stand sponsor—some just him, some with Fleming, then Jones.

"How long are they telling you?" Jones asked, looking at his leg.

"They can't say yet. I'm hoping five months."

"Before rehab?"

"Back playing."

"Tib and fib? You'd be doing well at nine."

When the photos were over he was released back into the throng. This was the longest that he had stood for, drunk for, in a long time, and he felt drained and increasingly woozy. There were still another twenty minutes until his taxi. He searched for Tom but could not see him. Every new person that approached him asked about the leg. He answered the same questions again and again until the injury became something separate from him that existed on its own, unconnected to the numb drift of his days and his nights, something which could be explained, defined, given a schedule and an end date that was not just a hopeful guess wrested from the club doctor to put out to the press.

He was woken up by Tyler shouting early the following morning. For some time he lay where he was, his leg throbbing under the covers. He tried to make out any words but gave up, deciding that it was gibberish. Tyler's constant babble never made much sense to him. Leah could understand it. She could listen to a stream of nonsense and know that he wanted the television or a Ribena, and he would look on in incredulity, struck by a yearning to be a part of it but feeling outside of them, a stranger. He waited for the front door to close. Even then he found it difficult to move. Pins and needles were shooting up his injured leg. His body felt heavy and a hangover was pressing at his temples. He would get up in a bit, he thought, and turned over uncomfortably to go back to sleep.

When he came out of the room there was a note from Leah on the carpet outside the door: "Going over to Mum's after nursery drop-off, back after I've picked him up again." He stared at the unfamiliar, measured handwriting and wondered why she had not sent him a text instead. He read it a second time, then let it drop to the floor, already anticipating the simple singsong of the laptop starting up.

Because of the function he had not looked at the message board since yesterday afternoon. The thread that he had been following was no longer at the top but he saw instantly that it had been added to.

Anyone noticed . . .		
Started by Town Legend	Replies:	14
20 Feb 2012 ≤ 1 2 ≥	Views:	218

Town Legend posted Mon at 11:20am
. . . that our form has picked up since Easter got injured? Coincidence?

Road to Wembley 2010 posted Mon at 12:32pm
Yes. Because he got injured at the same time that Wilkinson arrived.

Bald and Proud posted Mon at 12:50pm

Totally agree. The change in management is the reason for the turn-about in fortunes, together with the signing of Gundi. We've been crying out for a goalscorer all season and this guy is a class act.

Onetoomany posted Mon at 12:56pm

The Easter injury has no doubt helped but the turnabout has been too strong for it to be anything other than Wilko's arrival (& Gundi's). Just look at how things are now compared to a month ago.

20 January		P	W	D	L	F	A	Pts
21	Hereford United	26	6	7	13	25	41	25
22	Dagenham & Red	25	6	3	16	25	42	21
23	Plymouth Argyle	26	5	6	15	28	48	21
24	Northampton Town	26	5	6	15	32	54	21
25	TOWN	25	1	9	15	20	53	12
20 February		**P**	**W**	**D**	**L**	**F**	**A**	**Pts**
21	Plymouth Argyle	31	6	9	16	35	52	27
22	Hereford United	31	6	9	16	35	52	27
23	Northampton Town	29	6	6	17	34	57	24
24	Dagenham & Red	30	7	3	20	30	56	24
25	TOWN	29	4	10	15	27	55	22

Farris posted Mon at 12:59pm

Are you mental, Town Legend?

Town Legend posted Mon at 5:25pm

Probably true about new manager but what I mean was it can't just be coincidence things have picked up since Easter's been out. First half of the season Clarke wasn't getting the best from him and it probably affected the whole team. Be interesting to see if he fits into Wilkinson's plans once he's back fit.

Voice of Reason posted Mon at 6:04pm

Chris Easter was a non-league player, re-signed by a s**t manager with a charisma bypass who was misguidedly backed to the hilt by a chairman with more money than sense. Even if his career wasn't over he'd be getting nowhere near this starting eleven. End of.

Jamesy1987   **posted Mon at 8:05pm**
Didn't look like the chairman was backing Clarke to the hilt when he gave him his P45 ☹

Mary B   **posted Mon at 7:49pm**
Something I think's definitely been overlooked in all this is Bobby Hart coming into the team as Easter's replacement and the difference that has made. Jones + Hart = Leadership + Energy = Winning Combination.

The 13th Oyster   **posted Mon at 9:47pm**
Easter's pissed me off at times this season but at other times (Morecambe away) he's looked something like his old self. Don't fancy his chances of getting back in though.

Riversider   **posted Mon at 11:57pm**
Sometimes have been flashes like when he first came up from the youths but mostly he's disappeared in games. Was very poor Cheltenham away, Marlon Pack walked all over him. The main difference is Jones. With Easter out of the picture he's looked even better.

Whizzer   **posted Tues at 12:22am**
Drooling over Jones again are we? Are you related to him or something, Riversider?

Lardass   **posted Tues at 8:06am**
I genuinely don't understand why Easter comes in for so much stick on this forum. Even when he's going through a rough spell he never hides, and is this really a fair time to stick the boot in? He'd bleed the colors if you cut him open.

Towncrier Ian   **posted Tues at 8:22am**
Think that's what the doctors are doing to him right at this moment, mate 😂😂😂

Riversider   posted Tues at 10:00am

All I was saying is Jones is able to play his natural game now that him and Easter aren't looking for the same ball all the time, and we look a better outfit because of it. Yes, Clarke wasn't able to get the best out of Easter, but we'll probably never know if Wilkinson would be able to do any better. I am no relation to any Town player.

He continued to stare at the screen after he had read the final post. His skin pulsated against the cast. For a minute or two his hands stayed poised above the keyboard, before he started to type:

Town Legend   posted Tues, at 11:21am

Agree that neither of them were able to play their natural game under Clarke. Easter's natural game is driving forward but he was being made to provide defensive cover so that Jones could support the attack. Heard Clarke has given up trying to find a new post and has gone back to his van hire business! Best place for him IMO.

When he had sent the post he shut the laptop down and moved through to his bedroom, wanting to lie on the floor and stretch himself out for a few minutes before he went downstairs to see if Leah had made him any food.

14

The chairman came into the dressing room after a home draw against Accrington and told the team, while they continued eating lasagna from paper plates on their knees, that they would be spending three days at a country house hotel and golf resort before the second leg of the Paint area final against Charlton.

Tom got onto the coach on the Sunday morning and took his now usual seat, near the front, on the left. As the players shifted up the aisle and the air filled with the odor of them, Beverley swung in beside him. "Don't mind, do you?"

Tom moved his bag off the seat so that Beverley could sit down.

"I've got bagels and Connect Four on the iPad."

"Party time."

For a full five minutes before the coach set off, Beverley arranged himself. This was the third time they had sat together, though still Tom did not expect it and did not mind—was pleased, even, for the company. There was no edge to Beverley. He was easygoing and, after the mutual silence of room-sharing with Easter, talkative. The others had taken to him too. He was already part of the dressing-room banter bubble, and Tom knew from the conversations he sometimes heard on a Monday morning that he had been to the Hut a couple of times. He was popping open a large Tupperware box. Inside were two cling-filmed rows of bagels.

"Tuck in, mate. Steak and cheese, bacon and avocado."

They ate and played a couple of games of Connect Four, Beverley all the while half-involved in the meandering conversation going on behind them about spot betting and hair transplants. The bagels and their interest in the game had gone by the time they reached the motorway. Beverley put his headphones on. Tom stared out of the window, thoughts crowding in on him. Burning Liam's number at the sink. The lift home from the Town-supporting policeman after spinning his car. He was pulled from them by Beverley nudging his arm. "You ever play at Wembley, Tommy?"

"No. You?"

"No. You didn't play there with the England Unders?"

Tom shook his head. "I played in a final for the Under-17s, but that was at Burton."

"You think we've a chance?"

"Maybe. We are winning."

Beverley leaned his head back. He shook it slowly on the headrest. "Serious. If we do, I'm going to have twenty or thirty people down, going ape. Just amazing. I can't stop thinking about it."

Tom realized that he had not thought about it at all, not once. He pictured his dad telling his work colleagues, organizing the travel, buying Town shirts, sitting in the vast stadium with Rachel and his mum and Kenny and John, and he had to get up and shut himself in the toilet for fear that he would throw up his bagels.

The hotel was plush. Immaculate beaming staff greeted them on the gravel driveway. Once they had progressed through a reception area heavy with the aroma of immense pendulous flowers, the entire squad made immediately for the pool and spa area, where they aroused the unconcealed horror of a party of elderly golfing ladies taking tea at the poolside.

After changing and going up to see their room, Tom went with Beverley for a walk in the grounds. There was a landscaped pond. A ha-ha. A sparse orchard in which a well-built old man with a beard was making repairs with a length of twine while eyeing them through the branches. Before the evening meal the coaching staff sat everybody down in a large conference room to review the DVD of the first leg. The mood of the players was buoyant, frolicsome, their reaction to the goal on the recording every bit as joyous and physical as the celebration of the real event.

In the morning, following a training session at a nearby boarding-school facility, they were taken to the golf course. A rank of electric carts awaited them outside the clubhouse. They were split into groups of four, selected by Wilko. Tom was paired with Beverley, to play against Boyn and Daish. It was evident even by the time the foursome set off down the first fairway, the bouncing cart resounding to cheers as Boyn slipped the first four-pack out of his golf bag, that neither Tom nor Beverley had ever played golf before. They found Beverley's ball directly behind a horse chestnut tree. Beverley stood over the ball for some time, pondering. He decided to knock it back onto the fairway, but the ball jounced off the knuckle of the club head and smacked the tree, almost hitting him in the face on the rebound. All four collapsed in laughter. Tom then produced a succession of air shots from inside a deep bunker. On his fifth attempt he struck the ball out, and climbed up to see that it had landed in another bunker. When eventually they completed the hole they heard the distant ironic cheers of the following party. Boyn and Daish studiously marked the scorecards: Beverley 13, Pearman 15. Another round of cans was handed out and the cart trundled on to the next hole.

"You two, seriously," Boyn said, his voice wobbling as the cart traveled over a stretch of bumpy ground. "It's like playing with those old women." He was struggling to latch his finger onto the ring pull of his can. When he did, beer gushed all over him. "Crap." It continued to spout onto his lap. "I've just creamed myself, lads."

"Well, Boyney," Daish said from the driver's seat, "I've warned you before about your old-lady chat."

Tom sank back into his seat. Here, in the cold clean air of the middle of nowhere, pissed already, he was enjoying himself. He closed his eyes, letting himself soar with the purr of the cart, the merriment of the others.

He and Beverley improved, slightly, on the next hole, but then Beverley sliced a clump of soil from the perfect fringe of the putting green. Tom, Boyn and Daish, from their position beside the cart, doubled over at the sight of him, hands on hips, staring down at the wedge of earth lying on the velvet surface of the green, thick and rich as a portion of sticky toffee pudding. After six misses he holed the putt. Raising his hands in the air he ran over to Tom and put his arms around him in a bear hug. They jumped up and down together, shouting Tom did not even know what. Over Beverley's shoulder he could see Boyn and Daish watching them. He removed his arms from Beverley's warm torso and stood back.

The joking and the drinking continued for the rest of the round, though Tom was careful to avoid getting too close to Beverley other than to high-five or to consult, pointlessly, over shot choices. In the restaurant at dinner their performances and final scorecards— along with the confrontation between Bobby and Steven halfway through their own round—were the source of much amusement. Tom found himself included in the conversation to an extent that he was not used to. He tried to look unfazed by it. He joined in and to his own surprise was able to give a description of Beverley's attack on the second green which made both long tables shake with laughter. Boyn, sitting next to Tom, put an arm around his shoulder, and for a few floating seconds, clinched to Boyn's chest, Tom was empowered by a vision of how he must have appeared: one of them, normal.

They were permitted a single drink in the hotel bar after the meal before they went up to their rooms. As Tom climbed the grand staircase with Beverley, who had somehow managed to keep drinking all day and was hammered, he caught his reflection in one of the gilded mirrors and, in an upswell of unexpected happiness, smiled broadly at himself.

In the darkness, however, as he lay in bed and Beverley straightaway began snoring on the other side of the room, the feeling left him. His mind raced. Insistent choking desire tore at him—the thought of Liam's hands, his face, his body, the things they had done; the things which he blocked out over and over that he knew he wanted to do again.

———

With little to do at the hotel except swim, walk, go for a massage or play cards, the squad was restless by Tuesday, the day before the tie. After a short, sharp fitness session on the hotel's hedge-lined croquet lawn, then lunch, they dispersed. Some went to the television lounge. Some to bed. A small party—Price, Hoyle, Richards, Bobby Hart—escaped the hotel grounds and quickly became lost in their search for a village pub, ending up stranded by a reservoir. When they arrived back at the hotel sometime later in a taxi, Wilko was waiting for them in reception. He fined them two hundred pounds apiece. They ate the evening meal, each, to the initial confusion of the waiting staff, at a table on their own, and were sent to bed early. Once upstairs, though, they convened in Bobby's room and resumed a game of cards that had been running since the previous night.

All four were included in the starting lineup against Charlton. Tom was also selected. He deserved his chance, Wilko said at the breakfast meeting. And if they made it to Wembley, he pledged, those who had got them there would be the ones who played.

The Valley was by some margin the biggest ground that Town had ever played at. The team looked up in wonder at the stadium from the window of the coach when they pulled up outside it, and were then escorted inside.

During the warm-up, stretching for a ball, Beverley aggravated a groin strain that had been playing up over the past few weeks. He hobbled off the pitch, his inner thigh cramping, and Tom had to assist him up the few steps into the tunnel. Inside the dressing room he was helped onto a treatment table and the physio bent over him, syringing his groin, while Wilko delivered his team talk.

Even though the stadium was less than half full, the noise of the crowd flowed onto the pitch at kickoff. Charlton began positively, Town instinctively locking into rigid defensive lines, afraid to make a mistake or to venture forward other than by hauling long balls up towards Gundi. As a result they were at once under pressure. A Charlton midfielder loped forward and struck a powerful shot against the crossbar. Wilko's urgent calls from his technical area were lost in the building expectation of the crowd, and from a swift simple corner routine Charlton scored. The previously exuberant block of Town fans was swallowed by noise. Ten minutes later Beverley went to take a throw-in from deep inside Town's half. Nobody offered themselves for it, and Beverley, his arms tensing above his head, turned to launch the ball back to Hoyle—but an alert Charlton forward intercepted the throw and ran on to finish calmly through Hoyle's legs.

The team knew they were going to lose. They closed in behind the ball, determined to keep the score down. Tom, even when he came infield, hardly touched the ball. He chased and wandered as if drifting in a fog, the match and the crowd far away from him. The waves of sound, although loud, were indistinct, remote. The stands were set back from the pitch, and in the rising mass of blurred bodies he could not pick out any solo shouts, could not see the veins of any particular throat or forehead. Only after the final whistle did the rows of people take on a defined shape, when Wilko ordered the side to walk over and applaud the Town supporters. Their disappointed white faces shone in the roof lighting, clapping the players in response, resigned to the 3–1 aggregate defeat.

Cars sped in the gaps through the trees. Just inside the touchline of the pitch the squad was stretching on, a fresh molehill had emerged. A couple of pitches further out, Liam was pacing up and down, examining the ground inside a square he had marked out using the same colorful grubby cones that the team used for drills. Tom moved onto his front, concealing his groin. He pulled his feet against the backs of his legs, one at a time, pressing with secret discomfort against the mat, trying to make it go away.

He took his time in the dressing room and the canteen. He sat and ate next to Beverley, who had not trained and was on a pair of crutches because of the pain it caused him every time he took a step. He had not slept, he told Tom. The pain had become so bad during the night that he had got out of bed to go and sit on his sofa, where he had watched a whole series of *Only Fools and Horses*. Tom left when everybody else did and drove to the stadium. People were moving about inside the windows of the club shop but when he entered the bowels of the main stand the place was almost deserted. There was the faint echo of voices somewhere down the tunnels. An ancient aroma of muscle rub. A dusty light breaking through the gloom where the players' tunnel went out onto the pitch. He walked on to the dressing room, changed again, and once inside the empty gym pushed himself until his muscles failed.

Afterwards he returned to the training ground. He did not, though, turn his car onto the lane but pulled up on the side of the main road behind a van with a view of the opening in the hedge.

When the bonnet of Liam's car nosed through the foliage, Tom lowered himself in his seat. For several seconds he looked up at the sky, where motionless banked clouds sat above the treetops. When he inched back up, the car was away down the road. He waited for one, then another vehicle to pass before he pulled out.

He was able to follow without difficulty. Liam drove at an even, steady pace, as if still on the tractor. At one point the van in front of Tom turned off towards the town center, leaving only one car between them. He slowed, increasing the gap, and was brought to a halt by a set of traffic lights that Liam had already passed through. As he waited, the squalid reality of what he was doing caught up with him, and for a split second he considered turning back, but then the lights changed and the momentum of traffic moved him on. Minutes later he was looping past the identical new houses of Liam's cul-de-sac. He parked and watched from a careful distance as Liam unlocked his front door and went inside. After an hour and a half of no visible movement through the dark windows of the house and in need of the toilet, Tom left.

The following afternoon Liam took a detour from his route home. Tom, the blood vessels of his fingers beating on the gear stick, tracked him down unknown streets until they came to a retail park, in which Liam got out of his car and disappeared inside a B&Q. A wave of self-consciousness made Tom want hurriedly to leave. A large flustered woman, though, was in his rearview mirror, advancing on the car next to him, a toddler in the seat of her trolley full of lime-green cushions and spray cleaners. The woman was shouting at the boy. With the child still in the seat she opened her boot and began unloading into it. Tom felt the shunt of the trolley straying into the back of his car. He was almost tempted to pump his horn and scare them—to reverse sharply into the trolley and send the toddler spinning across the car park. They were still there, shouting at each other, when Liam came out of the store. He was carrying two large white tubs by their handles, forearms straining, his shoulders hunched and twisting. Tom waited interminably for the woman to wrestle her child into his car seat and reverse out, the trolley left where it was behind Tom's car, by which time Liam was long gone.

He had intended to sleep in on his day off, but once he was awake could not just lie there, so he got up, put on a tracksuit and set off for the stadium gym.

A few other players were in: Daish and Fleming, both returning from injury, who came over to talk to him while he warmed up, and Gundi, huge and immersed in headphones, who remained in front of the free weights mirror the whole time Tom was there. It was still early when he finished and changed, not yet midday. He came out into the car park and sat inside his car. Before his mind could begin to churn, he forced himself to go to the cinema.

The auditorium was empty except for a couple of fidgety teenage girls and a bald man in a leather jacket who fell asleep during the trailers. The film was loud, stupid, and once he made up his mind halfway through that he would go straight home afterwards he was able to give himself over to it completely, aching pleasurably in his seat with what was left of his protein shake and his box of chicken nuggets.

He had done it before, following someone like this. Propelled then by the need to despise himself after the two incidents with Craig. The memory of them, so painstakingly purged for two years, returning again.

The first time, in the gloom of the common that they had known together for years as a place of three-and-in and penalties and pilfered cigarettes, was so unexpected that they had gawked at each other for some time in bemusement, then Craig had bent in to kiss him again and Tom had felt dizzyingly alive and had known, as they touched, that there was something deeply wrong with him. The second, final, time—a couple of weeks later in Craig's bedroom while his parents were out at the pub—he could only recall fragments of, intensely: the taste of vodka, the Tim Cahill poster on the wall, the useless pot of Craig's mum's anti-wrinkle lotion.

They had avoided each other after that. Tom had kept to himself, shut away from his family, getting drunk on the alcohol that the older academy boys were only too happy to buy for him at a profit. One night he put a brick through the windscreen of a Ford Focus on a street near the common. And for a fortnight or more he had followed Craig, waiting in the cafe opposite Craig's sixth-form college until he came through the revolving glass doors, burning each time that he was with somebody, boy or girl. Thinking about the afternoon that his mum came up to his room asking for "a chat about something" still made Tom weak with fear. She had sat next to him on his bed and said that she and his dad were worried because they knew he was drinking, and he had felt such relief wash through him that he had put his arms around her and promised he was going to put an end to it. He felt like such an idiot, he had told her; he would focus on his football and nothing else from that moment on.

He was about to drive off from the cul-de-sac when a car parked outside Liam's house. A tall young man got out and went through the gate, producing a key and going inside. Even though Tom knew it must have been one of Liam's housemates he stayed on for a whole hour longer, his eyes fixed on the windows.

It became normal very quickly, following somebody. The risk of being caught, and his reasons for doing it, were already pushed to the back of his mind. By the end of the week he was practiced enough to maintain a five- or six-car distance, the occasional glimpse of the Nissan's green bodywork enough for him to keep track of it.

There was not, however, much variation to Liam's routine. He did not seem to have much of a life outside work. He set off early to whichever of the two grounds he was scheduled for, left nine hours later, sometimes went to DIY centers, and came home. Tom wondered as he sat in his car—conscious of the woman with her dog who had passed him earlier going in the other direction—what he did in there, on his own before his housemates came home. There were already several people in the cul-de-sac that Tom recognized. An Asian woman with a pram. A man who intermittently moved past a window in his dressing gown. The painter and decorator who owned the van in front of which Tom had today pulled up.

Liam was coming out of his front door. Tom, caught off guard, scooted below the dashboard. When he dared peep up Liam was getting into his car. He had changed into jeans and a sweatshirt. He drove off, and once he was at the junction of the main road Tom turned on his engine. Before long they were back at the retail park. Tom deliberated over whether or not to stay. He watched Liam walk away across the car park, moving past B&Q to go into a furniture store. Tom kept his sight on the entrance, waiting for his return, but seconds later Liam was visible through the glass wall of the upper level. He was walking past cafe tables, and Tom saw he was heading towards a woman, who was standing up to greet him. When the two figures hugged each other he saw with a jolt that it was Easter's wife.

A small child was eating at the far side of the table. Liam bent forward to say something to him, touching his hair, then returned his attention to the mother. They spoke barely without pause. Easter's wife turned sometimes to deal with the child but then instantly she was back, looking at Liam, both of them fully concentrated on what the other was saying. For a long time Tom did not take his eyes off them. The child finished his food, and Easter's wife got up to lift him out of his high chair and place him on the floor. He immediately made towards the window. The apparition of a miniature Easter appeared, pounding his tiny fists on the glass, and the image came back to Tom of Easter on the evening of their first room-share, trying to get the hotel window open.

His mother was coming for him. She crouched down to pull him back from the window, and the boy wheeled about to fling his arms around her. They looked out together at the car park. Tom did not even think to hide. His own gaze was directed past the pair at Liam, the static side of his head looking down at his cup.

When she turned away Tom started his car. He drove out of the retail park, away down the darkening streets. He took a wrong turn and became briefly lost before finding the main road into town. He stopped at an off-license and bought a bottle of vodka. Back inside the car he opened it and took a long drink, then put it underneath the passenger seat and drove on.

The small shaved lawns of the cul-de-sac were bathed in the orange glow of streetlamps. In one of the upstairs windows of Liam's house a light was on. Tom implored himself to leave, trying to drag himself out of the loud muddle of his thoughts, taking another pull from the vodka bottle.

Liam returned alone. When the Nissan's sidelights went off Tom took a final hit of vodka and got out. Liam stopped on the pavement as soon as he saw him. He waited for Tom to walk up.

"Tom," he said quietly.

Tom did not respond or look at him.

"You can't come in, you know."

"I know."

"This isn't like last time?"

"No."

Liam was studying him. He looked over to his house. "You didn't get in touch. I thought . . . I don't know what I thought. Didn't think I'd find you here again."

"We could meet up somewhere."

"Oh. Right."

"We can't be seen though."

"No, I know."

Tom stared at the road.

"You've got something in mind?" Liam asked.

"I've not thought about it."

"Look, you've got my number."

"I lost it."

"Right. If you want, maybe I could contact you."

"No, I'll do it."

Tom took out his phone. Liam glanced again at his house then gave his number.

Only when Tom was in his car and had taken another mouthful of vodka did he save it, under a made-up name, the only one that would come into his head: Gary.

15

The French windows of the clubhouse had been opened and the scent of curried chicken was wafting enticingly over the field. From the tacky plastic warmth of the stretching mats Tom watched the burly little assistant groundsman moving in and out of the ground-staff shed, his quick hands and busy energy so different to Liam, who was back at the stadium, no sign or sound of him present now to cloud the simple clear air.

The fitness coach called them over for a doggies drill and Tom sprang to his feet. By the time they broke for liquids the roots of his hair were crawling pleasingly with sweat. A bag of balls was released and a forgotten tingle of expectancy moved inside him.

They took turns at dribbling around a line of cones. The number two timed each effort. Tom's focus was total. He guided the ball nimbly around the cones, his brain, his feet, his toes inseparable. After two attempts each he had recorded the two fastest times. Wilko walked over and, in full view of the whole squad, pointed at Tom. "That, people, is what Premier League quality looks like," he said, giving Tom a wet pat on the kidneys that Tom could feel long into the keep-ball routine that followed.

Finch-Evans was struggling. Town were on top at home against Morecambe, leading 1–0 and pushing for a second, but the winger's every contribution was a mistake—a cross shanked into the crowd, a pass to Fleming without looking up that squandered possession— and by the closing stages of the half it was obvious that he was lost. The Morecambe left back stationed himself high up the pitch to attack Town's right and in injury time set up a chance for the tat-tooed number nine which was volleyed with enough power, just wide of the post, to take down an advertising hoarding.

Wilko did not substitute him at halftime. He wanted him to be a man, he said. To go back out and turn his performance around. Finch-Evans acknowledged these words with a slight dip of his head. Wilko then turned to the rest of the squad and clapped his hands. "Bloody superb. These are promotion material, and you're matching them, better than them, man for man, almost. A second goal kills them off, lifts us above the drop. Get out there and more of the same."

Finch-Evans lasted another eighteen minutes. A rumble of satis-faction went around the ground when his number was held up. He sloped across the pitch, only looking up from the grass to acknowl-edge Tom with an expression of humiliated relief on his face as they exchanged on the touchline.

The crowd cheered Tom's introduction. He received the ball just after play restarted and passed it forward, simply, to the feet of Gundi. A neat touch a few minutes later worked him a few seconds of space; he put his head up and spotted the overlapping run of Fleming—into whose path he played an easy measured ball. Each choice was suddenly clear. Uncomplicated. As if it had never been any different. Every part of him functioned at once. Even when he misjudged one cross, the conviction of the effort gave it the impres-sion of being intended: the ball floated over Bobby at the near post straight onto the impending forehead of Gundi and hurtled past the goalkeeper. Tom squawked with delight. Some of the players rushed to converge on Gundi, others to Tom. He could hear from amid the breathless thicket of them a thin chorus of "One Tom Pearman . . ." and he resisted the urge to look out into the crowd, to search the faces across the pitch, where the staff and scholars were gathered to one side of the disabled supporters' stall.

Some of the players wanted to go out afterwards. The win had moved the team clear of the relegation zone and they were in a mood to celebrate. Beverley tried to persuade Tom to go with them.

"Come on, man. You never come out."

"True. I'm pretty fucked, though."

"You played half an hour, mate."

"I know. My body's not used to it."

Beverley laughed. They clasped hands and Beverley pulled him close. "Next time, OK?"

Tom turned up the volume on his television. He took four deep breaths. The phone was cold against his ear.

"Hello?"

"Hello."

"Tom. How are you?" There was a faint electrical buzz on the line. Liam's voice sounded different over the phone. "Tom? You OK to talk?"

"It's fine. I'm in my bedroom," he added, as if he was a little boy gone upstairs to play after dinner.

"Good result today. You did well when you came on."

"I didn't expect to get that many minutes."

"They sang your name."

"I know."

Beneath the floorboards he could hear the Scottish boys going into Bobby's room.

"So. Are we going to meet up?" Liam said.

"It can't be anywhere in town."

"Obviously."

"No one can recognize us."

"Wigs?" Tom met this with silence. "OK," Liam continued, "we could go to some small place somewhere. You know Darm? It's this village a bit of a drive away with a couple of all right pubs."

Tom had heard of Darm. A few of the players carpooled from around there. "Is there anywhere a bit further?"

Liam laughed. "You're not that famous, mate."

There was the muffled sound of voices underneath Tom. He turned up his television still louder.

"There's a Beefeater," Liam said, "north up the dual carriageway, about fifteen miles away. That's about the most nothing place I can think of. What do you think?"

The commuter traffic moved slowly out of town. Tom turned on the radio, and loud dance music startled him. He had been too preoccupied on the way home from training to put it on, so it was still tuned to the station that Bobby and Steven insisted on every morning. He switched it off, alone again with the smell of his deodorant, the blatancy of his sharply combed hair in the mirror. He turned the radio back on, quieter, changing the station.

Liam's car was the only one outside the pub, parked beside a line of wheelie bins against a wall. Tom drove past to the far end of the car park, where a couple of other vehicles were positioned by the entrance to a hotel.

Liam was sitting in a corner, partially obscured by a partition. Tom walked over, glad at the choice of table, then at the handshake when Liam stood to greet him.

"What are you drinking?" Liam asked.

There was a pint on the table, almost half drunk.

"Lager's fine."

Liam went to the bar. He exchanged a few words with the barman, more than just the drinks order. He was wearing the same jeans and sweatshirt, Tom thought, that he had worn to meet Easter's wife at the furniture store. Tom looked around the bright room, at the fake beams and the pale brick pillars festooned with meal promotion placards that glimmered under the copper lampshades. A recollection of his first date came to him. In a burger restaurant with Jenni Spoffarth, the small quiet girl he had seen throughout most of his final year at school—happily, for the most part, at least when he had been able to ignore the hidden roiling desperation that ate at him on the occasions he had touched her slight, rosy body, and which had overcome him eventually one blus-

tery wet afternoon in an underpass on his way home after breaking
up with her.

Liam returned and placed Tom's pint on a coaster. "Good win,
that, Saturday."

"It was. Fair chance we'll be safe now."

"Couple more wins."

"Something like that."

Liam's right hand was splayed on the table, as coarse and yellow
in the table light as a starfish. He noticed Tom looking and with-
drew it.

"When did you start supporting Town?" Tom asked.

"Four. That was my first game. Five when I started going properly."

"A lot of games."

"Yep. Lot of shit football." He took a drink of his pint. "Following Town's the one thing that's always been, you know, simple." He
smiled. "Most of the time."

"Not when they released you."

"Not when they released me, no."

Tom nodded. He wanted to say that he knew how that felt. "You
ever miss playing?"

"Yes and no. Some of it, I do. Stupid stuff. Holding the ball in
my gloves. Shouting. I don't know if I'd even have been up for playing pro, though. You're supposed to be eccentric as a keeper,
but . . ." He looked off to the bar and said, "What about you? What
was your first game?"

"Think I was about seven. Rochdale, home to Hull City."

"Rochdale?"

"It's where I was born. Me and my dad used to support them."

"Didn't know that."

"We moved away when I was eleven, season after I signed academy terms. We used to drive in before that. There was a sixty-minute
rule for my age group that meant Rochdale was in the catchment
area. Took my dad the full hour to drive it, though. He used to drop
me off, drive back to Rochdale for work, then come back and pick
me up. It got too much in the end. That's why we ended up moving."

Liam was listening closely. "Must've been tough, not getting a contract after your family made a sacrifice like that."

Tom mumbled agreement and looked away. They became quiet. A man in a suit and sagging tie came into the pub. He bought himself a drink and made for a tucked-away alcove on the other side of the room. Liam continued to look over, even when the man was out of sight, and Tom took in the wide forehead, the smooth line of his jaw. A seizure of longing at the realness of this stranger across the table made him lean forward and jam his knuckles together until they hurt. He had no idea what Liam was thinking, feeling. There was so much between them that was unsayable. "Another drink?"

Liam drained the rest of his pint. "All right."

When Tom came back to the table Liam remained quiet. He seemed distant, thoughtful. Tom wondered if he was waiting for him to push the conversation. He tried to think of something to talk about. He took a long gulp of his lager, put the glass back on the table. The anxious need to understand why Liam had met Easter's wife wrung inside him, but there was no safe way of bringing that up. Apart from football, there was nothing. When a long time had passed, he said, "You're back at the stadium, then?"

"We swapped over, yes."

"How long will you be there?"

"Until the end of the season. And then I'll stay there, getting the pitch renovation done for the start of next."

"Must get a bit boring."

"It doesn't," Liam said, shaking his head. "It's my life, mate."

He said nothing more, and Tom could not think what his next question should be, so they lapsed again into silence.

Condiment holders were lined up along the steel shelf of an unlit hot pass. Wedged between two of them was a collection of breakfast menus displaying the logo of the hotel at the other side of the car park. Tom took another slug of his pint. He had drunk nearly half of it already and he knew that he should slow down. He needed to eat too, but he did not want to suggest it.

"Day off tomorrow?" Liam said.

"Yes."

"What will you do?"

"Not much. Relax. Go to the gym."

Liam gave a hum of response, and the topic was at an end.

They finished their drinks and decided against another. They walked into the dim cold of the car park, coming to a stop in front of Liam's car. It was still on its own beside the pub. The man in the suit must have come from the hotel, Tom thought, or been dropped off, or walked up the dual carriageway. Liam went round to the driver's side of his car and got in, shutting the door behind him. Panic tore through Tom, thinking that he was going to drive away, but he stayed there, completely still, not looking round, not looking anywhere.

Tom approached the passenger door and opened it. They sat in the darkness, unmoving. There was a machinery catalog in the door storage pocket. A floodlight above the car illuminated the path to the pub entrance, shining on the pebbledash of a shrub tub, the thick tarpaulin of a steak deal banner. Tom closed his eyes. At the touch of Liam's fingers on his thigh he tightened. There was the sound of their breathing. The dual carriageway beyond the car park. A thumb moved in a small gentle circle on his jeans. Tom could sense the warmth of Liam's face near his own and turned away from it.

His neck froze at the touch of Liam's lips, momentarily against it, then gone, leaving a cold tingling on his skin. The hand on his thigh moved over his own and they knitted together in a fierce cat's cradle as Liam pulled towards him, breathing at his ear. Tom twisted further away from the brazenness of his lust. The metal fence of a beer garden was diffused in the purple bloom of the hotel entrance sign. In the half-light a fox darted underneath the wheelie bins. A large dry fingertip ran across Tom's temple, around the hairline of his sideburn and onto his earlobe.

"It's OK," Liam said, sliding the finger over his cheekbone, pulling his face back round, and Tom realized that it was because he was crying.

He shut his eyes again, their lips coming together. His mouth was numb, sucking and pushing against the shocking muscular strength of Liam's lips. He forced himself not to let go to the dreadful intimacy of it, panning out until he was experiencing the whole thing from outside himself, outside the car, the image through the windscreen of two men's heads moving together in the dark.

16

Leah moved about the kitchen, taking the butter out of the fridge, putting the chocolate mousse in to set, making a salad, checking on the roast, the potatoes, Tyler. She and her mum had decided on a late lunch after his nap, but he woke up after only half an hour, out of sorts and needy for her attention, so she had put him in front of the television while she rushed around trying to get the preparations finished before her mum and Robert arrived. Chris was in the office. She had not seen him since he came out for the toilet a couple of hours earlier in an unwashed T-shirt, barefoot. She had considered reminding him again about the meal but wavered just as she was about to shout up, and then he was gone.

They arrived ten minutes early. Her mum greeted her and went straight inside to find Tyler. Robert presented her with two bottles of wine, which she took in each hand and found herself defenseless as he moved in to kiss her on the cheek and give her a cuddle.

"Been so looking forward to this," he said, coming inside, sizing up the living room. Her mum picked Tyler up from the carpet. Because they were early Leah had not yet had the chance to turn off the television, and as she looked for the remote she had the feeling of being caught out, occupying Tyler with cartoons.

"Something smells good," Robert said.

"Chicken," she said, and they moved through into the kitchen. Robert was wearing dark blue slacks and a matching short-sleeved shirt. There was no lady belt, she noticed with a little disappointment, as she had imagined that this might be something that she and Chris could talk about later, if he deigned to come down from his hideaway. They stood around the island, Robert and her mum making approving noises about the food, and she knew that they were already wondering where he was. For an instant she considered telling them that he had gone for an appointment—with the doctor, with his agent—but a flash of exasperation, always having to lie for him, stopped her. They might hear him upstairs anyway. Or he might sneak down to get himself a drink, a sandwich.

Tyler was crying. Leah's mum joggled him up and down, talking gently to him, then buttered him a slice of bread from the basket next to the salad. He took it from her and became quiet as he began eating it, and Leah was no longer sure whether he had not in fact simply been hungry all this time. He had not eaten much of his lunch. Either way, she thought, that was what it would look like.

"Can we help you with anything?" Robert asked.

"No. Well, you can open a bottle of wine if you feel like a glass now."

"Will do." Robert went into two cupboards before he found some glasses, the old ones, as those she had intended to use were already on the table. They went through to the living room. Tyler was calmer. He played with some of his toys on the carpet, then ran in and out of the kitchen when he learned that this provoked a response from Robert and her mum, sitting next to each other on the sofa. They kept touching, she noticed. Knees. Elbows. Robert's big hand briefly on her mum's thigh. She should feel glad, she thought. Her mum was obviously happy. But instead she watched them with growing irritation at their intimacy, at the naturalness of it.

"How's this guy getting on at his nursery?" Robert asked, even though he must have known all about Tyler's nursery through her mum.

"Loves it. He's getting one or two little friends there. I picked him up one day this week and they said he'd spent the whole morning following one little girl around trying to kiss her jumper because there was a pig on it." They laughed admiringly. She did not tell them that one of the staff had told her this because Tyler had pushed the girl over repeatedly and made her cry. There was a small noise from the floorboards above them. She could not tell whether they had heard and decided that they had not because they were riveted by playing with Tyler, Robert creasing and uncreasing his eyebrows to make him giggle. Leah got up and put some music on. "I'm just going to take the chicken out of the oven. Food's ready whenever you are."

She laid out all the dishes at one end of the dining-room table and carved the chicken while they came through and her mum sat Tyler in his high chair.

"Sit wherever you like," she said, arranging a large helping of chicken on Robert's plate before placing it, with a serviette-wrapped knife and fork, before him.

"Looks bloody marvelous."

"It does, Leah. No easy thing getting all this together on your own with this one around your feet."

"It was easy enough. It's just a chicken." She set a plate and cutlery in front of her mum. That morning she had laid the table with four individual place settings. She had got halfway through the task, before taking them all up again.

"It's a lovely room, this," Robert said, passing her mum the vegetables. "What an amazing table."

"We don't eat in here that much. Only really if we've got people round." She avoided looking at her mum, hoping that she would not pick up the subject, but she was happily engaged feeding bits of potato to Tyler. Although they had been in the house for coming up to a year, this afternoon was the first time anybody had been round for a meal. And Leah and Chris had only sat at the enormous rustic-effect table, bought one fraught sweaty afternoon at an Oak Furniture Land showroom, twice: the first time the weekend after they bought it, the second on her birthday, when Chris had cooked her beef Wellington and got into such a dark mood over how it had turned out that they barely said a word to each other the whole evening.

"Chris," her mum said.

He was there, in the doorway.

"Hi, Donna." He came into the room. He had put on a new T-shirt and a sweater. A sock. "Robert, yeah?"

Robert stood up from the table, joyful, overcome. He stepped towards Chris and for a moment Leah thought he was going to hug him too. Chris shook his hand.

"Sorry," Leah said. "I didn't know when you were—"

"It's fine, it's fine. I was just sleeping off my medication," he said with enough conviction for Leah to wonder for a second whether it might be true. They all watched him get a plate of chicken and potatoes, carrots, sweetcorn, bread, salad, and maneuver his cast under the table to sit down in the space next to her mum, opposite Leah and Robert. He had brought a bottle of Powerade downstairs with him, which he drank from now, and as he put it down and started to eat Leah could sense that he was already shutting down, going into himself again. She was moved by the need to help him, to reach out and pull him back, but almost as soon as she felt it, the urge was replaced by a hardness towards him, as she watched his lips, his mouth chewing at the food she had cooked, still not looking over once towards Tyler at the end of the table, who was starting again to cry.

"I don't know if Donna told you," Robert said after Leah's mum gave Tyler two kernels of sweetcorn to try picking up between his fingers, "but we've booked a holiday. Last night. We're going to go to Corsica. I was up for Paris, but your mum got her way." A look and a smile passed between them. Tyler started crying yet again so Leah got up and went to him. She took him out of his high chair and brought him to sit on her lap. She imagined Robert on the beach. The mound of his beer belly wet with perspiration. His big hands massaging sun cream into her mother, sliding up and down the backs of her legs.

"How long you going for?"

"Ten days."

They continued eating.

Tyler was whinging to get down. She lowered him to the floor and he went straight under the table. He could stand upright beneath it and he started running up and down its length, until Leah picked him up again. "No," she said. "Naughty." And felt immediately stupid for telling him off.

"How are the dance classes going?" she asked because she knew that they liked talking about them.

"Oh, I'm an embarrassment," Robert said, chuckling.

"It's true. He is." They tittered at each other.

"I'm like an elephant. An elephant that needs a hip replacement. But your mum, she puts the young girls in the class to shame."

"Shut up, Robert."

"You do, it's true."

Chris had finished eating. He was sitting, staring at the table. Leah put Tyler down, and he went off into the living room. "Door," he piped as he left. "Door. Door." It was the first time she had heard him say the word, but she did not mention it, in case her mum and Robert had heard him say it before. She started to clear the plates. Her mum got up to help her.

"I might go and see what the little man is up to in there," Robert said.

They left Chris alone at the table. As she followed her mum out of the room Leah looked back at him, still staring down, and she could not be sure whether he knew that they had gone.

In the kitchen her mum began washing up.

"Leave those, Mum. I'll do it later."

"I'll just do the greasy stuff. Save you a job."

Leah got the mousse out of the fridge. She put it on the island and peeled away the cling film. She looked at her mum. From behind she looked ten years younger than she was. The dancing, as well as all the other things she did for herself—swimming, Zumba, weekend walking trips—which she had never been able to do in the days when Leah's dad had controlled everything in her life, were keeping her trim. She was dyeing her hair too, Leah had noticed. And she must have cut down her shifts at the leisure center, because she was seeing an increasing amount of Robert through the week. Within minutes she had completed all of the dishes. She dried her hands, looking through to the living room, from where came the sound of

Robert making lion noises. She approached the side of the island where Leah was standing. Leah presumed she was going to pick up the stack of dessert bowls but instead she gently took hold of her hand. The two women faced towards the living room. Robert scuttled past the entrance on all fours, quickly followed by Tyler. Her mum was stroking the back of Leah's hand with her thumb.

"Are you OK?"

Leah continued to look through into the living room. Tyler came into view again, laughing, being tickled. His face, week by week, becoming the face of his nonexistent father.

"Yes." She pulled her hand away and picked up the dish of mousse. "You mind bringing the bowls?"

When they came back into the dining room Chris was not there. His empty bottle of Powerade sat on the table. Leah put the mousse down and spooned helpings into three of the bowls. Robert came in carrying Tyler. "Oh sweet Lord," he said, seeing the mousse. "Shall I put this guy in his high chair?"

"Please. He can have a little of this. It's got a bit of Baileys in it, though, so not too much." Leah dug a teaspoon into the soft pudding and walked over to hand it to Tyler. He appeared at first more interested in the spoon than the chocolate, watching it glint when he twisted his fist. When he did put it into his mouth, though, they all laughed at his face, screwing up with concentration then breaking into a smile. "More. More."

"Can he?" Robert said, taking the spoon from Tyler when Leah said yes.

They all looked up as Chris returned to the table. He got himself some mousse and sat down in his place. There was the sound of spoons on bowls. Leah passed the dish around so that they could help themselves to seconds. She asked if anybody would like coffee.

"Not a bad result yesterday," Robert said when she was about to go to the kitchen.

Nobody spoke. Very faintly, Chris nodded.

"Disappointing not to win, conceding that late, but realistically that's a decent point against a top-three side, and we're looking safer by the minute."

Leah could see her mum trying to get Robert's attention, but Robert seemed oblivious, and Leah wanted him to keep going.

"Bodes well for next season. With you back in the side, new keeper, couple of wingers, bit more strength in depth, I'd say we could even be looking at a promotion charge."

Chris did not move his eyes from his bowl. He slid his spoon from his lips and said quietly, "That's what they're saying."

"He's turned it round, Wilkinson. Breath of fresh air. Although what do I know? I'm just a supporter, and a fair-weather one at that, if I'm completely honest. What's he like to play under?"

Her mum was looking visibly agitated, glaring across the table at her boyfriend, and Leah felt a cold pleasure in the fact that, for all their touching and flirtatious glances, she was unable to stop him. Her mum said flatly, "Robert, I'm not sure Chris wants to talk about football while he's injured."

"He's better than Clarke," Chris said, raising his face.

Robert became enthusiastic again. "Right. I can imagine. Clarke's got his place in the history of the club, don't get me wrong, but he's a non-league manager. This guy Wilkinson knows what he's doing." A very slight smile appeared on Chris's face but he said nothing.

"I'd think about renewing my season ticket for next season if it wasn't for these dance classes." Now Robert did turn his attention to Leah's mum, and an expression of confusion came over his face when he saw the way she was looking at him.

"Leah," her mum said, "how was college on Thursday?"

"Yes," said Robert. "How's the project coming on? Computer design, isn't it?"

"CAD, yes."

"How many garments have you done now?" her mum asked.

"Three." She fixed her eyes directly on Chris, who looked down again at his empty bowl. "Me and Maria. There are going to be five pieces in total."

Robert bunched his eyebrows. "Remind me—it's jackets, yes?"

Leah did not take her attention off Chris. She sensed that he knew she was still looking at him, but he did not lift his face. "Yes. We're 3-D weaving and draping a series of women's jackets."

Tyler threw his spoon to the floor and began battering his high-chair tray. Robert went to him but Tyler pushed against his hands.

"I'm going away too, actually," Leah said.

"Are you?" Her mum looked over at Chris, who had not reacted. "To Milan."

"Oh, lovely. The two of you planning a weekend break?"

"No. On my own."

He would not meet her gaze and did not allow his expression to alter, but she knew that he was listening.

"It's a study trip at the start of my second year. I'm going to a trade fair."

Tyler was crying, but she did not move her eyes from Chris, even as her mum went to Robert's assistance and it was just the two of them left, opposite each other at the table.

17

The spring sunshine and continuing good form of the team ensured that three sides of the ground were bright with red and green before the kickoff of the penultimate home match, against Gillingham. The dull throb of a drum emanated from the back of the Riverside Stand, where half a dozen teenage boys had taken off their shirts in an energetic display of ribs and nipples and sparse clammy armpit hair. A one-minute silence was announced to mark the death of a former player. The drumming ceased. At the referee's whistle there was perfect stillness. The slightest involuntary sound was audible everywhere inside the stadium. A sneeze in the Kop. The quacking of a duck behind the Riverside Stand. Even, for those sitting closer to pitchside, the breeze shivering through the tinsel pom-poms of the eight child cheerleaders ranged around the center circle, whose metallic hot pants and crop tops flashed in the brilliant sunlight. When the referee blew his whistle again, the voice of the crowd rose to the sky like an explosion.

Wilko came onto the pitch to be presented, by Easter, with the League Two Manager of the Month for March award. With only five games left, Town were up to twentieth, and another victory would put them seven points clear of the relegation zone. On completing his duties, Easter circled awkwardly to applaud each stand and immediately left the ground, while Wilko returned to the dressing room, where he held aloft his dumpy little trophy and, to the surprise and evident distress of the players, dropped it into the bin.

When Wilko led the team out onto the pitch the goalkeeping coach waited behind until the room was empty, to retrieve the trophy from where it had nestled at the bottom of the bin among used bandages and energy drink bottles, and by the end of the day it would be situated on the manager's desk, between a photograph of his son and a similar award that he had won the previous season.

They won 3–1. Tom started the match and laid on the pass for Gundi's first goal. After his second a chant went up in the area around the bare-chested teenagers: "He's big, he's brown, he bangs them in for Town—Crocodile Gundi, Crocodile Gundi . . ." It came again, louder, more confidently, on his hat-trick, and had spread to the Kop and the main stand by the time the supporters began to troop away into the tight littered streets and temporary car parks around the stadium.

By Monday afternoon all evidence of the match was gone. The terraces were swept, the toilets scrubbed and power-hosed, lost phones and scarves and season-ticket wallets collected into a card-board box under the club secretary's desk. The banqueting suites, executive boxes, lounges, dressing rooms, referee's room, coaching offices, tunnels, were all cleared, vacuumed, sprayed, and at one side of the car park, piled against the skip by the ground-staff shed, seventy-four heavy-duty rubbish bags were twitching in the pleasant afternoon sunshine. Inside the unmanned control center at one end of the main stand, shifting CCTV images—the car park, the river footpath, the concrete bunker catering areas behind the terraces—showed no movement. Everywhere was quiet, unhurried. At rest.

Only in the match-day medical room, underneath the control center, was there any sign of life. On one of the two treatment beds, on top of which an elderly woman had lain with minor breathing difficulties for most of the second half against Gillingham, Tom was now sitting, his hands gripping the mattress, while the urgent bobbing head of Liam caused the wheels of the bed frame to yip and rattle below him.

Tom stayed on the bed as Liam undressed. The big rounded body was so unlike the bodies of the players—heavy and smooth, with wide raised shoulders and no trace of gym lines, no machined hardness. A goalkeeper's body. Tom watched him take off his socks, his underpants, and move into the shower room.

Tom took off his own clothes and stepped into the gray hissing cubicle. Water dripped from Liam's short thick fringe, from his nose, his ears. Tom moved to join him under the shower head. When the water began to run cold Tom turned it off, and the cubicle echoed only with the helpless ugly slapping of their bodies.

They dried off, dressed and returned the treatment room to order. Neither spoke; a building awareness of the locked door, the stairwell outside it, any passersby. They went over what they would say if anybody saw them together, prepared the fake note Tom would hand to Liam from Mr. Davey.

"You going to the gym?" Liam asked quietly, picking up the broom from beside the door.

"Yes. Won't stop long, though. There won't be many in."

"You'll be ripped soon, the way you're going."

Tom smiled back sarcastically, careful not to look camp. He spied through the keyhole into the empty stairwell, then signaled for Liam to begin sweeping the floor.

Outside no other people were visible. Tom walked along the touchline and through the fire door into the main stand.

The gym was empty. Very few of the players came in the day before a match. Although there was no need for him to stay, he decided to work out for a while. He peeled off his tracksuit top and stood in front of the mirror. His body was changing, his chest, his arms, noticeably bigger. His calves, when he flexed his ankles, two firm apples. He could feel it on the pitch, this change. Backing into the opposing fullback. Striking the ball. He stood sometimes now before this mirror or the one in his bedroom, marveling at the body in the glass. A body that he recognized as his own but not his own, one that belonged also to somebody else, belonged, two or three times a week now, to the shut-away room beneath the stand with its faded stiff sheets and its old medical smell.

He was lying on his bed watching football after one of his increasingly short phone conversations with his parents when there was a
knock on his door. It was unusual for anybody to come up to his
room, and for a few dazed seconds he thought that Liam was there.

It was Bobby.

"All right, Tom? Sorry yeah."

Tom was in tracksuit bottoms and no shirt. He noticed Bobby
look at his chest, then at the windowsill.

"They cactuses?"

"Desert cacti."

"You collect them?"

"Yes."

Bobby kept looking at the windowsill. One hand was bunching
repeatedly inside his pocket. "See, thing is, I'm after a favor if it's
all right."

"OK. What is it?"

"Can you lend me some money? Until next month just."

"How much?"

"Three hundred and fifty."

"Bloody hell."

Bobby was staring at him, his face all white attentiveness.

"It important?"

"I'd no ask otherwise."

"You need it all now?"

"If you can."

Tom wanted to ask what it was for but held back. "All right. I
can give it you the day after tomorrow, at training. Best not do it in
the house."

Bobby was at once full of boyish elation. "Spot-on, pal. You're
a mate. Thanks." He stepped forward to offer a handshake.

When Bobby had pounded back down the stairs Tom returned
to watching the match, thinking about what had just happened.
Both of the Scottish pair were on two hundred a week, which he
knew because of how often they complained about it in the back of

his car. Bobby was starting regularly for the first team now, although Tom doubted that his appearance bonus—if he was getting
one at all—was very much. Even for Tom, three hundred and fifty
was a considerable amount to lend, or would have been if his
spending amounted to more than fitful trips to the cinema and renewing the vodka bottle in his underwear drawer.

Bobby was still on a ten o'clock curfew. Tom was sure, nevertheless, that he had been out with some of the others after a couple of
games. He was becoming more a part of the squad than Tom was,
yet Tom still felt protective of him, of both boys. Outside the house
the pair had drifted towards different groups: Bobby to a small
band of first- and second-year pros, especially James Willis, a forward recently returned from two loan spells; Steven, who was rarely
selected for the first-team squad, to the scholars. The divergence
was most obvious on match days. Bobby would be restless by
breakfast time, especially before an away journey, during which he
would stay with his group, joking noisily and playing cards on the
coach. Steven, after the morning run-out with the other reserves,
stayed at home with the Daveys and would usually be watching
football or a film if he was still up when Bobby and Tom returned.

On the one occasion that Steven did train with the firsts for the
whole session, he struggled to keep up and compete. Near the end
of the session, his body visibly weakening, he attempted to head
clear from the edge of his penalty area and did not see Jones leaping to attack the same ball. Jones won the header, striking Steven
on the side of the head with his elbow as he went through him.
Steven shouted out and stayed down, floored. Play continued, and
as Foley kicked the ball upfield, Jones bent down to Steven and
clapped his hands twice above his face. "Get up. On your feet,
bitch." Tom, jogging past, noticed Bobby move towards Steven, but
when Jones came over and said something to him, Bobby turned
and ran off in the direction of play.

Hidden from the wind and showers and infrequent fits of sunshine during the closing weeks of the season, Tom and Liam con-

tinued to meet in the medical room. Since the evening in the pub they had seen each other nowhere else. Sometimes they simply lay together on the bed, holding each other. The first time this happened Tom had brooded afterwards that Liam might be losing interest in him, although he told himself that if they were normal people, able to go about in public, then there would be plenty of occasions when they would not be physical together—and it was during these times, together without the refuge of sex, that he felt most strongly the huge volatile weight of his desire, swamping, consuming him.

They had not spoken about the end of the season. About the end of Tom's contract and a summer in which, even if it was extended, there would be no reason for him to be at the stadium or in the town at all. If it was on Liam's mind as well, he was keeping it from Tom just as Tom was from him.

A family of ducks appeared one morning at the training ground. They announced themselves noisily, filing out of the bushes next to the pitch that the scholars were using, to congregate a short distance from the touchline as if intending to watch the session. Three of the ducklings made a break for the pitch. The youth team, and the firsts, who were assembled for a team talk not far away, all stopped to look at one of the scholars, a tiny lad with a closely shaved head, track and grab each bird in turn before carrying them, to a round of applause from both squads, in a precarious cradle back to the mother.

Beverley came up to Tom as they watched the ducks toddle away into the undergrowth.

"You off to the stadium after lunch?"

Tom hesitated. "I don't know. I might go home."

"I was thinking I'd do some gym. Go on, come with me. Let's drive over together."

Tom could see him in his rearview mirror all the way to the stadium, and he was unable to shake off a steadily building resentment at the small silhouetted head, singing behind him. He wondered if it would be possible to lose him—to push through a set of lights as they were turning red and speed away—but all the lights were green and Beverley stayed close behind him, and Tom knew that the afternoon was lost.

The disruption to his routine set him on edge, a feeling that only increased when he arrived at the stadium and saw Liam mounting the steps of the main stand with a shotgun. Beverley had spotted him too, and hurried down the touchline. When he got level with him he called up to Liam, "Fuck, mate, is that a gun?"

Liam turned, smiling. "Pigeons."

Beverley went up the gangway towards him. Liam did not appear to have noticed Tom.

"There's a load of them that roost up in the roof."

They looked up, then down at the fossilized waterfall of shit that clung to the back wall of the stand.

"We have to control them every month or so. Buggers keep coming back, though, here and the Kop. Pete takes them home and eats them or something." He gave a quick look to Tom, but his attention was on Beverley, clearly enjoying his fascination.

"Can I have a go?" Beverley asked.

Liam laughed. "I've seen your shooting, mate. You can watch, though."

Liam and Beverley went up the steps, squinting into the roof, where the scrambling movements of a pigeon could be seen above one of the rafters. Liam raised the shotgun. His Adam's apple coursed once, slowly, up and down. Beverley flashed a look of childish excitement at Tom. There came the violent report of the gun, then a rash of clangs as the pellets ricocheted inside the corrugated roof. Two pigeons took flight. Liam aimed again and fired—one instantly plummeted, dropping heavily onto the plastic seats. He spun and fired once more, but the second pigeon was away, disappearing over the pitch as the shot echoed through the stand.

Liam looked first at Beverley.

"That's mental," Beverley cried. "You allowed to do that?"

Liam shrugged. "We've borrowed a hawk before. That's something to see. Or if there's heavy rain and the river rises, all the rats get in the bottom of the Riverside Stand. We've shot bagfuls of them before, me and Pete." He continued looking at Beverley, then turned to peer again into the rafters. There was no movement that Tom could see, but Liam lifted the shotgun again, his body set perfectly still, his cheek hardening as his eye contracted, and he fired another shell.

As the echoes died, Beverley ran down the few steps to Tom, putting an arm around his shoulders. "Come on, man, let's work out. I'm fucking pumped."

Tom turned, not looking at Liam, and went with him.

Most of the players, regardless of the best efforts of the coaching staff, were already winding down. The dressing room was full of chat about summer holidays. Those players with partners or young children talked about spending time with them. Fleming, whose wife had given birth to their first child during the Morecambe victory, was moving back up north to be with them for the whole summer.

Those who were not contracted for next season, conversely, were playing and training with fresh intensity, with the result that the last couple of matches were played out to a manic tempo of torpor and frenzy that threw teammates, opposing players and referees alike. There were a couple of spats at the training ground. A scuffle, hugely exaggerated on Twitter according to Wilko in his program notes, broke out one short damp session during a seven-a-side non-contact game. It was increasingly clear which players were most likely to be let go. Three were now frequently asked to join the scholars: a couple of first-year pros who had never started and Febian Price, whom Wilko refused to pick even when Jones or Bobby were injured because his next start would trigger a clause that automatically extended his contract. They could usually be seen together, stretching, standing in a knot, eating together at one unhappy end of a canteen table. The bomb squad. Finch-Evans was soon to join their number. Wilko brought the players together after a warm-up and said that he wanted to do some set plays with small groups of attack and defense. He called out the names for each group. Finch-Evans was the only one left out.

"Finchy," he said, and everybody turned to look at the winger. "You've not had much game time of late, so you'll be better off getting some fitness work in over there."

The squad, and from the other pitch the little cluster of bombed-out players, watched him jog away across the field to where the scholars were listening to the youth coach organize a dead-ball routine.

Tom did not allow himself to dwell on the season ending, his contract expiring. He concentrated on his performances. The old determination to succeed had reentered him like a drug. He approached the team sheet with the expectation of finding his name there, an electric spurt running through him each time he saw that it was. He was able to busy his mind, just as he used to, by visualizing himself on the field, dominant, unstoppable, these fantasies sometimes blending with images of real moments in which he had impressed. His pass to Gundi for the first goal against Gillingham. A charge up the touchline in the same match, past one, two players, the groan of delight from the crowd, his foot in perfect control of the ball for fifty yards, keeping it never further than a few toes' distance from the white line.

He was sure there was new respect for him among his teammates. Especially the strikers, who knew that he could create chances for them. He had learned to anticipate Gundi's movement—where and when he would run into the box, which areas he wanted the ball delivered to. Gundi had developed a code for these deliveries known only to the two of them, which involved Gundi double-tapping on one or other of his formidable buttocks—right for a near-post cross, left for the far post—and it worked almost every time, simple as pressing a button.

But there was already talk of Gundi leaving. His agent had been in contact with three or four League One clubs—so Gundi said—and one in the Championship. The chairman made known to the media that he was going nowhere. Next season was about an historic promotion. The playing budget was going to be increased to two million. The Riverside Stand, to a design and time frame that he neglected to specify, was going to be demolished and rebuilt.

The final home encounter was televised because their opponents, Southend, were on the brink of going up. A crew arrived in the morning to erect a makeshift studio. They assembled it in one corner of the ground, above the disabled supporters' stall, ugly and functional as a shipping container. Town had climbed to eighteenth, and the players were told by Wilko and then by the chairman, making a surprise, inebriated appearance while they were coming out of the dressing room, that going into the summer with a win in front of the home crowd would be the perfect springboard for a promotion campaign next season.

Southend, however, charged into the game with a ferocity that the Town players were unready, or unwilling, to match. Steven and two other second-year scholars had been included in the starting lineup and were bamboozled by the onslaught. The noise of the Southend fans resonated about the stadium, largely because the chairman, keen not to pass up a financial opportunity, had in addition to the usual terrace given over several sections of the Riverside Stand to the away support, which had the effect of confusing one of the television pundits into believing, for most of the first half until a producer informed him otherwise, that he was in Southend.

Tom, despite the 4–1 defeat, put in a decent performance. His dad called afterwards to tell him that he was one of the few, along with Gundi and Beverley, to put up any kind of a fight. He was proud of him, his dad said. Tom's jaw tightened as he listened. He had turned his season round. You needed character to do that. Character and guts.

He lay on the bed. Liam's back was against his chest, their bodies pulsing together with the rise and fall of their breath. There were several dark orange moles on Liam's neck, standing from his skin like tiny nascent toadstools.

"Can I ask something?" Liam said.

"Nope."

But a few seconds later: "I'm wondering when we talk about next week."

"Next week, I suppose."

There was a pause. "Right. I get you. One match at a time, is it?"

"That's right."

On the afternoon before the concluding fixture Tom left the medical room and walked across to the car park. He got into his car and put on his seatbelt. He stared at the door of the medical room, incapable of starting the engine, driving away. After a couple of minutes the door opened, and Liam appeared. At the sight of the stooping figure brushing out the doorway, the unspoken faithfulness to their strategy, Tom's stomach hollowed. He got out of the car and stood beside it. Liam was immediately aware of him. He looked up, straight at Tom, who stayed where he was. Liam checked left and right, then rested the broom against a wall and came towards him.

They stood together by the open car door. For a few exhilarating seconds Tom thought that they were going to kiss. There was a noise. They both turned to see the fire exit door to the main stand shutting and Boyn and Daish advancing towards the car park. They stepped apart. Boyn and Daish looked over at them, then angled away towards their cars.

"I'll text you," Liam said and walked away.

Air was hammering in Tom's ears. He got into his car and sat, watching Boyn and Daish out of the corner of his eye. He tried to control the panic, still high in his chest, knowing that they had almost been discovered. The two players were talking to each other over their car roofs. They turned at the same time to look in the direction of Tom's car, then, in unison, they got into their vehicles and drove off.

18

The season closed with a 0–0 draw at Hereford. Hereford, who had needed to win to have any chance of staying up, were relegated. The somber atmosphere in the stadium and the tunnel when they left the pitch was uncomfortable, and the Town squad showered and changed quietly, conscious the whole time of the private sorrow on the other side of the wall. They ate their sandwiches, tidied, without instruction, the mud and paper plates from their bench spaces and left.

The second-year scholars' futures were dealt with two days later. Tom gave Bobby and Steven a lift to the stadium and told them he would take them back to the Daveys' once they had been informed. He sat in the main stand while the meetings took place. He remembered well what it was like, this day. He did not want to think about it. He surveyed the pitch instead, the avenues of battered turf along each wing, imagining them lush and smooth again, the roll of the ball on young grass. His attention, though, was drawn constantly to one side of the pitch, the door under the control center, and to thoughts about his own contract outcome.

After forty-five minutes he got up and made his way to the players' lounge. He knew right away, when he entered the room and one or two of the boys looked up at him, that the last thing they wanted at that moment was for one of the seniors to be there. It appeared that they had all been done already. Boys sat alone in all corners of the lounge. A few had their faces lowered to the floor; one was fixed on a piece of paper that looked like a certificate. Some turned away from him. Two that Tom recognized as the central defenders sat close together on a sofa, staring out of the window at the pitch. Tom dithered, wanting to say something to them but knowing that he could not. He went out of the room. Further down the corridor the small lad with the shaved scalp was sitting on the floor with his back against the wall and his head between his knees. It was like the scene of a disaster. He should not have come in here, intruding on their humiliation; he should have stayed in the car. Bobby and Steven, though, were not about, which he knew was probably a good sign.

Wilko was leaving his office, coming towards him. Tom slowed, ready to say hello, but Wilko continued past without acknowledging him. Doubts began niggling at Tom before he was even out of the stadium—that the manager had ignored him on purpose, that it had something to do with his own meeting next week.

Bobby and Steven were waiting next to the car. Tom walked up, unlocking the doors, and without a word the two boys climbed into the back. Tom got behind the wheel and they set off, but before the car park exit he slowed down and stopped. He turned to face them.

"You two OK?"

"He got a deal," Steven said straightaway. "Him and Spence. No one else." He looked out of the window, even whiter, Tom thought, than normal.

Bobby was unsure where, or how, to look, and was gazing into his crotch. "One year," he said, lifting his face up, "option of a second in the club's favor."

Tom could see that beneath the studied quietness he was bursting to talk about it.

"Well done," Tom said. And then to Steven, "Doesn't mean you're a bad player, you know. Plenty of other clubs out there."

He was aware, turning back round to drive them home, just how inadequate these words were. *You're going to be some player,* he might as well have added, *when you grow into yourself.* It had not felt like it at the time, but he had been fortunate ending up at Town.

Those eight boys had nowhere to drop to except for the sprawling expanse of the semipro, the amateur, the Sunday pitches, armed with a sports science BTEC and the realization that their dream was over. Three of the scholars that Tom had played with, he knew from his dad, had gone into the lower divisions of foreign leagues: Sweden, Denmark, Hong Kong. It was possible that one or two of the Town boys would try the same route and maybe even find their feet abroad, although his dad had told him more recently that only one of Tom's academy team was still out there—in the Hong Kong second tier—the others already returned, disillusioned, homesick.

Halfway into the journey, passing the leisure center, Steven put one freckled hand up to the side of his face. His chest was quivering in little shuddery movements. Tom turned up the radio. He wanted desperately to stop the car and get out to put an arm around him, to hold him and tell him that everything would work out, an impulse which as soon as he had it made him cling, sick and fearful, to the steering wheel even harder.

Steven went back to Scotland the next day. After his short and subdued final dinner Tom had gone down to the toilet and heard the muted comforting efforts of both Mr. and Mrs. Davey coming from the ground floor. How many times, he wondered, must they have been through this over the years? They were kind people, patient, understanding. They would be the same with him, he knew, if he ended up in Steven's position. And he thought then about the secret, through all these seasons of guidance and gentle consolation, which, Tom presumed, had been kept from them. Although that was another thing that had never come up between him and Liam—that had been tacitly left, like Tom's contract decision, unvoiced.

The day after Steven left the house so did Bobby, with a hangover, promising to return Tom's loan on the first day of preseason. Tom let it go; he did not want to discuss with Bobby the possibility that he might not be offered terms for next season. Bobby had been told that his digs would be held for him for another year if he wanted them but that he could look for his own place if he preferred. He went up to Scotland for the summer to think about it.

If Tom was awarded a new deal he would not, as a second-year pro, be coming back to the Daveys'. He set off an hour or so after Bobby with all of his belongings. The earnest faces and farewells of the Daveys stayed with him as he drove away into the sour humid afternoon. He was not looking forward to going home. The prospect of lying to his parents, his sister, for the five days before he had to drive back for his face-to-face with Wilko occupied him all the way up the motorway.

For the first couple of days his parents were incessantly around—followed him about the house, it felt to him at times—but he tried to put on a show of good humor. He became tense with the effort of it, counting the morning minutes before they left for work, Rachel for school.

He did not speak to Liam, but a string of text messages, short, neutral, often about the play-offs or the Town pitch, built up between them each day until his family returned home, and he would tell them about his jog, or say that he had been into the city to catch up with a friend, even though the idea of meeting anybody that he knew from home was unthinkable. He spent the afternoons watching television or on long runs with his music turned up to block out the recurring thought of Tuesday's meeting. After tea and often-curious looks from his sister across the table, then more television, he went up to his room and played on his Xbox as the exchange of text messages started up again. Each night before he went to sleep he deleted everything in his sent and received folders. He watched the messages tumbling away with a racing sensation that was like falling from a tall building.

One evening he came downstairs to fetch his top from the living room and overheard his parents talking in the kitchen. They were clearing up, his mum washing the plates and cutlery, his dad drying.

"He'll sort himself out," his mum was saying as Tom sat down on the sofa and observed them through the two doorways.

"I know. I know." His dad moved out of view briefly, putting away a plate, then came back to the drying rack, the pair of them quietly carrying on with clearing up. When the sink was empty of dishes and his mum let out the water she remained where she was, looking out of the window at the garden, her gloved hands resting on the sink top. Tom watched his dad move close beside her. She turned round, pulling off the gloves and setting them down. His dad placed both of his hands on her shoulders and they looked at each other for a moment in silence.

His dad smiled. "You look knackered, Liz. You're working too hard."

His mum shrugged and his dad's arms shifted slightly up and down. "No one else to run this new clinic. And we could do with the hours."

His dad's face moved towards hers and Tom looked away. When he glanced back his dad's arms were around her. For a few seconds their foreheads touched, then came apart. Tom stood up. Stealthily he left the room and climbed the stairs, a strange undertow of shame staying with him at having witnessed this private moment of tenderness.

His parents sensed his withdrawal from them. His mum was the first to bring it up, in the front doorway as Tom was coming back inside from taking the rubbish out.

"It's a horrible time, this waiting," she said. "You don't have to keep it all to yourself, though, love."

"I know." He gave her a smile as he came past. "Perils of not having a proper job, Mum," he said chirpily. "It'll sort itself out."

Then his sister. He left the door to his room ajar one day after coming up from tea and she came straight in without knocking.

"Fuckhead. Talk to me."

"About what?"

"About why you're being a fuckhead."

She was peering inquisitively about his room. "I'm not."

She glared at him, arching her eyebrows.

"You don't know what it's like," Tom said.

"No, I don't. I really don't. You could be a bit nicer with Mum and Dad, though. And Dad says you've been getting starts," she continued softly. "He says you've been playing well, and he should know because he checks out all the match reports every week. That means they'll want to keep you, doesn't it? Might offer you more money, even."

"Maybe. It's football, though. It's not like the real world."

She sat down next to him on the bed. "Somebody will, surely. Even if it's not them. Maybe some club up this way will want you and you can move back up north."

She put a hand on his knee and he flinched; she moved it away.

"There's plenty of lads who would kill to get where you have, you know. I bumped into Sammy D not long ago—I didn't tell you. He's got nothing. No qualifications, no direction, nothing. He'd been put on this workfare thing—he's been working at Homebase for six months for no pay and now it's finished all he does is go to the gym. He's bloody massive. At least you're still playing. Wherever you end up. And remember, in the real world what you earn is shitloads."

He looked at her. "How do you know how much I earn?"

"Oh, you know. The Internet."

On Sunday, the weather decent, the four of them went for a pub lunch a short drive away. Tom worked hard to put on a sociable front. They chatted—about Rachel's university offers, about Internet shopping—and he could see how pleased his parents were that he was not behaving strangely. He was becoming more adept at acting like himself. Splitting himself into two people: one that could be normal, a footballer, the other kept apart.

That night Liam texted to ask if they could talk. Tom called him in the morning from the park after going out for a run.

"I had a thought," Liam said.

"Go on."

"What time is it tomorrow, your meeting?"

"Eleven o'clock. I'm driving down this afternoon."

"And then what, are you going back up north after?"

"I don't know. Mr. and Mrs. Davey said I can stay with them if I want. But I've not thought about it." Whenever he spoke to Liam about them, which he tried not to do, he never referred to them as "your parents."

"The thing is, I've got leave from Wednesday. I can't get started on the pitch renovation because they're flogging all this Pro for a Day bollocks for another two weeks."

A jogger was advancing up the path beside Tom, checking her stopwatch.

"I thought maybe we could go away together," Liam said.

Tom waited for the jogger to go past. "What do you mean?"

"I don't know. Go somewhere for a few days."

"Where?"

"Somewhere further than the Beefeater."

He wanted to carry on running but the blood in his legs had turned thick. "I don't think that's . . . I don't think we can do that."

"Can you think about it? When the meeting's out of the way. We can just wait until it's out of the way."

"I want to roll you on for another season," Wilko said. "Same terms. Then we'll see where we are this time next year." Tom watched his agent write this down on a notepad. The air inside the office was rushing around his ears. "You've done well—I'll just say my bit if I can, please, before either of you chip in. You've done reasonably well. You've pushed on physically, and that's important at your age. You've pushed on mentally. Now we need to see you push on again, consistently, because next season is a big one for us and I don't want any passengers."

His agent took all of it down. One of his heels tapped on the floor. Inflamed skin gaped between the bottoms of his trousers and his Family Guy socks. On the folded-over page of his notepad Tom recognized the name of another player underlined amid the scrawl.

"Couple of points," his agent said. "One is terms; the other, are you bringing in anyone else in his position?"

"I'm looking to strengthen in that area, yes. I'm looking to strengthen in all areas. I can't guarantee anybody a place, but what I'm wanting from Tommy is for him to carry on where he left off— give me no choice but to pick him. The shirt's his to lose."

Twenty minutes later Tom had been offered a rise of two hundred pounds on his weekly wage, his win and goal bonuses unchanged but his appearance bonus to increase to a hundred and fifty. He had thirty days from receiving the offer in writing to respond. They would be in touch, his agent told Wilko, and Tom followed him out of the room.

Richards and Hoyle were in the car park. When his agent went off to talk on his phone, Tom walked over to chat with them. He could tell at once that something was amiss. Hoyle turned away as Tom approached, and Richards turned with him, speaking quietly into his ear, rubbing one hand over his back. Tom was too near now to steer away without it being obvious. "You two all right?" he said when he got to them.

"Yeah," Richards said. "I'm just telling him that he's a quality fucking keeper. Couple of seasons and he'll be playing at a higher level than any of us."

"For sure." Tom said. "You're a great keeper."

Hoyle, still facing the other way, muttered something that Tom could not make out.

"It'll work out for the best," Richards said to him. "Serious. You need to be playing first-team football now, this stage of your career."

Hoyle turned. He did not appear to be crying, as Tom had presumed. "Who for, Ash? The Dog and Duck?"

"Steady, mate. Don't get too far ahead of yourself."

Hoyle gave a phlegmy laugh, then lunged forward to hug Richards. Tom looked away until they released each other.

"What about you, Tommy?" Hoyle asked. "You get a contract?"

"One year."

"Good for you. You deserve it. Not like this jammy fucker. He got two years, if you can believe what he says."

They spoke about the players who had come in the day before—Finch-Evans, Price, Yates—all of whom, as Tom already knew from the message boards, had been released. He heard his name being shouted. His agent had finished his phone conversation and was signaling him over. "Best be off, boys," Tom said, hoping to avoid saying goodbye to Hoyle. He spun round with a quick salute to them both and made away across the car park to his agent.

They drove in their own cars to a pub on the outskirts of town to discuss the contract offer over a swift greasy lunch.

"We take it, yes? Or you want me to push for more? I'll be honest. It's a fair offer. You should take it." He went back to his fish and chips. Tom did not know if he was expecting an answer. At that moment it felt a very long time since the afternoon of the FA Youth Cup semifinal, when a posse of agents had been waiting for him in the car park by his dad's old Honda.

"I want to take it."

"Good. I'll straighten it out." He looked up, sucking in a chip. The tip of his nose was pink and peeling. "You need them to help you find a flat?"

Tom took a drink of his Coke. He had not allowed himself to think about that, about any of it, until now. "No. I'd rather do it myself."

He called Liam from the pub car park when his agent left.

"That's good news," Liam said.

Tom shifted the phone from his mouth, not wanting to give any indication that he was hurt by the unexcited reply.

"Have you accepted it yet?"

"It doesn't work like that. I've got a month to respond. My agent's on it."

"But you're going to?"

Tom paused a moment. "Yes." There was another moment of silence. "I'm up for the holiday."

"Yes? Any thoughts where?"

He was tempted to say, as a joke, nowhere gay, but he resisted. "I'm not fussed."

"Right. Leave it with me. I'll think of some options."

He decided against staying and drove straight home. That evening his mum cooked baked chicken burritos, the meal that for some reason had become acknowledged in the house to be his favorite. His family were overjoyed. They wanted to get Kenny round. His dad, getting more and more drunk, kept smiling over at Tom or clapping him on the shoulder.

For the rest of the week he affected to join in with the convivial atmosphere of the house, suffering their good humor, waiting for each night when he could go upstairs and be released to the solitude of his room.

19

They flew, separately, to Portugal. Tom had been abroad half a dozen times before, either with the England Unders or with his family to Spain, as well as one long wet trip to Rotterdam, when he and his sister had been at each other's throats the whole holiday. But now he sat looking out of the window as if on a plane for the first time. He felt a jittery excitement at the hills and forests and endless yellowed fields appearing beneath drifts of vapor, the outlines of towns and villages, traffic streaming in and out like ant trails. Halfway through the flight there was a short but intense spell of turbulence. The flight staff took to their seats near the toilets. The quiet old couple beside Tom joined hands on top of their shared armrest. Tom gripped tightly to both of his own, fixing his sight on the flaming ocean below, the flesh of his body already tearing open, defenseless.

Liam was waiting for him in the arrivals hall. He appeared out of the milling crowd in shorts and a T-shirt, his shins somehow already a deep pink. They greeted each other with a firm hand clasp that lasted a few seconds, a midair arm wrestle.

"Decent flight?" Liam asked.

"Mostly. Yours?"

"Good, yes. Easy. On time."

"It was hot as soon as I got out of the plane," Tom said.

"I know. Early heatwave, apparently."

They smiled at each other, recognizing, despite everything, the reassuring pull of the conventional.

"I've picked up the car," Liam said.

It was on the far side of the car park, outside the baking concrete hutch of the hire company.

"I didn't bring the paper bit of my license," Tom said when they reached the car. "Didn't even think, sorry."

"Don't worry, I'm all right doing it. Probably won't do much driving anyway. Depends what the resort's like."

Liam maneuvered out onto the road. Palm trees. Car horns. Peeling, sun-bleached advertisement billboards. The vents injected a gush of hot air into the car. He would not let himself be led through the holiday, Tom resolved. He would pay for drinks and meals, speak to foreign waiters, not shy away from tipping. The thought of Liam doing it all, expecting to, revolted him.

Their apartment was one of twenty arranged around a small pool and a rock garden. Under the cool relief of a ceiling fan they looked the rooms over, constantly watchful of each other. They took off their shoes and socks, and the white-tiled floor was deliciously cold underfoot. There was one main room with a bed, table and chairs and tiny kitchenette, a wet room with a shower and toilet, and a narrow low-walled veranda set at the back of the apartment to screen it from the others. They got glasses of water and moved out onto it. Orchards and scrub sloped gently down in front of them. A mile or so away were the brightly colored rooftops and apartment towers of the town. Beyond, steep wooded hills sheltered a lagoon, the hills speckled with whitewashed houses and the concrete and steel frameworks of half-built or abandoned buildings. In the distance, further out past the lagoon, was the hot sea, shining in the afternoon sun like the skin of a fish.

"What did you tell your family?" Liam asked when they had sat down on the scalding plastic chairs.

"That I'm in Portugal with a few of the squad."

Liam nodded.

Tom waited a moment, then said, "You?"

"Same, pretty much. Except Mum and Dad know most of my friends. I told them I'm with some of the people I met on my groundskeeping course. I'm not actually much in contact with them these days, Facebook a bit, but they can be useful for something to tell Mum and Dad."

They were both sweating. Liam rolled his glass across his forehead, and Tom studied his face for any sign that the hint at his sexual past was deliberate. Tom got up and went inside to refill his glass. Moments later Liam came into the kitchenette and stood behind him. He passed Tom his own glass to fill and their arms brushed against each other, but Liam took his drink and moved away to begin unpacking his bag. Tom went to do the same. For the next few minutes they arranged their things: toiletries, sun creams, insect repellents, unnecessary phone chargers, shorts, T-shirts and swimming shorts, their combined belongings tidily stacked and shelved independently as if they were roommates. Liam finished and went to the toilet. While he was in there Tom changed out of his jeans into a pair of shorts, unaccountably self-conscious.

They went for a stroll around the apartment complex. Birds sang from the bushes. A man was watering a bed of scorched flowers. Around the pool three English girls lay out on sunloungers pulled close to the edge, their feet dangling in the water. The afternoon was still hot. They walked for a quarter of an hour along a shadeless road into the town. When they got there it was pleasantly bustling. Cafes and bars fringed a narrow cobbled street, and there was a row of stalls displaying wooden trinkets and jewelry and decorative paper fans. A fish market at the beginning of a wide promenade of restaurants that smoked the air with grilling sardines and shellfish, leading to a long curving beach.

They had not brought towels, so they settled down on the hot sand next to a roped-off sunlounger concession. Tired from the heat, they sat quietly, looking out at the lagoon, absorbing the hum of the people around them. There was the lulling *tock-tock* sound of a bat and ball game at the water's edge. Liam was watching. Tom felt weak with a need to touch him. He did not understand why Liam had not yet come close to him. Tom stood up and told him he was going to get some drinks from a stand a short way down the beach.

He bought them each a bottle of Coke, pleased with how he handled the exchange with the vendor. On the way back he noticed two men sitting on the same towel. One was whispering into the other's ear, stroking his back. Tom hurried past. He returned to Liam and passed him a Coke, wondering if he too had seen the men, if he would have been perturbed by them if he had.

The sun descended towards a hill on one side of the lagoon, and the afternoon began to cool. They walked to a beachside bar and sat at a table on the sand for a beer. They talked about close-season transfer dealings, first Town's, then more generally, and had a second beer as the conversation turned to the upcoming European Championship, until the sun disappeared completely behind the hill and the temperature fell sharply.

On the walk back, Liam took Tom's hand. Tom squeezed it in response. At the approach of a shambling dirty truck they let go and moved onto the verge, and when it had passed Tom turned to kiss Liam, his body closing against him and neither of them pulling away at the loud, foreign honking of another passing vehicle.

Once inside the apartment they did not hesitate much further than the door. Their clothes fell to the tiles with little showers of sand, and Tom was fired with an awareness that nobody was on the other side of the door. Nobody even knew that they were there. Liam's hands were on his back, the pressure by degrees easing, drawing down his vertebrae, his tailbone. A few weeks ago, in the medical room, he had thought that he wanted this but at the last moment had not been ready, turning over and pulling Liam down onto the mattress. Now, though, he closed his eyes against the cool new sheets and heard Liam's breathing quicken, his lips touching the back of Tom's neck, whispering something imperceptible beneath the wild ringing of the crickets outside the apartment walls.

Tom gave a small cry of pain. Liam kept his hands around Tom's waist, slowing but not stopping, and gradually Tom let himself go, the unnatural sensation, heightened by the new sounds from Liam, convulsing through his body with an acute terrible pleasure that was almost unbearable.

The long bright days that followed belonged to a different life. The car remained under the palm trees by the entrance to the complex, untouched. They moved back and forth between the apartment and the beach, staying at one or the other for long, untroubled spells, not caring or noticing that dusk had fallen and they had slept through an afternoon. They would emerge from the apartment ravenous and devour a tableful of dishes at one of the colorful cheap restaurants along the beach or in the cobbled main street. They got drunk—Liam, to Tom's surprise, became drunk almost as quickly as he did—and stumbled, laughing, onto the sand to walk beside the lapping water.

In these moments, at night, on the beach, when few people were about, Tom was not uncomfortable with them touching or kissing. In the apartment he was becoming unreservedly intimate with Liam, but he was still uneasy at the idea of other people, even strangers, seeing them like that together. Liam teased him about it, sometimes pretending to attempt a kiss while they sunbathed on the beach. One evening while they were walking through the town he playfully called Tom a queer, and Tom fell into a silence that was only broken an hour later by Liam apologizing on the veranda and promising not to say it again. It did not help that they were made conspicuous by their, and especially Liam's, fierce red patches of sunburn. Or that there were several blatantly gay couples around the resort. Quite often they passed the two men that Tom had seen that first day on the beach. He made sure each time to move a small distance apart from Liam, wary of the possibility that the pair might acknowledge them in some way. He noticed two other couples, as well as a group of five Germans whom he presumed to be gay from the way they play-fought and posed endlessly for photos on the beach, although he wondered if that might just be what Germans were like, and he did not discount either the fact that they could be footballers.

One night near the end of the week, drinking cocktails in celebration of Tom's birthday on a low hammock seat outside a beach
bar, Tom asked Liam why he had chosen this resort.

Liam shrugged. "Don't know. Just what it said on TripAdvisor.
Cheap, good weather, chilled out."

"You researched it then?"

"Course I did. You didn't bloody do anything, did you?"

"Were there other places you looked at?"

Liam gave him a skeptical look. "Mate, this isn't a gay resort, if
that's what you're thinking."

"I wouldn't know. I've never been to one."

"You think I have?"

Tom sipped his cocktail. "I don't know."

Liam laughed. "Well, you'll be glad to know that I haven't. I did
find out that this place was 'tolerant,' or 'gay friendly,' or whatever
bollocks it said on the Internet. And I thought that would be about
right because I knew you wouldn't have wanted a more full-on
place. Me neither. They look proper dodgy."

"You looked into it?"

"Not for long."

They drank another cocktail. The group of English girls from
the apartment complex passed on the beach and waved hello. Tom,
tipsy now, pushed at the sand with his foot to swing the hammock.
"So, you've not been anywhere like this before?" he said.

"Like what—here?"

"Yes."

"I've been to Portugal before. We came when I was about thirteen. With my sister, I think. Andrew had moved out."

"No, I mean, with anyone else."

Liam smirked at him. "A man, you mean?"

Tom did not say anything.

"No, I haven't."

They were quiet for a long while, watching the dark shapes of
the fishing boats moored in the lagoon.

"You gone out with anyone before?" Tom said.

"Yes. Not many." He checked to see if that was as much as Tom wanted but gathered from his attention that he needed to hear more. "My first relationship was with a girl I went out with when I was eighteen. Lisa. I thought I was in love. I thought I was going to marry her. But then there was this thing—didn't go anywhere—with a boy after a youth tournament. That was a bit before I split up with Lisa. Why I split up with Lisa."

He looked across. Tom's face, although his heart was beating hard, showed nothing.

"Then it was all just confusing for a long time. I didn't know what was going on with me. If I'm honest, that's probably why I didn't try getting a trial anywhere else when Town released me. It's hard enough anyway. You're on the scrap heap. And then you think, right, if I'm . . . if that's what I am, then why am I going to put myself through a load of shit just to get a trial at some Isthmian League back-end-of-nowhere place?" He gave Tom a look that suggested he thought Tom might say something, but Tom kept quiet. "Anyway, about a year and a half after I left the club, I met this guy, Dan."

He stopped to drink the last of his cocktail and did not pick up the story, staring off instead through the palm trees to the looming mass of cliffs at one side of the lagoon. A band the color of rare meat covered his neck, although the white edge of his still strangely unburned chest was just visible above his shirt.

"Who was he?"

"Dan? Went out with him, on and off, about six months. He was in the year above me at school, but we didn't know each other then. We met at a party. Facebooked for a while afterwards, and then he said we should meet up. I didn't even know he was gay at first. It was difficult when we did start seeing each other. He was at university up in Lancaster, so we only saw each other when it wasn't term time. All his friends up there knew he was gay but nobody at home knew, and nobody knew I was either, so we'd meet up in secret. I think in the end the choice between having to hide or being somewhere he could be himself, plus the long-distance thing . . . Well, not much of a choice, to be fair."

He gave a short laugh and then he turned to Tom, his eyes clear and bright in his red face. "So, there you are, my life history. That enough of an answer for you?"

Tom tried not to let the thought of Dan bother him. The story, however, kept playing on his mind. A contrived image of Dan grew quickly into a presence that left the bar with them, walked alongside them on the road back to the apartment. Tom hungered for more details. Dates. Whether it had ended definitively or if there had been later, more occasional, meetings. If they were still in contact now. He knew that he could not seek any of this from Liam, though. While they returned, Liam asked him about his own past relationships. There wasn't much to tell, Tom said. A girlfriend, Jenni, a long time ago, who had moved away after school and married a military policeman. Nothing since. Part of him longed to tell Liam about Craig, but another, more careful part of him would not allow it. A vague guilt came over him at concealing Craig after Liam had shared his own past with him, but he was not prepared to let Liam compare some ancient episode with a boy and what was happening now.

Later, drunk, standing on the veranda looking out at the enormous black sky, Tom let Liam undress him then lead him through the doorway and guide him onto the bed. He waited for the sound of Liam's shorts buttons but Liam continued working his hands down the grooves of his back, over his buttocks, kneading, circling delicately with his fingertips, then with the increased sliding pressure of one unrelenting finger until an abrupt thick tide radiated deep inside him.

Liam sat next to him on the bed, still dressed.

"You didn't know about that, did you?"

Tom could only shake his head. "Do you wan—?"

"No, it's OK," Liam cut him off. "I need to sleep. I'm wasted."

In the morning Tom woke to find the other side of the bed empty. The door of the apartment was open, a square of sunlight on the floor. There was loud birdsong, as if the birds were inside. And then they were—two small hopping creatures pecking at the tiles of the kitchenette for a few seconds before spotting Tom and flying out. He lay on the bed for a while, waiting for them to return, then put on his shorts and went outside.

He found Liam at the pool, talking to the English girls. He was standing in front of their sunloungers. They were laughing as though at something he had said.

"Tom." Liam smiled over.

Tom hung back, staying by the corner of the pool. "Hi."

"Apparently this lot got hit on last night by some middle-aged American golfers."

"Canadian," one of the girls said, and the other two giggled.

They were all looking at him.

"Bloody hell," he said.

"You guys should come out with us tonight," one of them said from beneath her wide straw hat. The others chimed their agreement.

"You could protect us," another said, and they all laughed.

Tom could not tell whether they knew that he and Liam were together. But then Liam came round the pool and put his arm about his waist. They did not look surprised.

"What do you think?" Liam said. "Sounds fun."

"Yeah, it does." They were all watching him again, half-smiling. "We'll maybe see you out and about then." He turned to Liam. "Come on, let's get breakfast. We'll leave you to it. Enjoy the pool."

Liam was quiet as they walked up the path back to the apartment. They nodded hello to the gardener, the expecting Dutch couple, the ageless friendly owner, who waved back at them, crouched behind her huge panting dog. They all knew, Tom was convinced. Had heard them, probably.

"Don't you want to do that tonight?" Liam asked when they were inside, packing a bag for the beach.

"Yes, if you do."

"That was a bit rude, back there."

"Wasn't meant to be. I'm up for it if you are."

He was not in the least bit up for it. He had been instantly hurt, standing by the pool, that Liam was so keen to spend their final night with these girls. He fell into a brooding detachment while they went to the beach and lay out in the heat, indulging the feeling, finding a wounded pleasure in it. Doubtful thoughts took hold of him: that Liam had grown bored with his constant company; that he was staring at a man with a tattooed neck near the beach showers.

These notions were intensified by Liam's own silence, and Tom could not relax. He went for a long dip in the sea, becoming aware, as he swam against the powerful tugging water, that he had lost condition since the end of the season. He vowed to get started on building his fitness as soon as he returned home, and at once the inevitability of leaving this place pulled him down like a weight. He swam forcefully out into the lagoon, quickly becoming out of breath, sucking for air on each stroke but making his body continue to work, sensing the buried cords of muscle in his legs and buttocks, and the thought of playing football again, as if rising from the darkness below, impelled him onwards, out into the ocean. When eventually he stopped, treading water to catch his breath, the anticipation of playing, the determination to prove himself, was still there. And, when he started back for the beach, a spontaneous resentment too, towards Liam, for the disordering of how that part of his life could be.

He neared the shore, his knees brushing against the seabed. He climbed out of the water, wanting Liam to notice him, to watch him walking back over the sand. Liam, though, was reading his book. Tom sat down beside him. He rested his dripping body against Liam's side and got his own book out. He did not want to bring up the subject of that evening. He could imagine, if they did go out, how it would be. The girls assigning them the role of their gay companions, flirting, expecting them to be funny, wanting to dance. They would want to know all about them, and they would have to lie. A cover story would have to be prepared in advance. He pictured again the scene by the pool that morning and felt a reflex of anger at Liam for playing up to the stereotype.

They left the beach to go for what ended up being a long, tiring walk around the lagoon to the top of a hill, where they sat exhausted in a bar to share a bowl of little fried fish. While they ate, Liam, out of nowhere, said, "Have you told anybody about us?"

Tom was startled. "No. What, have you?"

"Yes."

Tom stared at him, instantly petrified.

"The friend I told you about. Leah."

"You've told her my name?"

"No. And don't worry. She's an old friend."

"She's Easter's wife."

"That doesn't mean she'd tell him."

They carried on eating. A crowd of dead fish eyes ogled him from inside their crunchy caskets.

"I wondered if you might have told your sister," Liam said.

"No."

"Leah's the only person I've told, you know. She couldn't believe it. I've never told anybody before." When Tom did not respond, he continued: "I've thought about it, but then every time I've known I just can't. Never seemed worth the risk of other people finding out. Not like I work in a hairdresser's, is it? There's my dad, for one thing. His position at the club. Not to mention my position. And don't even think about what would happen if the club found out I'm shagging one of their players. Can you imagine?"

Tom dipped a fish in mayonnaise.

"You should meet her," Liam said, animated. "You'd like her, I know you would."

Tom looked out at the lagoon. In the distance a huge white ship proceeded through the ocean. He had suspected this ever since he saw them together at the furniture store, but nonetheless hearing Liam say it had turned him cold with dread. Swelling beneath that too was the feeling that he had been betrayed, that Liam had put them at risk.

He tried to hide it from Liam, but he was unable to stop his foreboding and, as well, the sense that something vital had been lost. That it was no longer just the two of them; that whatever was going to happen between them when they left this place, somebody else would know. "I'm going for a lie-down," Liam said when they returned to the apartment. "I'm done in."

Tom went out onto the veranda. He sat, weary with the heat, watching a lizard—perfectly still on top of the wall—monitor a fly. He tried to keep his mind from Leah but could not. Even though he knew it was natural that Liam would eventually tell a friend, the fact that he had done so was shocking, disorienting. He told himself repeatedly that it was fair enough, it was normal, wanting to brace himself against the possibility that anything could come between them or mar the time they had spent together here, pissed off with himself for his earlier petulance, which had wasted most of their final day.

A slow wheezing was coming from the bedroom. He got up, causing the fly to drone away, though the lizard remained steadfast on the wall as Tom came past, through the doorway, to lie down next to Liam on the bed. Liam's neck, his sideburns, were damp. As they lay there, faces close together, Liam began to snore. Tom moved his body up against Liam's, letting his eyes close.

When he woke, Liam's arm was around him, although he seemed still to be asleep. Tom placed a hand on Liam's head. He stroked the hair above the ear with his thumb, revealing the ghostly white skin beneath. Liam came to, grunted, shut his eyes again.

"I do want to go out tonight," Tom said.

"Huh?"

"With those girls. I think we should meet up with them."

"You sure?"

"Yes."

They walked together through the complex. The evening was still hot. Children's voices, the sound of splashing, came from the pool. A barbecue had been lit on the Dutch couple's veranda, and the smell of cooking meat carried on the air. Liam apparently knew which was the girls' apartment. He walked up the path towards their door while Tom hung back, surprised at his assuredness, won-

dering whether maybe there had been some other interaction between Liam and the girls that he had not known about. The door
opened, and a girl with short dark hair was saying hello to Liam.
She had a towel wrapped around her. As she spoke to him in the
doorway another one approached, smiling, in only a skirt and a
bra—confirmation, Tom thought, that they did know he and Liam
were a couple. Liam was turning to come back down the path.

"We're going to meet them in a bar," he said, putting his hands
on Tom's shoulders and leaning in to kiss him on the mouth in full
view of the Dutch couple on their veranda.

They sat at a table outside the bar, on the cobbles. Across the
street, vendors were packing up their stalls. An African man knelt
before a suitcase, carefully placing into downy slots the artifacts
that a woman passed down to him.

"Last night, then," Liam said. "Cheers."

They knocked their beer bottles together. Tom waited for him
to say more about the holiday, about their return home, but nothing came. They watched the stalls coming down. Holidaymakers
were going up the street and into the bars and restaurants, some of
them still in swimwear, only now leaving the beach.

They were on their second beer when they saw the girls walking
down the street towards them. Tom watched their approach, ready
to take his cue from Liam, but upon their arrival Liam did not get
up to greet them and Tom was happy to stay in his seat. The girls
went inside to get drinks, and came back out a few minutes later
with a tray of beers and dark red shots.

"To holidays," one of the girls said. They held up their shot
glasses, then downed the contents.

"I'm Laura, by the way," the same girl said to Tom. "This is Eve,
and Jo."

"Tom."

Laura and Eve had similar short black hair, sun-bloated freck-
les. Tom had presumed that they were sisters, but early in the
conversation, Jo—small, blond, who had already attracted the attention of a group of shirtless boys walking up from the beach—

informed them that the three had met at university. They had been in the same hall of residence during their first year and were about to move into a house together.

"What about you guys," Laura asked. "What do you do?"

It struck Tom only then that they had neglected to discuss a cover story. He hesitated, waiting for Liam to answer.

"Tom's an underwear model."

Tom let out a breath of surprise, embarrassment. The nasty sweet belch of the liquor filled his nose.

"Cool," Laura said. She smiled at Liam. "Lucky for you, eh?" She turned to Tom. "And what about this one?"

Tom wiped his mouth. Composed himself. "He's a butcher."

For a moment there was silence.

"Wow. Butcher and underwear model. That's different. How did the two of you meet?"

Liam was grinning at him, and Tom understood that he was challenging him to answer, enjoying this.

"The Internet," Tom said.

Liam's hand was on his leg. After a pause, during which Jo noticed it there, Tom put his own hand down on top of Liam's.

"More drinks?" Eve made to stand, but Liam gestured for her to sit down and got up himself to go to the bar. A few tables away, a noisy party of men settled themselves in. Above the heads of the three girls a fat red sun dappled the forested top of the hills beyond the lagoon.

"How long have you two been together?" Eve asked.

"Couple of months, maybe."

"Oh, not long. Must be going well, then?"

He wondered whether they would have spoken like this to a straight couple, and for an instant he imagined Leah there sitting alongside them. "It is." He did not, however, feel annoyed by their nosiness. What he felt was drunk and, when Liam returned from the bar with another tray of the red shots, uninhibited. Anonymous. They downed the shots and he stretched over towards Liam to kiss him, enjoying the look of surprise on his face, uncaring of the girls, the other tables, the happy stream of people moving past them from the beach.

They went on to another bar, which was busier, louder. Some people on the other side of the place were dancing. Jo offered to help Tom get more drinks while the others looked for a table. She was more reserved than the other two, and she stayed quietly beside him while he ordered a round of vodka and sodas, a beer for Liam. For a moment, as they stood together, he felt an urge to talk to her, to speak he did not know what about, but the music was booming, and anyway a man had taken her attention, was saying something to her. A few men, he saw now, and he perceived in their regarding of her something expectant, untoward. He stepped up alongside her, facing the men.

"All right, fellas?"

They looked at him indifferently. Four older men in chinos, Hawaiian shirts unbuttoned down moist slack chests.

"Probably time to fuck off, isn't it?"

They stiffened, unsure how to respond. One of them muttered something into the ear of another and they turned, in sequence, to move off. Tom did not know what to do then. He looked back towards the bar. When he handed a couple of the drinks to Jo, she was smiling at him. "Thank you. Idiots, those lot."

"Who were they?"

"The Canadian golfers."

When they found the others standing near the entrance, Jo told them about the encounter at the bar. So odd did it sound to hear about what he had just done, he could not help but laugh, even before he saw Liam's reaction.

Laura and Eve indicated that they were going to join the dancers. Laura, departing, took Liam's hand. Liam did not resist and was sucked, still holding her hand, into the bodies. Tom watched the top of his head above the crowd, weaving away.

Jo touched him on the forearm. "Come on."

They slid through, following the slipstream that had not yet closed behind the others. Up ahead he could see Liam, already dancing. Something sudden rose inside him at the sight of him: the great feet stomping, arms flexed at the elbows into locked right angles, like a forklift. A small force field had opened up around him on the dance floor. Laura and Eve were dancing nearby, enjoying the show, but Liam appeared not to be aware of them or anyone else. Tom pushed towards him until he was at his side, copying his movements, stamping the ground, crooking his arms.

"You dance like a butcher," Tom shouted.

Liam began stamping even more vigorously, grinning madly. Tom followed suit, clapping—then, as the track changed, jumping, bouncing; Liam, the girls, the dancers around them jumping too, following Tom's lead. Liam wrapped his arms around Tom's middle, still bouncing. Tom put his mouth to Liam's ear. "Not the Hut, is it?"

Liam jumped harder, lifting Tom now with each spring. "Fuck them, mate." He turned his giant sweating face to Tom's. "Fuck the lot of them." Tom loosened his arm from Liam's grip and thrust it upwards with the beat of the music. Liam put his head back, laughing as they clung to each other amid the latticework of tan lines glowing in the dark, still bouncing, punching the air in unison.

They parted in the airport. Surrounded by the melee of the departures hall, Tom took hold of both Liam's hands and, in full view of all the gawping children and silently disgusted fathers, kissed him. He had planned this. Built himself up to it.

"Fucking homo," Liam whispered, and Tom kissed him again. They checked in, dropped off their bags. In the security line Tom watched Liam step forward towards the scanner. On one of his wrists there was a shocking white handcuff. The oddness of it rendered Tom, to the irritation of the man behind him, momentarily still. They would be back home in a few hours, he thought. Their time here was over, the separateness of it so distinct that it was already, not even out of the airport, beginning to take on the unreality of an illusion.

20

Mary B   posted Sun at 2:32pm

Plenty of rumours on here and on Twitter but anyone know if something concrete is about to happen? Heading for June already and we've not brought anyone in. Starting to get a bit worried.

Jamesy1987   posted Sun at 2:49pm

I have it on good authority that Sergio Agüero is about to sign for us on a 5-year deal. Only sticking point is we can't guarantee him a starting place because Jacob Gundi's just too ****ing good.

TTID   posted Sun at 3:16pm

👍👍

The 13th Oyster   posted Sun at 3:19pm

. . . and because Agüero's failed his medical for being an Argie grease-ball with fairy hamstrings.

Lardass   posted Sun at 3:47pm

There's no need to panic yet. No good business gets done when the players are on holiday. We've cleared out the dead wood, that's the key thing. There are plenty of good players—League One and Championship—out of contract now who will be looking for new clubs or trials. Wilko knows what he's doing. Keep the faith.

Riversider   posted Sun at 3:59pm

My contact at the club tells me that we are about to sign Maurice Lloyd-Day from Ipswich. Same source as told me about Gundi and I was the first to break that news.

Towncrier Ian   posted Sun at 4:24pm

He's big, he's brown, he bangs them in for Town, Crocodile Gundi! Crocodile Gundi!

Voice of Reason   posted Sun at 4:46pm

Sorry to say it Gundilovers but there's no chance in hell that he'll still be at the club come August.

Bald and Proud   posted Sun at 4:53pm

Peter Pascoe is saying the same thing about Lloyd-Day on Twitter. Says he was speaking to the chairman yesterday and MLD is the first of a number of new signings over the next few weeks.

Tommo   posted Sun at 5:01pm

It's true!! I was down at the club this morning and I saw Lloyd-Day in the car park.

Road to Wembley 2010   posted Sun at 5:28pm

Me too. He was having his medical. Didn't expect to see him in a Hyundai. Ipswich couldn't have been paying him much.

The 13th Oyster   posted Sun at 5:30pm

What are you two doing hanging around the club car park? Season's finished. Get a job you losers!

Whizzer   posted Sun at 5:44pm

As it happens I was down at Andy Jones's house this morning. Funny thing is, Riversider's car was parked in the driveway 😉

Easter looked at the time and saw that it was past two in the morning. A short while ago there had been a bout of wailing from Tyler's room. The sound had brought on a strange brief vision of going through to soothe him and be found doing so by Leah, but he had held back, knowing the boy would reject him. When he then heard Leah coming out into the corridor he had turned off the screen and waited in the total darkness for her to finish ministering to him.

He read to the end of the thread. There was no longer any activity on the forum but there were still seven users online. He stayed up for another half-hour, then shut down and shuffled cautiously along the walls to his room.

In the morning the usual routine: he got up late and went downstairs to the kitchen, where Leah had laid out breakfast and lunch for him, then through to the living room, the television, where he would stay until midday, when Leah would be on her way back to give Tyler his lunch.

Nobody from the club had been in contact with him since the season ended. His last communication had been with the physio and the fitness coach, who had given him a joint program to follow during the summer. The private physio he was paying for himself had taken one look at it and laughed. "You're a month or two off any of this, even without complications." The only player to have been in touch since the alarming rash of texts a couple of days after the injury was Boyn, who had sent him a message before the final game of the season—"Hope all good with you mate. Better things to come next season. You'll be back before you know it"—and another the day after the end-of-season awards night, taking the piss out of him for not coming and detailing the antics that had been got up to. He had replied simply, "Sounds like a laugh," not mentioning that he had not received an invite.

At twelve he heated his bowl of pasta in the microwave and went upstairs to the office. When he had positioned the red plastic toddler chair underneath the table and rested his cast on top of it, he ate, staring at the blank screen for a few minutes before turning it on.

Where have the squad gone on holiday? Started by Towncrier Ian 28 May 2012 ≤ 1 2 ≥	Replies: 20 Views: 56

Towncrier Ian   posted Mon at 8:14am
Anybody know?

The 13th Oyster   posted Mon at 12:31pm
Are you serious? Who cares?

Steve Tomkins   posted Mon at 12:39pm
Tenerife.

Dr. Feelgood   posted Mon at 1:00pm
Vegas.

Jamesy1987   posted Mon at 5:03pm
Chessington World of Adventures.

Mozza   posted Mon at 5:19pm
The Isle of Lesbos.

Towncrier Ian   posted Mon at 5:22pm
Explains a few of the performances last season.

The 13th Oyster   posted Mon at 5:50pm
Gundi's gone on safari with Jamesy1987.

Mary B   posted Mon at 5:58pm
I heard that Richards, Hoyle and Beverley have gone to Tenerife together. Most go away with their partners and families obviously, but it can only be good for team spirit if some players go away together.

Faz   posted Mon at 6:12pm

Good for the local brasshouse, I agree.

TTID   posted Mon at 6:35pm

Apparently Chris Easter was in Majorca.

Glory Hunter   posted Mon at 6:50pm

Apparently EastEnders is on tonight at eight o'clock.

TTID   posted Mon at 6:55pm

He was. Him and his wife and kid (who looks so like him it's freaky).

Town Legend   posted Mon at 7:23pm

How do you know?

TTID   posted Mon at 7:50pm

A mate saw them in the airport when he was on his way to Hamburg for
a stag do.

Mary B   posted Mon at 8:23pm

He still in a cast?

TTID   posted Mon at 8:48pm

Yes.

The holiday had been difficult. They had booked it before he got
injured, and when it came around he had tried to persuade Leah to
go on her own with Tyler, telling her that there would be no point in
him being there. He would not be able to do anything; he would just
be in the way. "You'll be able to lie on the beach," she had come back
with, "which is all I'm planning on doing." But when they got there
the leg was intolerable in the heat and the sand. For the first couple
of days Leah went to great lengths to try and make him comfortable, with cushions and cooler bags, snacks and beer, attempting to
make conversation when she was not running about after Tyler, but

by the third day he had retreated to the air-conditioned comfort of the hotel room.

Each morning, after they had eaten breakfast together on the balcony, Leah and Tyler made the walk to the beach or went down to the hotel pool. He would sit on their seventh-floor balcony, battling the feeble Internet connection, with an eye on them down by the poolside with the Scottish family that she spent every evening going on about. He watched her chatting and laughing with the husband, trying to hear what he was saying to her. Twice she took a dip in the pool with him while the wife supervised Tyler and their little girl. They swam slowly up and down then drifted to one side, where they rested their folded arms on the lip of the pool, still talking, close enough that their elbows were nearly touching. He had taken a shine to Tyler too, the husband, chasing him and the little girl between the sunloungers, lifting him up into the air to put onto his shoulders and jiggling him about while Tyler pissed himself laughing.

There were a couple of groups of young women who returned to the same spot by the pool at the same time each afternoon. For long spells he watched them too, and when Leah was at the beach he took to coming down to the pool just before they arrived. Whenever he lay down, though, he felt instantly stupid and cumbersome with the ugly dollop of his leg stuck out in front of him, and when he saw one of the women look at him and snigger to her friend, he went back up to the room, not to visit the pool again.

Bald and Proud   posted Mon at 9:45pm

Most of them will be back from holidays now. Preseason training starts in under five weeks. Time to get in shape for some hill running!

Tommo   posted Mon at 11:21pm

If getting slaughtered in the Hut helps getting back in shape then Hart and Willis are going to have no problem.

Town Legend   posted Mon at 11:29pm

Same pair were legless at the player of the season awards. Heard Hart fell off the stage when he went up to get his young player of the year award.

Bald and Proud   posted Tues at 8:06am

Are we supposed to believe this just because you "heard" it, Town
Legend? Can you tell us what reliable source it is that tells you these
things? Did he fork out for the £50 ticket, or did he "hear" it from someone else?

He paused, thinking that he had heard a noise downstairs. A couple of minutes later, hearing nothing more, he moved his hands to
the keyboard.

Town Legend   posted Tues at 12:27pm

Leah was home. He could hear her talking to Tyler. There was a
screech of pleasure. Running. He had an impulse to get up and go
down to see them, but it passed, the leg, his entire body, too heavy,
immobile. There were times when he sat there and his body was
just an object, a thing, as much related to him as the laptop or the
swivel chair. At other times he wanted to do damage to it. More
than once he had experienced the wild desire to ruin the leg for
good. To take off the cast and jump down the stairs. To crunch his
shin in a doorframe. In these moments he would go and lie down
on the bed, shaking until whatever it was that had come over him
had passed.

   He went downstairs when Leah called up to him. She was at the
entrance to the kitchen, searching for something inside the pram
bag. She did not see or hear him, and for a while he watched her
from the bottom of the stairs. He was gripped by a longing to be
near her, to touch her, but this was overtaken by the sudden understanding, as she raised her head and saw him, that he did not know
her.

When he went upstairs to do his stretches, Leah gave Tyler a box of
raisins so that she could dry up and put away the dishes. He finished them quickly and started whining at her legs for more, so she

picked him up and carried him upstairs for his nap. Once he was settled she headed down the corridor and saw, through the slightly open door to the spare room, that Chris was asleep on the bed. For a second she contemplated lying down beside him, but her courage immediately vanished and she walked on.

For the next hour and a half she lay on the sofa with her phone, browsing sites about Milan, most of which her mum and Maria had forwarded to her. She looked at photos of street art and boutiques and canalside cafes with a mounting excitement that felt, despite the fact that her mum had already volunteered to look after Tyler, illicit. At college last week she had asked Maria what she thought they would do there. Maria, next to her at the workbench, had given her a little nudge and said, "We're going to have some fun, mate," and Leah, though not quite certain what she had meant, had experienced a prickle of heat at her words. There was a creak from the floorboards upstairs. She tried not to let her thoughts shift to Chris, to work out when it was that he had last slept in their room. Ever since the injury she had been anxious for him not to think she was physically rejecting him, although any opportunity that she got she had spurned, at a loss, even more since the trial of the Majorca holiday, for how to get close to him.

Chris was still in the spare room when Tyler woke. Quietly, she went upstairs to retrieve him from his cot and brought him back down to get ready for an outing to a nearby lake which she had only recently discovered, where they went most afternoons now. The lake was small and clean, man-made, with a well-kept grassy bank along one side which attracted only the odd runner or dog walker, and two men who every afternoon sat fishing twenty yards apart, never acknowledging each other.

They fed the ducks, Tyler offering bread out of his fingers. When it dropped from his grasp the ducks stabbed around his feet and he ran back to Leah. "Hungy duck, Mummy! Hungy duck!" She laid a rug on the grass, assembled his toy farm and animal figurines, and sat down on a bench.

This afternoon was her first meeting with Liam since he had returned from his holiday, and it bothered her that she was so eager to find out how it had gone. They had met up a few times since he first told her his secret and on each occasion he had revealed a bit more: that he and the player were meeting regularly—she presumed, but did not want to ask, for sex; that the player was nervous about his contract; that Liam was developing strong feelings for him. Each of these disclosures she received with a display of quiet understanding, concealing her unease at the actual thought of it, the two men's bodies together, but always craving to find out more.

Liam still had not told her who he was. The day that he came out to her she had gone home and searched for a photograph of the squad on the Town website. She scanned along the three rows, but with no result except to muddle herself. Before long they all looked gay to her. Now, though, she had her suspicions. Little things that Liam had said—about his contract, his youth, a suggestion that he had lived in the north—had enabled her to narrow it down to three or four. She never pushed him to tell her. She did not want to risk this renewed closeness, this company that she was so unused to, despite growing increasingly uncomfortable at what he was telling her. He was never detailed or graphic, but she knew that the relationship was sexual, passionate, even. Before he left he had jokingly referred to the holiday as a sex trip, to which she had smiled and retreated to the pram bag for a bag of wet wipes.

Tyler was making a bolt for the lake. She jumped up and ran after him. She caught him well before the waterline and they had a short fight as she carried him back to the bench and he refused to give up a project to launch his duck and chicken on the water. She sat down, letting him sob into her stomach and stroking his hair for a long time until he calmed, his thumb in his mouth, the late afternoon sun perishing on the lake, radiating from the bald buttered crowns of the two anglers.

When she got to the furniture store Liam was already sitting down with a coffee.

"Weather was good, then."

"Oh yes," he said, picking up Tyler.

She went to the counter and came back as Liam was putting Tyler into a high chair. He told her about the holiday. The weather, the apartment, the resort, that they had enjoyed themselves. She fed Tyler a breadstick from a box in the pram bag, and they watched him suck and munch at it.

"It was just . . . don't know—normal."

"What do you mean?"

"It was normal. Like your holiday. Like any two people going away and doing all that stuff—lying on the beach, drinking beer, going to a restaurant."

Tyler finished the last of his breadstick and started crying.

"It's his dinner time. Stay here with him a minute, will you, while I go and get him something to eat."

When she returned with a small plate of sausage and mash, Tyler was out of the high chair, sitting on Liam's lap, snickering at some game to do with an object hidden underneath one of Liam's hands. The sight of Tyler on Liam's lap instinctively disturbed her. She put the plate down in front of the high chair and lifted him back into it. He clapped his hands in delight and grabbed for the pieces of sausage that she cut up for him.

"I know this might sound nuts," Liam said, "but I really am gay."

She stared at him, lost for something to say.

He laughed. "I mean, I know it for sure. I never completely thought that word about myself before, but I do now."

"What about him?" was all she could think to say.

"He's getting there."

Tyler dropped his fork on the floor. Liam bent down to retrieve it for him. The back of his neck was flaked and peeling. He wiped the fork clean and handed it back to Tyler, wiping his mouth as he did so. Watching them together, Leah was struck by the thought that she was shutting Chris out. That there was something wrong, unnatural, about allowing Liam this familiarity with Tyler.

"How are you, anyway?" Liam asked.

"Fine. The cast's still on but they say it might come off in the next couple of weeks." Liam was giving her an odd look. "Other than that we're good. This guy loves his nursery. He found a frog in the garden this morning and didn't want to leave when I came for him."

"I told him about you," Liam said. "That I'd told you."

"Oh. What did he say?"

"He's fine about it. Pretty much. I was thinking that maybe you two could meet each other."

"With you?"

"Yes, with me. What do you think?"

"If you want to," she said. And then swiftly, "So, what now, when the season starts again? Did he get a new deal?"

"Yes."

"So you're going to carry on, then?"

"Yes, of course."

"And keep it secret?"

"We managed before." He looked directly at her. "We can't tell anybody else, obviously. He'd have the whole world on his door-step. And no club would want him."

"And you?"

He laughed. "They'd be rid of me in a second. Probably with my bollocks floating down the river."

Liam texted her a couple of days later to ask if she fancied going out with him and the others that Friday. Through habit she was reluctant to bring it up with Chris. Since she had been seeing more of Liam, the full extent of which she had kept from Chris, she had been out several times with the group and she did not want him to get any kind of wrong idea about it. When she told him about the night out, however, he said that it was fine, and she got the impression that he was glad of the opportunity to be alone.

She dressed tastefully in black jeans and boots and a long-sleeved cream silk shirt. They ate together on the sofa, Chris resting the cast on the coffee table, angled so that they could see past it to the television. He seemed relaxed, she thought, although it was getting more and more difficult to know what was going on inside his head.

The first month or two of Friday nights after the injury had been the most difficult times. He had been at his most agitated then—before the now customary detached silence—painfully aware of the emptiness of his routine but unwilling to alter it. Even tonight they were still eating chicken breasts with mashed sweet potato and spinach.

She finished her food quickly, conscious of the squirt of perfume that she had put on. If he noticed, he did not mention it. He sat eating, watching the television, waiting for her to leave. There was a time when he used to be obsessive about her movements. The people she was with. Where. Why. They finished their meals. Chris started watching a film, and she got up with the plates. She prepared a bottle of milk, a couple of sterilized dummies and a parade of teddy bears, then she went to say goodbye and let him know that she would be back before midnight.

They were standing at the far end of the bar. She squirmed through the throng of tanned arms and legs, feeling, amid the noise and flesh, in her modest unrevealing clothes, old. When she reached her friends they hugged her in turn. Shona handed her a drink. Gemma asked if she was up for going to the Hut with them. The bar they were in was across the street from the club, and all of the young crowd around them would at a certain point pile en masse over the road towards the pair of cement Grecian pillars on the other pavement.

"Not tonight," she said. "Baby steps." She turned her face from them to Liam at the burst of irritation she felt at Gemma's gentle cajoling—"Go on"—as if she actually had a choice, as if their lives were in any way the same.

Liam came to stand beside her. The conversation moved quickly and lightly from one thing to another, involving all five of them, but she could feel his presence next to her. None of the others knew, he had told her on Tuesday, only her, and this had revived something in her, this revelation of trust, even as a vague grievance was also forming that forcing her to be complicit in this was not right, not fair.

A couple of drinks later, on her way back from the toilet, a man started talking to her. It was so long since anybody had come on to her that she was not prepared for it. He was short. Good-looking. He sounded Irish, she thought, or northern. He had a vain little beard. His circle of friends shifted away from them while he told her a long funny anecdote about a holiday that he had just returned from on which his bag was lost on the flight out. For the first half of the trip his mates had dressed him in clothes from a supermarket, giving him a different persona each day. A Frenchman the first day. Circus ringmaster the next. Finally, before the bag finally turned up at their hotel, a German lesbian.

They moved to the bar and he bought her a drink. She was determined not to tell him who she was. Fortunately, he showed no sign of asking her about herself. A small table with two stools became free. He gestured towards them and she nodded. As they made for the table she glanced towards her friends. They were all watching her, smiling. Mark gave her a thumbs-up. Even though it was a joke, she knew that if she left with this man, slept with him, they would be pleased. She thought about the closed door of the office and pity wrenched at her. It was all right for them, she thought—Mark, still going out with the teenage girl; Liam secretly shagging a footballer and expecting her to cover for him, to keep it from her husband—they could do what the fuck they wanted, it seemed, without any comeuppance.

The man was looking at her. "You coming?"

"I should probably get back to my friends."

He shrugged his shoulders and gave her a mischievous disappointed smile.

When she got back she laughed off their ribbing and stood next to Liam again.

"Still got it, then?" he said.

"Must have."

"Who was he?"

"James. Works for the council. Surveyor or something. He was all right, actually."

She pressed up against him as a couple of men pushed past.

"You tell him who you are?"

"No. I used to do that. It was the only thing that would get rid of them. Unless they were egged on by it. Now it's just embarrassing. They'd probably think, what—*she's* with a footballer?"

Liam shook his head. "Come on, let's dance," he said.

Surprised, because he never danced, she followed his broad back to the half-dozen bobbing girls on a square of floor by the DJ. Liam went into the middle of them and started to dance with heavy, clomping movements. She joined him, bumping against him. At the end of the song he put his face towards her ear and for an instant she thought he was going to kiss her.

"The guy, his name's Tom Pearman."

She stayed where she was, near his face. She had guessed correctly, almost, yet still a tingle passed through her at the revelation. The others were snaking through the crowd towards them. Shona and Gemma put their arms on either side of her and the five formed into a tight circle, singing to the music, then wheeling round at speed, joyously oblivious to everybody around them.

She closed the front door behind her as quietly as she could, but dropped her keys on the floor. As she bent down for them she heard crying from upstairs. Loud, desperate, abnormal. Alarm girdled her—the thought that Tyler might have been left distressed and unattended, maybe for hours. She ran through the living room and up the stairs, and saw with relief that Chris was with him, sitting on the carpet outside Tyler's room with his arms around the little body standing before him in giraffe pajamas.

"What happened?"

She hurried towards them, and it took her a few seconds to understand that the noise was coming not from Tyler but Chris. She stopped, afraid. He did not appear to have noticed her. The high, hoarse noise reverberated through the corridor. Chris's face was obscured by Tyler's head, on top of which one hand was pressed, its knuckles white over the soft motionless skull.

"Chris," she shouted. She fell to her knees. Tyler spun round and looked at her, frightened. He ran to her and began crying the moment he was in her arms.

"Chris?"

He had turned his face from her. He was no longer wailing, but there was a faint low whimper as he pulled himself with difficulty to his feet and, with one hand steadying himself against the wall, he shuffled away to his bedroom.

21

"You don't think it looks right?"

"It's your place. You do what you want."

"But you don't think it looks right?"

"No. I think it looks like shit."

Tom looked at him disbelievingly. He leaned the mirror against the wall of the entrance hall.

"What's wrong with it?"

"It's gold."

"So what?"

"It's gold and it's enormous. You might as well get a full-size portrait of yourself to go opposite. A bust or something."

Tom ignored him and went through into the living room. Liam followed and they sat down on the floor to drink their mugs of tea. The previous family had lived in the house for a long time, with all their own furniture. Apart from the mirror and his dumbbells in one corner, his cactus collection carefully assembled along the window ledge, the living room was bare. In the kitchen there were a few pots and pans, a tray of stained cutlery. Upstairs, a mattress in one of the bedrooms. The small Victorian terraced house was everywhere warped and cracked. There was a below-stairs toilet that Tom had to hunch over to use, Liam, the one time he had been in there, to kneel. At the end of the kitchen was a back door that opened onto a thin wild garden. The granny flat, Liam had taken to calling it.

The club had initially guided Tom towards an apartment in a modern block, and he was close to signing the rental agreement when he discovered that several of the other players lived in the building. He rang the club secretary, then the unimpressed letting agent, to say that he had changed his mind, and two days later, through a different agency, found this house on the other side of town from the first apartment and the Daveys' place.

Liam finished his tea and stood up. "Mind if I have a crack at the garden?"

"Go for it."

Minutes later Liam was outside wearing a pair of gloves that he must have had with him, ripping out thorns and weeds from the lawn borders. Tom sat on the back doorstep, where he was not visible to any of the neighbors.

Liam paused, puffing. "Not going to give me a hand, then?"

"Nope."

Liam shook his head and carried on. Tom took out his phone and idled on the Internet, every now and then looking up at Liam working his way around the garden.

"Here, listen to this," Tom said. "What do you think Sunderland made Stefan Schwarz put in his contract when he signed for them?"

"No idea."

"That he'd never travel into space."

"That for real?"

"Yep. I'm on this site with all these daft contract clauses players have had. Here. What did Sam Hammam put in Spencer Prior's contract that he had to do when he signed for Cardiff?"

"Don't know. Only shag women."

Tom ignored the comment. "He made him eat something," he said when Liam had stopped smiling. "What do you think it was?"

"A leek?"

"No."

"Daffodil?"

"No. A sheep's testicle."

"Fuck off. That's insane."

Liam kept on at the garden while Tom browsed for more funny football stories, telling Liam the best ones. In another garden somewhere a dog started yapping. Liam stopped to listen, wiping his face with his upper arm, then getting on again with the borders. Tom remained on the step, hungry now but powerless to get up from where he was, tracing Liam's every movement, absorbing into his own body each plunge of the garden fork, each sharp little exhalation at a yanked weed.

A short while later there was a straggly yellow pile as high as Liam's waist in the center of the lawn. "Done," Liam said.

"What am I going to do with all that?"

"Burn it. It's dry enough."

"Burn it? You nuts? Get the neighbors round, have a bonfire?"

"I'm just saying, I'd burn it."

Liam knelt on the grass and picked up some soil, crumbling it through his fingers. He crawled around, occasionally poking a finger into the borders, and something moved inside Tom that made him want to step into the garden and take Liam's face in his hands, heedless of everything: the neighbors, the yapping dog, the full frightening import of what he was feeling.

However, he could not afford to be reckless, a fact that he was reminded of one morning when he arrived at the stadium and sat for a few minutes in his car, watching, through a gap between the stands, Liam ride the tractor slowly towards the away terrace. A large knitted steel mat was attached to the tractor, glinting in the sunlight. The pitch, which the day before had been loose, turned dirt, was now a plain of sand across its entire surface. Tom got out of his car and walked towards the fire exit of the main stand. He stopped by the door as Liam smoothly maneuvered the tractor to come back in the other direction. Tom let himself become as rapt by the sight of him as Liam was in his work. Liam's eyes did not leave the imagined path in front of him—would not move, Tom knew, for minutes, hours, for as long as the job took.

Tom did not notice that he was himself being observed. The club chaplain was approaching from the car park. Tom started when he appeared beside him.

"Crackers, isn't it?" the chaplain said, and Tom understood that he had not been found out.

"Yes."

"You wouldn't believe they'll be playing football on there soon."

"No."

And for a time they stood there by the fire exit, the chaplain beginning to hum a low tune, luxuriating together in the sunshine.

With preseason still a month away, the ground was quiet. Inside the bowels there was only ever the occasional player in for the gym, or Wilko and his coaching staff, who would show their faces at the door to say hello, clearly impressed that Tom was in so regularly. A couple of times Wilko's son was with him, his father showing him the dugout, the dressing room, the St. John's Ambulance cupboard, stopping anyone they passed to chat for a while, and Tom, transfixed by the disabled boy, could not stop himself looking over even though he knew it was wrong, although never for long enough for anybody to notice or to be at risk of Wilko introducing the boy to him.

Liam was there every day, usually with one or both of the summer lads he had taken on. Often, after finishing in the gym, Tom went to find him. Sometimes he helped with some task or other. Now that Tom had his own house and there was no risk of them being found in their old seedy hiding place, they decided that it was natural enough to know each other, given Tom's stay at the Daveys'. As long as they were not seen together too often, nobody would suspect anything, they believed. They did not look gay, they told themselves. They spoke normally, behaved normally. Appearing to be friends was a more sensible ploy than pretending not to know each other.

There was the issue, however, of Liam's two housemates. From a life of rarely socializing more than once a week he was now out most nights, often not returning until the morning, if at all. Unable to think of any other way round it, Liam told them that he had started seeing a girl. Polish. A care assistant. Before long of course, although Liam rarely mixed with them outside the house, they would begin asking questions, and at that point he would probably have to feign a breakup. He and Tom had not spoken about what they might do then, but Tom had the sense that both of them were daring to imagine that Liam might, eventually, move out.

One evening, sharing a takeaway pizza on the tan leather sofa that they had earlier bumped and scraped into Tom's house, Liam said, "I should tell you something."

Tom stopped eating but did not look away from the television.

"On holiday, when I told you about Dan and all that, I should have said as well that I have had a thing with a player before. Once. I don't mean the boy after the youth tournament. Something else, but it was nothing, really. I'd actually forgotten about it."

"You've just remembered?"

"Pretty much. It really wasn't anything. Happened by chance. I met him online but I didn't know who he was because he gave a different name. Then when I got there it was one of the players who was with Town at the time. I'd just been promoted head grounds-man and I was as spooked as he was, to be fair. We agreed we wouldn't meet again and we didn't."

Tom's throat felt hot and stuck. The cold blue light of the television jumped like flames over the wallpaper. "Who was it?"

"I won't say, if that's OK. I promised him."

"You serious?"

"He's not here anymore. He left ages ago," Liam said and went back to his pizza.

"Online?"

"I didn't do it much. Couple of times after Dan."

When Liam had finished his pizza he got up and cleared away the box, saying that he was going home for an early night.

Tom sat staring at the television. He began to wonder whether Leah knew about this player. About Liam's Internet meetings. The longer he sat there, his mind working it over and over, the more he was convinced that she did. She knew his own name now, Liam had told him a few nights ago, an admission that Tom had not reacted to well. Instant gaping fear had made him shout at Liam, "Fucking joking, you idiot!" then become silent and ignore Liam's reasoning that it would only have been a matter of time anyway because Tom had agreed to meet her, and then, once Liam had gone home, kick the bathroom door so hard that he cut his toe and loosened the door hinge.

The night was muggy, and he slept poorly there on the sofa once he had taken his clothes off. His skin pulled against the leather, and pizza crumbs stuck to his face. Gradually the room turned orange from the streetlamp. In the morning the sun invaded the uncurtained window and he lay there stiff and uncomfortable, his plans for the day—buying furniture, helping Liam at the ground— seeming somehow pathetic.

There was a short-lived heat wave. Tom moved his dumbbells out into the garden. When he saw a neighbor watching him from an upstairs window, he moved them back inside. He kept meticulously to his fitness program, most days exceeding it. He jogged in the cool of the early morning, again at twilight, and worked out relentlessly either at home or at the stadium gym.

Following one hot breathless session, moving the fan in the gym as far as the cord would allow from one machine to the next, he went to get changed and see Liam. He found him in the forecourt of the ground-staff shed, lifting junk out of the skip and into the back of a van. He was sweating heavily. He saw Tom approaching and waved hello before turning back to his work.

"Hot enough?" Tom said.

Without looking, Liam pointed to the side of the shed, where a thermometer was nailed up by the entrance. It was thirty-three degrees.

"Bloody hell," Tom said.

Nobody else was anywhere about. In one of the brick bays behind Liam flies moved restlessly above caked piles of drainage sand. In another, broken-up pieces of asphalt from the footpath behind the Riverside Stand were softening. The air choked with the stench of them.

"What are you doing?" Tom asked.

"Beer money." He stopped and held up the drawer of a filing cabinet. "Probably sixty, seventy quid here. There's been staff and players in every day dumping all their crap. Doing their houses out before preseason starts. Me and Pete pull out all the metal and take it down the scrapyard. Give me a hand? There's a drink in it."

Tom got stuck in, ferrying the objects to the van that Liam hauled out of the skip: a radiator, two mangled garden chairs, a trampoline base, the tray of a wheelbarrow. A blackbird landed on the large, disused roller in one corner of the forecourt and inspected them silently, panting in the heat. Liam started whistling. When he handed down a rusted garden fork Tom could smell him through the smog of asphalt. Desire racked him, mixing, as he looked instinctively over his shoulder, with the certainty that it would always be like this—vigilant, precious, forbidden.

His parents were eager to come down and see his new place. They arranged to visit for a weekend shortly before the commencement of preseason. The day prior to their arrival Tom went over the house for any evidence of Liam. There was a shirt in the bedroom, which he hid in a suitcase. A pair of mammoth walking socks. In the garden he scattered a calculated array of stones and broken bricks to distract from the immaculate loamy borders that Liam was continuing to work on. The lettered coasters on his new living-room table, which he had bought with barely a thought—joy, friendship, unwind, cheers!—suddenly looked outrageously gay, and he went through both floors again, questioning his decor choices: the tan sofa, the purple cushions, the gold mirror, the patterned shower curtain, the glaring lack of girl posters.

His parents, though, were more perplexed at the house itself than his choices inside it. His mum thought that it was too out of the way. She was concerned that the club had advised him badly. His dad, running his hands over floorboards and cupboard panels, fingering window jambs, wanted to get straight to work on the place. He had brought his toolbox.

They spent most of the damp weekend doing the house up. Tom and his dad hammered, glued, pulled out rotted wood and idiot-job workmanship, while his mum cleaned or went into town for cookware and home furnishings. The busyness of it was enjoyable.

Working at his dad's side, fixing things, making intermittent conversation, felt reassuringly conventional, even if a sly discomfort did come over him when they were in the bedroom or downstairs putting a shelving unit into an alcove of bubbled wallpaper that Tom could still vividly recall the texture of against his palms and his chest.

On the Saturday night they ate a curry at the new table and drank lager from the off-license round the corner. Tom tried not to think about how much he missed them, how normal it felt to be in their company. They told him about their holiday in Ireland and the bed-and-breakfast owner whose son played for Chelmsford City. Tom gave them a carefully prepared version of his own holiday. Later, they moved on to his sister's upcoming first term at university, her new boyfriend and football. His dad believed that Tom could make thirty-plus starts this season. He expected that, he exclaimed, rapping the table. Thirty. As a minimum. A bare minimum.

Liam arranged an evening for Tom to meet Leah. Tom reluctantly agreed to a drink, and after some back-and-forth Liam suggested the three of them go to the Beefeater. Tom and Liam arrived together, early, and sat opposite each other on a bench at the back of the beer garden beside a collection of parasols heaped like corpses against the metal fence.

When Leah arrived Liam stood up but did not kiss her. She moved in next to Liam on the other side of the table and held out her hand for Tom to shake as they said hello. Liam asked her how her weekend had been. She said it had been fine: she had gone round to her mum's, and her mum's boyfriend had done a barbecue on the balcony with the neighbors. It occurred to Tom, with an unexpected flicker of jealousy, that she and Liam were in more regular contact than he had realized. He got up and asked Leah what she would like to drink. Her teeth, when she thanked him, looked as though they had been whitened. Her face was heavily made up, and she was wearing tight jeans, gold sandals and a low top that showed off a deep tan which Tom presumed to be fake.

Liam had entrusted their secret, their life, to this person, Tom kept thinking as he walked to the bar and ordered the drinks. He looked over at the two of them talking, more casually now that he was away from the table. He imagined again the little group of old school friends, Liam among them, chatting, laughing, gossiping.

"Your drinks, mate."

He took a note from his wallet. When the barman turned away to the till Tom shut his eyes for a few seconds, resisting the hot rushing panic descending through him that everything was changing and that he would not be able to stay in control of where it was all going.

When he returned, Liam was asking about Leah's son.

"He's not been sleeping that well recently. He's at my mum's tonight."

"How's Easter?" Tom said after a pause.

"He's fine. The cast's close to coming off. They discovered one or two complications, but at least it's not far off now." She took a drink of her wine, and there was silence again, which Liam did not attempt to fill.

"Good news about your contract," Leah said.

"Thanks."

"Could be an interesting season."

"The manager thinks we should be pushing for promotion."

"Think you will?"

"Yes . . . well, I don't know. Depends who he signs."

They slipped easily enough into a discussion about Town. Tom was surprised by how much she knew—about the players, tactics, the old manager, the new manager. He wondered if it was all second nature to her or if she had prepared. The conversation moved on to the European Championship. She had put money on Germany to win it. "No chance," Liam said. "Spain look quality so far. No one's going to stop them." She challenged him to a bet. They settled on twenty pounds and sealed it with a handshake that seemed to Tom flirtatious. It was unclear whether or not the subject—the reason they were all there—was going to be brought up. Tom was not going to do it; it did not seem as though she was either, and it was difficult to know what Liam was thinking, his eyes flitting from one to the other of them as if amazed to see them in the same place.

On returning from the bar with a second round of drinks, however, Leah said to Tom, "I hear the holiday was good."

"We were lucky with the weather."

"Me and Chris went to the Algarve once. It was lovely."

And with that they switched to the unpredictable summer they were having. Liam talked about the effect of it on the pitch renovation. The importance of a good irrigation program, of arriving early in the morning before it was hot to give the pitch a good drink. The four sprinkler heads, at eighty-five quid apiece, that Pete had gone over with the aerator. The topic of Tom and Liam did not come up again, although Liam appeared pleased when they got up to say goodbye. He kissed Leah on the cheek, and Leah, after a moment's hesitation, shook Tom's hand again, this time squeezing it for a second before she let go. She too looked pleased—or relieved—that the evening had gone well, or that it was over, or that he wasn't too gay.

They waited for her to drive away before getting into Tom's car. Liam leaned across to kiss him.

"You see?" he said.

Work around the stadium stepped up as preseason neared. Tom continued to help out occasionally, an hour here and there, never more so as not to raise any suspicions. Liam's days became longer. He often went back to his own house or did not get to Tom's until nightfall. Under his supervision, he and Pete, the two summer lads and, from time to time, a few of the scholars got through an enormous amount of work. The gangways of the stands were repainted. Cracked and faded seats were replaced. The new season billboards were put up around the perimeter, and a company was hired to asphalt the river footpath. The drooping, torn netting above the Riverside Stand that prevented balls from flying into the river was taken down, resewn, tautened. A whole afternoon was spent killing the weeds that had grown up through the terracing, the car park, the club-shop roof. Tom and Liam spent one happy Sunday morning kitted up in large yellow backpack sprayers, moving down the teeming borders of the new footpath as ponderously as a pair of astronauts.

All of this activity took place to a continuous backdrop of Liam grumbling about the changeable weather. He was forever staring over the pitch, making adjustments, fretting about irrigation and disease and root growth.

"You sound like a farmer," Tom told him.

"I am a fucking farmer," came the immediate response.

Tom took quiet pleasure in watching him work: his understanding of the pitch, both scientific and sensual. The gentleness with which he touched the grass or tested the firmness of the soil. Liam had known this stadium, this ground, his entire life, and it moved Tom to think that no other person knew it as intimately as he did.

Tom found him one morning after the pitch had been watered, sitting on a step of the away terrace. Tom sat beside him, and Liam pointed to where a fox cub was darting in and out of the glistening sward.

"Worms," said Liam.

The pitch—scarified, sanded, photo-documented, cored by two million miniature drainage channels, fertilized, scrupulously watered—had been growing half an inch a night since the overseeding program. Almost a month on, it resembled a meadow. The wind gusting between the stands caused glossy waves to course down its length. Butterflies were drawn to one section, where a cluster of wildflowers had migrated from the banks of the river. According to Liam, adamant despite Tom's skepticism, there was a visiting deer.

A thrilling tension was suspended over this time together at the ground—not touching, wary of how they spoke to each other, looked at each other. By sundown, when they could be alone, an intensity would have built up between them that neither could fully control.

The night before the grass was due to be cut, Liam phoned just as Tom was about to go to bed.

"Can you come to the stadium?"

"What? It's half eleven. Are you still there?"

"Just come. Park on the road."

Tom left his car a short distance from the stadium. He walked behind the dark block of the main stand. Liam was standing at the edge of the pitch. No lights were on anywhere and his face was in shadow.

"Is everything OK?" Tom asked.

"Come with me."

He led Tom down the touchline as far as the dugout, where he motioned for Tom to follow him onto the field. The grass reached almost to their knees. They waded through it, adrenaline surging into Tom's bloodstream. When they were somewhere near the middle Liam stopped and waited for Tom to reach him. He took hold of Tom's shoulders and pushed him down into the grass. There was the smell of diesel and dried sweat on him, the huge shadowy forms of the floodlights above his face as it descended towards Tom.

Afterwards, they went up to the control center. On one of the CCTV screens Liam rewound and played back the footage. Tom was unable to make anything out at first until Liam pointed to the two tiny figures moving across the grainy image, a scene from a horror film. Once they stopped walking they were barely visible, the only sign of them, moments later, a slight silvery pulsing amid the gray, as minute and regular as the winking heart of a fetus.

"Porn, mate."

But Tom was too paralyzed by the evidence on the monitor in front of him to find it funny. The ghost of his own body having sex with another man, on a football pitch—the act made real, recorded, until Liam pressed a button to delete it and Tom, as Liam gestured for them to leave, made him check the device again to make sure.

In the morning the stadium was busy. Preseason was less than a week away so there were players about, using the gym, picking up their new season recovery skins, paperwork, kit. When Tom arrived a small audience of players and club staff was sitting in the main stand, watching the cutting of the grass. Tom stood at the bottom of the stand for a minute, then went up to join them.

A strip ten yards wide had been mown down the pitch, smooth and enticing as a freshly shaved head. Behind the whining black mower Liam advanced steadily, exactly, his gaze locked ahead. A fountain of chopped grass sprayed from the rotary blade. The two summer lads followed a short distance further back, raking and gathering the crop into the big cardboard boxes that Liam had collected over the last month from the town's three supermarkets. Secret pride climbed inside Tom at the sight of all these onlookers captivated by the spectacle. A loud cheer went up when a startled bird flapped out of the grass. The summer lads turned to grin at the little crowd, but Liam did not flinch.

The mower proceeded slowly, a black sparkling beetle, moving up, down the pitch. Some of the staff got up and left. The players, though, all remained. For minutes at a time none of them spoke, held like Tom to their seats as more of the pristine surface was unveiled and the sharp green smell of it carried through the air.

22

The first morning of training was cool and overcast. Wilko assembled the squad in the lounge twenty-five minutes before he intended to address them, to allow the players to catch up and joke and eat the croissants and Danish pastries stacked on the breakfast trolley. The coaching staff regarded them with satisfaction from one side of the room. They appeared in good shape. It was obvious that the majority had followed their fitness programs. Only Foley had noticeably gained weight.

"I'm not going to make you run up and down every hill in the county," Wilko said once he had them sitting down. "Some of them. But not all."

There was an audible release of breath. All those who had been present a year ago had undergone a full fortnight of hard running—overtraining, the old manager had called it—before any playing resumed, by which point they were aching for the appearance of a football. Wilko wanted to get onto the pitch right from the off, he told them. To get into a rhythm. To acclimatize the new players to Town's style of play. There would be signings within the next week, he said. As it stood, there was only one: a lithe, beautiful Jamaican international defender, Maurice Lloyd-Day, let go by Ipswich, who had so far eaten four Danish pastries and spoken to nobody.

Five friendly fixtures had been arranged. Three of them were to be played in Ireland, where the whole squad was going to spend almost a week building match practice and team spirit.

For the rest of the morning they ran. Firstly around the pitches, then, in batches, between two lines of cones, sprinting to an escalating barrage of bleeps while the fitness coach noted down their times on a clipboard and the waiting groups stretched and swapped stories about their families and their holiday exploits.

By the second day it was evident that Bobby, Willis and Tom were considerably fitter than anybody else. Bobby and Willis reveled in the situation. They jostled each other for front position during runs. When they finished, sprinting the final yards to try and be first, they stood and waited for the rest of the squad, venturing tentative banter at them as they labored in. On the third morning, when the balls came out for a game of two-touch keep-ball, Bobby was knocked to the ground three times and Willis's foot was stood upon with enough pressure that the bruising ruled him out of the Ireland trip.

They departed under a sky of ragged thunder and sudden heavy downpours. Their base, Wilko told them on the first steaming coach, taking a break from leafing through dossiers of released players, was a college campus in the west of the country. On arriving it became clear that, with the students away, they had the place to themselves, and they were soon getting lost, or drunk, in the labyrinth of stale corridors and nondescript, disinfected bedrooms.

The first practice session was taken indoors, the outside pitches judged to be too boggy. Two trialists were in their number, both recently let go by their clubs: an eighteen-year-old former Premier League academy fullback, and a journeyman forward who had been sent off in January playing against Town and subsequently fined for offensive language and gestures towards the Town supporters. To begin with, this twosome stuck together. The young fullback was up to the speed of the fittest, but the forward had clearly not exercised for months. He heaved and sweated against walls, or toiled behind the jogging pack alongside Foley. At the end of a bleep test he disappeared into the toilets to throw up a stream of orange juice and honey nut cornflakes, and in the afternoon, when they went outside into the pale blanket of sunshine to use the playable half of one pitch, the other trialist moved stealthily away from him.

Most of the players had been put into single rooms, but a few, including Tom and Beverley, were in larger twins with en suite bathrooms. Tom had not foreseen how pleased he would be to see his roommate again. There was a kind of relief in how predictable, how normal, it was. They talked without effort for much of the coach and plane journeys and on the first night shared most of a bottle of Jack Daniel's, along with a selection of foreign cheeses and salami balls that Beverley produced from freezer bags. They spoke about the European Championship final, transfers, Beverley's holidays. Beverley showed him, anxious for his opinion, a neat new tattoo at the base of his neck—a tiny crescent. He and his girlfriend had got one each, he said, at an expensive parlor in the West End on one of their weekends in London. Tom wondered if the girlfriend was recent, and if Beverley would think that he was being rude or odd not to ask about her.

The Irish league was in mid-season. The first opposition side was quicker and more competitive than Town. Their physical approach caused the Town players to step out of several unrestrained challenges, and early in the game there was an angry exchange between the two managers on the touchline. Tom was up against a brawny left back who pinched his triceps twice in the opening minutes. When he tried to do it a third time Tom swung out an arm, hitting the man in the chest, and the referee galloped over to tell him to calm down. The supporters standing nearby chanted for him to be sent off. He turned round for the referee to make a note of his shirt number, booking him, and caught the left back smiling, giving a wink to the crowd as he jogged back into position. Egged on by the fans, his challenges became even rougher. After one heavy tackle Tom fell to the pitch and the defender looked down at him, stooping to bring his face close to Tom's.

"English poofter."

Tom lay on the grass, his heart pounding with terror. When he got up and play resumed he veered infield, distancing himself from the player and the enlivened crowd, until the man crashed into Fleming and Tom heard him say the same words to him as he went to ground.

At the final whistle—eight goals, ten Town substitutions, two further flare-ups between the managers—the players left the field exhausted. Wilko told them it was a good workout, and they retreated to the campus for massages and a long, deep sleep.

There was an announcement at breakfast. Two new signings would be joining them the following night, after the second friendly. Both were from Oldham, in the division above. The pair would add genuine quality, Wilko told them: Mark Munro, a striker, and Michael Grant, a right-winger. When the squad left the room Richards walked out alongside Tom.

"You've got your work cut out there, Tommy. I was with Grant at Millwall. He's class."

Tom did not say anything, but the news of Grant's signing had shaken him. It did not help when he read on the club website after lunch that the manager was keen to address the wide areas because he thought that Town were "a bit light in those positions." He refused to let himself worry, however. His form, his fitness, his hunger to succeed, were all strong. Stronger than at any time since he joined the club. Even when it emerged on Twitter that Town had paid Oldham two hundred thousand, a club record, for Grant, he tried to remain rational. The shirt was his to lose. If anything, the others' banter about his prospects helped: he understood quickly enough that it was the ones whose own positions were in some doubt who were giving him the most stick, and he was able to return it.

After dinner he went for a walk across the campus. There was a small hill at the far end of the grounds, which he headed towards with the intention, for the first time since getting to Ireland, of calling Liam. He walked up the hill, nervous anticipation building as he thought up one or two things to talk about and took out his phone.

Liam wanted right away to speak about Grant. "He's good, you know."

"I've heard."

"All you can do is keep doing what you're doing. And Grant can play left side too, is what the Oldham forums say, so you don't know what the manager's thinking is."

"Right. I didn't know that. Thanks. How are you, anyway?"

"Fine. Pitch looks fucking beautiful."

"I bet."

"No, I mean it really does. Dad says it's the best he's ever seen it."

"Good."

Tom looked down at the concrete blocks of the campus buildings, the rich wet countryside spreading out beyond them.

"I'm missing you," Liam said.

Through the windows of the college bar, Tom could make out the shapes of several players moving around the pool tables.

"Boring here too," he said. Then: "I'll be back on Friday."

There was a small noise of Liam's breath and Tom thought that he was probably smiling. "Friday, then."

"Yes."

Tom walked back down the hill. He recounted the conversation in his head, frustrated with himself, quiet anxiety playing on him that something had just happened, a moment, an opportunity that he should have taken.

The starting eleven, except for Tom and Bobby, was changed around for the second friendly. They won 7–0. Tom performed well, if it was possible to perform well in such a contest, scoring once and setting up two more before he came off at halftime in a mass substitution of all the outfield players. When the journeyman forward who replaced him injured his shin, Tom was put back on the field for the last ten minutes, and scored again. In the dark cramped dressing room word got around that the two new players had arrived. They had been in the stand watching the game. Tom listened for more information, content that Grant had seen him play so well.

The pair were in the clubhouse, where supporters, coaches and players from both sides were drinking and mingling. Wilko brought the new players over for a handshake with each member of the squad. Grant was black. For some reason Tom had not been expecting that. Automatically he made the assumption that Grant would be faster than him, that he would be a good dribbler—which is what people must have meant when they had described him as "class" or "quality," words that Tom had rarely heard said about a black player before, unless he was foreign.

But from the first moment Grant touched the ball the next morning it was obvious that he was a player. The session started with a non-contact game, and he seemed incapable of losing control of the ball. Whenever it was at his feet his first notion was to glide forward, and even though he was not in fact any quicker than Tom, he drifted with ease past his markers, cutting infield off either wing, his head always up, searching for a pass. His teammates responded immediately to his ability. Even Gundi found a new energy. Twice he ran on to one of Grant's through balls and rounded Foley to score. When he sprinted towards Grant to celebrate, Tom realized that Gundi would soon be giving him the buttock-crossing code, that they would probably invent new codes between themselves.

Munro too, was good, and Tom knew that it must have taken an attractive financial package to persuade them both to join Town. The two were naturally drawn into the company of Gundi, Jones and the other established players. The quiet Jamaican, Lloyd-Day, had also done well in the two friendlies, although he continued to keep to himself, walking about the ugly landscaped grounds in a different orbit to each of the bored little groups doing the same thing.

One breakfast time the trialists were taken aside, one at a time, and both sent home.

Tom sat with Beverley in the empty cafeteria playing a slow game of cards. Liam had not texted for two days. It was clearly a very busy period for him, yet Tom could not stop himself wanting to know if Liam was thinking about him. If he had been spending his free time with Leah. When Beverley left to go for a nap Tom went outside. Concrete sculptures rose at random from the stiff, browning lawns. Water sprung rhythmically from some of them or bled down smooth sides into underground tanks. He reached the shore of a small lake, on the other side of which stood Boyn and Daish, skimming stones.

"Hey."

It was Bobby, close behind him. "How's it going, Tommy?"

"Yeah, OK."

"No bad here, eh?"

They looked together across the lake. In the distance a bank of cloud was coming in off the coast.

"I was wanting to ask another favor. I know I owe you that three-fifty still, and I'm good for it, don't worry, but see, I was wondering if you could lend me a bit more, for now just."

"Really? I don't know if I can, Bob. How much?"

"However much you're able." He was staring at Tom.

"No, I don't think I can this time."

"Oh. Right-o. Fair enough. No bother."

Tom watched him walk away. He could have lent him the money without too much difficulty, but he had not wanted to. Bobby's new contract was probably more lucrative than his own, for one thing. But it was not so much that, or even that he knew Bobby was gambling, so much as an objection to Bobby's obvious inability to control himself. He wondered what Liam might say. He imagined telling him or Beverley or any of them—how easy it would be to let them in on it, to expose Bobby.

While they milled about before dinner he saw Bobby talking to Richards in a corner, the two of them turning their backs to the room, Richards very slightly shaking his head at Bobby. A nasty satisfaction crawled through Tom at the rejection on Bobby's face, his helplessness in the shadow of a problem which, no matter how much everyone might continue to praise his development on the field, was only going to get bigger.

Grant started the final friendly. Within minutes he was being double-marked—the spindly Irish winger tracking back to help out his fullback. Grant, although he dominated the pair, never tried to embarrass them. He was looking always for a teammate, for the right pass. Tom sat in the wooden dugout, impatient to get on. He could hear in his mind Liam's words on the phone: *He's good, you know.* The tiny drunk contingent of Town fans who had taken their holidays to follow the tour cheered Grant's every involvement, and when Tom did get put on, Grant remained, switching to the left flank. The spindly winger, flummoxed by the change, followed him across the pitch, so that for the few minutes until his manager shouted out new instructions Grant was being tailed by three of the opposing team. Even then, with Tom completely unmarked on the other side of the field, Grant was still the player his teammates wanted to get the ball to.

That final night they were allowed out in the town where they had just played, a small place that seemed to be located entirely along one short stretch of road. There were, however, eight pubs. In the second of them Tom spoke for the first time to Grant. Tom had been standing with Beverley and Richards when Grant got up from the table in front, just as the other two went off to the pool table.

"All right, buddy, you want a drink?" Grant asked him.

"I'm all right, thanks."

"Don't reckon you mind coming to the bar with me, anyway? I think there's some in here have never seen this many black guys before."

"Sure."

It did appear that some of the drinkers were looking over as they walked to the bar, but it was usual in some of the smaller towns the team visited for the arrival of twenty young men in designer jeans and stretch T-shirts to attract some kind of attention.

"Good cross, that, by the way," Grant said. "The third goal." He ordered his drink, glancing about, conscious of being watched, and an instinct of pity moved in Tom. "What's the standard like in League Two?" Grant asked. "Better than that, right?"

"Better than that, yes." Tom was surprised at how unguardedly he was talking to him. "You play left side much for Oldham?"

"Sometimes. Kind of prefer it. I can cut in and shoot more. My left back at Oldham was really attacking, so it worked well there. He could get up the outside and stretch defenses for me. I don't know if the manager here has decided how he wants to play me yet."

It hit Tom that Grant had been guaranteed a starting place. It had probably not even occurred to him that he and Tom might be competing for the same spot.

"What's he like, anyway, the manager?" Grant asked, stooping to pick up his drink from the counter. There was a long scar on the back of his neck, pink, like an earthworm.

"Pretty fair."

"Good. Suits me. I like fair."

With some difficulty, due to the squad having splintered across all eight pubs, they were collected at the designated time and returned to the campus. Tom told Beverley that he was going for a short walk to clear his head before going up to the room. He went towards the hill. Hiccups bolted in his chest. He lay down next to the lake and waited for them to pass. Above him a black seam of night, massed with stars, cleft the layers of cloud. By the time he stood up, he knew exactly the words he was going to say to Liam. He mounted the hill, steeling himself, and dialed. The call went to answerphone. An image came into his head of Liam out with Leah, laughing, their friends around them, Liam taking out his phone to look at the screen then sliding it back into his pocket.

When he got back to the room, Beverley was sitting up in bed. His face was shiny, the sides of his head damp.

"Still up?" Tom said.

"Yeah. Just thinking."

Tom sat down on his own bed. "What about?"

"I was piss-poor today, wasn't I?"

"I thought you played decent. Just a friendly. I wouldn't worry."

"Yeah, but I do, mate. Can't stop it. This time's always the worst, before the season starts. Just don't know what's going to happen."

Tom started taking his shoes off. He fumbled at the laces, which he seemed to have done up in some complex and confusing way. They would not come undone. He picked away at them and sudden annoyance flooded through him, through his arms, his fingertips—at himself, for doing them up like an idiot, at Liam. "You've nothing to worry about," he said. "Your place is nailed on. It's me should be worried."

"Grant, you mean?"

"Obvious he's a starter."

"Might play him on the left, though."

"He might play him on the left, yeah."

He gave up on the laces and tugged the shoes off from the heel. Beverley twisted towards his phone on the bedside table, probably to set the alarm that they had woken up to without fail on each of the five mornings, a whole hour before breakfast. In the light of his bedside lamp Tom could make out the fading red area around Beverley's tattoo. He tried to envisage the girlfriend, waiting with him in the tattoo parlor, but when he did so it was Leah sitting there, stroking a hand down Liam's wide white back.

"Bev? Can I tell you something?"

"Course."

He did not know what he was doing. He was drunk. But he could not stop the words from coming. "Know I said I'd been seeing this girl but we split up ages ago before you were at Town?"

"Did you?"

"Yes . . . think so, not sure, but anyway the thing is, though, it wasn't true. I wasn't seeing anyone then."

"OK."

"But I am now."

Beverley was looking at him closely, trying hard to understand.

"I am now, but it's not the same girl. It's not. Not the same."

"I'm not following, mate. Sorry. Bit pissed."

"It's not a girl," he said and wanted to laugh. The words came out of him and he did not care. He felt a surreal sense of abandon, as though he was talking about somebody else.

Beverley's face looked blank. He gave a short strange laugh, his eyes fixed on Tom's. "I'm not sure what you're saying to me."

"I'm saying the person I'm seeing is a man."

Beverley's expression remained blank.

"You're telling me you're seeing a man?"

"Yes."

"You shitting me?"

"No."

Through his drunkenness he was lucidly aware that he should not be doing this, that Liam would not want him to.

There was a strange smile on Beverley's face. "Fucking hell," he said and nodded very slowly. "Right, well, that's fine, mate."

Tom laughed.

"I would never have guessed that," Beverley said.

"OK. Good to hear, actually."

"Sorry, I mean—well, no, that is what I mean. I'd never have guessed that. Who is it, that you're seeing?"

"You don't know them."

Beverley sat upright in his bed. "Nothing changes," he said. "Right. Nothing changes. I'm not going to tell anybody. I'm not going to ask to stop rooming with you. Full stop." He held out his hand. Tom leaned over and shook it. "Nothing, OK."

For a few minutes neither of them spoke while Tom went into the bathroom to get undressed. He felt outside himself. Delirious.

"My cousin's gay," Beverley said when Tom got into bed. "We think he is, anyway."

They lay in silence. Beverley's bedside lamp remained on, as if keyed in to his thoughts. "What are you going to do?"

"Do?"

"You're not going to tell anyone at the club?"

"You fucking joking?"

There was silence again. Tom shut his eyes, although he felt a long way from sleep. Beverley, quietly, started laughing.

"What is it?"

"I'm just thinking about it. If you told them. The look on their faces." He turned out the light. But a moment later: "There any other gay players?"

"No. How would I know?"

"Point. Don't know. Hey, Tom?"

"Yeah?"

"Seriously, I'm . . . I don't know, I'm honored you told me that."

Tom opened his eyes. He stared up at the red pupil of the smoke detector. "This doesn't feel real," he said. "None of it feels real."

In the morning neither made any mention of the conversation. Beverley was exactly as normal—more obviously normal, in fact, in his perkiness and chatter, than usual. He stayed beside or near Tom throughout breakfast and the tour debriefing, and followed him onto one of the minibuses for the journey to the airport, where they occupied the same two seats as they had on the journey out, Beverley for a long time cleaning his iPad screen with a wet wipe, separating Tom from the aisle and the other players.

A vague shifting unease settled on Tom as he looked out of the window at the fields and hedges and drenched gray hamlets, the lifeless roadside pubs appearing, disappearing. He had no doubt that he could trust Beverley—he had known it as soon as the words had started to come, with a sureness that he could not possibly have imagined before—and yet the more he went over what he could remember of the conversation, the more it disturbed him, the more distant from Liam it made him feel.

Liam finished at the ground early and was at Tom's house by five. Through the living-room window Tom saw his car pull up at the curb. He went outside and met him in the graveled front garden, where, without saying anything, they kissed for a long time by the bins even as one of Tom's Bangladeshi neighbors walked past the gate.

They went inside, upstairs, and only later when they sat down to eat the burgers and chips that had been in the freezer did Tom tell him about Beverley.

Liam was taken aback. "Why didn't you tell me you were going to do that?"

"I didn't know. I hadn't planned it."

"So, what . . . you just got pissed and told him?"

"I wasn't pissed."

"You were fucking pissed, mate. I heard your answerphone message."

"Oh, so you listened to it then?" Tom turned away towards the window. "It felt right, that's all. He's not going to tell anyone."

"How do you know that?"

"I just do. You did it. You told someone."

Liam pushed his chair back. "You think any of this is fucking easy for me? Do you think you're the only one that ever has a hard time dealing with what they are?" He stormed into the kitchen. Seconds later the fridge door closed with a thud. When he appeared again at the doorway, though, he looked calmer.

"I've known Leah for years. She's my friend. This guy Beverley has been at the club for, what, five months? He might be all right but he's a teammate. You don't know him." He went back into the kitchen. Tom left him alone. Stupid injustice welled inside him, working into anger as he deliberated going through to appease him and imagined the scene, two gays making up after their tiff.

Liam did not go home to his own flat. He stayed the night, but in bed they were quiet and remote, not touching or saying good night. By the morning Tom's anger was already turning into anxious self-doubt—that Liam would draw away from him, that everything was going to change and it would be his fault. But Liam's mood had also altered. "I went too far," he said. "I'm sorry. Let's forget it."

Tom moved up against him, overwhelming relief pouring through him at the words, at the simplicity of the apology.

23

The shading stripes were mown in and the naked field marked out. Liam framed the playing areas with string and rolled brilliant white lines onto the surface—the touchlines, halfway line, center circle and penalty areas materializing bit by bit, clean and perfect as icing. With a brush he painted the center spot, the penalty spots. When he had repainted the goalposts he knelt to trim the grass around each of their bases with a pair of kitchen scissors, then collected up the trimmings with his hands and put them into his pocket, like a keepsake.

Tom could tell, during the quiet times that they lay in bed or watched television, that Liam was thinking constantly about the pitch, and in these moments Tom's attention too would turn to the new season. He made targets for himself: assists, goals, appearances. He visualized himself playing, in a system with Grant on the left sweeping inside and looking for Tom to make a run.

When the starting eleven for the final friendly was put up on the wall of the dressing room, however, he was not in it.

From his position in the dugout he could see the outline of Liam, up in the control center, staring out at the grass. At Tom's level, in the sunshine, the pitch shone like a body of water. Two Wolves players were warming up close to him, passing a ball between them. The path of it, after each exchange, appeared as a visible line over the sward.

Just before kickoff Wilko promised Tom a run-out, but when, on sixty-five minutes, Richards was taken off and Grant switched to the left, it was Willis who was brought on, and the formation adjusted to a 4-3-3 that Tom had no place in. He watched, showing no sign of his delight when the two Wolves wingers capitalized on the change, continually attacking the green exposed flanks of the Town defense. Tom was put on for the final three minutes. He was given no positional instructions and touched the ball once. On returning to the dressing room he did not bother to shower and changed straight into his clothes in order to leave as soon as the manager's talk was over.

The last training session before the season opener was brisk. Focused and fun, according to the number two. He made them play a game that he had devised at a previous club in which two five-a-side matches were played simultaneously, across each other, with a shared center circle and four sets of goalposts. The exercise quickly became chaotic, then hostile, and was only partly improved when the number two remembered that the game required the use of two balls, not one. When it was over, Wilko—who had spent the morning on the sidelines, observing, talking on his phone, calling individuals over for short private conversations—asked Tom to come and see him once he had changed and eaten.

"You've bulked up," he said when they were sitting down together in his little windowless office. "That's good. You won't get bullied as much now."

"It was part of my fitness program."

"Good. Tom, I've got a proposal for you. You're in good shape. You look sharp in training. I don't want you to lose condition. I'd like you to go out on loan."

Tom shifted his eyes to the wall. His lungs stopped, as though he had just been punched in the chest.

"I need you to have game time, and there's a couple of Conference teams, good outfits, who have been on the phone."

"My agent—"

"I've spoken to your agent. He's up for this. You should speak to him, obviously."

There was a flip chart behind the manager's head: CHELTENHAM. HOTEL FRI NIGHT. NOBODY TO LEAVE DINNER TABLES UNTIL (AJ, MM, JD) GIVE OK—£30. NO MOBILES AFTER 11 PM—£30. DRESSING ROOM TO BE LEFT TIDY NOT DISGRACE—£40.

"Tom? First thoughts?"

"What if I want to stay and compete for my place?"

Wilko nodded. "I'll be up-front, Tom. You're not in my plans." He gave Tom a sympathetic smile.

Tom thrust his knee into the angle of the table leg, desperate not to cry. "I've just signed a new deal." His voice broke on the final word.

Wilko was nodding again. "Things change very quickly in football. I didn't know Michael Grant would become available. I didn't know that the player I've signed this morning would become available. It's no disrespect to you, Tom, to say that these are higher-level players."

"What's my level then? Non-league?" he said and at once shrank back from the whinging faggoty sound of his own voice.

"I don't loan to rival teams. Never have. And these are good sides, Tommy. Both of them get the ball down. I'll make sure to guarantee you a starting place. One month with an option for extension or permanent transfer, and a callback clause in case I get an injury. Sleep on it. I don't need you to come in for the match tomorrow."

Tom closed the door and stood in the dim passageway. From the far end of it the sound of studs was building as the scholars came in from the pitches. It echoed towards him like a downpour. He stayed where he was until the corridor returned to near silence and there was only the far-off noise of cutlery being tipped into a tray. An occasional shout from the dressing room. For an instant he wanted to kick or punch something. A wall. The noticeboard. The line of urine samples on the floor beneath it. But he could hear Wilko moving around inside his office so he walked quickly away, down the passageway, out of the building.

He sat in his car for some time. On the training field the assistant groundsman was replacing divots. Tom took out his phone and texted Beverley. Seconds later, his phone rang.

"What are you going to do?" Beverley asked.

"Don't know."

"What did he say if you turn it down?"

"Frozen out. Not in his plans."

There was the thrum of people and faint scrambled music at Beverley's end. "I'd go. Don't see you've got a choice. It's shit, yeah—you're living in a hotel, you don't know anybody, you don't know what's going to happen after—but what else are you going to do? If a manager's decided he doesn't want you then that's you bombed out. I know it, believe me." He waited for Tom to respond and when he did not, said, "It's not fair, Tom, but that's football. Where are you? Do you want me to come and meet you?"

"No, it's all right, thank you."

Later, at home, he heated up a pasta ready meal and sat down in front of a television film that he had never heard of. He got a text from Liam, late—"Still here, final touches . . . be glad when it's ten to five tomorrow!"—which he did not reply to. He finished his meal, watched the film for a while before giving up on it, washed up and went to bed.

In the morning he worked out then moved restlessly from one room to another. There was nothing to do. Nowhere to put himself. The sly indulgent thought of Liam finding out from somebody else, and of other people gradually learning what had been done to him, gave him little respite. The other players would be focused on the match anyway, on their own futures. The fans would be excited about Grant's debut and the arrival, made public that morning, of the latest signing: Dominic Curtis, another right-winger, who before a knee injury had been a Welsh international. The supporters would see the logic in moving Tom out. As for his family, he could not bring himself to speak to them.

Town won 2–0. Tom listened to the commentary on the local radio station. There was no mention of his omission from the squad. Curtis had not been registered in time for the game so Grant played on the right. The commentators could not go on enough about the improvement he had brought to the team. He was involved in both of the goals. Tom could hear the crowd celebrating them, distantly through his open window, seconds after the muffled eruption on the radio.

Liam called after the match, when his divot team had finished repairing the pitch. He had not known that Tom wasn't in the squad, he said. He did not understand why Tom had not told him. He wanted to come over.

They sat at the table with the cans of lager that Liam had brought round. Tom told him about the meeting with Wilko. About the loan. Liam listened, saying nothing while Tom spoke. Tom studied his face for a reaction but could not see one.

"I'm sorry," Liam said when Tom had finished. He put his hand out on the table but Tom did not move to touch it. There was a sharp wounding enjoyment in these small rejections that made no sense. He did not even know why he was doing it.

Liam took a drink from his can. "I think you've got to."

"Go on loan?"

"Yes."

"Both those clubs are more than a hundred miles away."

"What choice is there? Your deal's only a year. Sit it out and you'll end up nowhere. Least this way, if you do well, there's more of a chance that you'll get back in. Injuries, cups, all that."

"You want me to go?"

"Fucking of course I don't want you to go. I'm just trying to be realistic, Tom."

"Right. Not you has to move away, is it, though? You can just carry on like normal."

"Except you won't be here. So it won't be normal."

"Nothing's normal anymore," Tom said quietly.

"What does that mean?"

Tom paused. If everything had been normal, the thought flashed through his mind, then he would have been concentrating on nothing but football for the last year and none of this would be happening.

"I mean I've forgotten what normal is," he said. "All I know is it's not this."

The next day was dry and hot. They drove some distance along the coast and set up on a windless busy beach. They ate ice creams. They swam in the sea. They walked up the slope behind the beach and lay in an embrace on the hot shifting sand of a dune at the edge of a golf course. Liam ran his hand over Tom's neck, his back, and Tom felt his senses heighten at the pressure of his touch, the roughness of Liam's fingertips against his skin. He felt childish, petty, for pushing him away and held tightly to him, needing, on this glorious sunny day, away from the club, the town, to let Liam know that he was there, that he did not want to be apart from him.

They met Leah for a drink. The same pub. Same time. Probably, had it not been raining, it would have been the same outside table and seating arrangement. During the first round of drinks the three of them struggled for something to talk about—the weather, Leah's upcoming trip to Milan—that would last for longer than a minute or two. When Leah went to the toilet Tom and Liam reached instinctively towards each other. On her return their hands were still held together on the bench. They pulled apart but not before she noticed—with, Tom was sure, a fleeting look of distaste. She did not say anything, yet the shared knowledge that they had parted because of her hovered unspoken about the table.

In the toilets she had apparently come up with several questions for Tom. She asked about his house, if he had finished doing it up yet. About the mood among the squad and the win on Saturday. To Tom's surprise she asked if the manager had said anything to him about the signing of Grant and Curtis. "It's a result for the chairman," she said, "getting those two to drop to League Two. They'll be on as much as Gundi, I'd bet."

Tom did not know how much Gundi was on. He wondered if it was possible that she did.

"You can only keep doing what you're doing, you know," she said.

"You sound like him."

"Well, he's right."

A man walked past the table on his way to the toilets, starting to pull at his belt before he reached the door.

Tom stood up. "Another drink?"

Just before they left the pub, Leah turned to Tom and said, "Can I ask you a favor?"

Tom tried to look unperturbed. "Yeah, sure."

"There's a few things at the club I wonder if you could pick up for me, for Chris—his kit and stuff."

"No problem. He wants his kit?"

"That and whatever else there is for him. Just so he's got it all. No one from the club has been in touch with him about it. He'd come in himself but I thought I'd save him the journey."

"I could drop it off for you."

"That's OK, I can come down to the training ground."

They exchanged numbers. She said that she would be in touch in the morning and thanked him. When she said goodbye to Liam a look passed between the two of them that made Tom think they had plotted this in advance.

They arranged to meet after training on Friday. She came into the clubhouse with her son, who, close to, now looked so much like Easter that Tom was instantly forced into the thought of him: of Easter at home on the sofa with his leg up on a table, dressed in full kit. The child was in a pram. Tom did not know how to greet him. He did not know how to greet either of them.

"Hi," he said.

"Hi." She did not move forward to kiss him.

He directed her towards the pair of beaten-up plastic chairs against one wall of the reception area. On one of them was the sports bag that contained Easter's things, a tag attached to a handle with 19, his new squad number, written on it. The child began agitating to get out of the pram. When Leah lifted him out and set him down he ran straight to the entrance door, left open for the breeze, and tried to push it shut. She went to tell him to stop as a group of players appeared from the passageway. All of them glanced down at her, crouched speaking firmly to the boy, as they made their way out. Most must have known her, Tom thought, and he could sense that she was aware of them, preoccupied as she was with the writhing child. Boyn came next into the reception area, and Leah turned her face towards him. For a second they looked at each other without speaking, until she turned again to the boy and Boyn came over to Tom. He put his lips almost to Tom's ear. "Easter's missus," he whispered. "You dirty little boy, Tommy." He gave Tom a squeeze on the arm and a small smile, and walked out of the building without looking down again at Leah and her child.

Tom picked up the bag. "I'll walk out with you."

He knew, as they headed towards the car park, that they were being watched.

"How's his leg doing?" he asked, moving closer to her.

"The cast is off now. He's started his rehab."

"That's good. He must be pleased."

"You'd think," she said and walked on without saying any more. Tom considered, not for the first time, that there was something closed off about her, this woman that Liam trusted so much, something discomfiting.

They arrived at her car. She took the child out of his pram and loaded him into his seat. Tom thought he should fold down the pram for her and put it into the boot but was not confident about all the buttons and levers. He stood and watched her do it. He put the bag into the backseat, next to the child. She closed the boot and they stood together beside the car.

"Thank you," she said.

"No bother." He stepped forward to put an arm awkwardly around her. He breathed in the smell of her perfume, holding her slender stiffening body until she drew away and got into the car.

Leah started the engine, observing him walk back to the clubhouse. The ease with which he carried his secret, going back inside to mix with the others, suddenly incensed her. This other player—Beverley, the one Liam said that he had told—was he comfortable, she wondered, with being made party to it? Did it not bother him, what they were doing, that they were getting away with it and expecting him to just carry on as before—socializing, rooming, showering with Tom? Everything continuing as usual, just as Liam expected from her. If Chris or any of the others found out, she had a good idea what their reaction would be. Alek Boyn, who had blanked her just now but obviously thought pretty damn highly of Tom. Thought that he was normal, one of the boys.

She drove away down the lane. On one of the pitches ahead of her half a dozen scholars were taking it in turns to punt balls from the halfway line towards a set of unguarded goalposts. She slowed to watch them. When one of the boys struck the crossbar she understood from the group's response that this was the point of the game. Through her open window she heard the shouting as the boys piled on top of the successful player. There were no other vehicles on the lane. She brought the car to a standstill, the view from the clubhouse blocked by a hedge. The giddy romp of their bodies sprawling over the grass. They were only a few years younger than her, these boys. If they were to see her there, she asked herself, would they know that? One of them, the one who had hit the crossbar, was clambering out from the heap. He darted across the field. Seconds later all the others were in pursuit. As they closed on him he jinked one way, then the other, until finally they were upon him, one big boy jumping onto his back and bringing him down, prompting another happy pile-on.

"Mummy, Mummy!" Tyler yelled, startling her. She turned around to shush him and set off for home.

She parked on the driveway. Upstairs, the blind of the office was down. She tried to think whether it had been like that when she left the house. She could not remember. She could not be sure, she realized, that it was not always in that position now. More than ever, they kept to their own areas of the house. When she cleaned and on the rare occasions she still brought him up snacks and cups of coffee, she had begun to feel like an intruder, and because he was always in the house she had taken to cleaning his rooms less and less often. They were getting dirty. There was a smell. She had noticed that Tyler too sensed the privacy of those spaces. He no longer shouted through the doors or beat on them to be let in, and he had a couple of times referred to the spare room as "Daddy bedroom," a phrase that she was fearful he might repeat at his nursery or in front of her mum.

She carried Tyler inside.

"I've got your stuff," she called up the stairs.

He came down straightaway. He looked at the bag, taking in the tag on the handle.

"Thank you," he said and knelt down to open the bag and pull items from it: sweat top, wet top, vests, recovery skins, socks, underpants, and his playing shirts, which he held up, staring at the back of each of them, the number, before bundling everything once again into the bag. She thought about Boyn and Tom whispering about him, or her, and she wanted to go towards him, but she held back. He got gingerly to his feet, picked up the bag, and returned upstairs.

Tyler was bawling at her. She gave him a bag of grapes and sat down on the sofa behind him while he ate them in front of a cartoon. The rest of the day, the evening, stretched ahead of her. She thought about calling Liam later, but then she imagined him with Tom, talking, kissing, touching.

"More, Mummy, more, Mummy." Tyler was climbing up her legs, pulling at her shorts. "More gape, Mummy. More—"

"Oh, shut up, Tyler. Just fucking shut up."

Immediately feeling guilty, she reached to console him, but he did not cry or come to her for comfort. Instead he moved slowly, deliberately away to sit on the floor in front of the deranged beeping creatures on the television and put his thumb into his mouth. She got up from the sofa and knelt behind him, cuddling into his back.

"I'm sorry, Ty." She pressed her lips to his skull. "I'm sorry. Mummy's not in a happy mood," she said very quietly into his hair. "Mummy's not very happy."

Chris came down later to eat dinner with her. They sat on the sofa together. At one point, leaning forward for his glass, he knocked the remote control onto the floor and she noticed, from his stomach, the definition of his arms, that he was not keeping to his program. Her mind went to the ex-pros that she had seen at functions and in the players' lounge. Their bellies and jowls and painful locking knees; their faces, vaguely recognizable, puffy with inactivity. She wanted somehow to tell him that everything was going to be OK, but the idea of speaking to him so intimately was inconceivable. His body, his future, their future, sex, finances, all now were walled off.

Increasingly she was worried about money. He was clearly not receiving any appearance bonuses, and there was a possibility his contract contained a clause in the club's favor regarding injury. She had never seen his contract. She did not know if he had ever seen it. There was no way of knowing exactly how much money was left. Although the accounts that she had access to did have money in them it always confounded her there was not more. And as for how much the mess of stocks and investments that his advisers had set up for him was worth, she was fairly sure that he had little idea himself. What would he do, she asked herself on an impulse, if she left? Her blood quickened as she allowed herself to contemplate this. A spark of secret pleasure came and went. He would not cope; that much was clear. He was not coping now. She watched his cheeks working at a mouthful of chicken and sweet potato mash and she yearned for something that they could talk about, just to hear his voice and know that he was still there, that they were both still there.

The party traveling to Milan were all booked onto the same flight. Most of them took the same train connections to the airport but she went separately, meeting them at the check-in desk. They had all brought less luggage than her. She watched them for a few seconds from a short distance away, regretting her bulky suitcase, until Maria noticed her and waved her over.

Maria sat next to her on the plane. The eleven others and their course tutor were paired up on the seats ahead of them, ordering glasses of wine, chatting.

"You having one?" Maria asked when the steward approached their seat.

"Best not."

Maria frowned. "Why? You're on holiday."

The steward, listening to their exchange, leaned over and placed two glasses and two tiny bottles of white wine onto their seat trays. "Oops," he said. When he departed, smiling to himself, Leah's first thought was of Liam and Tom having sex.

Maria's boyfriend had recently been laid off, she told Leah. They were having difficulties with the rent, and she was worried she might have to leave the course before getting her diploma in order to go full-time at her job. "Or," she said, "Nathan could get off his arse and look properly for one himself. Anyway. So, your husband end up looking after your little boy then?"

"He can't," she lied. "His leg's broken. Tyler's with my mum."

"Oh, right. Hey, can I see a photo?"

"You sure? It's a pretty ugly break," Leah said, giggling, realizing that she was pissed already.

The hotel was close to the exhibition center. From the window of her room Leah could see its spiraling glass turrets, and in the distance the city—a dreamlike horizon of basilicas and towers and palaces, the cathedral, a castle, mountains. She stood for a while staring out at it, then showered, changed and went downstairs to meet the others in the lobby to go out for dinner. They ate near the hotel in a pizza restaurant full of television screens which, despite its proximity to the trade fair, was almost empty. Afterwards, the group was keen to go on. Leah left them to it, telling Maria that she was tired, slipping away for the hotel.

She found out at breakfast that they had not gone very far. All of the places they had walked past had been quiet, or they had not been sure whether they were actually bars, so they had ended up returning to the hotel and drinking there.

They went straight to the exhibition center after breakfast. Inside, everywhere was noise and activity. They clustered together, looking to the tutor, who simply smiled and said, "Go explore."

There was a very long central walkway through the exhibition space. They went down it, peering into the pavilions on either side, which were filled with colorful displays. Half an hour later, when they came to the end, they turned and walked back the other way. They found a cafe and sat down, ordering coffee and sparkling water. One of the students, Sarah, produced a plan of the fair and everybody leaned in to study it, discussing which pavilions and exhibitors to visit. Maria asked Leah if she would like to go with her to take a look around.

They left the cafe together, Leah pointing them towards the knitwear pavilion. Smiling faces greeted them when they entered it. Spinners, knitters and machine-makers were lined up beside their displays, explaining and demonstrating to other visitors. Leah did not know where to begin. She followed Maria to a table draped with yards of material. Maria held up a length of intricately patterned organic wool. "This is beautiful." She put it down and walked to another table, a Japanese-looking woman advancing to talk to her, while Leah stepped towards a wire tree hung with cardigans. She felt slightly light-headed, dazed by the abundance, her mind beginning to run with thoughts about the fabrics and what could be done with them as she walked around, examining, touching. "It's just amazing," Maria said when they came together in front of a woolen clock in the center of the pavilion. "We're here surrounded by all this stuff that's going to inform trends before designers even know what the trends are going to be. I can't get my head round it."

They went to the leather pavilion, where a workshop demonstration was taking place. Maria purchased several samples from a very blond man in jodhpurs. At the next pavilion, silks, Leah bought a couple of samples of her own. They found a place to eat lunch and sat on stools at a counter, watching the crowds.

"I'm going to finish the course," Maria said.

"You should."

"My head's full of ideas."

"Mine too." Leah took a bite of her mushroom pastry. "We should put some of them together, you know. When the course is over."

Maria looked round at her. "OK. Deal."

Leah turned away to the mass of people as she drank from her bottle of water, aware that she was blushing.

They visited more pavilions, collecting samples and stumbling into a seminar on the 3-D printing market, which they stayed until the end of. By mid-afternoon they were exhausted. They met up with the others at the arranged time and place and returned to the hotel.

In her room, after a short nap, she made a Skype call to her mum on Maria's laptop. When the call went through Tyler's face filled her screen. He was hitting the keyboard and did not at first notice her. She could hear her mum in the background: "It's Mummy. Look, it's Mummy." Then Robert: "Lift him up, Donna. He can't see." Her mum pulled Tyler back and he sat on the floor waving his arms about, then lurched forward for the keyboard again.

"Tyler," Leah called. "Tyler."

He looked up. For a couple of seconds he was confused, but then a joyful smile broke out over his face. He flung himself at the screen. It filled with his nose, squashed up against it. Leah pressed her own nose to Maria's laptop. She screwed her eyes closed, spoke his name again. When she pulled back, he was scampering away. Her mum's face appeared, and Leah briefly turned the screen away from herself, not wanting Robert to see her wiping her eyes.

"Hi, Mum. He giving you the runaround then?"

There was laughter from her mum and from Robert. "You could say that, yes."

When she had said goodbye she sat for a while on the bed. Her fabric samples were piled on the table in front of her. Eventually, she went over to them, smoothing her hand over the top one. For the first time since leaving home she wondered what Chris would be doing at that moment. She could see him at the computer, the desk around it littered with coffee cups and the stained Tupperwares of the meals she had stacked up in the fridge for him. The thought of telling Chris about the conversation that afternoon with Maria, the admission that she sometimes had fantasies to do with designing, a career, the future, was unreal. He did not know about any of that. He did not even know who Maria was.

The others were downstairs in the hotel bar. Maria beckoned her over to where she was talking to Sarah and a couple of the other women and Richard, the only man on the course.

"I was just telling this lot what your husband does for a living."

"I can't believe you never told us," Richard said. "I love football."

"You a Town fan?" Leah asked.

"No, don't be daft, I support a proper team. But I love football."

Maria put a glass of wine into Leah's hand and turned back to Richard. "Who's your team, then?"

"Arsenal."

"Get to see them much?"

"Not as much as I'd like, no."

"When did you last go to a game?"

Richard smiled. "Few years ago, maybe."

Maria put her hand on his forearm. "Shit, Rich, you really do love football."

Towards the end of the first year, once she had decided that Richard was not gay, Leah had begun to suspect that there was an attraction between him and Maria, and as she watched them together now, teasing and laughing, the shamelessness of it riled her—making her want, before it passed, to bring up Maria's boyfriend, just as Maria had brought up Chris.

"We've been given a tip," Richard said to Leah. "Barman's told us about a place we should go to. An actual bar this time, apparently. What do you reckon?"

"Yes," she said. "Sounds good."

The bar turned out to be one of the places that the others had passed the previous night. There was no sign on the outside. When they went in it was dimly lit, busy, full of Italians. Two large plates of cured meats sat on the marble bar counter. They bunched inside the doorway until an effortless young woman in a couture dress came towards them and without being prompted asked in English for the group to follow her. She led them into a second room, gesturing for them to take the area in one corner among the casual disarrangement of heavy leather sofas and glass tables. Leah headed with Sarah and Richard towards the far side by a window, then checked herself, thinking the seats would be filled before she reached them. She took one end of a sofa instead, next to Maria.

"So," Maria said once the kerfuffle of ordering drinks from the hostess was out of the way, "what do you think, then? Me and you putting our heads together when the course is finished?"

"I'd like to."

"It could be small, you know, to start with. Get a little collection of things together. Set up an Internet operation, something like that. Do it from my flat—or yours, if you like."

Leah took a sip of her cocktail. From the far side of the group, Richard looked over. She pictured Maria arriving at her house, the surprise, embarrassment, on her face at the size of it.

"There'd be no money in it, obviously," Maria said. "Not at first. So Nathan would have to get off his arse."

"It might help him to, you never know."

"You never know." Maria held up her glass. Leah touched her own against it, trying to ignore the apparition of Chris, the idea of asking him if she and Maria could use his office.

"You know I've never done anything like this before, right?" Maria said. "I wouldn't have a clue what I'm doing."

"That makes two of us." Leah slid the gleaming cherry from her cocktail stick and put it into her mouth. "I wanted to open a shop once," she said. "A salon or something. But then Chris got transferred, and I had Tyler, and I sort of forgot about it."

"Guess you have to go wherever he goes, do you?"

Richard was looking over again.

"In a way."

"Some commitment, that."

"It's not for long, really, if you think about it. A footballer's career doesn't last long."

"No, I suppose it doesn't," Maria said, before changing the subject: "So, you enjoying being on holiday?"

"Yeah." Then, more quietly, "Different to my last holiday."

"Must be good having a break from being a mum."

She could see Tyler's face on the laptop screen. "It's just different with a kid. You're kind of always on duty." At once she felt guilty and stupid, for saying it—for the suggestion that it was Tyler she was having a break from—although Maria had turned her attention away to the group. There was a small burst of laughter, and as Sarah shared a joke with Maria across the tables, Leah's mind turned to those days by the pool with Tyler, conscious of Chris up there on the balcony, watching them. The days spent with the Scottish couple, Andrea and John, whose little girl had befriended Tyler over a stone collection; their ease together, the unspoken teamwork of their parenting. Her own awkwardness, explaining to them that it was too hot, too cramped, too slippery around the pool for Chris's leg when she knew, because she had seen him one afternoon when she had come back from the beach for Tyler's sun cream, that he went down there and that Andrea and John had probably seen him too at some point.

Leah had hidden behind the balcony railing that day while Tyler wailed at her from behind the sliding door, watching him eye up the girls on the other side of the pool. And what she had felt, at the same time as acknowledging to herself that there was definitely something wrong with her, as she saw his self-consciousness, his humiliation at his non-functioning body, was pity. Then anxiety, already foreseeing the time when the leg would be healed and he would return to football, to playing away matches, training trips.

They stayed at the bar for a couple of hours until they became hungry and found out that the bar did not serve food, except for some confusing arrangement to do with the meats on the counter. So they returned to the hotel and ordered pizzas. Somebody— Richard, she thought—got the barman to bring over two bottles of Prosecco. She had come to realize, even before they arrived back at the hotel, that it was her, not Maria, that Richard had been looking

at. He caught her eye again now, pouring one of the bottles of Prosecco, and as she met it she let herself smile back at him.

She remained sitting at one end of their long table, next to Sarah
and Maria, joining in occasionally with their conversation about
the plan for the morning, every now and again giving a look over,
knowing each time that he would return it. But the moment she
admitted the electric possibility of it, here, in a hotel, away, she was
at once consumed by guilt. She looked away, infuriated, knowing
that she could never do it, cross the line. And the thought came to
her again of Liam and Tom greedily fucking each other somewhere,
unbothered by what they were doing, getting away with it.

24

Tom listened to most of Town's first half against Plymouth in his car, until the transmission began to crackle at the limit of the station's range. He drove the rest of his journey in silence, turning the radio back on only to tune in for the full-time results shortly before his arrival at the loan club. Town had won 3–1. He parked in the stadium car park, empty because his new team was playing away, and he was greeted by the chairman's wife. She shook his hand, then hugged him. "We're delighted to have you," she said, uncomfortably close to his ear.

She took him on a short tour of the ground. There was one main, wooden stand. The other sides had a makeshift appearance. Along the opposite touchline were strung three small huts of different sizes and construction materials. Behind one goal was a small terrace, and behind the other a grass bank, along the top of which a row of beer garden parasols had been planted. The chairman's wife was amiable, full of conversation. Tom remembered that he had never sent the Daveys a gift or a card. He had intended to, but it was too late now. He was shown the dressing room, the players' tunnel, and then, with a wide proud smile that stretched her thin eyebrows, the pitch.

"We all think that this might be our year," she said with grandmotherly chumminess before they parted.

He drove to his hotel. He checked in, went up to his room and sank onto the bed, a peculiar sensation that he was in the same room, the same hotel, as a year ago seeping through him.

The club, despite Wilko's assertion that they were a well-run outfit on the rise, with a bit of money, playing the right kind of football, were an obvious two levels below Town. The training ground was a rented section of a boarding school's sports fields. Pupils took games and PE lessons in the afternoons, so three pitches were available for the football club to use each morning at the far side of the school buildings, next to a railway line running along the top of a brightly littered ridge beyond a high barbed-wire fence. The grass was thick and healthy, too long for football. On Tom's first morning he struggled initially to gauge the weight of his passes. Sprinting was difficult, heavy; his studs were too short for the turf and he twice went over on his ankle attempting sharp turns.

The squad was smaller than Town's. There were only seventeen players, most of them young. Tom counted seven or eight who were probably recent youth-team graduates. They were, in the main, welcoming. When it was mentioned that he was a Premier League academy product some of the younger ones crowded around him, wanting to hear about the experience. He gave his spiel, recounting more the words he had spoken before than the actual memory, which now felt so distant it did not seem real. The senior players were watchful of him. The only one who approached him to talk was the newly signed forward, who had been on trial with Town in Ireland. He came across immediately to shake Tom's hand and joke about how out of shape he had been on that tour. "I was in bits," he said. "Proper fucking mess."

Tom went at the session with gusto, determined to prove that he was better than this, than them, that he used to play for a Premier League club, for England age group teams. Once he had adjusted to the grass he began to show a few neat touches, and it was obvious that he could pass the ball better than anybody else there. The manager, a large old man, breathless from the first minute of the session, stopped the practice match to point at Tom. "Watch him. See. Time. Head up. Pick your man." Tom turned his eyes away, embarrassed, furtively proud. He worked even harder, raising his level further still. He immersed himself totally in the hustle of training, frantic not to slow down and let the sensation of being lost take over.

Near the end of the warm-down he moved alongside the journeyman forward, who started a conversation about injuries. As they stretched, the manager moved between the players, placing a hand on or around their shoulders, speaking quietly to them, a fat grandad. Some of the young players meandered off to chat to the little groups of schoolgirls who had finished morning lessons and walked out across the grounds. A few boys looked on as well, but from further away, lounging and laughing on the grass, making fun of the squad from a distance.

There were new, expensive gym and changing facilities at the school, but the squad based itself in an old circular wooden pavilion fitted out with a basic kitchen and one narrow table with benches down either side. During the practice match the injured players had gone in to put jacket potatoes into the oven. These three were now—while Tom lay on the grass turning and stretching his ankle, watching the players flirt with the schoolgirls—busy heating beans and grating cheese into a large bowl in the center of the table. The squad ate in two shifts, still in their kit. Noisy rebounding laughter filled the cramped space. At the end of the meal they drove, those with cars giving lifts to those without, to shower and change at the stadium.

Tom returned to his hotel. He watched television and played a computer game on his laptop until Liam called him after work.

"How did it go?" he asked.

"Fine. They're rubbish."

"It's non-league, mate. Are you OK?"

"Yes. Think so." For a while they were quiet. "We're at home Saturday," Tom said. "I could drive back after the match. Spend the rest of the weekend."

He sat each night in the restaurant of the hotel eating one of the three healthy choice options from the oversized menu. Liam occupied his thoughts constantly. Tom stewed over what he might be doing at any particular moment, trying to take comfort in the steady reliability of Liam's routine. He ate through the watery limp meals, disbelieving what had happened. Nothing made any sense: that his career was in pieces and he was here, adrift in a place where nobody was aware he existed. Cold, shooting doubts came at him without warning, but the next moment he would want to laugh hysterically, a lunatic in the corner of the restaurant behind a clown menu. Nobody knew him. The anonymity of it was as shocking and weightless as an ice bath.

After eating he went up to his room to go through a sequence of repeated actions: drawing the curtains, getting his kit for the next day ready on the chair by the desk, emptying, refilling the kettle. Everything in the room seemed fake, like stage props. He regretted leaving his cacti behind. The collection was something real. Safe. On top of which he was worried about them. Liam, for a grounds-man, was surprisingly useless with houseplants.

The players arrived at the ground only an hour before the kick-off of Tom's first match. Some had traveled, already in their strip, on trains and buses with early fans on their way to the stadium bar. The manager read out a scouting report on the opposition, half a dozen printed-out pages, crumpled and stained, that Tom suspected had not been altered from previous seasons. The other team was dangerous at throw-ins and corners. Set pieces generally. There was a big black boy up front, all elbows. A veteran left back, a plodder.

The manager looked at Tom. "Get at him. Get at him until his legs go."

In the opening exchanges Tom was able to beat his man without difficulty, regardless of his legs. Fifteen minutes in he delivered the cross for the first goal. He won a penalty, inducing the fullback into a clumsy challenge when Tom stepped outside, inside, outside him. The penalty was converted, and the hundred or so home support-ers behind the goal sang his name: "Pearman's too good for you, Pearman's too good for you . . ." When the one-hut contingent of away fans responded with the same chant Tom experienced a moment of searing clarity, a split-second rapture in which he knew with absolute certainty that all of this, being here, was only temporary.

At halftime the supporters behind the goal moved in a procession around the pitch to position themselves on the grass bank behind the other goal. From the restart the ball was played to Tom, who ran towards them, teasing the miserable hunching fullback, switching the ball from one foot to the other, relishing the stupefied anguish on his face, willing the chant, the catch in the supporters' collected breath as it started up again.

They won 3–0. Tom was named man of the match. He showered, changed and waited around in the tunnel until he was taken to the bar to pose for a photograph with a bottle of champagne and the owner of a car dealership.

It was seven o'clock before he was able to leave, past nine when he got home. Liam met him at the front door. They kissed for a long time against the entrance hall wall.

"You better not have killed my cacti, you fucker."

"Oh shit," Liam said, grinning, "was I supposed to be looking after them?"

There was a lineup of boots and a tin of wood stain on newspaper in the hall, a bunched fist of keys on the second step of the staircase.

"Been making yourself at home, then?"

"I have."

They went through to the living room. The cacti were healthy. In the kitchen a meal was waiting in the oven. Liam took it out and plated up: chili con carne. They drank the champagne, which was by now warm, and Tom told him about the match. Liam, to Tom's disappointment, listened quietly, nodding, seeming more interested in his food than in Tom's performance.

In the morning Tom went out to a cafe and returned with bacon sandwiches and a paper. They sat on the sofa to eat. Town were playing very well, Liam told him. The new players, he said, were outstanding. Dom Curtis, if it wasn't for the dodgy knee, would be in the Premier League. Tom, who already knew from the Internet how the new players were performing, could not help but detect the note of excitement in Liam's voice. He had met up with Leah shortly after her return from Milan, he said. She had been a bit odd and distracted, and he had not seen her since, probably because her head was buzzing with ideas and plans from the trip, he thought. And his parents had spoken about Tom over lunch last Sunday, saying what a nice lad he was. There were three new boys now, Liam said, who had not spoken a word for almost the whole time that he was there.

They read the sports pages, watched some of a touring car championship on the television and went upstairs a final time before Tom left.

It started to rain while he was on the motorway. The traffic slowed. Through the wet film of his windscreen the red burst blossoms of taillights filled his vision. He began to feel drowsy, listless—brought to his senses by the booming horn of an articulated lorry in the lane beside him.

The training pitches were marshy and yielding. Tom presumed they would be considered unfit for ball work, but after a conversation between the manager and his number two a bag of balls was brought out and a few players were instructed to carry the two sets of goalposts from the pavilion to positions beneath the rugby posts. Even in his longest studs Tom found it difficult to keep his footing. Mindful of injury, he ran about at half pace. The number two, reading this as laziness, shouted at him during a give-and-go routine, "Come on, princess. One decent game doesn't mean you're special. Get moving."

Tom itched to turn and tell him to fuck off, the amateur idiot, but he kept quiet. He upped his work rate slightly, part of him hoping to go down injured just to prove himself right, superior to all this.

In the stadium dressing room he kept to his usual corner to change after his shower. As he was putting his socks on, one of the defenders walked across, naked, and stood directly in front of him to talk to another player. Tom was intensely conscious of the penis in front of his face. The beads of water dripping from the end of it. He looked down, taking off his socks slowly, putting them back on again. He looked up when the man walked away, and watched his bright hairless bottom, testing, goading himself.

A few nights previously an unfamiliar member of the hotel staff had waited on his table. Tom had formed the impression that he was gay. There was a moment when the man had looked at him pointedly, and the idea that he had made the same assumption about Tom had made his chicken and bacon salad churn in his stomach.

Later, the knowledge that the man was possibly there in the hotel troubled him enough to keep him from sleeping. He was aware of a black shapeless fantasy that he could not allow to develop because he could not trust what it might mean, what he might be capable of.

He played in an FA Cup qualifier against a team, a town, that he had never heard of. It rained heavily shortly after kickoff, and the supporters on two sides of the ground moved to shelter underneath the ash tree in one corner. Early in the game Tom scored the first goal and automatically sought out the away fans to celebrate, before becoming unsure if there were any.

By the time he got back to his hotel the restaurant was closed. He opened the Bible drawer in his room, where he kept a small store of food: biscuits, cereals, peanuts, Nutri-Grain bars, energy drinks. He sat on the bed and ate handfuls of cereal straight from the box. On the bedside table his phone was flashing. There was a text message from Wilko: "Saw got goal today, well done, keep it up." Apart from Beverley, who had texted before Tom's first match to wish him luck, nobody had contacted him until now. Energized, he rang Liam. There was no answer. He considered calling him again, but when the short recording of Liam's voice finished he left a message and stayed awake for a long time waiting for him to phone back.

The other players liked him, he thought. He was easy for them to place: quiet, keeps to himself but not in an arrogant way. After a midweek draw against Weston-super-Mare Tom was again named man of the match. There were some joking complaints from the rest of the team about how they might as well give up any hope of champagne because Tom was obviously giving blow jobs to all the local businessmen. Although glad to be included in their banter, Tom knew that he had not in fact played well. With each game he was working less hard, seeking less the movement of the forwards. Instead of running the line and tracking back he would loiter, waiting for the ball to come to him—and when it did his first thought was usually to show up the fullback, or his own teammates, with flicks and dummies and unexpected one-twos. Or he would take the ball forward on his own, so disconnected from the match that even as he drove into the unprotected space his mind would be alternating between determination to prove himself and a quick self-pity that saw no point in trying.

It was over two months since he had seen his parents. He should have felt happy to be visiting them, or at least guilty that he did not. Instead, a resentful mood gripped him as he traveled up the motorway to spend a rare fixtureless weekend away from Liam. He arrived on the Friday evening in time for tea. After eating and the television, his mum went to bed and his dad got out a bottle of whisky which John had given him years ago as a fortieth-birthday present but had been lying on top of the kitchen cupboards ever since.

They sat down in the living room, the television off, and his dad poured two glasses, handing one to Tom.

"Oh, do you want ice?"

Tom paused, wondering which was the correct way to drink it.

"I'm fine, thanks, Dad."

"OK. Don't think we have ice anyway." He pushed back into his seat, sipping, frowning. Tom waited for him to speak but his dad remained quiet for some time. He looked tired—older, in the overhead light, than when Tom had seen him last.

"Things are going well then," his dad said.

"Fine. I'm playing OK."

"Playing well, I've read."

Tom drank, trying not to wince when the liquid passed his lips. "And Town are monitoring my form, so they know, even though the level's crap."

"The level's not important, Tom. It doesn't matter, the level. It's how much fight you show to get back in." He patted his chest. Tom swallowed, the whisky burning in his throat.

They clinked glasses.

His dad leaned back in his seat and took another sip, scowling. "Always bloody hated whisky," he said.

In the morning his parents were in lively spirits in anticipation of his sister arriving. She had moved out a couple of weeks ago, although her course was yet to start, and they were hoping that today she would bring her boyfriend home with her. Fergus. She had been dating him for a few months but they were yet to meet him.

She arrived on her own. Their parents overcame the disappointment with a battery of questions—about her new accommodation, whether she could do the drive home in less than three-quarters of an hour, and about Fergus, joking that she was obviously ashamed of them to keep him away so long.

That afternoon their dad drove them all to the good fish and chip place. Once they were seated Rachel explained again that Fergus was at his own parents' house for the weekend. He said hello. He was looking forward to meeting them all. It occurred to Tom that she had been going out with Fergus since about the time that things had properly started with Liam—if the holiday marked the real beginning, and not the medical room, nor the early brutal passionate encounters in the shed.

When the waitress came over to take their order he had an erection and missed the first thing she said. He forced his knuckles against the edge of the table. The waitress was a jolly type, his mum's age, and whatever she had just said it had clearly been addressed to him. She continued smiling at him for a moment and his family laughed.

"He's in the clouds, this one."

Rachel gave an exaggerated nod.

"I'll bet you've broken some poor young girls' hearts," the waitress said. There was a curry sauce stain on her black apron. On top of her head her hair was piled into a lifeless swollen ball in a disposable cap, like a bag of grass cuttings.

"He's a footballer," his sister said.

"That right?" Tom waited for her to ask who he played for, but she turned towards his family. "Go on, then. Four cod and chips, is it?"

When they returned home he saw that he had a missed call from Wilko, and he went up to his room to listen to the voicemail. It had been sent at half past five, asking him to ring back. Tom checked Town's result on the Internet and saw that they had won again, 3–1.

Wilko answered straightaway. "Tom, good, I wanted to speak to you. How are you getting on down there?"

"Fine, thanks. No match today."

"I saw. I'm getting good reports on your form, Tom. You're pleased with how you're playing?"

"Yes."

"Good. I'm low on bodies here, so I'm thinking of recalling you. Grant's been out with a niggle and Dom Curtis's knee isn't right. We're managing him through games with injections at the moment, but it's looking like we might need to send him to a specialist to sort the problem out. So I need to get bodies into the building. I could use the loan market, but I've got my own player here, in good form, and I know you can do a job for me."

"As cover?"

"Shirt's there to be won, Tommy. Always. Shirt's there to be won."

The team were on the coach. In the background he could hear laughter—through it, distinctly, Beverley's voice: "Oh, come off it, man."

"When do I need to be back?"

"We've no midweek game so how about you sort your things out tomorrow, take Monday off to drive back, and I'll see you first thing Tuesday."

Later that evening he went out for a drink with his sister. They walked to the pub down the road, their dad's local. Rachel got the first drinks in. While he waited for her at a table he imagined how and when he would tell Liam about his return, becoming jittery with the need to share the news with him.

Rachel stayed at the bar chatting a while to the barmaid, then the landlord, and Tom distracted himself by marveling at how at ease she was with everybody, his little sister, how unlike him she was. Now that they were away from their parents, he thought that she might be more likely to talk about Fergus. Their parents' interest in him, he guessed, would feel over the top to her. He could understand that, though. When she was sixteen she had started seeing a man who was almost thirty, divorced, with a child. The three months that they were together had been hard on their parents. The man was manipulative. Deceitful. They blamed themselves, something that Tom had always been uncomfortable about, believing that they had provoked her into it. They hated the man. There had been an occasion, near the end, before he left her, when he had rung the house. Their dad had answered the phone and shouted, yelled, at the man, and cracked the Formica of the telephone table with his fist.

When she came to sit down he told her that he was pleased things were going well with Fergus. "Good to see you've found a normal one," he said.

She smiled and took a sip of her wine.

"So, he nice then?"

"Look, Tom, I know you won't tell them this, but please don't tell them this."

"OK."

"Fergus is great. I really like him. He's in my room at uni right now, though. He's completely normal, seriously. You'd like him. But he's had . . . he's got a few issues. He's on medication. That's part of the reason he couldn't come, actually."

Tom listened intently, intrigued, guiltily pleased.

"Anyway, that's all I wanted to say."

Tom studied her face a minute, not wanting to harass her.

"If you like him," he said finally, "then I'm sure Mum and Dad will too."

"Until they find out he's mentally ill."

Tom took a long drink of his pint. When he put it back onto the table his hand was shaking. He kept it gripped around the cold base of the glass. "They'd probably prefer him to mine, anyway."

She was at once alert. "You're fucking kidding? Go on. Who is she?"

He looked out at the room. He felt out of control. Floating. He made himself focus on the bar straight ahead of him, the greased gleam of the beer pumps, the barmaid setting off the glass washer. He pictured his dad sitting on a bar stool, talking to the landlord.

"It's a fella, Rach. Not a girl."

He did not move his gaze from the bar. Two men came up to the counter at the same time; there was hesitation, a joke, one gesturing for the other to be served first. His sister's arms were around him. She kissed his temple, buried her head in his neck. For a few seconds the sensual memory of Liam made his organs feel as though they were collapsing inside him.

When she lifted her head she was crying. "Oh, Tom, I'm sorry."

"For my loss?"

She did not laugh. "That you've never been able to admit it."

"It's not been long. This has all happened recently."

"Then I'm sorry about that too."

She was still crying. The barmaid had noticed. The landlord too, Tom thought.

"How long have you been seeing him?"

"About four months."

"Who is he?" He could see quite plainly the curiosity on her face.

"Liam. He's called Liam."

"Nobody knows, I'm guessing."

"No."

"You going to tell Mum and Dad?"

He looked away at the door opening, an old couple coming in. He gave a slight shake of his head. "You can't say anything, Rach. Not to Fergus, not anyone."

"I'm not daft, Tom."

When he turned back to her a smile was playing on her lips.

"What?"

"Nothing. Just thinking."

"About what?"

"This explains the muscles then. I'd thought you were on steroids or something."

That night he was woken by her at his bedside, touching his shoulder.

"It OK if I come in with you?"

He squinted through the dark at her. "Bit weird."

"I'm off early in the morning and then I won't see you for ages."

He moved over against the wall. "Go on then."

They lay facing away from each other on the shared pillow, backs pushed together, silent except for their breathing.

Into the darkness Tom said, "What do you reckon Mum and Dad would think if they came in and found you here?"

"At least it's not a man."

Driving back for his final night at the hotel, speeding underneath the bare sky, he planned how he would tell Liam—about his sister, that he was back in the team, that he was coming home. Near the end of the journey he stopped at a service station—the idea of the hotel menu's healthy choices box, the gay waiter, enough to make him pull off the motorway.

He sat at a window to eat a chicken burger, surveying the car park, the roofs of lorries racing along the other side of a high screening hedge. The urge to call almost made him pick up his phone, although he knew Liam was at the Daveys' that afternoon.

He finished his meal and went to the toilet. On his way out he came to a halt beside a coin-operated massage chair two little boys were playing on and took out his phone.

He stared into the dark recess of arcade machines on the other side of the gangway, a bald man slowly raising a gun with both hands as Liam's recorded message came on. Tom hung up and moved away, restless, still hungry, and returned to the counter to buy himself a second burger and chips.

He got back to the hotel early in the evening. He went up to his room and settled down on the bed with a cup of tea and a bar of chocolate to call Liam. The phone was poised in his hand when it started to ring. It was Beverley.

"Tom, how are you? Mate, something's happened."

His first thought was that Liam had been in an accident. Machinery. A blade. The shotgun.

"I don't go on forums anymore because they're full of twats, but some of the boys do and there's a thread. Tom, look, man, I'm really sorry—you've got to know it's nothing to do with me. I've not told anybody. None of it's about you, either. I've been through most of it and you don't come up once."

Tom could not at first work his throat to speak. He sank back against the headboard. He felt unbalanced, the ceiling spinning. Outside the room people were coming past in the corridor. A loud scrape from something being trailed against the wall. A child squealing in imitation of an ambulance siren.

"Does it say who he is?"

"Yeah. It does."

The door to the next room shut. The thump of it ran through the walls, through the headboard, into his skull.

"There's a lot of stuff being said in the dressing room, Tommy, I've got to warn you."

Tom ended the call and put the phone on the bedside table. He stared at it for a while, then went to sit at his laptop on the desk beside the restocked hospitality tray and the bottle of champagne from his last man-of-the-match award.

> Explosive news
> Started by Town Legend,   Replies: 287
> 7 Sep 2012 ≤ 1 2 3 4 5 6 →˙ 16 ≥   Views: 4,008

Town Legend   posted Fri at 8:40pm

First of all this is a totally serious post and 100% true.

I have recently found out that one of club members of staff, the head groundsman, is gay. Fine, each to their own and all that BUT I have it on very good authority that he has had a gay relationship with a former player at the club. I don't know who before you ask.

Silver Fox   posted Fri at 8:44pm

Utter rubbish.

The 13th Oyster   posted Fri at 8:51pm

Least believable post ever. Somebody wanting a bit of attention are we?

Town Legend   posted Fri at 8:53pm

Have I ever been wrong about anything I've broken on here before?

Riversider   posted Fri at 9:03pm

Why wouldn't it be true? It's well known there are gay footballers who are afraid to come out, so not unlikely that one of them might have played for Town.

Town End   posted Fri at 9:20pm

The main point is if this has happened once then it could happen again if it's true about the groundsman, and if it does then the unrest it would cause in the dressing room would threaten to destroy any hope of promotion.

Dean Thorneycroft   posted Fri at 9:24pm

True. Plus we'd be a laughing stock and a target for every contingent of visiting fans.

Silver Fox   posted Fri at 9:25pm

Target? Come off it. "Does your boyfriend know you're here?" and all that stuff Brighton fans get? Just a bit of a laugh. I'm hardly shaking in my boots.

Riversider   posted Fri at 9:30pm

Worth pointing out it's against club rules for a member of staff to have a relationship with a player. This shouldn't be any different if the relationship is gay. Town would look weak if they treated it any different.

Towncrier Ian   posted Fri at 9:47pm

So who do we think the player was then?

Lardass   posted Fri at 9:55pm

So one of the club staff is gay. He once had a thing with somebody who no longer plays for us. So what? In the real world outside football no one would bat an eyelid, it's just because football (and this forum) is stuck in the dark ages that it is a talking point. No wonder he kept it hidden.

Tommo   posted Fri at 9:58pm

Sounds like he's not the only one hiding in the closet, Lardass 😊

Towncrier Ian   posted Fri at 10:00pm

If it is found to be true and the groundsman is searching out gay players then he should be got out of the club. The impact on the dressing room would be massive. Imagine if a married player turned out to be secretly gay and the fallout that would have.

Shakes86   posted Fri at 10:16pm

Charlie Lewis. Look at the way his form tailed off after promotion and how quick we got shut of him.

Tony Slalom   posted Fri at 10:20pm

Can u tell us which players form didnt tail off after promotion?

Onetoomany   **posted Fri at 10:32pm**

Do we know that it was last season? If we look at all the players who
have left the club since then, that means

Chris Gale

Charlie Lewis

Reece Elan

Febian Price

Simon Finch-Evans

Michael Yates

James Willis

Of those my money would also be on Charlie Lewis.

Towncrier Ian   **posted Fri at 10:36pm**

Finch-Evans.

Bald and Proud   **posted Fri at 10:50pm**

Are you seriously speculating about who might be gay? How mature.

Onetoomany   **posted Fri at 10:59pm**

Surprised nobody has pointed this out yet, but if it became known that
a player was gay then he would immediately lose any transfer value
because what manager would want to sign him?

Road to Wembley 2010   **posted Fri at 11:07pm**

Who is this groundsman anyway? Do we know anything about him?

Jamesy1987   **posted Fri at 11:09pm**

He's gay.

TTID   **posted Fri at 11:17pm**

😁

Mary B   **posted Fri at 11:34pm**

He turns out a damn good pitch.

Dr. Feelgood   posted Fri at 11:41pm

He's been head groundsman since the promotion season. Been at the club for years, used to be in the youth team, goalkeeper I think.

Steve Tomkins   posted Fri at 11:57pm

So there could be any number of players going right back to the youth team that he's slept with.

Voice of Reason   posted Fri at 12:00am

You'll have seen him on the pitch before games. He's a big guy. Wouldn't have picked him as a fudge packer but totally fits that he was a keeper.

Tom's hand was shaking as he moved the cursor and clicked again, onto the most recent page.

Gull's Beak   posted Sun at 4:59pm

Chant for Saturday (to tune of Row Row Your Boat): "He mows, mows, mows the stripes, neatly in the grass, But when he's in the dressing room he takes it up the a***!!"

Towncrier Ian   posted Sun at 5:15pm

Genius.

Faz   posted Sun at 5:19pm

Love it.

Steve Tomkins   posted Sun at 5:46pm

Is it just me, or does anyone else think Jacob Gundi might be gay?

The 13th Oyster   posted Sun at 5:55pm

I can think of someone who would like him to be.

Glory Hunter   posted Sun at 6:20pm

Gay Gundi? I'd like to see you tell him that to his face. Here's betting he'd smash yours in.

Gull's Beak   posted Sun at 6:36pm
Or you might get lucky and he might smash something else in. (#Back-
door)

Tom started again at the beginning of the thread and read through
every page.

He closed the laptop and walked in a daze across the carpet to
lie down on top of the bed. His hands and forearms, his legs, shuddering. There was noise all around, footsteps on the ceiling, more
voices in the corridor, a television somewhere that seemed as
though it was inside the room. An impulsion to ring his sister almost made him get up for his phone, but he could not move. He
remained where he was, eventually pulling one side of the covers
over himself.

The two burgers spat and grumbled inside his stomach. He
wanted to put on the noise of the television but the remote was over
on the desk. Behind his head a child was crying, and a woman
shouted. "Now!" he made out, muted through the wall. "Now!"
The voices moved along the wall until they were on the other side
of a connecting door, even louder. Tom watched the door, rigid
with anticipation, expecting it at any moment to open.

He woke disoriented, not knowing how long he had blacked out
for. He was cold but sweating, the back of his head throbbing
against the pillow. Outside the window the car park was dark.

He got off the bed and went into the bathroom. He took off all
his clothes and stood naked in front of the mirror. He stayed there,
motionless, the ceiling light humming faintly above his head, his
strength failing, until it was a muscular effort to stay upright and
his legs buckled beneath him.

On the cold shock of the tiles he curled into a ball. He could see
the underside of the sink, where it had not been cleaned and the
pipes were knotted with dust. There was a pain in his temple where
it had struck the floor. He strained his neck to lift his head off the

tiles, then there was a new bolt of pain as it came down again, once, twice, then again and again, the steady pounding rhythm resounding about the small smooth space, his brain thickening with absurd relief each time it beat on the floor.

He lay on the tiles. There was a ringing. It stopped, and he was surrounded by silence. Moments later it came again. He labored to get to his feet, but it was too difficult, so he walked on his knees to where his phone was lying on the bedside table and picked it up.

"Tom?"

He knelt on the carpet, propping himself against the bed. He willed himself to speak, closing his eyes against the thundering in his head. "I called earlier," he said at last.

"I was at my parents'."

A thin line of blood was trickling down his forearm. There was the sound of running from behind the wall. His hand squeezed around the phone.

"Have you seen it, Tom?" Liam's voice was unsteady.

"Yes."

He could see the big white face, searching his.

"Where are you now?" Tom asked.

"Training ground."

"Working?"

"No."

Tom pulled himself up to sit on the bed. "Are you in the shed?"

"Yes." There was a tremor in Liam's breath. "Been waiting to shut myself in here all day."

Tom tried to think of something to say but there was nothing. Liam made a small moaning noise that Tom angled away from his ear. "I keep thinking about my dad," Liam said. "Reading it."

"He reads the forums?"

"How do I fucking know?"

Tom could hear him moving about. Footsteps echoed inside the shed. There was what sounded like the fridge door shutting.

Neither of them spoke. Tom listened for any noise on the other end of the line. There was only the clobber of blood in his temple.

"I've been recalled," he said, and all the words that he had been intending to say rushed through his mind. "I'm driving back tomorrow."

Liam began to say something, but his voice faltered. Tom waited for him to continue, pushing the phone hard against his ear, but all he could hear, more distantly now, was the thin broken sound of Liam fighting to stay in control of himself.

25

"Listen to this."

Curtis walked across the room to where Easter was stretched out on a mat and lay down beside him.

"What am I listening to?"

"Here. Just listen."

Curtis lifted a straightened leg into the air, then, slowly, bent it at the knee to lower his foot. The knee made a loud creaking sound, which continued until he placed his foot flat onto the mat.

Curtis turned his face to him. "Sounds like a bag of marbles, doesn't it?"

"Sounds fucked, mate."

They stayed there on the floor, arms pressed together, staring up at the crusted air-conditioning unit. "Oh yes," Curtis said, "it's fucked all right."

Easter regarded Curtis's knee. The lumpy leathered lines of old operations above and below it. A secret pleasure entered him at the point where his own leg—repaired, strong—rested against its neighbor.

"You're starting ball work this week, though, yeah?"

"Yep," Curtis replied. "Getting back out there. Best thing for it, they keep telling me. Until it bursts again."

Easter rolled himself up into a sitting position. "Right. I'm due in for the fizz. See you in a bit." His own rehab complete, he had been joining in with ball work, little by little, for a fortnight with no aggravation. Every day he had sensed a power, a control, returning. It increased with each painless warm-down or word of praise from Wilko, each piece of banter with the others. And now every time he saw the cowering faggot groundsman, emerging, disappearing back into his hiding hole. Whenever there was a sighting or some joke about him, he was ridden with an excitement that was almost uncontainable. It was in these moments that he felt the strength, the muscular, sexual capability of his body most intensely. He looked across the field and wanted to overpower him—somebody, anybody. To take a girl to her bed and hold her down. A couple of times, late at night on leaving the office urged by the thrill of gathering views, two thousand, five thousand, ten thousand in less than a week, he had gone into Leah's room; watched with hot fascination the sudden startled fear on her face when she woke beneath him.

He ate lunch in the canteen with Curtis before the squad came in. His progress report, he told Curtis, was still all clear. He would be ready for competitive matches in a week or two. The manager, he went on, had already spoken to a couple of clubs about arranging a reserve fixture just for him to get in some game time. Curtis nodded without reply. They finished their fish fingers and fruit salads, and when the squad came past the window Easter saw in the distance the ground-staff shed shutters rolling up. He looked with a smirk across the table, but Curtis was away with himself, making shapes with his spoon in the pool of his fruit salad liquor.

Driving was a wonder. Even now, after almost a month of it, the motion of his feet and ankles caused a sleek ecstasy to travel up his leg, the same feeling as when he struck a ball, the nerve endings of his toes freshly routed through the once-thick black wall of snarled tissue. He had gone out on several long drives, down the coast, the motorway, just for the satisfaction, the control of it, the action of his body merging into the action of the car. He eased out of the car park, glancing out of the window across the field, and he was able to put everything else—the afternoon's community visit, the spew of chat from Curtis in his passenger seat—out of his mind.

They arrived half an hour later at a one-story concrete school for excluded pupils, or spastics—something to do with the manager's son—neither of them could quite remember. A pupil referral unit, they were informed by the deputy head, waiting in the car park to escort them in. They passed through a high galvanized fence and he was reminded, looking up at the gaudily painted spikes along the top of it, of the front of the Riverside Stand when he was very young, not even at school yet, his dad still alive— a memory of following the players' movements through the red and green spears, the first stirrings of longing filling the whole of his little body.

"This to keep trouble in or out?" Curtis asked.

"Bit of both," the deputy head replied and led them into the reception.

Signing the visitors' book, he noticed a block of names that he did not recognize, all, according to the "From" column, representing Town, and it dawned on him that this must be the place he had heard the scholars complaining about, to which they were bused and shepherded into a separate building, then shepherded and bused away again without even getting to look at any girls, all in service of their BTECs, a qualification he'd known nothing about during his own time in the youths.

They were introduced to a PE teacher and a trio of unspeaking children, then taken outside through a gray landscape interrupted at random intervals by single-room prefab huts.

"Jesus," Curtis whispered to him. "It's like a fucking army base."

"It's like the old training ground," Easter said and smiled at his joke, the speed of it.

They went into the further of two paired buildings, through corridors and into a bright hall thumping with children. He stepped closer to Curtis. "You're going first, mate."

"No shitting way." But when the deputy head turned towards them Easter was already moving aside, indicating Curtis.

Curtis went up onto the low stage and waited for the deputy head's efforts at lessening the din to have some result.

"So, that fence," Curtis began when the room fell to a tolerable mumble, "that to keep you lot in, or them lot out?"

There was an uprising of laughter, and he had them. Easter forced his heels into the floor, bringing a cord of pain up his leg.

The arrangement was that Curtis would speak for a few minutes about the health choices of a professional sportsperson and then he would talk about the day-to-day life of a footballer. Unlike, as was becoming clear, Curtis, pacifying them with his jokes and his comedy Welsh accent, Easter had prepared nothing, and as he looked out at the crowd he began to hear his own breath moving in and out of his nostrils. When finally he walked onto the stage to the reverberation of Curtis's applause, his leg was throbbing with the memory of sponsors' functions, pitch presentations . . .

"I've been out injured the last eight months," he began, reciting the words he had been repeating in his head for the last two minutes into the microphone, "so day-to-day life has pretty much been computer games and Internet porn for as long as I can remember. But they probably don't want me to tell you about that."

After that it was easy.

He slipped into a current of empty words, as if he was speaking to Pascoe or the club website drones or any other of the no-hopers they were obliged to perform for, and as the words took care of themselves he was heedful of his audience's spellbound attention, the unquestioning awe with which they were gaping at him. He recognized the ambition of the boys, the same as the youth teamers', to be like him; to be him. It had crossed his mind too, while Curtis was speaking, that some of them would be Town fans. They would have been on the message board. Everywhere, in the schools and pubs and construction sites and offices of the town, people were talking about it, what he had done, what he had revealed.

He had not known what to do with it at first, when she told him. She had come back from Milan acting strangely, avoiding him—a bitchy remark one day when they passed in the corridor that it would probably be more convenient for him, wouldn't it, if he moved all of his clothes into his own room—and he had grown more and more suspicious that something had happened while she had been away. But when he came across her in the kitchen the next day, slumped against the island, just staring at the wall, he had gone to her out of instinct, putting his hand on her waist, asking her if everything was OK. "There's something I need to tell you," she had said.

He was instantly angry with her. Which made no sense, he knew as soon as he left the house and got into his car, going over her words, ending up driving to the coast. He had just not been expecting it. He had become so convinced that something had happened in Milan, had got himself ready to confront her even. But that night he went into her room while she was asleep and got into bed with her, apologizing, stroking her face, moving up against her. Then for days afterwards he had hesitated, deciding what to do. And it had come to him, as clear as anything, watching the hefty pervert calmly driving about on his tractor, that he was the one, just him, who needed to be exposed. If he let slip who the player was then from the off it would only be about Pearman, that would be all anybody would be interested in, and the faggot groundsman would get away with it. Because there had been another player too, Leah had said, who he had met online and had left the club, so who was to know how many others he might have preyed upon? And once he had made the decision, watching Liam for the rest of the morning strolling about the place as if nobody could touch him, he had felt the determination to punish him for what he had done, to make him pay, take hold.

He scanned the row of older pupils at the back. He held the gaze of one girl, who shied away, then another, who met his eye and gave a small nervous smile. For a few seconds he spoke directly to her, burning with the belief that she was completely in his power—helpless, surrendered to him.

There was loud applause when he finished, cheering, more than Curtis got. Then a long irritating period of standing about next to the PE teacher, during which he watched the children teem out of the hall, looking for the girl but not locating her through the mayhem of faces and hair and limbs.

26

The chairman, the three executive directors and the operations manager stepped out from their glassed-in box shortly before kick-off to sit at the top of the main stand. There was some surprise among the nearby supporters but, with the general mood lightened by the team's form—undefeated at home, second in the table, through to the third round of the League Cup—the picture of the five men uncomfortably shuffling along the top row caused a ripple of good humor to filter through the stand. A season ticket holder ten rows down stood and yelled up, "First game you've watched in a year, isn't it, Mr. Chairman?" There was a smattering of laughter. Other supporters, who had not noticed the board members behind them, turned round. Some clapped. The chairman smiled and gave a slight, pope-like wave.

Five days earlier these same men had gathered around the chairman's table for a meeting which Mr. Davey and, for the appearance of evenhandedness, the other associate directors, had not been made party to.

"Get Saturday out of the way, that's all we can do," the chairman had said from one end of the table.

"Agreed. Don't give it any oxygen and people will lose interest."

"As long as it doesn't happen again."

"Calm down, David. It's a rumor. And not one any of us believes for a second either."

"What about the players?"

"The players aren't the problem."

"The players are always the problem."

There was hummed agreement then a tentative knock at the door. "Yes," the chairman called out, and the club secretary came in with a tray of coffee. They went quiet, their eyes following her around the table.

"Ban them from social media," the operations manager said once she had left. "For a couple of weeks. Warn them they'll be fined, heavily fined, if they go on Twitter."

"And the groundsman?"

There was a pause. A circle of heavy forearms bore down on the table. They waited for the chairman to speak.

"Nothing we can do. Not yet. Steer clear, let him get on with his job, don't give him any attention."

"But we keep him away from the ground on Saturday, yes?"

"Obviously. Tell the assistant he's in charge."

When the Tannoy sputtered out the loud music that signaled the entry of the teams, the main stand turned its interest to the pitch and the appearance of the newly adored players. Michael Grant, despite pre-match speculation, was fit to start. The board watched him shuttling back and forth, stretching his torn back with the fitness coach. They admired his physique, his athleticism; they noted the camaraderie of the team too, as the players grouped together in a nest of huddled temples, before the referee walked to the center circle and the warm beery anticipation of the stands closed around the pitch.

If in some enclave of the Kop or the Riverside Stand there was any shout or chant about the groundsman, it did not break through—and certainly nothing came to the attention of the board members, jammed together on their plastic seats, as time went on more and more content at how the whole problematic episode appeared to be petering out. Their cause was aided by the award of a contentious penalty to Yeovil early in the match, which incited the crowd to fill any lull with outraged abuse of the referee, the linesman, the cheating Yeovil winger. Gundi equalized with a softly flicked header. Five minutes later Mark Munro scored a second, and a charge of righteous solidarity electrified the place. Even when Grant rose from a challenge clutching the small of his back and hobbled through the closing minutes of the half, the crowd remained happy, distracted.

In the dressing room, Wilko, the fitness coach and the physio crowded over the body of Grant, rubbing and fingering at the shining flesh above his coccyx, assessing whether to strap or inject or replace him. They were in agreement: with the team ahead and an important away match in three days, there was no value in risking further injury.

Wilko walked over to Tom, sitting on the bench under his peg.

"What did I tell you, Tommy? Shirt's there to be won."

After forty-five minutes inside the hot clamp of the dugout, withering at the outbreak of every chant outside, Tom crossed the touchline and lost himself inside the match.

He ran his wing with unloosed energy. When he had the ball at his feet he could disappear—the pure release of the crowd's standing, growling mass propelling him onwards, through and beyond the stupid green legs of his opponents—unsuspected, safe. His adrenaline carried him each time a pace too far, sometimes to the irritation of his teammates, but he nonetheless came off the field to the acclaim of the Riverside Stand when he went with Beverley to acknowledge them, and he received from Wilko—as he passed the exhausted referee leaning against the wall of the tunnel with his head beneath his forearm—a single nod, followed a second later by a wink.

He drove home desperate to hold on to the uncomplicated joy of victory, hungering for the next match, to be again part of the unit, distanced from everything else. He turned into his street, the dying sun penetrating the dusty glass panels above the line of front doors, annoyed that somebody had parked in his usual space outside the house, realizing, his stomach hollowing, that it was Liam.

He pulled up half a dozen houses short and stared at the dark shape above the driver's headrest inside Liam's car. He checked his phone, but there was no message. He stayed there, watching Liam's silhouette, and the thought came to him that it was not possible for two people to truly know each other. A gap would always be there, however strong the pull between them.

The brief satisfaction of the afternoon had vanished. He got out of his car, walked quickly down the pavement past Liam and went into his house, closing the door. A minute or so later Liam was knocking.

Tom opened the door. "Fuck's sake, why were you waiting out there? Get inside."

Liam slipped past Tom into the living room and stood at the window, next to the undrawn curtain. Tom rushed to pull it closed, and Liam, wrongly guessing Tom's intention, moved towards him. For a split second Tom was powerless, yearning to be touched. Then he stepped back and wrenched the curtain across the window.

"We said it wasn't time yet."

"I wasn't going to come. I haven't been there long."

"You shouldn't be here."

Liam, looking at the carpet, gave a faint sigh. "I listened to the match."

"There was nothing. I didn't hear anything."

"No. Me neither. None of the players said anything? Yeovil?"

"No. But I was on the bench first half."

Outside, a large vehicle was coming down the street. Its shadow traveled slowly across the curtain.

"You played well. Possessed, they said on the radio."

"Something like that."

There was a look on Liam's face, the beginnings of a smile, which Tom retreated from, going into the kitchen. It assumed that it was to do with him, with them, how Tom played; that everything was connected to them. But as he stood by the fridge and Liam came to stand behind him he felt himself letting go, knowing that he should resist yet unable to prevent Liam from kissing the back of his neck, placing his large deliberate hands on his sides.

"No." But Tom's own hands were on the fridge door, and he heard one of his protein shake bottles tumble from its shelf as he allowed himself to be pushed against it, closing his eyes in expectation, and again he had the sense of unfurling—of being released, for a time, from himself.

Liam's fingers closed around his trachea, then let go, and when Tom after some time opened his eyes again they were on the other side of the kitchen and he did not know how that had happened.

They went back into the living room and sat down on the sofa. After a few minutes sitting silently together, Tom put on the television. The normality of it all made him want to laugh. "We should eat," he said.

"You got anything in?"

"Not really. Bag of apples. Protein shakes."

They agreed on fish and chips. Tom left Liam on the sofa and went to get it.

The shop was empty. He ordered two cod and chips from the young Chinese girl and watched her getting it together, the quick skillful action of her hands with the chip shovel and the curry sauce, her sister and her mother talking in the back room, the father behind them in a filthy bib, reading a newspaper spread on a table.

"Tom Pearman?"

He turned around, panicked.

"It is. Bugger me. It's Tom Pearman."

Three men his dad's age stood gawking at him from the doorway.

"Fish and chips, mate? That Wilko's secret, is it? Pints and takeaways?"

The men laughed, looking at him.

"Tell you what, boy, you've improved some. Month of nonleague and you've come back a new player."

They were all agreeing. The straightforward familiarity with which they were talking about him was unnerving, weird.

The girl called over to him from the counter: "Fish and chips twice, two curry sauce."

He took the carrier bag, feeling precisely the weight of his two portions. The men were studying him, and he was struck with the conviction—that came, fleetingly, as respite—that they knew: the bag made it as obvious as Liam standing there with him.

"Good luck, Bristol, Tuesday. We'll be there. Proper fans, us."

He hurried, almost running, home, looking back frequently to make sure that the men were not behind him. When he arrived at his street there was nobody about anywhere but he was still unable to shake the sensation of being followed. In each of the front windows lights and televisions were on, families congregated on sofas eating and staring, and he wanted right then to be with his own family, to be in their wordless company, not having to think. He let himself in, submitting as he sat down beside Liam to the knowledge that the pieces of his life were never going to fit. He watched the big hands tear into the paper, popping the little lids of the curry sauce pots, and it was all so clear, Liam smiling at him and passing a pot, the impossibility of being one person, instead of all these different people running and hiding from themselves.

Liam left at midnight, after *Match of the Day*. They kissed for a long time in the hall and Tom thought for a moment that they were going to have sex again, but Liam pulled away, moving to the door. "You're right," Liam said. "No chances."

Tom looked through the spyhole at him trying to be inconspicuous, his dark bulk stepping softly past the bins, head down, teasing open the gate, checking the street, and a surge of hopeless devotion bled through him, making him stay there, shaking against the door, long after Liam had got into his car and driven away.

27

On Monday morning the club secretary, shortly after sitting at her desk to begin going through the pile of squad photographs that each of the first-team players was supposed to have signed for a mental health charity, received a call from a tabloid journalist. He had been given a tip-off, he told her, that the head groundsman at the club had been involved in a homosexual affair with a player there. He had read the official message board thread. He intended to write a piece. He was ringing to ask if the club wished to comment, and if he could speak to the groundsman.

Half an hour later, she phoned him back with a statement:

We have a policy of tolerance and openness at this club. It does not matter the sexual orientation, color, or any other issue to do with our staff, whether that be a club employee or a player. Any employee, or fan, or anybody else connected to the football club who is found to act in a discriminatory way towards a person because of their difference would be promptly and severely dealt with. We are pleased and proud, however, to say that such a situation has never arisen here.

And no, the groundsman would not be available for comment.

They were satisfied enough with the statement, drawn up between the club secretary, the chairman and the operations manager in the sweaty leather interior of the chairman's Jaguar, that they decided to put the same words on the club website and Facebook page, should any piece be published. The official message board was closed down by lunchtime. "No announcement, no noise," the chairman instructed. "We should have bloody done it a week ago. Years ago." The club secretary also suggested flying a discreet rainbow flag somewhere within the stadium—other clubs had done it, she pointed out—probably on top of the disabled supporters' stall.

The only remaining matter, for the time being, was the groundsman.

Liam sat in the quiet cool dark of the shed. Through the opening at the bottom of the roller shutters a line of sunlight irradiated the concrete. He let his eyes rest on it, listening for any sound coming through the slit.

The squad were on the other side of the field, beginning a second circuit of the pitches. He got up and went to the fridge, where he took out the carrier bag containing his lunch—ham sandwich, sausage roll twin-pack—and returned to his position behind the tractor.

The sandwich remained poised in his hands while he waited, forecasting the squad's progress, past the clubhouse, the goal line of the far pitch, the long stretch along the road fencing, until he could hear the rumbling earth. His thumbs dug into the bread. They were alongside the shed. He counted the seconds, and for an instant he thought that they had passed until there came the violent clatter of palms on the shutters. The space filled with the roar of it. And then it was gone. A trail of laughter as they carried on down the side of the pitches. The sandwich lay squashed in his lap, both of his hands braced for some time longer against the smooth neck of the tractor.

He ate what he could of his lunch, made himself a tea, slowly relaxing with the small familiar sounds of the fridge door, the kettle, the cars on the road dulled by the thick wall. In a few minutes the squad would begin their drills on the clubhouse pitch and he could get to work. He drank his tea, looking about the shed, putting his mind at ease with the steady ordering of his tasks: cutting down the branches overhanging the fence, patching the fox holes, changing the rotary mower's blade.

He had understood straightaway the reason for the operations manager's phone call last week, asking if Pete might benefit from getting some match-day experience and take charge of the Yeovil game. To his surprise, it had come as a relief to have it taken out of his hands. There had been no mention of further home matches, but he knew that sooner or later he would have to be there. To sit in the stand. To go onto the pitch to replace the first-half divots. Pete had not called to debrief him after the match. They had hardly spoken at all in the past week, except for one short, tight conversation about sand bands that had left him drained with anxiety, certain that Pete was in the know.

In one corner of the shed last season's unrenewed billboards leaned, ready to use as bad-weather platforms for pitch repair work. He let his eyes rest on the top one: WILSON'S TYRES. Behind it, ABC SECURITY, THE YARD WINE WAREHOUSE, PEEL DAVIS LOCK AND KEY SOLUTIONS, CENTURION PLANT HIRE, a list of premises that he could no longer go into without an awareness that their staff, management, customers all knew, that they had been gossiping about him. About his dad. His gut caved at the thought of his parents, a few nights ago at their kitchen table, speaking gently and wanting to hug him, shushing him when he began pathetically to cry, like one of their released lodgers. His mum's face against his own. "Why could you not tell us, Liam? We don't understand why you couldn't tell us." His dad beside her. "It'll blow over. Don't worry. It'll blow over, will this."

"The fuck it will," he had muttered, unable to look at him.

He got up and went to the door, opening it a little. The squad were grouped by the French windows, listening to the number two. At the back, partly obscured by the dense tanned head of Jones, he could make out Tom. Through the limbering necks and shoulders he was standing perfectly still, his eyes set on the number two. Liam continued to watch, craving some minute supple action of his body, but he did not move.

Tom had not called last night. It was the first time they had not spoken since his return a week ago. Liam had stayed up debating whether or not to ring or text, but could think of nothing new to add to their previous conversations. They would tell each other that they were OK. That they could not meet again yet. It felt to him, even more since Tom's coolness on Saturday, as though they were both waiting for something but that neither of them knew what it was.

There had been a lot of banter in the dressing room on Tom's first day back, he had said, but less the following day, and—even if Liam was not entirely able to believe him—there had been little obvious reaction directed towards himself other than the game of rattling the shutters and the occasional shout above the mower on that first morning when he was foolish enough to go out onto the grass while they were warming up. The forum thread, threads, had mostly fractured into myriad battlegrounds of jokes and abuse between posters, and in his thorough and constant searching of the Internet he had found no other reference anywhere. A hope was beginning to grow within him that maybe it would, indeed, eventually blow over. But then he thought about the crowd. Alone and exposed amid the eyes and noise. The breathing white wall of the terraces, surrounding his pitch.

The squad were walking off towards one of the goal areas. He watched for a moment longer, seeking Tom, before his attention was broken by the sound of his phone.

His dad was already waiting for him at a table near the back of the cafe.

"Liam." He got up, smiling, and sat down again. "You've not had your lunch yet, have you?"

"Sort of, but I'll eat."

Although he had managed some of his sandwich and one of the sausage rolls, the prospect of a cooked meal was appealing. It was over a week since he had eaten in the canteen, and his evening meals had been reduced to delivered curries and Chinese, or pizzas pried from the gray fur of ice at the bottom of the Polish minimarket's chest freezer. When his housemates were at home, he ate in his room. He listened to them from upstairs, coming and going to their jobs and girlfriends just as before, a little conversation around the kettle in the early morning, a little more in front of the television on the nights they were in together. If they knew anything about what was going on, they had not brought it up; neither was a Town fan.

"What do you want to eat?" his dad asked.

"Not sure . . . Lasagna. Chips and salad. Cup of tea."

"Top man." His dad went up to the counter and ordered the same for them both. When he returned he gave Liam a swift pat on the shoulder before sitting down.

"So," he said. "I spoke to the chairman earlier."

"Right."

"There's been something of a development, and I'm not going to cushion it because I don't think there's much in it. OK?" An old woman near the door started coughing loudly, repeatedly. When she had finished, he continued. "There was a call this morning from a journalist. He's heard something about what's gone on, so he said, and he's wanting to talk to you. But you're best not to. And then there's no story."

"There won't be a story, then?"

"There might be something, I don't know, but without you I don't see that there's anywhere to go with it. Sounds to me like your typical opportunist hack, sniffing around. Just don't speak to him, simple as that."

"I don't want to speak to anybody."

"Good. Well, that'll please the chairman."

"Sent you to stop me, then, did he?"

"He did, if I'm being honest. But that's not why I'm here. I wanted you to hear this from me, is all. The thing is, you've not technically done anything wrong, but if you spoke to the press then he'd probably call that bringing the club into disrepute, and then you could guess where he'd go from there."

"Technically."

"I'm thinking about it from the club's perspective, son. You know that as far as I'm concerned, your mum's concerned, you've done absolutely nothing wrong."

He tried to make eye contact but Liam turned away. Across the room, the old woman was gripping the arm of her chair and was then seized by another fit of coughing. Fine wandering clouds of spittle were lit up in the light from the glass door, chasing after one another in the sunshine.

"What are they saying in the boardroom?"

"I've not been involved until now. I'll tell you this, though. If they try and do anything to you I will reveal every dirty little secret they've got. Referee sweeteners, illegal cameras, illegal payments to parents, attendance fiddling, the lot."

The man was coming with their lasagnas. Liam did not look up at him when he put them on the table. He was a Town fan, Liam knew. Sometimes, if he got a bacon sandwich here on his way in, they spoke about matches, players.

"I don't know how to talk about this with you, Liam."

"About what?"

"Any of it. But you know that you can. I'd like to, if you would. To be honest we're still trying to understand why you've never talked to us, any of us—Andrew, Sarah—"

"You've told Andrew and Sarah?"

"We've spoken, yes. Haven't they called?"

Liam plunged a fork into the middle of the microwaved lasagna and put it into his mouth, letting it burn at the smooth tight membrane of his palate, and without warning he was thinking about Tom—Tom's tongue pushing between his lips, sliding into his mouth.

"Is there anything that you want to talk about?"

Liam shook his head.

"Fair enough."

His dad reached across the table and placed his hand, palm down, alongside Liam's plate. For a few seconds it stayed there, then he pulled it back. The old woman was getting up. She shuffled over to the table by the counter where the papers were. She leafed through them, finally picking one up and taking it back to her place. She began to read it and Liam could not take his eyes off her, until she grumbled to herself, "Last week's," and slapped it onto a neighboring table.

His dad left him outside the cafe after making him agree to come over for dinner one day later in the week. From the moment he said yes, Liam's mind was on their three new lodgers, angst building again as he thought about how far his disgrace might have spread through the intact beating organ of the football club, the town, the media, the unending veined possibilities of the Internet.

He drove the few minutes to the training ground, calming down on the lane at the sight of his empty pitches, the patterns of shadow over them from the early autumn sun riddling through the trees. He tried to block the journalist from his mind. When he reached the shed he turned off his phone, putting it on the shelf of machinery keys, and pulled on his gloves.

After each morning of high alertness, waiting for the players to leave, afternoons were a mercy. The smallest task took him out of his head and into a rhythmical green world of lines and calculations and chemicals, the instinctive nurturing of his land.

He did not look at his phone when he picked it up at the end of the afternoon. Only when he got home, via the Polish minimarket, did he turn it back on again, in his room. There was a missed call from an unknown number. He lay down on his bed, fighting the compulsion to call Tom, knowing that he could not burden him.

He phoned Leah, remembering, as her recorded voice kicked in, that she might be at college for one of her new module evenings. He left a message, asking if they could meet up, and went downstairs before his housemates came home, to cook his pizza.

The morning was still dark when he searched the Internet again. There was nothing. He checked again an hour later, and left the house early to drive across town to an Indian newsagent's, where he inspected all the papers that did not put their full content online, as well as the ones that did, once more, in their printed versions. There was still nothing.

By lunchtime the unknown number had called twice more. He switched his phone back on while he ate and immediately deleted the voicemails as well as a text which he tried not to look at but glimpsed the opening: "Sorry to contact out of . . ." Again his first thought was to speak to Tom, about anything, not even to mention the journalist, but again he talked himself out of it. Tom would be getting ready to board the coach to Bristol. This news would disrupt his concentration, the new focus he had found since coming into the manager's favor. Besides which, it was possible there would not be a piece, so to involve Tom now would be selfish. Because it was not about Tom. Tom had not been exposed. As far as the forum rumor was concerned, it was about Liam. And a former player. It did not have anything to do with Tom, apparently, but instead with that one night years ago. The memory, so long buried alongside the other transgressions of his youth, kept resurfacing now, perfectly preserved, as palpable and alive as it had been in the moment he had followed the man into the darkened hotel room, watched him undress in the thin green light of the alarm clock, heard the catch of his breath at their first touch. And it was the very exposing of himself—the truth of it—that made him want to keep Tom on the outside. A quiet acceptance of shame that was embedding itself inside him, which was not theirs, but his, his alone.

At home, in his room, he deleted the new voicemail from the unknown caller, then phoned and left another message for Leah. Tom texted late that night, when the coach got in: "Started tonight. Good draw on balance. Wilko pleased how I played." Liam replied, "Good stuff, well done," sent it and tried to go to sleep, realizing, as the murky presence of the journalist entered the room, that this was the first time a Town match had ended and he had not known the score.

28

Leah sat on the bench by the lake, beside the space on the grass that the pram would normally occupy. Liam had not wanted to meet at the furniture store or a pub, or anywhere else but here, her lake. And even in this secluded place, she thought, watching his approach underneath the line of trees, he appeared wary, looking every few strides at the two men fishing by the lakeside. They had not seen each other in the week and a half since the phone call when she had sat up in bed whispering weak reassurances to him, hoping that Chris was not listening through the wall.

He sat down next to her. "Who are they?"

"The fishermen?"

"Yes, those two."

"They're fishermen."

Liam looked from one to the other.

"They're always here," she said.

The man nearer them swung back his rod, then launched it at the water. A gentle ripple moved across the surface.

"This is probably a cruising place, the way things are going."

She thought she should laugh or punch him on the arm, but caution held her back. "This isn't a cruising place," she said.

He was unshaven. Hair that she had never seen before ran scraggily down his thick throat. He was wearing a dirty red and green

T-shirt, a brown sports fleece over the top. Even now it still amazed her that he was gay.

"The papers know," he said.

It took her a moment to fathom what he was talking about.

"There's something in the papers? What, about you?"

"No, not yet. But there might be. There's some journalist who's been on to the club. He wants to speak to me."

She was about to ask if he was going to agree but caught herself, registering from his expression that it was the wrong question. "How does he know?"

He shrugged. "Doesn't matter now, does it?"

When he first called, this had been the thing that he had been most worked up about. *Who? Which fucking arsehole? Who?* And after the dreadful pause of her realization, as he recited the post to her, all she had been able to say was, *Maybe Tom told Beverley about the Internet thing?*

"What does Tom think?" she asked.

Liam shook his head. She resisted asking him anything further. On the road a car beeped, and they both turned to see it speeding past a cyclist—the cyclist lifting a finger at the disappearing vehicle.

"We've not spoken for a few days," Liam said. "He's getting starts. He's doing well."

She struggled to find an appropriate thing to say. "It'll all be forgotten in a week or two," she said, and stared hard at the lake, hating herself.

But after a silence he stood up and, to her surprise, kicked her foot playfully. "Thank you."

She watched him walk back to his car, parked on the grass by the road, and wondered if she had given him what he had been in need of. If he had begun to suspect her. She would call him later, she decided. Suggest that she come round to his house one evening and cook them some dinner. It was darker now and getting cold, but she was unwilling to leave the bench. To drive home and change the sheets. *Let him change his own fucking sheets,* she thought with a gratifying sureness and stayed on the bench, feeling the pleasing solidity of it under her bum. But she had to pick up Tyler. She had almost forgotten; he was over at her mum's so often since she had stepped up her college work.

Her mum would never say she was too busy for him of course, but it was plain enough that she could do without him under her feet at the moment. Two weekends ago Robert had proposed at an expensive restaurant in London, and the wedding planning was already in full swing. "Hardly front page" had been Chris's response when she told him. Already, six months before the scheduled date, she felt jaded by the inevitability of having to worry about him being there, him not being there. Robert, in her mum's kitchen, one sunburned paw on her arm, had told her very earnestly one morning that they had decided not to hold the wedding on a Saturday. "Nothing is more important than family," he had said, giving her the strong impression that he was trying to communicate the fact that they were family now, the two of them, and she had thanked him and let him leave his hand on her arm, unexpectedly comforted by the thought.

She got up. Instead of going to her car, however, she started towards the lake.

From the shoreline she could see the ducks clumped in a soft brown heap on the bushy knob of land that protruded into the water on the other side. Without thinking, she took off her pumps. Her socks. She stepped into the lake. She stood with the water around her ankles, her handbag still over her shoulder, cool velvet stones beneath the soles of her feet, and she imagined diving in— the cold shock of it—swimming to the other side to cuddle in with the ducks.

It was paranoia, surely, this thing about the journalist. Liam was being dramatic. Even if the media were aware, she could not imagine that anyone would be interested, not without a footballer, without a name, without Tom. She considered that for a moment, the dark water lapping at her ankles. Liam hiding alone in his bedroom while Tom carried on with his life without any consequence of what he had done, still getting away with it. She had known, the moment the words had spilled from her mouth, that she should not have told Chris. There had been no relief in it. No closeness. And it was at once obvious to her that he would go after Liam, given the years of coldness towards him. Though she still did not understand why whoever it was that Chris had told had not outed Tom as well, unless out of some pathetic deluded loyalty to the team, to football. Chris's first reaction had been to shout at her that she was lying, she was a stupid gossiping slut. Then he had stormed out of the house. The next time she had seen him he was on top of her, pulling down her pajama bottoms.

There was a cry. A yell, away to her right. One of the anglers was staggering, splashing, into the lake. She stepped out of the water and ran towards him, barefoot over the grass. She was half-way there before she grasped that he had caught a fish, yet she kept on, walking now, compelled by a strange new force that took her ever closer until she was almost beside him, watching him rooted in the shallows, staunchly reeling it in. The fish's side broke the surface, then went under again. Somehow, despite seeing these men every time she had visited the lake, the now-visible fact that there were fish in there astounded her.

He had it in a net and was laboring to pull it out of the water, over the grass, onto a mat. It was enormous. As big as Tyler. The man straddled the fish on the mat, looking at its face, in shock at the miracle of it, as if at a child that he had not been expecting to deliver. Until now he had not appeared to notice her or the other angler closing in from the other side, but he looked up as she bent down to him now and his face shone with simple unburdened joy, euphoric. She was on her knees, her arms around his neck. "I got a bloody whopper," he said quietly into her shoulder. "I bloody well got a whopper."

When they released each other he seemed still too overcome to be even curious at the out-of-the-blue appearance of a woman running to hug him. They got to their feet and stood with the other man. Together they looked down at the massive beached fish slowly opening and closing its mouth.

"What is it?" she asked.

"Mirror carp," the other man said. He glanced down at her bare feet. "Thirty pounds at least. Biggest I've ever seen." He held out his hand to the catcher. "Congratulations. Incredible."

The catcher went into his bag and took out a digital camera. He held it out to her. "Do you mind?"

With the assistance of the other man he lifted the creature up, supporting it under its belly, his arms shaking with the effort. When she had taken four shots he squatted down to rest the fish on top of his knees. "Do you want to take one for yourself?" he asked. "For your boy?"

She opened her mouth to refuse, but as she looked at him, gripping his fish against his legs, she got out her phone and swiftly took a photo.

He let the fish slump to the ground. "Right then. Best get her weighed."

She watched the men struggle to maneuver the thing into a hammock, which they raised together using two bars. "Bang on thirty-eight," the other angler said, and the two men exchanged a look that contained a world of meaning she was not party to before she went over to help them return the fish to the lake. As they began to shunt and slide it towards the water's edge, flattening a slithered trail across the grass, a powerful notion came over her that it was Chris, the deadweight of his foul body, that they were moving.

When they got it into the shallows it did not move. They stood watching it, and she was sure that it was dead, but then it spasmed, flipped and was gone, away into the black lake.

Without the fish, the two anglers looked awkward.

"Well done," she said and turned back to walk to the bench, picking up her socks and pumps from beside the water.

She sat down and pulled on her clinging socks. She looked up a final time at the men, both now silently, individually, packing up their bait boxes, their foldout stools. The catcher, when he was done, knelt for some time over his things. He was looking at the photographs, she realized, and as she stayed watching him, this stranger she had held in her arms, compassion pulled at her, followed, rushing, by a sudden decisive joy that rose from the core of her.

29

The piece was printed two days later. It was short, a small square of words in the top corner of a page above the betting tips and the next day's fixture listings. The longest of the three paragraphs was an edited-down account of the club's statement. There were no names. The "rumored affair between a former player and a member of the ground staff" did not feature any more prominently than the news that Town had shut down its official message board due to a series of homophobic and racist postings.

The players became aware of the story immediately. Boyn, sitting in the lounge eating a bowl of cereal, shouted, "Lads, look at this," and they hurried to surround him. For several immobile seconds they read it together, waiting for somebody to react.

It was Easter who broke the spell. He snatched the paper from Boyn's lap and rolled it up. He turned to Tom beside him and jabbed the paper into his stomach, then, beside Tom, into Beverley. "It's you, you faggots," he shouted, and chased them through the lounge, spanking them on their bottoms. "Come on, admit it, we all know it's you." The pair exploded into the same frenzied laughter as the rest of the squad, taking cover behind the breakfast table, and the tone for the rest of the morning—excitable, uncertain, watchful—had been established.

———

Easter woke early the next day and lay in bed for a few minutes, marveling at the tranquillity of his leg. Not aching, not doing anything, just there. He flexed it at the knee. Then again. He took in a deep breath, letting his lungs fill. Exhaled. The perfect machine of his body, functioning. He swung out of bed, wondering if it was early enough for Tyler to still be asleep and Leah alone in bed, but then he heard them together downstairs, Tyler whinging at her for something: milk, food, attention. He got dressed quickly and went downstairs, not looking through into the kitchen, let himself out of the house and drove away.

Powering through sleeping villages, fields, the vigor of yesterday was still with him—the way that the others had looked to him, needed his direction, his sureness. He would sit among them on the coach to Aldershot today. It did not matter that he was not yet ready to play. He was more relevant, more vital, than half of the ones who were. He pulled into a petrol station and saw on the forecourt the Saturday papers stacked in their plastic boxes. He went in and bought a copy of each one. When he got back into his car he resisted the temptation to look. He sat them in a pile on the passenger seat and set off again for home.

He installed himself at his desk and lined up the newspapers in front of the lifeless void of his laptop. The first couple had nothing. In the *Sun* a tiny item that was almost identical to the previous day's. The next three papers, nothing. Then, in the *Guardian*, a half-page feature of interviews with gay members of staff at football clubs—a cook, a ticket office manager, a barman, a Congolese steward who had never, he said, received any abuse on the terraces, or at least not for being gay. He skimmed uninterestedly through their profiles—it wasn't a thing; most of their colleagues were unaware of their sexuality; they just got on with their jobs—hunting out anything more than the one-sentence introduction at the top that mentioned Town. When he was sure there wasn't anything, he moved on to the next paper. Although he was well aware that none would give details, anything specific, he continued to comb through, searching, on edge.

He flicked through the raft of sports pages inside the *Express* and tensed. The familiar few lines were there, then an interview with "the captain," Jones: "To be honest it's the first any of us have heard about it. It's a lot of fuss over nothing, really. People's private life is their own business. We just concentrate on the football. And if a player said he was gay, which isn't what's happened here, we'd probably just think, fair enough, so what? It's got nothing to do with winning football matches."

He could see Jones bantering with the journalist. The private preparation with the chairman before the interview. Heat rose to his face. Nowhere, in any of them, was there any mention of the original forum post. Below the desk, pain was slugging up his leg, though when he reached down to rub the length of his shin he could not be certain whether the pain was real or the phantom of his injury. He pushed the interview away from him and glowered at the inert laptop. Then, standing up, he gathered up the pile of newspapers and went downstairs.

In the kitchen he stuffed them all into the bin.

He had a sense that Leah was behind him, and when he turned she was there, in the doorway. She was looking at the swinging top of the bin but said nothing.

"Tyler asleep?" he asked.

"It's ten o'clock. He's playing in his room."

She remained in the doorway. There was something odd about her that made him reluctant to walk around her to leave the room, so he went to the fridge. He had not had any breakfast, he realized, and he was hungry, thirsty. He opened the fridge door and took out a two-pinter of milk.

"I've decided to move into Mum's, Chris."

He unscrewed the top of the milk and took a long swallow. The bottle still in his hand, he scanned the shelves. There was a packet of ham. Prawns, defrosting. Two bags of grapes. A small bowl of last night's leftover sweet potato mash. He closed the fridge door and looked at her. Something fierce, determined, passed over her face. Then she was just looking at him plainly.

"This about him?" he said.

"What? About who?"

"Your mate."

"I don't know what you're talking about."

He took another slug of milk, watching her over the top of the bottle, and he could see she was telling the truth. He laughed quietly. She was as blind as the rest of them.

"That's it? You're laughing? Aren't you going to say anything?"

"What do you want me to say?"

"I don't know. You never say anything."

She was going to cry, he thought. To come to him and cry into his chest. But after he put the milk onto the kitchen counter and wiped his hand across his lips he turned back to the doorway and she was gone. He stood there, looking into the living room, being sucked upstairs to the laptop until his legs weakened, remembering, his strength unspooling from him at the thought that the forum was gone and she would probably be straight on the phone to him, the faggot groundsman, the useless fat goalkeeper, as he had once been. And now he could not hold it back. It was coming at him—breaking free. The journey home from the youth tournament, the ferry, standing on the deserted deck with the relentless brutal sea hemorrhaging in his ears as the big white face pressed against his own, lips, breath, fingers reaching, terrified, down for each other.

He turned the car round and reversed to the edge of the viewing point. There was nobody about. He got out and walked to the back of the car, where he stood before a mass of nettle bushes still stirring from the last of the exhaust fumes, and stared out at the sea. His chest was heaving. He looked for the ferry but could not see it. Anger built deep inside him as he searched, and then he saw it, a dot swelling on the horizon, advancing towards him.

He took in several deep, lunging breaths. "Pathetic," he shouted. He listened to the echo of the word carry in the wind towards the sea and die. He brought the base of his fist down on the car roof. "Fucking pathetic," he shouted again, the rhythm and force of the words helping to bring his chest slightly under control. There was a head. Two heads. Walkers, over on the cliff path, looking at him above the sea scrub, turning, hurrying away.

He watched them flee with their dog down the coastal path, fading to two tiny bright dots, disappearing.

30

There was an atmosphere on the coach to Aldershot that made Tom apprehensive. It was the mood of yesterday after they had seen the newspaper article, only quieter, solidified. He had not fully recovered or slept, and in the hush of the coach he was acutely sensitive to every movement and mumble around him. An unspoken togetherness breathed through the seats. It was partly the confidence of winning so frequently, being joint top of the table, but there was something new, a grave unity, a low bristling violence that wanted to prove itself, push against something.

He had not spoken to Liam about the article. It was a week now since their last conversation, when Liam had slipped out of his house into the night. After yesterday's training Tom had driven straight for home and the Internet, and had spent the rest of the day, then the night, on or around the sofa in a state of wired agitation which gave way occasionally to fragmented intervals of half-sleep. He woke in the dark at one point from a vision of the three men from the fish and chip shop reading the newspaper that was so real he had to slap himself on the cheek before he was convinced that they were not in the room with him. By the morning, when Liam had still not been in contact, he was fluctuating between the uneasy possibility that Liam was waiting for him to call, and a wild hope that he did not know. He decided not to risk telling him. And there was a match to prepare for. A series of safe, repeated actions to perform, to slip into.

Beverley twisted towards Tom. "I used to play for these, once. I tell you that?"

"No. When?"

"Month loan a couple of seasons back, when I wasn't getting near the team at Vale. Nice club. I was up for signing but they couldn't offer anything secure."

"When can they?" Tom said.

Beverley smiled, nestling back into his headrest. Somewhere behind them a murmuring that Tom had been conscious of for the last few minutes expanded into a spurt of laughter. Then another.

"Bev, Tommy, come look at this," Jones called over a couple of rows of heads, and despite the clotting terror in his chest, pride at being wanted invaded Tom.

There were too many grouped around the cramped table space for everyone to look together at the object of amusement. They queued up in the aisle, passing Bobby's phone down the line. At each exchange there was an expression of delight. A thumped headrest. A jerk backwards. "Jesus, Bobby." Most took a second or two to understand what it was they were looking at. Tom, though, when the phone came to him, knew instantly—as if it was exactly this that he had been expecting. On the screen was a photo of the ground-staff shed, its far wall a glaring flash of white against the black sky of the training ground. In big bright red lettering was painted, HOMO HUT. He passed the phone on to Beverley. Below them Bobby was recounting how he had done it, giggling anew at each high five and fist pump. There was a snort of laughter beside Tom, and he turned to see Beverley shaking his head in admiration.

None of the coaching staff came to find out what was going on, recognizing perhaps the value of the bonding. The group eventually filtered away, Tom following Easter, pausing to let him take his seat, noticing through his own stupor that Easter was talking to himself. Tom went back to his own place. He squeezed his eyes closed. For the rest of the journey everything around him was suspended, far away. Except for the sporadic gentle tremor of his seat, which he knew was Beverley chuckling.

He could not get into the match. He could not find the part of his brain that was just for football, and as he tried he found instead only the kaleidoscopic repeating image of the vandalized wall. He attempted to boil his actions down to the basics: control, touch, look for the strikers. As a tactic it was surprisingly effective. Gundi and Munro, in undisguised competition with each other, chased down everything. Tom spun one weedy lob into the corner, which an Aldershot defender attempted to shield out of play, but Gundi shouldered him off the pitch and pulled the ball back to Tom, who looked up, crossed simply for Munro, and it was 1–0. The flat continuous din of the Aldershot support continued undiminished, looping to the beat of a single military drum, drowning out any other crowd noise apart from the jubilant Town fans in the horse-shoed paddock in one corner, singing about Munro, Gundi and even, briefly, Tom. They disappeared en masse two minutes before halftime for the food van in the car park, and after the restart when Tom went over to collect the ball from a supporter ecstatically clutching it above her head, he saw the rows of fans holding their hot dogs and pies. As he waited for the woman to toss the ball and everybody looked at him he was suddenly emboldened by the thought that none of them knew. Nobody knew it was him.

"Give us a bite," he shouted.

They all heard him, laughed, sang his name again. For a few seconds he was cocooned in relief.

It was so near the end when the Aldershot winger was sent off that some supporters were already leaving. As he walked off the pitch, shaking his head, griping to himself, he looked back and said, "Bunch of queers," loudly enough for half a dozen Town players to sprint towards him. Within seconds there was a melee. Foreheads, eyeballs, captains separating the antagonists then squaring up to each other above the little scrambling referee.

Wilko banned any mention of the incident during the journey back. "Three points. Job done. We go home, we concentrate on the positives, we go again." But Tom could sense them dwelling on it, their anger chuntering beneath the surface in the soft yellow light of the coach.

He stayed inside his car for some time, watching the dusky movement of traffic leaving the stadium, the kit man hauling metal crates from the belly of the coach, the driver sitting at the top of the steps, having a smoke. He was the last person remaining in the car park when Liam called. The blue light of his phone strobed the inside of his car as he stared at it, ringing, ringing, then silent.

Once home he went straight to the under-stairs cupboard and pulled out the cardboard box of DIY odds and ends that his dad had left there. He emptied his kitbag onto the floor and repacked it with items from the box, then went into the kitchen to get more things from under the sink.

In the long pauses between the sound of cars from the road there was a dead stillness to the training ground. The graffiti was written on the back wall of the shed, out of sight from the clubhouse and the entrance, and Tom wanted to know, drawing nearer, just who exactly the stupid lumping twat had thought would read it. Or if it was solely for Liam. Or—the quick chilling thought passed through his mind—for them both. He rounded the shed, halted by the sight of the words. They had been sprayed on, he saw now. Bobby must have planned this: shopped for a canister, deliberated over the wording. Tom could not pull his eyes away; they bored into the slogan, the wall, and slowly he grew sure that Liam was in there. He stepped up to the wall and put his ear against it. He could hear nothing inside, but he remained in that position, his skin gradually becoming indistinguishable from the brick, from Liam's body pressing up on the other side, pulsating at his ear. The rush of something big on the road beyond the trees, a lorry, a coach, jogged him.

He lifted his face from the wall. He walked around the shed, his cheek tingling, and called through the shutters: "Liam." And again, louder, "Liam."

When there was no answer he returned to the far wall and set to his task.

The letters shrank at the first touch of the spirit, and he thought that he was going to get it all off, that Liam would arrive on Monday and would see nothing but the bare wall. However, after his initial success it was soon obvious that it was not going to be erased completely and that a muted layer would remain, smeared at the edges, like a halo, the words as blatant as the fact that somebody had tried to remove them. He scrubbed harder, working for minutes at a single letter, his breathing becoming ragged—and as the thin pink dribble of spirit slid down the wall, he was once again scouring at himself in the Daveys' shower, bleeding, desperate for it all to go away.

31

One week and one victory on, when a fourth goal went in and the Town following were again rejoicing, a low complaint started to spread through Barnet's stadium. Some supporters in the main stand were on their feet for the first time in the match, their mouths tightened into small puckered circles, like a thousand blown kisses.

A distraught middle-aged man wearing the Barnet team shirt, his own name glued across his shoulders, reached into his pocket and yanked out his season ticket. The teenage boy in the next seat looked up to see him wagging the yellow plastic wallet high above his head. There was a flapping sound as the pages came together, then, with a grunt and a momentary loss of balance on the narrow step, the man threw it at the pitch. It arced and fluttered and fell short of the grass. He looked about him. With the exception of his son, who was steadfastly ignoring him, nobody seemed to have noticed.

"What do they think?" the man said to no one in particular. "We want to pay to watch this rubbish every week? Watch ourselves get hammered by a team of gay boys?" He did not sit down. He shook his head, gazing at the season ticket lying on the runoff track. Behind him annoyance was building. "Sit down, pal," someone shouted, and he did.

One of the Barnet substitutes, warming up, spotted the season ticket and bent to pick it up. He looked at the jowly bespectacled face inside the sleeve and raised his head to peer into the crowd. There were a few outbursts of banter, token insults, before he walked down the track to hand it to a steward. The man watched all of this. He sat quietly until halftime when, having changed his mind or unable to think of anything better to do with his Saturday afternoons, he approached the steward for the return of his season ticket.

He was up again, though, when Town scored a fifth goal. Richards, who had been heckled throughout the first half by two boys in the next block, poked the ball into the net and ran across the pitch to celebrate in front of his detractors. The man, observing this, leaped up and screamed, "Does your boyfriend know you're here?" and began laughing, looking round at his son, who was scowling at his own feet. The two boys heard the refrain. They stood up, conferred and began to chant, "Down with your groundsman, we're going down with your groundsman . . ." The tune was picked up by some of the home supporters behind the goal, and for a short merry interlude it bounced happily about the seven sheds. The Town supporters, once they had picked out the words, clapped ironically and could think of nothing in reply.

Tom did not know whether Liam was aware of the chanting. There had been some in midweek too, at home, but Tom had presumed from the presence of the assistant groundsman with the divot-forking scholars at the edge of the disabled supporters' stall that he had not been at the game.

He had not listened to any of Liam's voicemails. Occasionally there was a text simply asking him to call, which he deleted, but the voicemails were all still there, a store of them building, secreted in a buried compartment of his phone.

He told his sister, when she called him, that Liam had not been in contact for a little while. They were keeping at a safe distance, he said each of the three times she phoned in the week that she found out what was happening. She did not say how she had heard, and he did not ask, fearful—although it had not come up during Tom's few very short conversations with him—that it was from their dad. She was thinking about coming down to see him, she said.

"You don't need to. Everything's OK."

"How can it be OK?"

"It is. Things are actually going pretty well at the moment. I'm starting every match."

"I saw the forum, Tom. It was ugly. Fergus managed to pull it up, somehow, after it got closed down." Into the silence that followed, she added, "He doesn't know that it's you, by the way. I didn't tell him."

But Tom was cold with alarm that another person knew, a person he had never met, who was mentally ill. He was angry at himself again for ever having told her, for telling anybody. It had been a mistake, he could see now.

"Seriously, Rach, I'm fine."

"What about Liam?"

"He's fine."

"Really? He's been hung out to dry. He's getting slaughtered. Not like I'm the right person to give anybody relationship advice, but surely he needs you now, Tom. He's your boyfriend."

Even when she had gone, the word lingered unhappily, causing him to slightly recoil every time he heard it.

A penis appeared one morning, shaved into the grass, as spontaneous and impeccable as a crop circle. Nobody noticed it at first, during breakfast and the squad meeting, because the outline could not be made out from ground level through the French windows, so it was only discovered when Easter and Curtis were sent up to the storage room above the canteen for new stretching mats. A few minutes later everybody was cramming into the little room, striving for a view out of the single cracked window. On the clubhouse pitch a detailed set of genitals had been mown very exactly into one of the halves, contoured all the way around—head, shaft, neat globular testicles—by a painted white line.

Amid the excitement they turned to Bobby.

"Don't look at me. Serious. It's pure class but it's no me."

They looked at one another, anxious to hail the prankster, but nobody came forward. It was a mystery. They charged from the room and out of the building for a closer inspection.

The coaching staff, taking advantage of the find, made them warm up by running around it, and turned a blind eye to the ceremony, initiated by Jones, of each man kissing the tip on completion of a circuit, so that by the end of the run a small damp patch had developed where the phallus neighbored the far touchline.

Several players, still in the canteen at the end of lunch, stayed to watch Liam repair the pitch. They stood by the window as, for the first time that day, he came out of the ground-staff shed and walked the mower towards the butchered grass. Nobody spoke, so entranced, moved even, were they by the spectacle. And after the earlier shock of the giant intruding cock, the strangeness and upheaval of the past few weeks, there was something about the sight of the groundsman slowly tending to the pitch, trimming the grass to the same level, spraying and massaging a substance into the white line, which was also, perhaps, reassuringly normal.

There was plentiful conjecture about who it had been. It was a supporter. It was a rival supporter. It was an ex-player, *the* ex-player, or the groundsman himself, some believed, because who else could have done it so well? The assistant groundsman. And there followed a theory that there was a feud between the two groundsmen. That they were both gay.

They awaited more practical jokes, but none came, so they engineered some of their own, usually reverting to the easy bets of old banter: rattling the shed shutters, hiding somebody's clothes while he was showering, gay pornography on the groundsman's windscreen, on each other's windscreens. Each joke, each windup, bound them, protected them. The inescapable feeling that they were being laughed at in the stands, on the Internet, in dressing rooms—and they knew from former teammates that this was the case—brought the group closer, at the same time as it made them restive with a need to react. The bond between team and fans too had grown tighter, their defiance stoked by the remarkable run of winning, winning, winning, three points clear by early October.

The supporters, following a short threatening summit between the board, Peter Pascoe and the local paper's sports editor, were praised for their vociferous support of the team, credited by the chairman, manager and carefully selected players with being able to win matches on their own. The national press, however, were refused any more contact. A new fans' forum, mediated by the club, was heralded. The rainbow flag above the disabled supporters' stall was, without fanfare, taken down.

Any initial disappointment at failing to draw a big-name opponent in the third round of the League Cup was outweighed by winning the tie with an outstanding victory at Colchester. Tom headed the final, fourth goal of a match in which Bobby scored his first senior hattrick. At the final whistle Bobby was so overawed—shaking the hands of Colchester players, hugging Wilko and all the coaching staff, fist-pumping the Town support—that he ran off the pitch forgetting to collect the match ball. When, ten minutes later, the referee came into the dressing room to deliver it to him, Bobby stepped through the almost hushed space to receive it, ignoring the giggles, with all the gobsmacked reverence of a child getting a visit from Father Christmas. The ball remained tucked under his arm throughout the post-match sandwiches and, despite various teasing attempts to steal it, stayed on his lap for the whole of the coach journey home.

The chairman invited the whole squad to watch the fourth-round draw together on a screen in the players' lounge the following evening. He laid on a free bar. A curry takeaway. They gathered around the television and, at the release of the sixteen numbered balls into a dark glass dome, the players, the chairman and the coaching staff put their arms around each other's shoulders. On the screen there was some banter between the two ex-pros appointed to draw the numbers when it turned out one of them had left a ball in the bag. The balls were jostled. The first hand went in. Town were the first team out. They were at home to Tottenham Hotspur. Still knotted together, the semicircle began to bounce up and down, bawling out joyous exclamations that soon coalesced into a chant: "Bring on the Tottenham! Bring on the Tottenham!"

A vague residue of the line was still bouncing around the room a few minutes later with most of the squad on their phones, calling, texting. Tom already had messages from his dad and Kenny and John, and another from an old academy friend: "Back in the big time, buddy!" He moved over to the pitch window. He replied to his dad, and waited with his phone in his hand for a moment after pressing Send.

When he returned to the ruckus by the bar, Beverley ran up to him. He put his arms around Tom. "I'm fucking buzzing, man. I've never played against a top-flight team, Tommy. I didn't think that would ever happen for me."

Beyond Beverley's ear, Easter, standing apart from the main group, was talking to the barman: ". . . for their academy if I'd wanted to." Tom watched the barman nod and move away to pass out bottles of beer to the rabble at the counter, while Easter walked off, heading for the door. Beverley released Tom to go and high-five Richards. Tom took out his phone again, checking the screen. As he was putting it back into his pocket, Boyn hoisted Bobby onto his shoulders. They started a jig around the room. Boyn, tittering so much that he nearly dropped Bobby onto a table, was singing something that was difficult to hear until Bobby picked up the words and sang it out himself, loud, unabashed. "Oh I'd rather be a faggot than a Yid. Oh I'd rather be a faggot than a Yid . . ." Beverley dashed over to join them, and the chant flared up briefly before the operations manager hurried across to tell them to stop, having realized that some of the other players had started filming.

Bobby scored again in the next league match, and on the same day was shortlisted for divisional player of the month. Ever more he was emerging—on the pitch, in the dressing room—as a leader. He was a full inch taller than when he joined the club. And stronger. He had been in the gym every day of the close season and was now one of the most well-built players in the squad. This new strength had bred in him a confidence. He wanted the ball, hunted it, screeched for it even when Jones was near, because it was Bobby, they all recognized, who had become the driving force of the team.

Scouts had started to come and watch him, including one from the Scotland Under-19s who had been at each of the last two matches. His sugar daddies, Bobby joked before anyone else thought of it.

With Yates gone and Easter largely ignored, the others looked increasingly to Bobby as the jester, and because Bobby was developing into a player of real potential who would likely not be playing for Town beyond the season, he started to walk about the place as respected and untouchable as a captain, regardless of the fact that he now owed considerable amounts of money to several of the squad.

The other player promoted from the youth team, Sam Spencer, stayed as close to Bobby's side as he was able. He said very little, but in the mornings after they had traveled together in Bobby's car from their shared flat, they could usually be seen talking in the lounge before the rest of the squad arrived, and on the rare occasions that Spencer was in the traveling party for an away match, he would sometimes be let into Bobby's clique of cardplayers gambling up and down the motorways. The rest of the time Spencer was mostly on his own. One day, though, when Bobby had stayed on the field at the end of the session to talk to Wilko, Spencer looked up in surprise, gratitude, at Bobby coming through the dressing room straight towards him.

"All right?"

"All right."

Bobby stood smiling before him. Slowly, from behind his back, he produced a brush and a tin of boot polish.

"Pin him down."

The nearest four or five men pounced upon the boy and pulled him to the floor. When he was fully restrained, pinned down on his front, a scorched red line was visible curving down his back where it had scraped the bench. His pants were tugged free. A hand, Beverley's, offered itself through the fray to press his head against the tiles to prevent it from rearing up.

Tom found himself with the left ankle. He helped turn Spencer onto his back and pushed down with both hands on the foot, mirroring Easter on the other side. Easter looked across at him, an expression of devilish collusion in his eyes that Tom did not meet. There was a bout of renewed thrashing that made it difficult to keep hold, so he shifted his full weight onto the arch of the foot, and from within the shrieking and sobbing there was a yelp of fresh pain, at which Tom eased off a little. Bobby knelt over his flatmate and instructed Tom and Easter to pull his legs wider apart. With one hand he took hold of Spencer's penis and, with a deftness that made Tom's innards contract, moved it aside so that he could apply the polish to his testicles.

"Bob. Bob, please, fuck off. Bob, please."

Tom watched the serious unsmiling concentration on Bobby's face, his precision with the brush unaffected by the slippery chaos of skin, or the wet piercing cries that rang about the tiled room. *You didn't paint the wall this carefully, you cunt,* Tom thought, forcing the foot harder to the floor, willing Spencer's hot streaming pain to be his own.

"He's got a stiffy!" Beverley cried. "Look, he's got a stiffy!"

And it was true, almost. Bobby stopped stroking the brush up the underside of Spencer's penis, which stood, for a second or two, before collapsing with a damp black kiss onto his pelvis. The noise in the room increased. People leaped back—Tom too, horrified. Spencer, however, gave no sign that he was at all conscious of his sorry erection. His reedy little rib cage pushed up against his whitened chest. One sideburn was matted with snot. From beneath him a rivulet of blood was trickling along the grouting of the floor tiles, quickening and thinning into the remnants of shower water shaken free from forty happy stamping feet.

The days that followed were bright and relaxed. With the Tottenham tie only a couple of weeks away and the spirit of the group high, the banter was relentless, undoubting. A kind of order had been restored with, at its foundation, Sam Spencer. He went by any number of names at first but, eventually, simply faggot. The joyful skip of the two syllables accompanied him everywhere he went and, because nobody other than Bobby had any real cause to say much else to him, the word pealed out on its own, racing past him on a sideline, echoing down a corridor. Bobby laughed along but did not join in. He started sitting with Spencer in the canteen before driving him home, and Tom wondered what they said to each other inside their flat, whether they spoke at all.

Although Tom also did not take part in the banter, except for occasionally, tactically, the focus on Spencer was enabling him to behave more easily around the other players than he had in the near month and a half since his return to the club. He skulked less on the outside of phone huddles, joke huddles, coming at last into the thick of them. He stayed for longer in the canteen. One afternoon when he was among the last group to leave Beverley got up to go to the tea urn and brought a mug back for Tom with his own, and when Richards, then Lloyd-Day departed, the two of them were left alone in the canteen.

"Mate, you know I don't mean any of it, yeah?" Beverley said.

Tom frowned, appearing confused, although he understood perfectly well and was already working out how to end the conversation.

"All this bullshit with Spence. I don't mean anything against you. It's just a laugh. It doesn't mean anything."

"I know."

"Probably half of them don't really mean anything by it. They don't know what they're saying. They just know they've got to say it. If you see what I mean."

Lesley popped her head out of the kitchen to see if anybody was still in the canteen. Seeing them, she smiled over.

"You doing all right, Tommy?" Beverley asked.

"Yes."

"Sure, yeah?"

Tom nodded.

"All this faggot stuff," Beverley continued more quietly, "it's nothing. It's just a word. You know that?"

"I know. We don't have to talk about it."

And he did understand. Whatever it did or did not mean, he was outside it. It had become so normal to hear the word being sung out that he had ceased almost to think anything of it, and if he did—a sudden image of the lacquered erection—it was with a quick virtuous contempt of Spencer, a sentiment which, although he did not wish to explore it, he knew was converging in his mind with Liam. In the vacuum of being apart, the two humiliations—Spencer's, Liam's—were coupled, a fact he was reminded of daily by the banter of the squad.

Liam had not been at the training ground or the stadium pitch for over a week. The night before Spencer's initiation Tom had received from him a flurry of missed calls, voicemail messages, then a couple more the next morning and none since. Still he would not listen to the messages. He sometimes allowed the desire to hear them to intensify, testing himself, and he felt renewed strength each time he succeeded in leaving them there, suppressed inside his phone.

Spencer was not present for training the Friday before a home match. Tom knew that they would not see him again. During a break between drills he went over to Bobby to ask if he had heard anything.

"Gone, mate."

"For good?"

"That's right. Wilko lined a club up for him someplace, non-league or something, but Spence said no. Thinks he's done with football. They settled with him on his contract. Bet they screwed him too. Boy doesn't even have an agent."

Senseless anger moved inside Tom at Bobby's flippancy. He had an impulse to ask him about the money that he still owed, to embarrass him, shame him in front of the others. A ball rolled over from one of the pitches. Bobby trapped it with his sole, kicked it back.

"Probably best thing for him," Tom said.

"Aye, probably."

The others, if they had noticed Spencer's departure, were similarly unruffled. They were ready to move on, had already moved on, from Spencer and from the whole unnatural recent period. The world, too, they sensed, was no longer watching them. The media had abruptly lost interest, and although there had been something of a chant during the last match, it had mostly died by the time it reached the ears of the Town supporters. As far as the squad, the fans, the board were concerned, everything was again as it should be, unshakably normal.

32

Tom was woken by his phone downstairs. He had taken to leaving it in the living room, using instead the old alarm clock that he had kept from his academy days, and his reflex, coming to, was of indignation that his dad or Rachel had broken his ten hours. But when it went off a second time, a third, he trained his sight on the ceiling and locked his focus, breathing firmly, evenly, visualizing his actions on the field that evening. It stopped ringing after the fifth call. He collected himself, accepting that he would not be able to go back to sleep, and got out of bed.

He made himself go into the kitchen without looking at the phone. He put together his breakfast: a small glass of goat's milk with a two-egg goat's cheese omelette and, on the side, a packet of pineapple pieces, a combination he had picked up from Beverley along with the necessity of eating as soon as he was awake. Through the doorway, as he ate standing up at the kitchen counter, he could see his phone on the living-room table. When he had finished his breakfast he went to the sink and filled his watering can, then, going through, he tested his cacti on the windowsill, pressing the soil of each with his thumb, measuring out different portions of water, one by one. He was just about to leave the room again when his phone rang once more, the sound cutting through his resolution. He walked across and saw that it was his dad.

"Feeling good?"

"Decent, yeah."

"Big night ahead."

"It is. Mum there?"

"Not yet. She should be finishing up at the clinic about lunchtime. We'll set off soon as we've eaten."

"Rachel there too?"

"Oh yes. Your sister is very excited. She's just on the stairs. She's saying she's looking forward to watching some players she's actually heard of."

"Very funny."

"Sold out tonight?"

"Capacity. Biggest gate in the club's history. There's people in the paper who've flown in from all round the world. This one guy's come over from Australia."

His dad went quiet, and Tom wondered for a moment if he was taking these details down.

"I thought your lot might have been on *Focus* at the weekend. Preview of the match or something. Nothing, though." For a few seconds he was quiet again. "I've been thinking the last couple of months, actually, that Town might have been on it. Moment's passed now, though, I suppose, with all that business."

Tom's arm tautened. He straightened it then brought the phone back to his ear. He had waited for this during each phone call since the newspaper article. Every time, he had cut the conversation short with some excuse before his dad might bring it up, saying that he was about to eat or Wilko wanted them in early or there were roadworks on the way to the stadium. This morning, though, he felt calm. He did not have to lie because there was nothing to say.

"It has, I think."

"Strange period, eh?"

"Was a bit."

"Spirit in the camp still good?"

"Better than ever. Solid. Lot of fuss over nothing, really. We've just been concentrating on the football."

"That's good. Smart manager, Wilkinson."

And with the concrete recognition that his dad was plainly not avoiding anything, a sharp clarity expanded inside Tom's brain, pushing open a clean space in which he was able to see himself distinctly as the person that his dad, everyone else, was able to see.

"Better keep winning, or some club might come in for him," his dad said.

"Wouldn't it be his fault if we stopped winning?"

His dad laughed. "See your point. See your point."

"I should go get ready, Dad."

"Right, yes. I should get lunch ready, anyway, for when your mum gets back."

"Tell her hello, will you?"

"I will. We'll see you after the match then. Good luck tonight. Love you, son."

"Bye, Dad."

His fingers curled around the phone.

He looked at it in his hand. He took several strong breaths then selected voicemail, and cleared his messages.

"All right last night, wasn't it?"

"It was," said Liam.

"I felt like a teenager, getting back in, stumbling about in the dark trying not to wake Mum up."

She had got in a little after four, more drunk than she had been for years, groping for the kitchen light switch, then, when she could not find it, along the walls and the counter for the fridge and the fridge handle, knocking the list of invitees to the floor, happy, drunkenly unencumbered, even as she reached for the array of foreign cheese and remembered that Robert was here, in bed with her mum; Tyler was here, asleep in a cot in her old room. Although, when she eased open the door to her bedroom and tiptoed in, he wasn't. Panic sobered her instantly, her eyes adjusting to the dark—but then she saw him, asleep on the bed, humped against her mum. She walked over and kissed them both, lifted Tyler into the cot and got in beside her mum. She did not stir. Leah found out later in the morning that Tyler had been up half the night.

"Hut's not changed, then," she said.

"Changed? You're joking? There's one of the mirrors in the gents that's new. Old one got glassed or something. Headbutted. How you feeling today?"

"Pretty rough. Hangover with a toddler, you should try it. What about you?"

"You know. Keeping it together, just about."

Robert came into the kitchen, saw her sitting at the kitchen table and winked. He had been to the shop and bought her a large bottle of Diet Coke. She watched him go to the cupboard for a glass.

"Your mum's still at the play park with Tyler," he said in an exaggerated whisper, pouring her a drink and bringing it over to the table.

"Thanks, Robert."

He walked off to her mum's bedroom, humming, and she wondered if this was what he would have been like if she was sixteen, bringing her Diet Coke to nurse her hangovers, or if he too would have shouted and backed her into the corner under the boiler until she cried and pleaded and threw up on the carpet.

"I'd like to come over later, before you set off," she said.

"You don't have to."

"I want to. Mum's still with Tyler, and I should take him off her hands for the afternoon, but I could come round to see you off when I've got him in bed. Just for a bit—I won't get in your way or anything."

"I'll be at my parents' by then. My dad's driving up with me tonight."

"I'll come to your parents' then."

The traffic became heavier as she made her way across town. She had forgotten about the cup match. She put on some music and continued her slow progress through the center. In front of her, long clean scarves drooped from the back windows of a four-by-four BMW that had joined from the coast road. She got a little closer and saw the heads of two children singing and clapping in the back. The vehicles crawled past a beer garden full of Tottenham supporters, drinking, laughing, calling out to one another under the golden sprawl of an uplit tree, and her mind turned to last night, the sweaty giggling tangle of it, how overjoyed they had all been when she told them. "So," Mark had said, "let me get this right. This one's suddenly gay and then two minutes later you're leaving your husband, and you expect us to believe that the two of you *aren't* having an affair?" Later, once they had bullied Liam into going to the club, Mark and Shona had given them a wink, passing them in the corridor on the way to the toilets, where she and Liam had stopped to talk for a moment away from the noise of the club. Liam had leaned into her, drunk. "How's it feel then, telling that lot?"

"All right. Thought it'd be weird or I'd feel guilty or something, but actually it's fine. Just feels normal now, in a way."

"Because it's the right thing."

"I know."

"Because he's a cock."

She turned her face away. "Don't, Liam."

A group of young women was coming down the corridor. Liam pushed against her to let them through. "Fair enough. Sorry. Why've you waited this long to tell them, anyway?"

She shrugged. "Says you."

"Fair point."

"Waiting for the right chance, I suppose. It's not like I speak to them on the phone much."

"What, mean you don't call them up every five minutes to ask if they've remembered to eat their lunch and change their clothes and go to the toilet?"

"Shut up," she said, and when she looked up into his tired smiling face she thought for an instant that she was going to confess to him. She knew just as quickly, though, that it would be senseless, that it would wreck everything. And Mark and Shona were leaving the toilets anyway, coming towards them.

"Hey, lovebirds," Mark shouted, "stop loitering. Gemma's at the bar. Black sambucas. If we're having a send-off, then let's do it fucking properly. Come on."

The BMW was turning off down a side street. When she came past she looked down it and she could see the stadium at the bottom, illuminated. The main stand dominating the houses. She could not halt the thought that Chris was in there. In her mind she could see him in the players' lounge with the other non-involveds, smiling for the directors and sponsors. Putting a front on. Her resolve, so secure last night, weakened a crack. She needed to be stronger, she told herself. There was no point reassuring herself that he would be OK. It was just her own need for proof that she was right, that she was doing the right thing. Last week during a tantrum Tyler had started shouting for him: "Daddy. Where Daddy? Where Daddy?" When she had eventually managed to soothe him she had gone into her bedroom and cried, letting herself—with her mum out and Tyler in front of the television—weep for a few minutes, coming to understand that this was the only time since they had left that Tyler had noticed Chris was not around. And that he had shouted like that before—"Where Daddy? Where Daddy?"—when Chris had been in the house.

He was not at that moment in the players' lounge, but in the dressing room. It was not Wilko's way, separation. They were all in it together, as one: the firsts, the injured, the unfit, the banned. He was sitting underneath a peg that had not been hung with a shirt for nine months, watching. Many of those around him were quiet. Others were threaded with nervous energy, headphones on, a silent disco of footballers bouncing inside their private universes.

Wilko made a show of including him and Curtis by mentioning them during his team talk. Praising their commitment to the cause, their importance to the unit. Easter looked across at Jones and Bobby sitting tightly together, then around the room at the circle of faces, and he recognized the hunger, the belief, of a promotion team. He looked at Tom, who was listening intently to the manager. As if sensing the eyes on him, Tom glanced over, gave a cursory smile and turned away again. Easter's hands squeezed his kneecaps as he kept staring at Tom, challenging him to look back.

To look him in the eye with some sign of admission. But he was too wrapped up in Wilko's words—to give everything they had, not to think about the occasion, to just go out there and enjoy themselves.

Everybody was nodding. He was nodding, he realized. He could hear the Tottenham players coming out of their dressing room and he wondered whether Wilko knew that he could once have gone there. He had been given the opportunity, and he had chosen not to. He would never have met Leah if he had gone, it came to him for the first time, although he did not know if that meant he had made the right or the wrong choice. He tried to picture her. The girl he had met at the school party—giggling, wanting him, pulling him into Katie Wheelwright's downstairs toilet—but however he tried to conjure the image of her as a girl, or now with Tyler, he could not get a proper fix on her, on the two of them together; he could only see her with the faggot groundsman.

Wilko was on the other side of the room, giving instructions, encouragement, to Jones and Bobby. Jones clapped his hand on Bobby's thigh. Easter closed his eyes. He was not a part of this. The unit. He was nothing here. He let his eyes remain closed as the specter of his own future appeared before him. The contract that would expire and release him at the end of the season, discard him to the market, a non-league club maybe coming in for him, near, or far from here, from Leah, from Tyler. They were gone now, either way. That was clear enough. There was no point fighting to get them back. It was too late even if he wanted to. He opened his eyes. Above Jones's head was a motivational poster he had not noticed before—THE MAN ATOP THE MOUNTAIN DIDN'T FALL THERE—and through the haze of controlled breathing and Deep Heat he could see them all falling as one, arms and legs locked together, a circle of butt cheeks dropping through the clouds. But he was drifting away. He saw the others landing softly atop the mountain, high-fiving, their faces getting smaller while he continued to fall. Sneering down at him. Ignorant of the fact that it was him who had protected them, so far, protected the one opposite him refusing still to meet his eye.

The sound of the buzzer cut through his reverie. The electric bleat of it made him coil up, his muscles forgetting, for a second, that they were not needed.

He hung back while they queued up at the door and the liturgy of blessings started: "All the best, all the best . . ." Then he got up and went down the line, each face a portrait of captured fear and excitement. Ashlee Richards, Bobby Hart serenely inside himself, an object of muscular calm, Tom Pearman—a union of young players brimming with form and self-assurance, all so certain of their bright futures. He paused in front of Tom, not releasing his hand straightaway, holding his gaze until the momentum of the line took him away. Easter followed them out into the dim tunnel, which a few seconds later was immersed by the noise of the crowd as the team filed onto the pitch. He stayed behind after Curtis and the other non-involveds had headed off for the players' lounge, until there remained just himself, alone, watching the winking bullet hole at the end of the tunnel.

In the turning outside his parents' house Liam stood at the side of Leah's car, his face towards the stadium, listening to the distant weather of crowd noise rolling and rising above the thin prattle of the Tannoy. The team was being announced. It was not possible to decipher the names, yet he could not help straining to hear.

Leah looked at him over the dusty roof. "You look knackered, mate."

He grinned. "Enjoyed myself, though."

He had not expected to. He had not wanted to go on to the Hut, but they had persuaded him. It was a double leaving celebration, they had implored, prancing about, jumping on Leah, pinching her bottom. *And I'm the queer,* he had thought, shaking his head but agreeing. He was afraid of being spotted, that from the thick of the drunken mob on the dance floor a chant might start up. Or that he would be beaten up. Or propositioned. For the first couple of hours until he began to relax, he had clung to Leah at the bar, believing, even though he knew it was impossible, that he had seen the flash of Tom's face among the packed dancing crowd.

"What now then?" he said.

Leah gave a frown of confusion. "What, me?"

"You, yes."

"I'm cooking dinner for Mum and Robert when I get back, then some wedding planning with them. Meeting Maria, my college friend, at some point tomorrow."

He flicked a dead leaf at her across the car roof. "Not what I meant, but fine. One match at a time then." And the memory of Tom, breathing onto his neck, hit him so heavily that he had to put both hands onto the car roof to support himself.

His dad was approaching through the garden, carrying two loaves of bread and a four-pinter of milk.

"What's this?" Liam asked.

"Your mother."

His dad stepped onto the pavement and unlocked the boot of his car. "Are you sure you won't stop for a cup of tea, Leah?"

"I'm fine, thank you. I'll be getting back in a minute."

"Fair enough. Don't go without saying cheerio," he said and went back to the house.

Leah turned again to Liam. "Have you heard from him?"

"No."

"Does he even know?"

Liam shrugged his shoulders. "I don't know."

She reached across the roof and he let her take his hand. The shape of a hut, faintly visible on her own wrist, was still prominent on his.

"I'm going to go in and say goodbye to your mum and dad."

He watched her go through the garden, then turned in the direction of the stadium. The four towering lights burned in the gloom. He listened closely and could make out the tendrils of a chant, a yellow fog of lungs and throats dissipating over the rooftops. From where he stood, a slice of the metal cladding on the Riverside Stand was visible. He could feel the exact texture of it. The smoothness of the panels. The cracks inside which a silt of dirt and skin and shredded paper had compacted. His hands ran down it—the blind intimacy of his fingertips over rivets and chewing-gum scabs; the protruding stanchion of the floodlight at the base of the wall, bursting through the ruptured brickwork like the root of a tree. The foot-worn concrete at the bottom of the terrace, brightened with trails of arrival and tea-bar visits, celebrations, slow disappointed exits.

He closed his eyes, remembering, from nowhere, lying with Tom on a dune. He touched the grass of the pitch. His palms skimmed over the thick pelt of sward, anticipating every dip and curve, every change in moisture, intuiting the invisible line across the surface beyond which the grass weakened in the winter shadow of the Kop. There were scars everywhere, known only to him. The toughened sinews of perished tubing. Tender patches of new growth over old wounds. He could feel the aliveness, the intricate biology of it, and it was his, even as the pressure of his touch against it abated, lifting, it would only ever be his.

Leah was coming around the car towards him. When she was at his side she reached up to cradle his face in her hands and leaned in, unhesitant, to kiss him on the mouth. In the press of her lips and the small alien nose against his, something inside him released. He put his arms around her, his cheek sliding against her face, and there were his parents, frozen beside the rhododendron. He broke into laughter. When Leah, turning round, saw them too, a pair of bewildered garden gnomes, so did she.

From the stadium a throttled roar swept through the dark.

"You'll call me?" Leah said.

He turned back to her. "Yes."

"Call me tomorrow." His dad was coming out of the garden, laden with tea bags, coffee, biscuits, margarine, still more bread. "Set my mind at rest that you've got enough to eat."

His dad put the supplies into the boot and took from his mum, arriving behind him, a set of pots and pans.

"What are you doing?" Liam said. "I'm not going camping."

"Essentials," his mum said. "Until you get a chance to do your first shop."

"When are you leaving?" Leah asked.

"Any time now. Probably a three-hour drive, so we won't get in till late, but I'm not meeting the principal until eleven tomorrow. Dad's going to come along, make the introductions."

His dad moved over to them. "I've told Ian I'll have lunch with him afterwards, if that's all right."

"Yeah, fine. You can set him at ease that I'm not going to molest any of his students," Liam said and saw straightaway that his parents were not ready for that kind of humor.

"We'll just be telling each other old stories. Boring stuff. But I'm sure he'd be happy for you to join us, if you want, get to know him outside the college."

"Thanks, Dad. We'll see."

"OK," Leah said, "I'm going now."

She got into her car. Over the rooftops there was another roar, this one quieter, drowned by the sound of the starting engine. His parents stood beside him and they watched her drive away.

"Right, shall we?" his dad said, opening the door of his own car. "No need for a convoy, is there?"

"No, I'll meet you in a service station somewhere for a quick coffee break. I'll ring you."

Everything he had imagined saying to his mum was at once lost in the soft warm armful of her. He did not need to speak, understanding now each of those silent private moments that he had peeked in upon in the kitchen. Except when he parted from her he did not feel like one of those boys, lost, failed; he just wanted to get onto the motorway.

He could sense beside him the sad stranded ghost in the passenger seat.

"Fuck them, mate," he said aloud and started his car, an unfamiliar anticipation permeating him as he mouthed goodbye to his mum on the pavement and pulled out to follow his dad's car onto the road.

He was inside the match, joined bodily to the fast-blooded life of it, performing without thought—feints, tricks—actions that he would not normally attempt even in training. It had been his cross, a low cut back into the feet of Munro, that had created the goal, and since the Tottenham equalizer it was Tom that the players, the crowd exhorting them to regain the lead, were putting their faith in. His name rang from three sides of the ground. When the referee blew for halftime he fought the instinct to look up at the little loyal row of his family in the main stand, his breath becoming uneven as impermissible caged thoughts threatened to escape and he walked towards the tunnel with his sight trained immediately in front of him, on Beverley, the top of his crescent tattoo.

Inside the tunnel Beverley stopped and waited for him. "This is fucking unreal," he whispered to Tom while the impassive celebrity faces of the Tottenham team moved past them. "It's fucking unreal, man."

Tom went to his place inside the dressing room. He could not focus on Wilko's talk. The space about him was fuzzy. He felt shut off from everything around him, trapped inside himself. Wilko was stepping up to him. "This boy. Get this boy on the ball." He walked away to talk to the defense and Tom did not hear the rest. When he did glance up, Easter was staring at him from the non-involveds' corner, so he put his head down again, waiting for the buzzer, desperate to get back out onto the field, to never have to leave it.

They were put under heavy pressure early in the second half. Tottenham began with a new intensity, hitting the post after one long passing move which the Town players, some already flagging, chased uselessly. There was a lull in the noise of the home support; the Tottenham fans awoke. When another Spurs attempt on goal went narrowly wide, Bobby let out a bellow of encouragement to the regrouping Town players, then, turning and clenching his fists, to the Kop. The crowd responded. One of the Tottenham forwards, smirking to a teammate as he jogged back, was confronted, his route blocked, by Bobby's face. The noise inside the stadium increased again. Play became scrappy, each Tottenham move broken down by a boot, a lunge, a furious tackle.

Tom hovered on the fringes, waiting. He could hear his heart battering but he was in control of himself, he thought, composed, capable of blocking out everything: the disjointed match, the faces

of his parents, his sister, the seats at the edge of the disabled supporters' stall, the medical room, the grass.

He spotted the opening a split second before his marker. He
darted into the space, taking Gundi's through ball in his stride—
and in that moment, free, running in on goal, he was at school, he
was on the common, the only thought in his mind the certainty of
what he was going to do with the ball. He took the shot early, before the goalkeeper went to ground, and he did not even see the net
move; he saw the red length of the keeper's neck, the crowd swimming, a plastic bottle high in the air, twirling and catching the beam
of a floodlight. From somewhere in the Kop there was a small explosion of shredded paper, like a shot bird. Amid the whirl of noise
and movement he looked up at the black sky and let out a scream
which he was unable to hear and which did not stop, but kept on
coming, emitting from him until his throat burned and it became
no more than a dry howl, tears running down his face as his teammates were upon his back and he crumpled to the earth.

ACKNOWLEDGMENTS

I would like to thank Peter Straus, primarily. I don't know quite how he does it, but his instinct and his loyalty have enabled me to write uninhibited by anything for the past decade, and I greatly appreciate it.

On the books side of things, I am grateful to Michal Shavit, for her belief in this novel; to Ana Fletcher, Ellie Steel, Kat Ailes and Joe Pickering at Random House in the U.K.; to Ellah Allfrey and Mary Mount; and for this U.S. edition of the book to Melanie Jackson and Sam Nicholson. I feel that the novel has found a very good home here.

Also to Adam Brown, Sarah Boyall and Jonny Goldspink, for sharing their experiences with me, and to Adrian Hassell for lending me his workspace.

On the football side of things I would like to thank the following people for their insights and anecdotes: Riz Rehman and the Zesh Rehman Foundation, Megan Worthing Davies, the Justin Campaign, Rob Hassell, Trish Keppie, and Liam Davis. And especially Ian Darler and Max Rushden, both of whom gave me more stories than I knew how to handle.

Thanks too, for helping facilitate some of these conversations, to Alex Goodwin, Jason McKeown, and Sheena Hastings.

Finally, to BP and to JG, for giving me their time and knowledge. I would like to thank you more fully here, but am wary of the football world's tendency to see things in simple terms, and I would not want a straight line to be drawn between some of the saltier episodes of this novel and yourselves, your clubs. The time that I spent with you both, though, was vital to my understanding of this world.

And thank you, always, to Tips.

ABOUT THE AUTHOR

Ross Raisin was born in West Yorkshire. His first novel, *God's Own Country*, published in 2008, was shortlisted for nine literary awards, including the Guardian First Book Award. In 2009, Ross Raisin was named the *Sunday Times* Young Writer of the Year. In 2013, he was selected as one of *Granta*'s Best of Young British Novelists. He lives in London.

ABOUT THE TYPE

This book was set in Sabon, a typeface designed by the well-known German typographer Jan Tschichold (1902–74). Sabon's design is based upon the original letterforms of the sixteenth-century French type designer Claude Garamond and was created specifically to be used for three sources: foundry type for hand composition, Linotype, and Monotype. Tschichold named his typeface for the famous Frankfurt typefounder Jacques Sabon (c. 1520–80).